VOLUME 1

The Legend of the Lamp

A Novel by
TINA MONSON

This is a work of fiction. Although some of the places are real, the characters, names, events and dialogue are not to be construed as real.

tina@soundsofzion.com
visit us at www.soundsofzion.com

Printed in the United States of America
Second printing August 2007

ISBN: 1-933098-18-X

10 9 8 7 6 5 4 3 2

ACKNOWLEDGEMENTS

THIS BOOK could not have been written without the support and assistance of a few very special people.

Suzette Jensen, my sister and editor who once again offered her invaluable support, long hours, and large supply of red pens. Thank you.

A special, heartfelt thanks to Kay Curtiss, for her encouragement, ideas, and travel on my behalf, making sure the details of this book were correct.

In addition, I would be ungrateful if I didn't extend a special thanks to Doyl Peck, for his sleepless nights reading the manuscript, his suggestions to make the book better, and for bringing to light his favorite words, but especially for his patience. Thanks, Doyl for being such a great friend.

Last, and most importantly, to my wonderful family, Kreg, Carson, Carter, Sierra and Bristol, without your love, support, and ideas, I would never have been able to complete this story.

FOREWORD

THE IDEA FOR THIS BOOK began over Christmas when I happened to notice an old lamp sitting on the fireplace mantle in my parent's home. When I asked where it had come from I heard a fascinating tale, almost too good to be true. My father told me the story about how this lamp was originally owned by Prescendia Huntington. When she married Heber C. Kimball, she brought the lamp with her. The lamp was then passed from generation to generation until it reached my Grandmother, Thelma Kimball, who then gave the lamp to my father. (Who hopefully will someday pass the lamp to me!) The real story began when I learned that this particular lamp was one of the actual lamps that Joseph Smith used while translating the Book of Mormon. I knew that my ancestors were involved in helping to bring forth the Church, I just didn't realize how involved they really were. As he told me the story, my imagination ran wild.

Although the lamp written about in this story is real, this novel will never be more than a figment of my imagination, and is a work of fiction. My hope is that you will love the idea enough to research your own genealogy, searching for the hidden adventures, courage and intrigue surely hidden in your own family's history. Enjoy!

CHAPTER ONE 1

HANNAH STARED at the bright yellow clock as it dangled precariously, slightly off center, from an old rusty nail on the wall. The nail had been forced at an angle into the cracking mortar which held together the brick walls of the old church house. She watched as the second hand crawled at a snail's pace past every second. Taking a deep breath and letting it out loudly, she noted the time.

"There can't still be ten minutes left!" she thought to herself. "I'm sure when I looked five minutes ago, we only had ten minutes left. That clock can't be working correctly."

Anxiously, she reached to her wrist and pulled back the blue sleeve of her sweater to reveal her most prized possession. Buckled around her wrist was a small, ragged, dirt-brown leather wristband that held together her Great-Grandma Kimball's watch. The watch was old and weathered, but it had a beautiful silver exterior, engraved with intricate designs and a gray mesh face. Adorned in a circle close to the face's edge were roman numerals carved from brilliant white sandstone. In the center of the watch was a large, arrow-like spindle that slowly clicked away the seconds. On each side of the face were two smaller spindles. Hannah thought one represented the days of the month and the other might reflect the moon's rotation, but she had never known exactly how to tell.

As she compared the time on her watch and the time on the wall clock, she found they were exactly the same. She still had nine minutes left before early morning seminary ended. Hannah closed her eyes in frustration, rolling her head to the left and then back to the right, trying to stretch her neck. She took another deep breath, hoping that might help keep her eyes open. Her desire to curl up into a ball and go back to sleep was almost more than she could stand, especially with today's boring lesson. Resting her elbows on her desk and holding her head in her hands, she tried to force her eyes open with her thumb and forefinger. But somehow her eyelids seemed stronger than her fingers, and her eyes slammed shut again.

"If this lesson doesn't get interesting really fast, I'm not sure I can keep myself awake one minute longer. This is so boring," she thought, as she half-heartedly tried to listen to what her teacher, Brother Hutcheon, was saying.

She continued to force her eyes open and stared blankly at the indentations and lines on the white brick wall surrounding the clock. Changing her focus occasionally to watch the second hand slowly maneuver its way around, ticking away one more minute. Leaning back in her chair, Hannah rubbed her blurry, pale-blue eyes, attempting to bring them back into focus. With little success, she held her hand to her mouth trying to cover the uncontrollable yawning and wondered, "When will I truly ever need any of this old information? How could the early years of the church and westward trek of the saints and leaders ever be anything I need to remember? I'm already a member and I have a testimony. I don't need to learn this stuff. I'm sssoooo bored."

Suddenly, a loud bang echoed through the room. Brother Hutcheon, annoyed by the inattentiveness of Hannah and the class, slammed his course manual down in the center of Hannah's desk. Startled by the noise, Hannah quickly sat up straight, placed her hand on her heart and took a deep breath. She blinked her eyes, trying to wake up and suddenly realized that Brother Hutcheon was leaning over her desk. With his nose not more than six inches away from her face, she looked directly into his dark green eyes and screamed.

"Hannah, am I boring you with all this information?" he asked gruffly.

Her heart raced with fear, and her breathing grew more rapid every second. She glanced toward the course manual on her desk and quietly said, "Nnooo, I was trying to listen—honest."

Brother Hutcheon stood up straight, grinned and asked, "Listen? Are you sure? I'm not positive you or anyone else in this room has heard one word I've said today."

Hannah nodded her head and answered, "Yyeesss, I've listened. But, I'm confused. Why do I need to know this information, and when would I ever use this stuff?"

"What information?" asked Brother Hutcheon, testing Hannah to see if she had truly been listening to his lesson.

"The information you've been talking about," she replied evasively.

"All right, Hannah," he said, as he moved away from her desk. "Would you please come to the front of the classroom and tell the other students what I have been talking about for the last thirty minutes?" asked Brother Hutcheon, as he pointed to the front of the classroom. "If you can tell me about today's lesson, then I will be glad to explain why this information is so important for you and the class to know."

Hannah was irritated. She quickly stood from her chair, pulled the course manual from his hands and confidently strolled to the front of the classroom. With her heart pounding rapidly, she casually pulled the hair off her shoulders and slipped a scrunchie from her wrist around the long, blond strands. She cleared her throat and opened the manual, flipping the pages quickly to early Mormon history. Then she started rambling to the class about early church history and the struggles the leaders and members had endured.

Impressed with her confidence, Brother Hutcheon shook his head, smiled and walked to the front of the classroom. He took the manual from Hannah and said, "You are quoting the correct chapter, Hannah. However, that's not exactly what I was talking about." Turning to the students, Brother Hutcheon continued, "Class, I know this is your last day before summer vacation, but try to stay focused. This information will come in handy one day, I promise."

The bell rang unexpectedly, startling everyone, including Brother Hutcheon. He dropped the manual, which caused an even louder bang as it fell on the floor. The kids laughed. They stood up from their chairs, gathered their belongings and scurried quickly toward the door.

"Wait class, wait a minute. No one has been excused yet," Brother Hutcheon bellowed, as he bent over to retrieve his lesson manual. "I know it's your short summer vacation, but don't think for a minute that you don't have homework."

Everyone in the class stopped and moaned.

"Moan all you want, but since none of you listened in class, you will need to read as homework: Doctrine and Covenants, Section One through Section Six, and in your course study manuals, Lessons Three and Four on Joseph Smith's history. And, so that you are all perfectly clear on the homework, 'yes' we will have a test covering the required reading the Monday you return to school," he finished, almost smirking.

"Brother Hutcheon, are you serious? Homework?" asked Hannah.

"Yes, Hannah, I'm serious, you all have homework. There will be a test the day you return, which will be worth one half of your term grade. Be prepared, I would hate to give you a failing grade. Seminary isn't as much fun when you have to retake my class for a second time in the fall."

"Because of summer school, we only have a short, summer recess, Brother Hutcheon. I need a break from homework!" protested Alli, Hannah's best friend.

"I can't find anywhere in the scriptures where the Lord or prophets state you don't need to study or read your scriptures during summer recess. However, if you can show me a scripture that specifies there should be no homework given during summer recess, I will be glad to reconsider your homework assignment," said Brother Hutcheon, holding up Alli's scriptures.

"Funny, Brother Hutcheon," replied Alli, as she snatched her scriptures and turned to leave the classroom. "You know there's no such scripture."

Brother Hutcheon walked to his desk, smiling as the remainder of the students quickly wrote down their homework assignments. He grinned as he heard several students mumble under their breath as they strolled out of class. "Remember class," Brother Hutcheon called. "Summer school is a privilege, and was designed so that accelerated students like yourselves, can participate in sports during the regular school year."

Hannah yawned, still struggling to stay awake. She walked back to her desk, gathered her papers and stuffed them into her backpack, threw it over her shoulder and started for the classroom door.

"Hannah," called Brother Hutcheon.

"Yes," she replied.

"Did you write down your homework assignment?" he asked.

"I have a good memory," she answered, smirking. "Besides, I heard every word you said today in class. Sssooo, if you're as good of a teacher as you think, I should ace the test after summer recess is over."

"Well, you know that I'm the best teacher in seminary, but in case your memory fails you during the break and you can't remember everything I said, I wrote the assignment down for you," he replied, holding out a small, white piece of paper. "I know how taxing these two weeks of vacation can be on teenage brain power."

Hannah really liked her seminary teacher. She had known him since she was a little girl and he had always been a good friend to her family. She knew he was only teasing her, so she walked quickly back to his desk, took the paper from his hand, crumbled it in to a ball and pushed it into her pants pocket. She scrunched up her face, tilted her head to the side and said, "Thanks a lot, Brother Hutchcon." As she turned to leave, she remembered that her mom had told him they would be leaving on a church history road trip. She wondered if that was why he had chosen church history as the topic for seminary today.

Hannah moved in slow motion all day long. She counted down every minute of every class, impatiently waiting for her two-week summer recess to begin. The last bell finally rang, signifying the end of the day and the start of vacation. The bell also marked the beginning of the dreaded church history vacation she was being forced to go on with her family. Her mom, Sarah, her older brother, Hunter, and her younger brother, Hayden, along with her mom's younger sister, Shirley, would be leaving in a matter of hours, and Hannah had no way to escape. Hannah, a sophomore at Cross Creek High School, would have to spend her sixteenth birthday somewhere in New York at a pageant she was sure she did not want to attend.

"The Hill Cumorah Pageant," she muttered under her breath. "Who wants to be there on their sixteenth birthday? No friends, no cake, no presents and to top it all off, I have to be there with my brothers. At least Aunt Shirley is cool," she said, trying to console herself.

Hannah stood up slowly from behind her desk. She flipped her, long, blond hair over her shoulders, gathered it all together and tied the strands into a bun. She grabbed her blue and maroon gym bag next to her chair, pulled her brothers letterman's jacket off the back of the chair and slowly wandered into the halls of the school. They were already filled with a frantic maze of students racing toward their lockers. She walked slowly toward her locker, watching everyone around her quickly hurrying home, obviously excited to start the two-week recess.

She dreaded the endless hours in the motor home dealing with her brothers and the torment they were sure to give her. She thought about the boring music that would be playing and the meaningless conversations Mom and Aunt Shirley would be having. Hannah was sure there was nothing to look forward to in the next two weeks—not even her birthday.

"I wish Mom would let me fly out to New York in a few days and meet them for the Pageant, like Dad and Uncle Gary are doing," she thought to herself.

She was pondering her dilemma as she arrived at her locker. She opened it and unloaded the books from her gym bag and placed them inside, knowing she would not need any of them. She grabbed her dance bag and slammed the locker door closed. Turning around Hannah leaned against the cold, gray metal door and let her mind wander as she waited for her brother, Hunter.

"Hurry up, Hannah," yelled Hunter, as he slammed his locker door closed, startling his sister. "We're gonna be late getting home. You know Mom wants to leave as soon as we can, besides, you know where the car is parked. You didn't need to wait for me here."

"Yes, I did," she thought quietly to herself. "I'm not going to wait at the car for the next thirty minutes while you socialize. And, quite frankly, I'm in no hurry to get home to start this two-week nightmare."

She watched Hunter's soft, wavy, blond hair as it swayed back and forth as he walked. Bouncing his basketball at his side, he moved toward the school parking lot, laughing and joking with his friends from the basketball team along the way. Hannah knew he would leave her if she was not ready and at the car when he was ready to go, so she hurried to keep Hunter in her sights.

"Hannah, Hannah," called a voice from behind her.

She twirled around to see Alli running to catch up with her.

"What's up?" Hannah asked. "I thought you would be gone already."

"Well, did you call your mom?" she asked.

"Call my mom? For what?"

"I thought you were going to call your mom and see if you could stay at my house, instead of going on this trip," Alli said.

"Oh, I'm sorry, I completely forgot to tell you," Hannah replied. "I did call her."

"Well, what did she say?" Alli asked excitedly.

"She said I have to go. This is a family trip, and I have to be part of it," Hannah answered sadly.

"I'm sorry, Hannah. I was hoping she would let you stay," said Alli, trying to console her friend.

"You know the worst thing?" Hannah asked.

"No, what?" replied Alli, as they walked toward the parking lot and Hunter's metallic-blue Pontiac Firebird.

"The ride in the motor home is going to be so boring. I'm not going to have anyone to talk to besides Hunter and Hayden. This is going to be the worst vacation anyone has ever dreamed up," Hannah said dejectedly.

"I think the worst part is having no friends around to hang out with on your birthday. That's what is going to be a real bummer," added Alli.

"Don't remind me. I bet my mom thinks this trip is my present, so I'm not even sure I will be opening anything," replied Hannah sadly.

"Come on. You better start looking for something good about this trip or you will have the most miserable time of your life. And you better hurry before Hunter leaves you," said Alli, as she pointed to Hunter sitting in the driver's seat. He was revving the engine as loud as he could, trying to get Hannah's attention.

Hannah and Alli raced toward the car. As they reached the door, Alli hugged Hannah and whispered, "Good luck. Hurry back—I'm gonna miss you." She stepped away from the car and watched as Hannah threw her gym bag and Hunter's jacket into the back seat and then climbed in the front.

Hannah waved to Alli and yelled, "Remember, I will have my cell phone. If I can, I will try to call or text message you in a few days and let you know how everything's going!"

Alli continued to wave back to Hannah until Hunter's car was completely out of the school's parking lot. Smiling, she turned and walked to meet her mom at the car.

"This is going to be the best surprise ever," said Alli, as she opened the door.

"Yes it is. It was sure nice of Hannah's mom to invite you to meet them next week in New York," replied her mom.

"The hardest part is going to be pretending to feel bad for her every time she calls."

"Be careful. You know this is a surprise, and you don't want to give it away."

"I know," Alli said chuckling. "Hannah is going to be so excited when I'm there for her birthday."

CHAPTER TWO

AS HUNTER STARTED UP the motor home, Mom and Aunt Shirley loaded the last few bags. They quickly made sure they had packed everything needed for the trip and climbed into the motor home.

"All right kids, the refrigerator is on, the cupboards are packed with food, and I've got the map," said Aunt Shirley, falling into the passenger seat. "With as much stuff as we have to bring, I'm sure glad that I don't have any kids to pack for yet!"

"Only one errand left before we can get out of town," said Mom.

"The motor home is already full of gas, Dad and I filled the tank last night," said Hunter. "So, what errand do we need to run?"

"We need to go to Grandma and Grandpa Kimball's house," answered Mom. "She called and asked us to stop by before we leave town today. I guess she has some family history information she needs from Nauvoo and she'd like us to look for it in the city cemetery while we're there."

"City cemetery?" shrieked Hannah. "Are you kidding? I don't want to stop at the cemetery while we're on vacation."

"Yep, the cemetery," answered Mom.

"Oh, this trip keeps getting better and better," Hannah muttered under her breath. "I still don't understand why I can't stay home with Dad."

"Yeah, me too, Mom. I want to stay home with Dad. You know you're making me miss the summer basketball tournament," interjected Hunter. "I would really like to stay and play in it—especially since my team is still undefeated."

"That's enough you two," responded Mom. "We've already been down this road. We're all going on this trip together and your father will meet us in a few days. Who knows, maybe you both will have learned something about the Church and the Gospel by then. Heaven forbid you three strengthen your testimonies."

"I thought we attended seminary every day for that," muttered Hunter, as he popped the motor home into gear.

"I'm serious you two. That's enough," Mom replied sternly. "You're both going to have a miserable trip if you don't change your attitudes right now."

"Attitude? I don't have an attitude," said Hunter, as he drove slowly down the driveway. He smiled and waved at his two younger sisters who were playing at the neighbor's house until Dad returned home from work.

"Look, Hunter and Hannah, I promise the harder you fight me on this trip, the more stops we will make, and the longer we will spend studying church history," said Mom. "Now, knock it off, and let's have some fun. Okay?"

"Why aren't the younger girls going on this wonderful road trip?" Hannah asked in a grouchy tone.

"I have already explained that to you, Hannah. Your Dad and I felt that you three older kids would actually enjoy the road trip. We also hoped you might have fun spending time with Aunt Shirley and me," replied Mom.

Hunter, Hannah and Hayden knew they would have fun with Aunt Shirley, she was always fun to be with. Aunt Shirley was their mom's youngest sister. She was only a few years older than they were, so being with her was like being with an older sister. But still, how much fun could they have with her or anyone on this trip?

Hannah and Hayden sat sulking quietly while Mom and Aunt Shirley planned the adventures for the day. They were deciding where the first stop would be while Hunter drove straight for Grandma and Grandpa Kimball's house. The next thirty minutes passed slowly.

Finally Hayden blurted, "Mom, would you please put on some music, I'm practically falling asleep back here," he complained.

Without a word, Mom paused for a moment from her conversation with Aunt Shirley, chose a station everyone could agree with, and then turned to continue the discussion with her sister.

As Hunter merged onto Highway 163, Hannah knew they were only ten minutes away from Grandma and Grandpa's house. She dreaded the long hours of driving they would have to do before they reached their final stop. Hunter parked and Hannah and Hayden hurried out of the motor home.

Excited to see Grandma, everyone raced toward the door to find the five-foot-two, black-haired, dark-brown eyed fireball they all called Grandma. As they threw open the front door and screamed Grandma's name, the kids were startled to find her housekeeper, Maria, looking straight at them.

Hannah gasped in terror. "Oh, Maria. I didn't expect you to be here!" she exclaimed, frightened by her presence.

"Me neither, Maria. You scared me!" said Hayden, shaking.

Maria smiled and sweetly said, "I'm sorry to have frightened you."

"What are you doing here?" asked Hunter, as he walked in the door. "I thought you only worked here on Mondays."

"Well, your grandmother has asked me to come on Mondays and Fridays. Now I will have a chance to see you more often," Maria replied, as she smiled and wiped down the fingerprints on the front door.

"Do you know where we can find Grandma?" asked Hayden.

"Somewhere," Maria replied. "I'm not sure."

Excited to see her, Hayden and Hannah pushed past Maria and ran into the front room to search. With no sign of her anywhere, Hannah called, "Grandma, Grandma, save us!"

"Save you?" she asked, as she tapped Hannah on the shoulder from behind.

Hannah spun around, uncertain as to how Grandma had mysteriously appeared behind her.

"Yeah, save us," chimed in Hayden. "Mom is making us go on some horrible, boring, terrible, ten-day-long church history road trip."

Grandma Kimball smiled, put her arm around Hayden's shoulder and said, "This could be one of the most interesting trips you ever take."

"Interesting?" asked Hannah. "So far the trip has been miserable. I've fallen asleep three times in less than an hour. I can hardly wait to see what the rest of the trip is like."

"I think the trip is going to be *lots* of fun!" said Hunter sarcastically, as he rolled his eyes and strolled into the room.

Grandma couldn't help smiling at Hunter's animated actions. Trying to be positive she said, "Oh, come on, you guys. I only wish that I could go with you. The trip is going to be great fun. I went on a similar trip with my parents and your Grandpa's parents when I was only a few years older than you are right now and I had the best time of my life."

"Sure you did, Grandma. You don't have to try to make us feel better," said Hannah.

"I'm serious. That's when your Grandpa told me about the Legend. I'm sure you've all heard your mom talk about the Legend of the Lamp. Maybe with the knowledge you gain from this trip, you can search for the clues and try to solve the mystery. That's what I did when I went on this trip."

"The what?" questioned Hayden. "Legend of the what?"

"Yeah, a Legend? I've never heard Mom talk about a Legend," said Hannah.

Just then, the screen door screeched as Mom and Aunt Shirley walked in, startling everyone. "Hi, Mom," called, Sarah and Aunt Shirley together.

Grandma quickly hurried to the door and hugged her two daughters as they entered the house. "I was just going to tell the children about the Legend of the Lamp," she said. "Don't tell me, Sarah, that you haven't told them about the Kimball Family Legend yet. The Kimball family has been trying to solve the mysterious Legend for almost one hundred and fifty years now. I would've expected my own daughters to pass the story on to my grandchildren, in hopes that someday the mystery might be solved," Grandma scolded, as she placed her hands on her hips.

"Mom," Sarah said loudly. "I've never told them about the Kimball's Legend because that's all it is—a Legend. I've watched Dad try to find information on the Legend for years, and he's never found anything. Besides, I don't want the kids to think we're only going on this trip to solve that old thing. I'm not even sure there is a Legend. I think the story is something Great-Great Grandpa Heber C. made up," she said, holding her hand to her mouth and trying to cover her smile. "I think he was trying to entertain his own children, and somehow that silly story turned into a great family Legend."

"What old Legend? What story?" pestered Hannah. "Would someone please tell us what you're all talking about? Is there really a Legend about a lamp?"

"Oh, come on, you wouldn't be interested in that old story anyway. Just forget Grandma even mentioned it," said Aunt Shirley, as she put her arm around Hannah's shoulder. "Grandpa has been telling that old tale for years and years now. I think he has only ever found one clue from the Legend, and that discovery was very recent. I'm not sure, but I think Grandpa might have made the Legend and the entire story up himself. There's no way that story could ever be true, or I'm sure someone would have found something by now."

"Mom, you knew about a family Legend, and you didn't tell us about it?" scolded Hannah.

"I don't want you children to waste your lives searching like Grandpa has, and as his father did before him," she replied.

"Does Dad know about this?" asked Hunter.

"Are you kidding? That is the first thing Grandpa told him about when we were married," Mom replied.

"What did he think about the Legend?" questioned Hannah.

"He was very excited, but your mom has sworn him to secrecy," replied Aunt Shirley, grinning from ear to ear.

"Thanks, Shirley," Mom said crossly. "Thanks for telling my secrets."

"Well, they should probably at least get to hear the story, they are part of the Kimball posterity."

"What's the story already?" Hayden asked anxiously. "Let me decide for myself."

"Yeah, what is the story?" asked Hunter, scowling at his Mom. "You're not telling us something, Mom, I can tell by the look on your face."

"Wait, wait a minute," said Mom. "We're not going to worry about Grandpa's old stories. We're going on a modern-day road trip in the motor home, and we are only planning on learning about real church history. We're not looking for some treasure or Legend. We're going to have a fun and educational family trip."

"If we search for treasure, this *could* be a fun family trip," Hannah said sarcastically.

"I want to hear the story, Mom. Come on, please?" begged Hayden. "What's it going to hurt if we hear the story?"

"Darn that ol' grandpa of yours and his silly story," replied Mom, shaking her head. "I guess you can hear the story, but that will be the end of the mystery! We will not be searching for the Legend's long lost treasure or anything else. Is that understood? You may be Kimballs, but I don't want you to waste your lives looking for something that doesn't exist."

"Okay," replied Hunter.

"I hear you, Mom," said Hannah.

"I want to hear about the story. Someone tell me. Grandma, please tell me," squealed Hayden impatiently. "Mom said it's okay!"

"Well," started Grandma proudly, "the story started after Moroni gave Joseph Smith the gold plates and instructed him to translate them. Once they were translated, Joseph Smith was told, on two different occasions, to show the gold plates to two groups of men—the three witnesses and the eight witnesses."

"Come on, Grandma, get to the good stuff. We already know all that," said Hunter. "What is the Legend?"

"Oh, I guess you're right. You would know that stuff—especially since you're in Seminary. You know, Grandpa is a much better storyteller than I am. Why don't the three of you go find Grandpa and ask him to tell you the story? He knows every word of the Legend by memory, and he can tell the story much better than I can," she said, as she sat down on the piano bench.

"Remember kids, this is only a fun story Grandpa likes to tell. There is no way it could be real, and we will not be searching for the Legend on this trip. So please don't get your hopes up. Now hurry," Mom said with a stern face. "Find Grandpa quickly, I don't want to be here all day. We need to get on the road before it gets dark outside. We need to stay on schedule."

"Hey, the three of you are looking suspicious. Are you guys making this up to get us excited about learning church history or something?" Hunter asked skeptically.

"I guess the only way to find out is to hear what the Legend is for yourself," Grandma replied, unable to control the smile spreading across her face.

"I'm not sure about you, Grandma, I think you're up to something," said Hunter, grinning.

"You're right, Hunter, I am up to something. I don't want the searching for the Legend to stop with your grandpa. How exciting would it be if the Legend was true and the Kimball family found the treasure?"

"Very exciting, Grandma," Hunter replied.

"Mom," interrupted Sarah. "Please don't get them too

excited. Relatives from several Kimball generations have searched for this treasure and found nothing."

"Is Grandpa even home?" asked Hannah, her curiosity now peaked. "I haven't seen him anywhere."

"Hannah, Hunter, Hayden, please promise me that you won't get your hopes up for a treasure. There may not be one," warned Mom.

"We won't, Mom. I promise. Now, where is Grandpa?" asked Hunter.

"Grandpa is in the Blue Room," Grandma replied excitedly.

"Where?" asked Hannah.

"Back in the Blue Room, where all the antiques are kept," she answered.

"Are your sure you want us to go to the Blue Room?" asked Hayden. "You've never let me go in there before."

"I hope you're big enough not to break anything," said Grandma. "Everything in that room was handed down by Kimball ancestors, so please be very careful."

Hannah, Hunter and Hayden looked at Mom, hoping the look on her face would somehow reveal a hint to the truthfulness of the Legend. Unable to find any answers from Mom, and unsure whether to believe Grandma, they suspiciously maneuvered their way through the front room. Slowly moving into a long, narrow hallway, they quietly walked between the numerous pictures of Kimball's hung on the wall. At the end of the hallway they climbed twelve stairs, finally reaching a large landing. Staring toward the closed door at the back of the landing, Hayden, Hunter and Hannah silently hoped the Legend was true.

"Do you think Grandma is making up a story about the Legend?" Hayden asked inquisitively.

"I'm not sure any of what Grandma or Mom are saying is true," replied Hunter. "They both looked a little suspicious."

"I thought so too," said Hayden. "But it sure would be fun if the Kimball family had a Legend they've been trying to solve."

"We don't even know for sure what the Legend is," replied Hannah. "Maybe it's something silly we've already heard in Sunday School or something."

"We should be able to tell by the look on Grandpa's face if the story is true," said Hunter, as he opened the door. "Grandpa! Grandpa, are you in here?" he called.

Grandma, Sarah and Shirley peeked around the corner into the hallway and watched as the three nervously walked toward the Blue Room. Grandma smiled as she watched them slowly disappear, one by one, up the stairs.

"Finally, something that interests them about this trip," said Aunt Shirley. "I wasn't sure we were even going to make it out of town."

"By the time they leave here, your dad will have them sure that old letter of Brigham Young's is real. They will be determined to learn more about church history, just to see if the Legend could be real," replied Grandma, still smiling.

"I sure hope so," said Sarah. "On the ride out here, the tension was so high I wasn't sure if we should go or not. I don't want them to have a horrible time or hate church history."

"I'm sure their excitement level will rise a notch or two when Grandpa is through with them. Now girls, I really do need the two of you to help me find some genealogy information," said Grandma, as she turned and walked toward the kitchen.

CHAPTER THREE

AS THE THREE skeptical teenagers entered the Blue Room in the southwest corner of the house, they found Grandpa asleep in an old, hand-carved, wooden chair. They looked at each other, then, Hannah whispered in a soft voice, "Grandpa, Grandpa, are you awake?"

Suddenly a deep, gruff voice rattled through the room. "Yes, I'm not asleep—my eyes are!"

Hannah smiled and said, "Hi, Grandpa. How are you?"

"Well, to what do I owe the pleasure of seeing three of my wonderful grandchildren?" he asked, as he reached out and hugged Hannah.

"I guess Grandma needed some help with genealogy, so we stopped to see her before we leave on our trip," answered Hunter.

"Your trip?" asked Grandpa, unsure what Hunter was talking about.

"Yeah, our church history trip," said Hannah. "You know, the one that is going to make it so that I am not home on my sixteenth birthday."

"Not to mention, the trip that is making me miss my summer basketball tournament," added Hunter. "And we're ranked number one in the region."

"Are you missing anything important, Hayden?" asked Grandpa, noticing him standing quietly behind Hunter.

"Nope, I'm getting lumped into the older kid's trip because I turned thirteen last week," Hayden replied, as he moved from behind Hunter and took hold of Grandpa's hand.

"Hey, Grandpa, what is the Legend that Grandma was talking about downstairs?" interrupted Hunter.

"Legend?" Grandpa asked in a squeaky voice.

"Yeah, a Church History Legend?" asked Hannah. "You know, the Legend of the Lamp or something like that?"

"You mean Grandpa Heber C. Kimball's Legend?" he asked, sitting up excitedly.

"Yes, Grandpa. The one you have been telling all of your kids about for years," said Hayden. "You know, the one Mom says isn't real."

"Nope, I've never heard of that before," Grandpa replied, smiling and shrugging his shoulders.

"Grandpa, come on. Grandma said you would tell us," insisted Hayden. "She said something about the Legend of the Lamp."

"Oh, oh, I remember that one!" he answered, raising his eyebrows.

"What is it anyway?" asked Hunter, looking at Grandpa

skeptically. "I'm not sure Grandma, Mom or Aunt Shirley were telling us the truth downstairs."

"I'm not sure if I should tell you. Grandma said I can't have any more of the family thinking there's this great Legend that leads to lost treasures of the Church. She said when I tell that story, all I do is send my family members off on wild-goose chases, making them ruin their lives searching for something that doesn't really exist."

"Well, does it exist?" Hayden asked excitedly. He watched Grandpa's face carefully as he clasped his hands together tightly in anticipation of the answer.

"Yep, I think so," answered Grandpa, as he leaned back further in his rocking chair. He smiled as he rubbed his chin with his hand, as though deep in thought.

"Okay, then tell us about this great Legend. We are old enough to decide for ourselves if the Legend is something that really exists or not," insisted Hunter. "Besides, Grandma sent us in here for you to tell us the story, so that if we decide it's real, we might have fun on our vacation—like she did when she was younger."

"Yeah, come on, Grandpa. Tell us," encouraged Hannah. "Grandma said it's all right."

Grandpa sat motionless for several minutes, pondering what Hannah had said, then, finally answered, "Well, okay, if Grandma said I could, then I will tell you. But, you have to promise never to tell any one else about the Legend. This has been a Kimball family secret since Grandpa Heber C. Kimball was alive. All right?" he asked, leaning forward in his chair and looking sternly at his grandchildren.

Excited to hear about the mysterious Kimball Legend, the three quickly nodded their heads in agreement.

"All right, you better sit down," Grandpa instructed. He rocked forward in his chair, placing his hands on his knees.

Excitedly, Hannah, and Hayden sat cross-legged in front of Grandpa's wooden rocker, while Hunter, acting cool, chose to lean against the wall and fold his arms. They all watched as Grandpa quietly stood up from his chair, walked over to the window and carefully pushed it closed. Next, he pulled the blinds closed and shuffled to the door. He grabbed the handle and pulled it open, quickly sticking his head into the hallway and searching to see if anyone might be listening. With no one in sight, he quietly pulled the door closed. As the handle snapped shut, he reached to the top of his head and pulled down his reading glasses carefully maneuvering them into a comfortable position on his nose. Eagerly, he moved to the bookcase and quietly searched for a book. Finally finding what he was looking for, he held up a large, burgundy book with gold lettering.

"What's that, Grandpa?" asked Hayden. "Is that the Legend?"

Grandpa smiled and held up the book, showing Hayden the title.

"Shakespeare? What does he have to do with Heber C. Kimball?"

"Nothing really," whispered Grandpa, as he knelt down next to the kids.

He opened the cover of the Shakespeare book to reveal a small metal key taped to the inside.

"What's that key for?" asked Hannah.

"You'll see," replied Grandpa, as he pulled the key from the cover, leaving the book sitting on the floor. Slowly, he stood up and brushed his gray hair back away from his face. Without another word, he turned and shuffled to the far west corner of the room. He stood in front of a beautiful, hand-made armoire. Using the key from the book, he unlocked the armoire doors and opened them, revealing several beautiful antiques.

"Hey, that's a pretty lamp. Is that what you're getting?" asked Hannah, peering around Grandpa's shoulder.

"Nope," he replied, looking back at her. "I'm looking for this." Reaching up toward the top of the armoire, standing on his tippy toes, he stretched and barely made contact with the top of the armoire. He patted the top softly until he located another key. They watched curiously as Grandpa held up an old, rusted key. It was round, about six inches long and had three short teeth at the end. With excitement in his eyes, Grandpa quickly lifted an old metal box from inside of the armoire and placed it softly on the blue carpet. He slipped the metal key into the lock and turned until there was a distinct click.

Once the lid was open, he reached inside with both hands and retrieved a small, dark brown journal that had a very weathered, leather cover. Wrapped around the small journal was a long, thin strap. It was tied into a knot, keeping the contents of the book secure. Clutching the book tightly, he walked back to the rocker and sat down. Several anxious seconds passed without a word.

Hunter could no longer stand the suspense.

"Grandpa, are you awake? Tell us the Legend already! I'm gonna go crazy," Hunter insisted impatiently.

Grandpa peered over his glasses, grinned and replied, "I'm excited that you want to know. I was afraid this Legend would be forgotten after I was gone. I'm already afraid that some clues may have been lost or forgotten over time."

"Well then, quit stalling and tell us," demanded Hannah.

"All right, all right," replied Grandpa, as he held up the small, brown leather book. He untied the strap and carefully turned the fragile pages, which had yellowed with age.

Searching only a few seconds, Grandpa found the page he was looking for and started. "Located in your Great-Great-Great-Great-Great Grandfather, Heber C. Kimball's personal journal is an entry dated May 15, 1855. This is where the Legend begins. The journal entry is fairly long, but I need to read you the entire page...

"'Today was an uneventful day, which I gratefully appreciated after the unexpected events of the last week. I arose as usual at 5:30 a.m. and tended to my regular chores around the house and yard. I even found time to work on Vilate's list of chores. She smiled as I crossed off several of the items in desperate need of attention. I haven't seen her smile much recently, with all of the sickness in the town. She is still the most beautiful woman I have ever met. After a hard but productive day, I am lying in bed, preparing to turn in for the first

time in months at a respectable hour. With only...

"'Well, what was I writing? The time is now 1:00 a.m., and I am not sure, after the tale I've just read, if sleep will actually come tonight.

"'Sister Elizabeth Cowdery, wife of Oliver Cowdery, very unexpectedly knocked on the door around 11:00 p.m. as I was completing my journaling and preparing to pray. She brought with her a sealed envelope from her husband. As she delivered the envelope, a tear trickled down her face. She told me of her husband's passing and the promise she'd made to him to keep the envelope secret and personally place it into my hands.

"'When she made the promise to him, she never expected it would take her a few years to reach the Salt Lake Valley, nor did she anticipate the struggle she would have bringing the letter from Richmond, Missouri. I asked her why the envelope was so important, and she shrugged her shoulders saying, "Oliver never told me. The only thing he would say is that the contents of the envelope would be very important to the Church, something he had to do to help bring forth the fullness of the Gospel."

"'Satisfied that she had keep her final promise to her husband, she hugged Sister Kimball and I, smiled with relief and disappeared into the dark, as mysteriously as she had appeared. As I held the letter in my hand, intrigued by its contents, I again retired to bed before opening the envelope. I wondered what could be so important that she would travel across the country to personally bring it to me. I carefully sliced the edge of the envelope open to reveal several pages of handwritten text, which read:

"'Dear Brother Heber,

As I lie ill in bed, surely close to my return to our Father in Heaven, I've been inspired in a dream to relate an unbelievable tale to you. I shall not attempt to pen to you the feelings of my heart, nor the majestic beauty and glory which surrounded me in my dream on this occasion, but believe me when I say that what I am about to tell you is the truth.

"'In my dream, the Spirit revealed to me that, because you are faithful and steadfast in your testimony, and because you are a man to be trusted in all things, the time has come for me to reveal a secret charged to me by the Angel Moroni himself. Moroni told me that because of events that will happen in the future, it is imperative that you be informed of those things, which are to come, and which will directly affect your posterity in regards to my secret charge.

"'As you are aware, I acted as scribe for Joseph Smith as he translated the Book of Mormon by means of the Urim and Thummim. I beheld with my eyes, and handled with my hands, the Gold Plates from which the Book of Mormon was translated. I was chosen, with Martin Harris and David Whitmer, to be a witness to the authenticity of the Gold Plates. While these are well known facts, they are only two of the many assignments given to me while in the service of Joseph Smith.

"'As I dreamt, the Spirit impressed upon my mind that I should relate to you a secret assignment—something only the following four men knew: Joseph Smith, Jr., Martin Harris, David Whitmer and myself. After Joseph was allowed by the Lord to show the Gold Plates to the eight witnesses, he was required by Moroni to return the gold plates to the Hill Cumorah—a hill of considerable size. We were not to replace them where Joseph had taken them from under a rock on the west side of the hill, but to a place revealed to us as we approached the hill. It is for this reason that I write you this letter.

"'As we neared the hill, Joseph and I were overcome by the Holy Spirit, and were suddenly unable to stand. We sat in the grass at the base of the hill. With little energy, I tried to speak but was unable to utter the smallest sound. Several hours passed in this same manner, and I found myself crying in my mind to my Father in Heaven for help. Then suddenly, Angel Moroni appeared saying 'By the light of the lamp.' As I did not understand what he meant, I asked, 'What?' And again, the angel spake saying, 'By the light of the lamp.'

"'Moments later, Joseph and I witnessed the Hill open, and we proceeded to walk into a cave in which there was a large and spacious room. I do not know whether the light in the room came from the sun or by some artificial means; I only know that the cave was as light as noonday, and the room was very warm. Glancing at my strange surroundings, I observed a room full of treasures—treasures beyond anything I could imagine. "'I watched as Joseph laid the gold plates on a large, wooden table in the center of the cave. Under the table was a pile of plates as much as two feet high and what looked to be wagons full of plates placed all around the room. The sword of Laban hung on the wall, along with the breastplate. I saw the

Urim and Thummim and many other relics in the room, far too many for me to list.

"'Joseph and I were overcome by the Spirit again, and I found myself in fervent prayer to the Lord. Within minutes, I heard Moroni whisper the words, 'By the light of the lamp', only this time he revealed what was to be required of me. During the last dispensation, before the return of the Lord, many events written of by the prophets of old would come to pass. In order for these events to occur, the treasures hidden inside the Hill Cumorah would have to be revealed, bringing to light the missing information needed for those prophecies to be fulfilled.

"'Moroni then stated that Joseph and the Three Witnesses would be responsible to devise a series of clues, showing the path back to the Hill Cumorah. Each clue would lead to the next and would contain the information needed for future generations to return and claim the vast treasures in the name of the Lord.

"'Angel Moroni then placed a charge upon us that we should never speak of this to any other person besides those names listed above, except if we were told to in a vision.

"'As I have now been told in vision to tell you regarding this most precious secret, and I know my time on this earth is nearing its end, I pass Moroni's charge on to you. In your hands lie the clues needed to bring to pass the returning of the Lord.

"'Your great-great grandchildren will bring honor and glory to your name, as long as they remain as faithful as you. Protect these clues, even with your very life, and prepare your children's children to do the same. Never speak outside your own home of this to anyone. And beware, there are those who would lay a cunning plan to destroy these clues. Satan and his followers will try to alter the hearts of your posterity.

"'Be diligent in teaching your children and grandchildren by the Spirit in the ways of the Lord. Remain faithful in all things. Be trustworthy, and hold tight to your testimony of the gospel. If you do these things, your posterity shall be blessed for your sake. Remember always to stay 'By the light of the lamp'.

"'With that, I awoke from my dream and found that I had slept almost the entire day.

Brother Heber C. Kimball, may the Lord, our Father, bless you and your posterity for all time. Such is my prayer, in anticipation of the return of our Savior to the earth. Such is the desire of my heart.

Your eternal friend,

Oliver Cowdery'

"'As I read the letter, I was shocked at its contents. Then I realized why Oliver had been so insistent that Sister Cowdery personally deliver the envelope to me. I'm not sure exactly what I will do. Prayer always brings the answers.'"

As Grandpa paused, Hayden nervously asked, "Is that all?"

"Yes," answered Grandpa. "That's all of it."

"Are you sure there aren't any other entries?" Hunter persisted.

"None, and I've read every word written in all of his journals."

"Are there any journal entries that mention the saying 'By the light of the lamp'?" asked Hannah.

"No," replied Grandpa. "Nothing more is mentioned in any of Heber's journals."

"What do you mean? There have to be more entries," interjected Hunter. "Are you hiding something from us, Grandpa?"

"No, Hunter. That is why this tale is a Legend. No one knows if there's any truth to the story. However, your Great Grandpa told me, before he died, that the Legend of the Lamp was the treasure of all treasures, and it would bring to pass a great and marvelous work."

"How did he know that?" asked Hannah.

"I'm not sure. But according to him, that was what Heber said before his death."

"There is not a lot of information. How are we supposed to find the treasure with so little to go on?" asked Hunter.

"Yeah, I didn't hear any clues in the letter," complained Hannah.

"That's right. Nothing other than Oliver's few hints," replied Grandpa. "But Angel Moroni thought that was enough."

"What about the clue that was found? Didn't Aunt Shirley say something about a clue?" asked Hayden.

"Yes, she did," said Hunter. "What was the clue she was talking about, Grandpa? She said you found something recently."

CHAPTER FOUR

"ARE YOU SURE you want to get involved in this treasure hunt?" Grandpa asked warily. "You may never find any more clues. There is also a good possibility that if clues ever did exist, they may have been lost or destroyed by now."

"Grandpa, did you find a clue?" Hayden asked excitedly. "Come on. Please tell us."

"I think that I did," he replied proudly.

"A clue that suggests this Legend might be real?" questioned Hunter.

"I'm not sure, kids. Maybe we better stop here with the Legend. I don't want you to spend your lives trying to find the treasure as many of the Kimball's have done. After all these years, there is only one known article that suggests the tale might be real," Grandpa answered nervously.

"No way, Grandpa. I don't want to stop now," said Hunter.

"Yeah, Grandpa. Maybe we can help find the treasure.

Oliver Cowdery's story said that Heber C.'s posterity was destined to find the treasure," Hayden exclaimed excitedly.

"I guess that is true," replied Grandpa.

"Maybe no one was supposed to find the clues until now," suggested Hannah. "We could be the posterity Oliver spoke about."

Grandpa smiled, took a deep breath and looked at his three grandchildren. He could not deny he was nervous, but excited, to pass on the Legend.

"I remember when my father told me about the Legend. I was as hopeful for it to be real as you are."

"So, what was the clue that you found?" interrupted Hunter. "Let's get moving on this. We could possibly find the treasure tonight."

"Yeah, what was the clue you found?" questioned Hannah. "Quit stalling and tell us."

"All right, but I know that my father, grandfather and great-grandfather spent most of their lives looking for anything that would indicate the tale was true, but never had any luck. I've also spent a good portion of my life searching for this treasure, and the clue that I've found isn't completely translated."

"Well, tell us what it is already!" shouted Hayden. "Maybe we can help."

"Are you really sure you're interested?" Grandpa asked through a smile. "All of this Legend stuff may be a figment of your old grandpa's imagination."

"Come on, Grandpa. Quit teasing. Interested? Yeah, I'm interested," responded Hannah.

"So am I, Grandpa!" yelled Hayden, jumping to his feet. "Show us!"

"Come on, Grandpa. What is it?" asked Hunter, raising his eyebrows and elevating his voice in excitement.

"Well, I'm not sure. What if you three can't keep a secret and someone else finds out about the Legend?" Grandpa replied skeptically. "I already think someone outside the Kimball family may be out there looking for the treasure right now."

"We can keep a secret, Grandpa. We promise!" squealed Hannah, shaking uncontrollably from the excitement.

Grandpa smiled and leaned forward in his rocking chair. He stretched out his arms and grabbed Hannah's shaking hands. Holding them together tightly, he said, "Maybe, you kids are taking this Legend too seriously. I don't want to ruin your lives. You need to remember that I'm the only Kimball still alive that believes there's any truth to Oliver's letter," said Grandpa worriedly. "I've even written the brethren at the Church offices regarding the Legend, and they have assured me that no such treasure exists. Maybe I oughta stop with this story now before you get too caught up in this mystery and treasure. Besides, I want you to be able to enjoy your vacation and not worry about the Legend."

"NO, Grandpa!" Hannah yelled insistently. "Come on. You've got to tell us now. Pllleeease," she begged.

"Yeah, Grandpa, I won't be able to get the story out of mind if you don't tell us," insisted Hunter. "I guess if you don't tell us, I'm going to have to start looking without your help."

"Well...okay. But remember, no matter what, the letter I'm going to show you does not make the Legend true. In fact, I'm not sure what or how much of it is true, and no one outside our family can know anything about the Legend."

"Okay, I won't say a thing," replied Hayden, as he held up three fingers signaling the Boy Scout promise.

Without another word, Grandpa stood up abruptly from his chair. He looked sternly at his grandchildren, then wiggled his mouth to the left and to the right, as though in deep thought. He took in a huge breath, filling his chest full of air, and then slowly softened the stern look on his face as he released it. "Oh, okay," he said.

They smiled excitedly and quietly watched as Grandpa again opened the door to the Blue Room and cautiously peered into the hall. Startled to see Maria staring back at him, he jumped in fright.

"What are you doing, Maria?" he asked. "You about scared me to death."

"I'm sorry, Mr. Kimball," Maria replied. "I am only dusting the pictures before I vacuum."

"Don't worry about these old pictures, they're fine," he snapped, as he continued to peer down the hallway. "This is my area, and I don't need it cleaned," he barked.

Maria nodded, then rushed down the stairs toward the front room. Absolutely sure she was gone, and that no one else was watching or listening, Grandpa closed the door. Shaking his head in frustration and mumbling underneath his breath, he quickly walked to the window. Again he looked for anything suspicious. When he found nothing, he quickly pulled the curtains back together until all of the light from outside was extinguished.

"What are you doing, Grandpa?" asked Hayden. "Why do you keep doing that?

"Yeah, who are you looking for?" asked Hunter. "Is there a problem?"

"I'm only being cautious," Grandpa replied. "Lately, I've noticed a few things missing or out of place here in the Blue Room, and I want to make sure no one is watching or listening."

"Things missing?" asked Hannah. "Like what? Legend stuff? The clue?"

"No, not the clue. I've hidden the clue well—where it will never be found. The missing objects are odd– several old books, an antique coin, Grandpa's pocket watch, and a few other random items. It's almost like someone has learned about the Legend and they are searching for clues to its whereabouts," he replied. "I'm getting nervous. Maybe this isn't the right time for searching."

Ignoring Grandpa's comment, Hunter asked, "Do you know who it is?"

"I don't know for sure," Grandpa replied. "But, I do have my eyes on a few suspects."

"Who then?" asked Hannah.

"I better not say until I know for sure," he answered.

Without another word, he walked over to the roll-top desk that Grandma called her secretary and popped open a secret door. He slowly reached inside and removed an old, brass castle key with three teeth, which was heavily tarnished. Again he paused, looked around the room and motioned for the kids to be absolutely quiet.

Grandpa finally walked across the blue, shag carpet to the small closet in the Southeast corner of the room. Opening the door, he stepped inside the closet and reached toward the top of the door. Just above the door-frame, he took hold of a tiny, blue cloth and pulled a small section of the drywall away, revealing an old, metal box. Quickly pulling the shoe-size box from the opening, he placed it on the floor.

He smiled as he reached in his pocket and retrieved the small key which he slipped inside the lock on the box. With a quick turn, he opened the box and retrieved a small, carefully–folded piece of paper. He left the box on the floor and hastily returned to the rocking chair, holding the paper tightly in his hand.

"Grandpa sure has a lot of hidden keys," whispered Hannah.

"Is that the clue, Grandpa?" Hayden asked in a soft voice.

"It sure is," Grandpa replied quietly, as he cautiously unfolded the white, half-sheet of paper.

"What does it say?" asked Hannah.

Grandpa looked up and smiled. "It's exciting to think the Legend might have some truth, isn't it?"

They nodded, anxious for Grandpa to read the clue.

Grandpa whispered, "I hoped something more had been written somewhere. With no other place to turn, I started an Internet search on, 'Articles written about and by Heber C. Kimball'. Hundreds of sites were listed. So, one by one, I searched through every article. On one of the sites I searched was a letter written by Brigham Young to his son. I almost passed over the site, unsure if the letter would have anything to do with the Legend, but afraid it might, I pulled up the article. Oddly, the only information on the site was that the letter had recently been found in an old box of documents, and the owner never had the time to translate the letter. Intrigued, I downloaded the letter. The message I saw was written in a language I had never seen before."

Grandpa carefully laid the paper on the table and continued. "Although I couldn't read the words, I hoped this was a clue to the Legend. Over the last several months, I started researching the writing and found that Brigham Young commissioned three men to create a language. This new language would be helpful to the Church by simplifying the spelling and reading of the English language, making learning to speak and read English easier for converts from several different countries. I was surprised to find that the three men who wrote the language were Parley P. Pratt, Heber C. Kimball and George D. Watt.

"According to the internet site, this letter never reached Brigham Young's son. In fact, it never was sent to his son, as Brigham Young died the day it was written. The Deseret Language died when Brigham Young did and was dropped from use in 1877. I finally found a copy of the alphabet a few weeks ago, but I have not translated all the lines yet. Here is the letter I printed," he said, holding up the paper.

"Dear Son,

I wrote this letter in the Deseret alphabet in an attempt to keep the contents private. Several years ago at the funeral of Heber C. Kimball the following events transpired. Because I feel this letter to be important I've returned to my journal so that I can give you a full account.

June 22, 1868—Today was an exceptional day for me with the passing of my dearest and most trusted friend Heber C. Kimball. As I gazed one last time at his face the visions of my childhood flashed before my eyes bringing a multitude of tears. I know that he departs to a better place, but I will miss his contagious and mischievous laugh.

As I turned to leave the funeral ceremony Prescindia Huntington Kimball his wife pulled at my arm and quietly handed me a small note. She quietly said, 'Heber fell asleep forever clutching this paper in his tightened fist. I attempted to read the letter, but was unable to do so. Upon further examination, your name is the only word written in English. I know what great friends you two have been and I hoped this letter was meant for you.'

With that, Prescindia turned and disappeared into the crowds of people. Curious about the letter, I opened it and found that Heber had written the entire note in the Deseret Alphabet. As the crowd of people at the funeral desired my attention, I quickly stuffed the letter into my pocket, excited to read the contents at a later time.

the letter later that evening, I placed the note inside knowing one day I would follow through with Heber's requests. Sadly, I have not had time to give the note another thought. As you know, I have become more and more ill and I'm trying to get my affairs in order. I know that my time to return to our Father in Heaven is growing near. As Heber C. Kimball asked, I wish to return his last letter to his children. However, as the text is written in the Deseret Alphabet, which is not as well known as I would like. I believe it is my duty to translate his letter before returning it to his children. Although returning this letter is my desire, due to my failing health, I am in desperate need of your assistance. As soon as you have the time, please translate these writings for me, that I may remain a trusted friend to Heber and return the letter to his posterity. I appreciate all that you do for me in the service of our Lord.

Your loving Father'."
'Brother Brigham,

As you are the most trustworthy man I know, I am entrusting to you the fate of my posterity. Please guard this letter with your very life for my sake. When my children have grown, please return to them this letter that they may continue the work of the Lord. I appreciate all that you have done for me, during my life and now even in my death.

"'By the light of the lamp,
That Joseph Smith owned,
Flickers the start to a map
That shows the way home.

While the light shines the brightest
With the wick fully soaked,
Your journey begins
When the chimney starts to smoke.

In the dark find the secrets
That will open the past
To a people long forgotten
Bringing forth ancient prophecies at last.

Kimball Posterity,

Remain faithful and all shall be revealed. Pray for the Lord's guidance and pay close attention to every detail. Search with the Lion, yielding unending courage.

Make me proud,
Heber C Kimball'"

"What language is this, Grandpa?" asked Hunter. "I don't recognize it."

"That is because very few people know of this language," Grandpa replied. "It is the language I was telling you about a minute ago called the Deseret Alphabet."

"Have you been able to translate the writings correctly?" asked Hannah.

"Well, I think so. I have translated most of the letter already, and it seems to make sense."

"Is it hard to translate?" asked Hayden.

"A little," replied Grandpa.

"Are you sure this letter is a clue to the Legend?" asked Hunter.

"Yes, I am now. Let me read to you what I have so far so that you can see," Grandpa replied.

"'Dear Son,

I write this letter in the Deseret Alphabet in an attempt to keep the contents private. Several years ago, at the funeral of Heber C. Kimball, the following events transpired. Because I feel this letter to be important, I've returned to my journal so that I can give you a full account.

"'June 22, 1868—Today was an emotional day for me with the passing of my dearest and most trusted friend, Heber C. Kimball. As I gazed one last time at his face, the visions of my childhood flashed before my eyes, bringing a multitude of tears. I know that he departs to a better place, but I will miss his contagious and mischievous laugh.

"'As I turned to leave the funeral ceremony, Prescindia Huntington Kimball, Heber's wife, pulled at my arm and quietly handed me a small note. She said, 'Heber fell asleep, forever in this life, clutching this paper in his tightened fist. I attempted to read the letter, but was unable to do so. Upon further examination, your name is the only word written in English. I know what great friends you two have been, and I hoped this letter was meant for you.

"'With that, Prescendia turned and disappeared into the crowds of people. Curious about the letter, I opened it and found that Heber had written the entire note in the Deseret Alphabet. As the crowd of people at the funeral desired my attention, I quickly stuffed the letter into my pocket, planning to read the contents at a later time.

"'Below is the letter that she gave to me. After reading the letter later that evening, I placed the note aside. I knew that one day I would follow through with Heber's requests. Sadly, I have not had time to give the note another thought. As you know, I have become more and more ill and am getting my final affairs into order. I know that my time to return to our Father in Heaven is drawing near. As Heber C. Kimball asked, I wish to return his last letter to his children. However, as the text is written in the Deseret Alphabet, which is not known as well as I would like, I believe it is my duty to translate his letter before returning it his children.

"'Although returning this letter is my desire, due to my failing health, I am in desperate need of your assistance. As soon as you have the time, please translate these writings for me, that I may remain a trusted friend to Heber and return the letter to his posterity. I appreciate all that you do for me in the service of our Lord.

Your Loving Father'."

"So, Heber had a letter in his hand when he died, and his wife gave the letter to Brigham Young?" asked Hayden.

"That's right," replied Grandpa.

"So, where is the letter?" asked Hunter.

"Right here," said Grandpa, waving a piece of paper in the air. "I'm going to read what I have translated from the letter so far."

"Oh, I am so excited. What does it say?" asked Hayden impatiently.

Grandpa smiled and replied,

"'Brother Brigham,

As you are the most trustworthy man I know, I am entrusting to you the fate of my posterity. Please guard this letter with your very life for my sake. When my children have grown, please return to them this letter that they may continue the work of the Lord. I appreciate all that you have done for me, during my life and now even in my death.

"BY THE LIGHT OF THE LAMP
THAT JOSEPH SMITH OWNED,
FLICKERS THE START TO A MAP
THAT SHOWS THE WAY HOME.

WHILE THE LIGHT SHINES THE BRIGHTEST
WITH THE WICK FULLY SOAKED,

YOUR JOURNEY BEGINS
WHEN THE CHIMNEY STARTS TO SMOKE.'"

Grandpa paused, looked up at the kids and smiled.

"Well, keep reading. What's next?" asked Hunter impatiently.

"That's it. I don't have any more of the letter translated yet. But, I'm getting closer," he said proudly, as he laid the small paper with strange writing on the table.

Hannah picked up the paper and looked over the unfamiliar letters and shapes. Then she held the paper up for Hunter and Hayden to see.

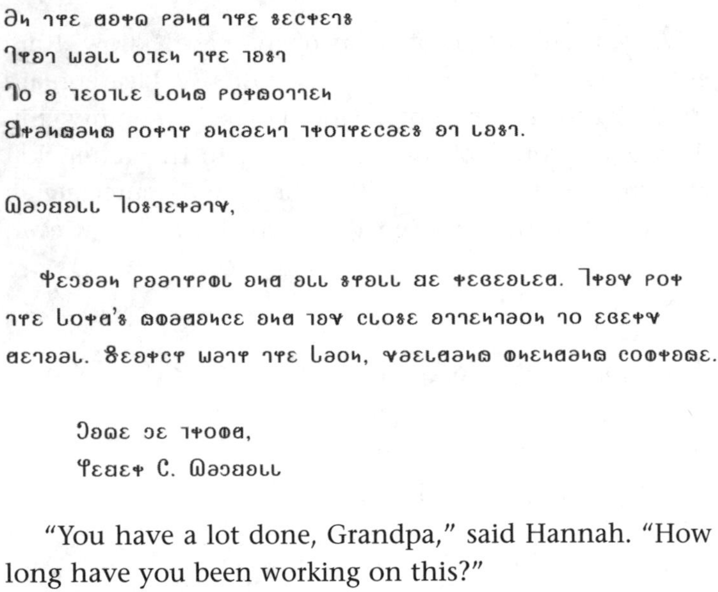

"You have a lot done, Grandpa," said Hannah. "How long have you been working on this?"

"Everyday for the last several weeks," he replied. "I'm

not very fast with my eye sight, but I'm getting it done."

"We can help you finish translating the letter, Grandpa," Hannah suggested excitedly.

"Do you have the time?" he asked. "I don't think the translation would take you three as long as it does me."

"We have until Mom calls us," replied Hunter, as he pulled the paper from Hannah's hand.

"Yeah, come on, let's hurry. I bet we can finish it if we hurry," said Hayden.

"Where is the key to translate the words?" asked Hannah, ready to start translating.

Grandpa smiled. Without a word, he hurried to the metal box still lying on the floor. Lifting the lid, he retrieved a small, brown book and held it up for his grandkids to see. The tan cover had several pictures on the front. At the top, in bold print were written the words ***Deseret Alphabet.*** Directly underneath the words was a sketch of a beehive wrapped in swirling leaves and vines. Several words in the Deseret Alphabet were written in the middle of the cover. And in the center at the bottom of the cover was a sketch of the Salt Lake Temple, also surrounded with leaves and vines.

As Grandpa walked back to the kids he asked, "Who has a pencil?"

Suddenly, there was a crash from the closet. Startled, Grandpa dropped the book and Hannah screamed. Grandpa was sure that someone was listening to their conversation. He spun around to see who was behind him. With no one in sight, he walked back toward the closet and yelled, "Who's in there?" With no response, he again demanded, "Who's in there?"

"I don't think anyone is in there, Grandpa," said Hunter, walking toward him. "Look! I think it was the lid to the metal box slamming shut."

Grandpa looked at the box and took a big, slow breath. "I think you're right, Hunter," Grandpa replied, still shaking with fright. "I guess I'm nervous. I'm finally finding information on the Legend and I really don't want anyone else to find out anything about it."

"I really thought someone was there, Grandpa," said Hannah. "That really scared me, too."

"I guess it doesn't hurt to be on the cautious side," said Grandpa, holding his heart and smiling. "You all need to remember to be very careful."

"Hayden, run downstairs and get a pencil, will you please?" asked Hunter.

Hayden jumped to his feet and said, "Sure, I'll be right back."

He threw open the door to the Blue Room and ran down the stairs toward the front room. He almost ran over Maria, who was sitting at the bottom of the stairs. As Hayden moved to the side to miss her, his big feet caught on her apron and sent him tumbling forward—straight for Grandma's flower stand. Hearing the noise from upstairs, Hannah and Hunter walked to the edge of the landing and watched as Hayden slowly sat up, picking leaves out of his hair.

"You okay?" called Hannah.

Hayden looked up to the top of the stairs and said, "I hurt everywhere. I'm sure that's gonna leave a mark!"

"Do you need some help?" asked Hunter.

"No, I got it. I'll just pick up the dirt and put it back in the planter. It's all good," Hayden replied, shaking his head as he stood.

"Are you all right, Maria?" asked Hannah.

"I'm fine. He didn't hit me when he fell," she replied. "I will help him clean up the mess."

Maria scurried to her feet and helped Hayden pull the leaves and debris from his hair. Hunter and Hannah quickly turned and walked back into the Blue Room. They were ready to get started on the translation.

"All right, let me take a look at what you have done, so I can see what still needs to be translated," said Hannah. She picked up the paper and started reading. "Well, Grandpa, the translation almost looks complete. We only need to finish the last few lines of the clue and the last paragraph." Reaching her hand out to Grandpa she said, "Let me see the page of translations so I can lay these two pieces of paper next to each other."

Grandpa handed her the paper and watched as she laid the two pages side by side.

"Let me help, Hannah," said Hunter, as he sat next to her on the floor.

"Okay, you write down the letters that I translate as I say them."

"I can do that as soon as Hayden gets back with the pencil," Hunter replied.

A minute later, Hayden burst into the room yelling, "Come on. We've got to hurry. Mom is on her way up to the Blue Room. I think she is ready to go."

"Give me the pencil, quickly!" shouted Hunter, holding his hand out to Hayden.

Hayden placed the pencil in Hunter's hand and quietly walked to where Grandpa was standing. The two of them eagerly watched Hunter and Hannah work.

"Are you ready, Hunter?" asked Hannah, as she looked at him and smiled.

"Yep, come on. We've got to hurry," he nervously replied.

"You're right, Hunter, but we need to get this right," said Hannah as she looked at the letter. "I'm going to read everything that we have so far."

"'Brother Brigham,

As you are the most trustworthy man I know, I am entrusting to you the fate of my posterity. Please guard this letter with your very life for my sake. When my children have grown, please return to them this letter that they may continue the work of the Lord. I appreciate all that you have done for me, during my life and now even in my death.

"BY THE LIGHT OF THE LAMP
THAT JOSEPH SMITH OWNED,
FLICKERS THE START TO A MAP
THAT SHOWS THE WAY HOME.

WHILE THE LIGHT SHINES THE BRIGHTEST
WITH THE WICK FULLY SOAKED,
YOUR JOURNEY BEGINS
WHEN THE CHIMNEY STARTS TO SMOKE.'"

"Okay, starting where Grandpa left off, the first symbol translated is an, *i* and then *n.* The second word is *the,* and third word is, *D, a, r* then *k*. The fourth word, is *f, i, n, d,* the fifth word is *the,* and last word is *s, e, c, r, e, t, s*. That's it for that line."

"The translated sentence reads, 'In the dark, find the secrets'," said Hunter. "I'm ready for the next one."

"Line two, first letter *t,* then *h, a,* and *t.* The second word is *w, i, l* and *l,* and the third word is *o, p, e,* then *n.* The fourth word is *the,* and finally, *p, a, s,* then *t.*"

"All right, that translated sentence reads, 'That will open the past'," said Hunter. "Next line?"

"The next line starts with…"

Suddenly everyone heard Mom yell, "It's time to go. Come on, you three. I want to stay on schedule."

"Just a minute, Mom," called Hunter.

"No, now," insisted Mom. "We need to hurry. Enough with the Legend."

Panicked, Hayden asked, "What do we do? I don't want to leave yet."

"We can't leave, we're not quite finished," said Hannah.

"I'll go see if I can slow her down for a minute. You three hurry and finish," said Grandpa, as he opened the door and headed down the stairs.

"Keep going, Hannah, or we're never going to get this finished," Hunter said anxiously.

Hannah agreed and started again. "The first letter is..." Nervously, she looked back and forth at each page and could not find the right letter. "It is...I don't know."

"We're all right, Hannah. Don't worry. Grandpa will slow Mom down a minute. Relax and start again," reassured Hunter.

Hannah took a deep breath and started again. "The first letter is... is a *t* and then *o,* the second word is *a* and the third word is, I'm not sure. Umm, I think a *p* then *e, o,* another *p, l,* and then an *e.* Next word *l, o,* I think an *n* and then *g.* The last word is, oh boy, let's see, an *f, o, r* then *g, o, t, t, e* and then *n.*"

"Nice job, Hannah," said Hunter. "Okay, that sentence reads, 'To a people long forgotten'."

"How many sentences are left?" asked Hayden.

"One more line and then a paragraph," replied Hannah.

"Let's finish that last line, Hannah," suggested Hunter.

"Okay, the first word starts with a *b* and then the *ri* sound, then *g* and *i, n,* and *g.* The second word is *f,* then *o,* then *r, t* and *h.* The next word is, *a, n,* then *c, ie* sound, *n* and *t.* The forth word is *p,* then *r, o, ph* sound, then *e, c ie,* sound and *s.* The fifth word is *a* and *t,* and the last word is *l, a, s* and then *t.*"

"Okay, the sentence reads, 'Bringing forth ancient prophecies at last,'" said Hunter.

"Read the entire paragraph, will you please?" asked Hannah.

"IN THE DARK, FIND THE SECRETS
THAT WILL OPEN THE PAST
TO A PEOPLE LONG FORGOTTEN,
BRINGING FORTH ANCIENT PROPHECIES AT LAST.'"

"This is so cool," said Hayden. "I wonder what the treasure could be?"

"I don't know, but you're right—this is very cool," answered Hunter.

"What do we do now? Should we continue to translate with out Grandpa here?" asked Hannah.

"Yeah, I think we better. We need to have all the information we can," replied Hunter. "Hayden, run downstairs and see how Grandpa's doing while Hannah and I finish the letter."

Hayden nodded, turned toward the door and said, "You better hurry, I don't know how long Grandpa can keep Mom busy."

CHAPTER FIVE

HANNAH AND HUNTER quickly continued translating the letter. Hannah worked on one line, while Hunter worked on another. They hoped to decipher the entire letter before Mom wanted to leave. Meanwhile, Grandpa and Hayden tried to keep Grandma, Mom and Aunt Shirley busy.

"I wonder if anything is really missing from the Blue Room, or if Grandpa is imagining things missing because of the new clue," said Hunter, glancing around the room.

"I was wondering the same thing. Grandpa seems to have a pretty good handle on everything that is in here," replied Hannah, as she tried to focus.

"Yeah, he does. But what if the lack of clues in his search for the Legend has made him so cautious about the clue he just found, that he is seeing things that aren't really happening?" wondered Hunter.

"I don't know, but the Legend means so much to him and the Kimball name that Grandpa would do anything to keep it safe," she replied. And I'm sure if anything is missing in this room, with as much time as Grandpa spends in here, he would know."

"Then who would be taking things out of this room?" asked Hunter.

"Who would know about the Legend besides the Kimball family?" questioned Hannah.

"Grandpa said he had written the Church leaders and that they told him there was no treasure. Could someone from the Church be after the clues Grandpa has?" asked Hunter.

"I can't imagine that," replied Hannah, shaking her head.

"Then who?"

"What if the letter he wrote never made it to the Church offices or was delivered to the wrong address?" asked Hannah.

"Then it could be anyone," responded Hunter. "That's a scary thought."

"That is a scary thought. We're gonna have to be very careful. If someone's breaking into Grandpa's house and getting into the Blue Room without anyone knowing, they already have more information about the Legend than we want them to have. We could be in real danger," Hannah said nervously.

"What if the house is bugged, and someone is listening to us? Or what if they have video cameras in here?" asked Hunter, as he anxiously looked around the room.

"Are you trying to scare me, Hunter?" Hannah asked, scowling at him.

"No, I'm trying to make sure we don't get caught off guard," said Hunter.

"Well, if someone is listening to us, we better be careful about what we say out loud," Hannah replied. "In fact, we better be careful about everything. If this Legend has any truth to it, we could have more than a few bad guys after us. We could have a lot of people after us—good guys and bad," Hannah reasoned.

"I'm finished with these lines. Are there any more?" asked Hunter, handing the paper to Hannah.

"No, that's it. I've translated the rest already," she answered. She took the paper from his hand and quickly copied the lines he had translated to her paper.

"Read it to me," Hunter insisted. "What does it say?"

"Hold on, I'm almost done," she replied. "I'm trying to see if we made any mistakes."

"Let's go with what we have. We don't have a lot of time," Hunter replied.

"Okay, see if you think this sounds right," she said, holding up the entire translation.

"'KIMBALL POSTERITY,

REMAIN FAITHFUL AND ALL SHALL BE REVEALED. PRAY FOR THE LORD'S GUIDANCE, AND PAY CLOSE ATTENTION TO EVERY DETAIL. SEARCH WITH THE LION, YIELDING UNENDING COURAGE.

MAKE ME PROUD,
HEBER C. KIMBALL'"

"That's so cool. Heber C. wrote a letter to us," said Hunter, smiling widely. "We are his posterity."

Hannah smiled and agreed. "Yes, he did. That is pretty cool."

"Alright, what do we do now?" asked Hunter, looking around the room.

"Well, with the letter Heber left behind for his family, he includes a clue. I guess we should start with that."

"Okay, read the clue from the beginning. Let's get started," Hunter replied anxiously.

"Before we do, shouldn't we go check on Hayden and Grandpa?" asked Hannah.

"Maybe, but if Mom sees us, she's gonna want to leave on the trip," responded Hunter.

"Let's sneak down the stairs and look into the front room. If we don't see anyone, then we'll come back and work on the clue. Okay?" asked Hannah.

"Yep, that sounds good," replied Hunter.

Quietly, the two opened the door. Hannah slowly stuck her head out to make sure no one was there.

"What was that?" she asked, as she jumped quickly back into the room.

"What was what?" asked Hunter, as he stuck his head out the door.

"I thought I saw something," she replied, shaking her head back and forth.

"I didn't see anything. I think you're seeing things," replied Hunter, as he pushed passed Hannah, rubbing the top of her head with his hand. "Come on, we need to hurry."

Hannah pushed Hunter's hand away and said, "Don't, I know I saw something. I'm sure of it, Hunter."

The two carefully maneuvered their way down the stairs toward the front room. They paused only for a moment when they heard the front door open and slam shut.

"Who was that?" asked Hannah.

"I don't know. I can't see the door," Hunter replied.

"I can't see anyone. I think we should try to decipher the clue," said Hannah.

"I do too," said Hunter. He peered around the wall, looking for any sign of Hayden or Grandpa. "I'm worried that we might need Grandpa's help, though."

"So what do we do?"

"Hey, look. There they are!" yelled Hunter, as he jumped behind the sofa and pointed toward the window.

Hannah and Hunter watched as Mom, Aunt Shirley, Grandma, Grandpa and Hayden stood on the front lawn and stared at the motor home. Mom shook her head, almost as though she was angry. She placed her hands on her hips as she listened to Grandpa talk.

"I wonder what's the matter?" whispered Hannah.

"I don't know, but it doesn't look good," replied Hunter. "I wish we could hear what they're saying."

"I think we better go find out," suggested Hannah, as she moved from behind her hiding place and walked toward the front door.

"Yeah, I think you're right. I don't want to start this trip with Mom mad at us for the first three days," replied Hunter. He stood from his hiding spot and followed

Hannah out the front door.

"Hey, Mom. What's the matter?" asked Hannah, as she walked out the door and through the grass toward the group.

Mom looked over at Hannah, almost in tears. Without saying a word, she pointed toward the back tire of the motor home.

"We've got a flat tire," replied Hayden, as he turned his face away from Mom and smiled.

"Oh, man. How did that happen?" asked Hunter, looking very concerned.

"I don't know, sweetie. I guess we ran over a nail or something," Mom replied, in a squeaky voice. "So much for staying on our schedule."

"Well, what do I need to do to fix it?" Hunter asked, as he started to roll up his sleeves and walk toward the tire. "Do we have a spare?"

"You don't need to do anything. Grandpa already checked, and the spare is flat as well. So, I called your Dad and he called Triple A to come and fix them both. Dad said they should be here in about twenty minutes," Mom answered.

"Good," said Hunter. "We should be back on track soon."

"That's not too bad," said Hayden, patting Mom on the shoulder.

"I know that's fast. I just didn't want to get a slow start on our first day," Mom replied sadly. "I hope since we have a flat tire now, we won't get one while we're traveling."

"Oh hey, with the way Aunt Shirley drives, we'll make

up the lost hour in no time," said Hannah.

Mom made a feeble attempt at a smile, patted Hannah on the shoulder and said, "I guess you're right. Aunt Shirley is a crazy driver."

"Hey, wait a minute. That sounded like someone made a joke at my expense," responded Aunt Shirley, as she started to chase after Hannah. "You better take that back!"

Hannah ran screaming toward the house as Aunt Shirley continued to chase her. She ran through the front door, slammed the screen closed and locked it to keep Aunt Shirley from coming in the house.

"Grandpa, I had a question about one of your books up in the Blue Room. Could you help me, please?" asked Hannah.

"I'm still gonna get you, Hannah," Aunt Shirley warned, as she tugged on the screen door. "Don't think you've escaped."

Hannah smiled at her through the screen and said, "We'll see about that, Aunt Shirley. You're not fast enough to catch me! Grandpa, can you help me please?" she called again, anxious for him to protect her.

"Sure, Hannah," he answered. "I will be up as soon as the guys get here to fix these tires."

"Oh, I can wait for them, Dad," said Mom. "Why don't you go get my cute kids excited to go on this road trip for me. I think you're the only one who can do that."

Grandpa smiled and asked, "Are you sure?"

"Yes," answered Mom. "Now get out of here."

Grandpa grabbed Hayden's hand and said, "Come on.

Let's go see what your sister needs. You too, Hunter, come with me."

Mom smiled as she watched her two boys' race to the front door toward Hannah. She knew Grandpa loved the Legend and was excited to share it with his grandkids. As they raced in the house, Grandpa ran by Hannah toward the Blue Room. As he reached the stairs, he slowed down slightly.

"So, tell me, how does the clue end?" Grandpa asked excitedly, as he fell into the old rocking chair, completely exhausted.

"First, tell me what you did to the tires," Hunter said, grinning suspiciously. "I know you did something. Dad and I checked them both last night when we filled up the motor home tank with gas."

"Me?" replied Grandpa. "I would never do something like you're suggesting."

"Yeah. Right. I know you did something," Hunter replied.

"Well, I don't know what you could mean," said Grandpa, acting suspicious. "So, come on, tell me what the rest of the letter says."

Hannah quickly pulled the paper from her pocket, unfolded it and read,

"BY THE LIGHT OF THE LAMP,
THAT JOSEPH SMITH OWNED,
FLICKERS THE START TO A MAP
THAT SHOWS THE WAY HOME.

WHILE THE LIGHT SHINES THE BRIGHTEST
WITH THE WICK FULLY SOAKED,
YOUR JOURNEY BEGINS
WHEN THE CHIMNEY STARTS TO SMOKE.

IN THE DARK, FIND THE SECRETS
THAT WILL OPEN THE PAST
TO A PEOPLE LONG FORGOTTEN,
BRINGING FORTH ANCIENT PROPHECIES AT LAST.'

'KIMBALL POSTERITY,

REMAIN FAITHFUL, AND ALL SHALL BE REVEALED. PRAY FOR THE LORD'S GUIDANCE, AND PAY CLOSE ATTENTION TO EVERY DETAIL. SEARCH WITH THE LION, YIELDING UNENDING COURAGE.

MAKE ME PROUD,
HEBER C. KIMBALL'."

"Is that all of it?" Grandpa asked, as he slid to the edge of the rocker.

"Yes, that's the rest of the letter," replied Hunter.

"What does it mean?" asked Hayden. "We don't have a lot of time before Mom has those two tires fixed."

"Let's think about this. What could the clue mean?" asked Grandpa, rubbing his chin. "I need to think."

"Grandpa, do we know what lamp the clue refers to?" asked Hunter.

"No," Grandpa replied.

"We know that the lamp belonged to Joseph Smith. Does that help?" asked Hayden.

"I'm not sure. Let me think for a minute," replied Grandpa, as he stared into space.

"If we find the lamp, the clue says that it will have a map," said Hunter.

The kids watched as Grandpa sat motionless in his rocker, staring at the wall for what seemed like a full minute before he finally blinked his eyes. Hannah, nervous from the silence in the room, started to pace back and forth, wondering what she could do to help.

"Sit down, Hannah! You're making me nervous," said Hunter, in a grouchy voice.

Hannah ignored Hunter and continued to pace until Hunter could not stand her nervousness any longer.

"Hannah, sit down," he yelled, as he walked to where she was standing. He forcefully helped her to sit on the ground.

Hannah pushed his arms away from her shoulders, but remained on the floor. Anxiously waiting for Grandpa to say something, she noticed the lamp that was in the armoire. She stood up and walked to the lamp. Carefully lifting the tall, brass lamp out of the armoire, she noticed the intricate designs carved in the brass from the base to the top. She also saw some etching in the glass ball.

"Where did this come from, Grandpa?" she asked, as she held up the lamp.

Grandpa looked up and gasped as he noticed her holding the lamp. "Be careful, Hannah, that lamp is very, very old," he insisted nervously.

"Where did it come from?" she asked again.

"That was a lamp that Prescindia owned," he replied.

"Prescendia?" asked Hayden inquisitively.

"Prescendia was Heber C. Kimball's wife."

"Where did she get it?" asked Hunter. "Why is this lamp so important?"

"I'm not sure. My understanding is that this might have been one of the lamps that Joseph Smith used when translating the Book of Mormon. That's why this lamp is your Grandmother's favorite lamp."

"How did Prescendia get Joseph Smith's lamp?"

"All I know is that the lamp was given to Prescendia before she married Heber, and it has been passed down from generation to generation since."

"How did Grandma get the lamp?" asked Hayden.

"I can't remember exactly. But I believe my Mom, Mae Wallace, who loved your grandma more than anything, gave her the lamp before she died. Grandma loved the lamp so much, she brought it up into the Blue Room and hid it in the armoire so that nothing would happen to it."

"Would Grandma know more about the lamp?" asked Hannah. "Maybe your Mom told her something about it when she gave it to Grandma."

"I'm sure she would tell us anything she knows," replied Grandpa.

"Would you ask her for us? Maybe this lamp is the lamp we are looking for," suggested Hannah.

"Sure, I can ask Grandma what she remembers about the lamp," Grandpa agreed. "Wouldn't it be exciting if this was the lamp we were looking for?"

Not waiting for a response, Grandpa immediately turned to the door, pausing only long enough to say, "I'll be right back. Remember to be very careful with everything in here. I don't want anything broken."

They watched as Grandpa slowly shuffled out the door and down the stairs, calling Grandma's name before he was even out the door. As soon as Grandpa was out of sight, Hayden walked over to the lamp and intently stared at the intricate designs. Reaching his hand out to feel the texture of the etched glass, Hannah startled him when she yelled, "Hayden, Grandpa said don't touch. We don't want to break this lamp."

"I'm not going to break it," Hayden responded defensively.

"I know you're not. I'm not going to let you," she replied, holding the lamp close to her body.

"Let's get a closer look at the detail on the lamp, Hannah," said Hunter. "Bring it over and set it down on the table where it will be safe."

Hannah agreed by nodding twice. She carefully walked toward the table, holding tightly to the round base.

Hunter hurried to clear the stack of newspapers from the table, then helped Hannah steady the lamp as she gently set it down. The three kids stared at the lamp in silence, hoping there might be a chance that this could be the lamp mentioned in Heber's letter.

"This lamp is neat," said Hayden, looking at the engravings on the round base. "Wouldn't it be cool if this was the lamp we needed?"

"Cool and totally unrealistic," snapped Hannah. "We'd never be that lucky."

"Unrealistic, Hannah," said Hunter. "But totally cool!"

"Look at the lion etched into the glass," said Hannah, pointing to the glass. "That is totally cool."

"And so is this piece. I wonder what it's for?" questioned Hunter, as he wiggled a small, metal lever about the size of a cotton swab.

"I don't know, but be careful wiggling it so much! This lamp is old," said Hannah, as she watched Hunter continue to move the lever up and down.

"Do you think this lever is what controls the wick?" he asked, still lifting the lever up and down, then left and right.

"On these old oil lamps, I'm not exactly sure. But I think the lever your messing with looks a lot like the levers used to lift and lower the wick. The lever is used to soak the wick in oil, so that it can be lit easily," replied Hannah. "Now, be careful. Don't break the lever or you'll ruin the lamp."

"I'm being careful, Hannah. I'm only trying to figure out how this old thing works," replied Hunter, as he continued to fiddle with the lever.

"The clue says the wick needs to be fully soaked. That's all I'm doing—fully soaking the wick—in case this is the lamp from the letter," he said, smirking at Hannah.

"If this was the right lamp, and we soaked the wick, what would we need to do next?' asked Hayden.

"The clue states that the light shines the brightest with the wick soaked. So that must mean that we need to light the lamp, so that it can shine brightly," replied Hannah.

"So, light it then," suggested Hayden.

"Should I light it before Grandpa gets back?" Hunter asked nervously.

"Yeah, light it already," urged Hayden.

Hannah shrugged her shoulders, lifted her eyebrows high on her face and nodded her head slowly.

"Hayden, run to the kitchen and get some matches as quick as you can," Hunter said excitedly. "Maybe I will light the wick."

"And be quiet," called Hannah.

Hunter continued to lift the wick up and down with the lever. He hoped the oil in the lamp was still good and that he was soaking the wick properly. Barely a minute passed before Hayden burst through the door and ran into the room.

"Here are the matches," he panted, holding them up for Hunter to take.

Hunter stopped moving the wick up and down, grabbed the matches and set them on the table. He carefully lifted the frost-colored, glass bulb off the top of the lamp, revealing a small opening. He set the bulb gently on the table. He then raised the lever, bringing the wick barely above the small, brass opening. Reaching down, he grabbed the matchbox and took out a match.

"Are you ready?" he asked, with a smile on his face that reached from ear to ear.

"Light it all ready, Hunter!" yelled Hayden, shaking from the excitement.

Hunter struck the match across the box. Suddenly, a splash of light flickered through the room as the match stick lit. Holding the match to it, the oil-soaked wick was on fire within seconds. He picked up the glass bulb and placed it back on top of the brass base. Then he checked carefully to make sure the bulb was fastened on securely.

"Now what, Hannah?" he asked, looking at the brightly shining lamp.

"The clue says that the journey begins when the chimney starts to smoke and the dark reveals the past. I don't know for sure what that means," she admitted.

"I think it means the clue must flicker when the chimney smokes, but only in the dark," said Grandpa, as he startled everyone when he walked in the door.

"You scared me, Grandpa," said Hannah, shaking. "I didn't even hear the door open."

"Did you find out where this lamp came from?" asked Hunter.

"Yes, I did. Hayden, open the window a little so the smoke can escape, but leave the blinds closed so the room will be dark."

"Where did the lamp come from?" Hannah asked excitedly.

Grandpa quickly switched the light off, closed the door and walked toward the light of the lamp. As soon as Hayden had cracked the window and pulled the blinds closed tight, Grandpa signaled for everyone to come closer.

"Grandma told me that this lamp once belonged to Joseph Smith and was given to your Great-Grandmother

Prescendia by Joseph himself. She owned it when she married Heber," he whispered. "The lamp has passed down from generation to generation, until it was given to Grandma."

"So, could this be the right lamp?" Hunter asked excitedly.

"I guess that's possible," Grandpa answered, still whispering.

"Why are we talking so quietly?" asked Hayden.

"I don't want anyone to know that we might have the lamp from the Legend," he replied. "If someone is stealing things from the Blue Room, I don't want them to know about the lamp."

"What are we looking for? How will we know if this is the right one?" asked Hannah, studying the details of the lamp.

"I've been thinking about that," replied Grandpa. "The clue states that when the lamp is lit and starts to smoke, a map would flicker in the dark."

"Flicker where? How?" asked Hunter.

"I don't know. Can you see shadows or anything flickering?" asked Grandpa.

"There's too much light in here. I bet the clue means the map would flicker at night or in the dark," offered Hayden.

"If I turn the wick up, would the lamp provide more light?" asked Hunter, as he again started to lift the lever and raise the wick.

As the wick moved further up out of the oil, the lamp began to shine brighter and brighter. Everyone watched as the lamp flickered and cast shadows around the room.

"Shadows are flickering everywhere. How do we know which shadow is part of the clue?" asked Hayden.

"We don't even know if we have the right lamp," responded Hannah.

"Does the clue say to do anything else?" asked Grandpa.

"No, not really," answered Hannah.

"Look!" yelled Hunter. "Didn't the clue mention something about the smoke?"

"Yes, the clue states that our journey begins when the lamp starts to smoke," Hannah replied eagerly.

"So, what do we do now?" asked Hayden. "The lamp is smoking."

"I have an idea," said Grandpa. "Let's move this table closer to the wall and see if the lamp casts a shadow."

"Ooohhh, good idea," replied Hannah, jumping to her feet.

Carefully, they each picked up a corner of the table and carried it over to the wall. After they set the table down, Grandpa scooted the lamp as close as he could to the edge of the table. Then he slowly turned the lamp, looking for any sign of a map to appear on the wall. He had turned the lamp in a circle three times, when Hannah suddenly yelled, "Stop!"

"What is it?" asked Hunter.

"Grandpa, back the lamp away from the wall a little," she said.

"Can you see something, Hannah?" asked Hunter.

"I don't know for sure," she replied. "Grandpa, turn

the lamp around again, really slow."

Grandpa nodded and started to turn the lamp in a circle.

"The lamp is not bright enough," Hannah said. "If the light was a little brighter, I think I could see something."

"Well, I can turn the wick up even brighter," said Hunter.

Hunter grabbed the lever, just as Grandpa turned the lamp again. Hunter was startled by a loud snap, suddenly holding the small, brass lever in his hand.

"Hunter, you broke it!" screamed Hannah. "I told you to stop playing with it."

"I didn't mean to break it," he replied angrily. "I'm sorry, Grandpa. I was trying to help."

Grandpa stopped turning the lamp and quietly took the brass lever from Hunter's hand.

"Can we fix it?" asked Hayden, as he looked into the hole on the lamp caused by the missing lever.

"I guess we can try to fix it," Grandpa replied nervously. "Maybe we better turn on the lights for a minute, while I look to see if the damage is repairable. And whatever you do, don't say anything about the lamp being broken. I will try to fix it before Grandma knows."

Hannah ran to the wall and flipped on the switch, throwing a bright light across the room.

"All right, Hayden. Let me see if this piece will snap back into the hole," said Grandpa, examining the small piece to see where it fit.

"Hang on a minute, Grandpa. I think I see something in this hole," replied Hayden. He squinted one eye slightly, trying to see inside the small opening.

"Let me look," said Hunter, pushing at Hayden's shoulder.

"No, let me look," demanded Grandpa, pulling the lamp closer toward him.

With the lamp still burning, Grandpa turned it to the right so he could see into the small hole. Several nervous seconds passed as Hannah, Hunter and Hayden quietly watched Grandpa inspect the small opening in the lamp.

"Hannah, get a pair of tweezers out of my bathroom," Grandpa said.

"Is something in there?" she impatiently asked.

"I think Hayden might be right. I can see something wedged inside here," Grandpa replied. "How exciting!"

Anxiously, Hannah turned and ran toward the door. She nearly flattened Maria as she threw open the door and ran into the hallway. As the two crashed, Hannah fell into the wall, knocking down two pictures. Maria fell backwards and threw the furniture polish into the air as she tried to catch her fall. Unable to stop, she landed squarely on her backside and watched helplessly as the small, metal can landed directly on Hannah's head.

"Is everyone all right here?" asked Hayden, as he ran to see what had happened.

"I think I'm okay. But I'm not sure about Hannah," answered Maria.

With tears in her eyes, Hannah handed Maria the small can and looked at the two antique pictures she had knocked to the ground. She rubbed her head, trying to stop the pain. "Boy, Hunter, you broke the lamp, and I broke everything else," she said, trying not to cry.

"What lamp? Did a lamp get broken?" asked Maria. "Do you need help cleaning up something?"

"No, nothing," replied Grandpa, as he walked out of the Blue Room, closing the door behind him. "Nothing was broken that I'm sure can't be fixed. Now, Hannah, are you okay?" he asked, trying to change the subject.

"Yes, I think so," she answered, rubbing her sore knees.

"What about you, Maria?"

"Yes, I'm fine," she replied. "My head has stopped spinning."

"Did you need something?" Grandpa asked, wondering why she was by the Blue Room again.

"No, I came to tell you the men are here to fix the motor home," she answered.

"Did Grandma Thelma need me to come help her?" he asked.

"No," Maria answered. "I just thought you might want to know."

"We will be down in a few minutes then," Grandpa replied abruptly.

With that, Maria stood up, turned and walked down the stairs toward the kitchen. Grandpa helped Hannah to her feet. He then picked up the two pictures that had fallen and handed them to Hunter.

"Take these into the room please." Then he turned to Hannah and asked, "Do you think you can still handle getting those tweezers for me?"

Hannah smiled and nodded. "Yeah, I'll be right back," she replied, as she turned and walked down the stairs toward the bathroom.

CHAPTER SIX

GRANDPA, Hunter and Hayden walked back into the Blue Room and waited patiently for Hannah to return with the tweezers. As they waited, Grandpa continued to inspect the delicate designs engraved all over the lamp. Nearly five minutes had passed before Hannah finally re-entered the room.

"Grandpa, I couldn't find the tweezers, but I did find these. Will they work?" Hannah asked, holding up a pair of needle-nose pliers.

"We can try," replied Grandpa, holding out his hand for the pliers.

Hannah quickly placed the tool in his hand. She watched as Grandpa carefully slid them into the opening and tried to retrieve the object. Hayden climbed onto the table to get a better look, while Hannah and Hunter peered over Grandpa's shoulder. Grandpa cautiously clamped the pliers onto the object and started to pull gently. Unable to budge the item, he pulled with a little more force. He wiggled his hand back and forth, hoping to break the hidden object free. Suddenly it moved, revealing a small edge outside the hole. He released the grip on the pliers and set them on the table. Then Hayden took hold of the protruding edge.

"Oh, wait. Be careful. Don't pull too hard. I'm afraid it might tear," Grandpa said, nervously holding up his hands.

"I'm being careful," replied Hayden, as he pinched the edge between his fingers and began to pull. "Hey, this feels like material," he announced, surprised by the object's texture.

Hayden pulled slowly, as everyone watched him gradually work the object free from the lamp. Laying the small, napkin-like cloth on the table next to the lamp, he was now sure they had the right lamp and that they had found the next clue. He carefully examined the odd-colored material, which was torn and frayed. With no recognizable markings, he turned the cloth over, hoping something might be on the other side.

"What is it, Grandpa?" he asked. "I thought there would be a map or clue or something."

Grandpa looked at Hayden and shrugged his shoulders. "Maybe this is only a buffing cloth for the brass."

"Why would someone hide a cloth inside the hole?" asked Hunter.

"I don't know," he admitted. "Maybe this cloth has nothing to do with the Legend."

"I think we need to focus on the clue," said Hannah.

"The clue states that we need to find a map hidden in the dark, not a cloth in the oil well."

"I bet Hannah is right," said Grandpa. "I think we need to turn the lights back off and see if we can find this map."

"What about the cloth? Should we put it back inside?" asked Hunter.

"No, let's leave it for a minute," replied Grandpa. "Hannah, turn those lights off, will you please?"

Hannah quickly turned off the lights as Grandpa placed the lamp closer to the wall. They searched for any trace of a map flickering on the wall. Several minutes passed with no sign of a clue.

"What do we do, Grandpa?" asked Hayden. "I don't see any sign of a map."

"I'm not sure," he answered, as he sat back down in his chair. "You know, I'm not sure if we even have the correct lamp."

"Should we read the clue again?" asked Hannah, not wanting to give up so quickly.

"Yeah, we're not quitting this easily," replied Hunter.

Hannah walked to the stack of papers on the floor, picked up the translation and started reading.

"BY THE LIGHT OF THE LAMP
THAT JOSEPH SMITH OWNED,
FLICKERS THE START TO A MAP
THAT SHOWS THE WAY HOME.

WHILE THE LIGHT SHINES THE BRIGHTEST
WITH THE WICK FULLY SOAKED,

YOUR JOURNEY BEGINS
WHEN THE CHIMNEY STARTS TO SMOKE.

IN THE DARK, FIND THE SECRETS
THAT WILL OPEN THE PAST
TO A PEOPLE LONG FORGOTTEN,
BRINGING FORTH ANCIENT PROPHECIES AT LAST.'

"'KIMBALL POSTERITY,

REMAIN FAITHFUL, AND ALL SHALL BE REVEALED. PRAY FOR THE LORD'S GUIDANCE, AND PAY CLOSE ATTENTION TO EVERY DETAIL. SEARCH WITH THE LION, YIELDING UNENDING COURAGE.

MAKE ME PROUD,
HEBER C. KIMBALL'"

"What does he mean by, 'Search with the Lion'?" asked Hayden.

"I think he means to be brave," replied Hunter boldly.

"I don't know. I think he means never give up," said Grandpa.

"I think he means both of those things," said Hannah.

"Well, do you think it could have any reference to the lion engraved on the glass?" asked Hayden, pointing to the engraving.

"Hey, I hadn't noticed that," Hunter said excitedly. "I'm positive this is the right lamp now."

"I guess it could. But, what does the Lion mean?" asked Grandpa.

"Hey, look!" shouted Hannah, pointing to the table.

"What? What are you pointing at?" asked Hayden.

"The cloth. Look at the cloth," she replied excitedly.

As they looked down at the cloth, they saw the most amazing sight. As the lamp's light flickered and splashed upon the cloth, a tiny line appeared. As the light changed, the line disappeared and reappeared in another area. They watched in silence for several seconds, amazed at the dancing, black lines.

"Can you see that?" Hannah asked.

"Yeah, I can!" screamed Hayden. "This is so cool."

"Ssshhh, Hayden," insisted Grandpa, holding his finger to his lips. "We don't want anyone to know that we found something."

"What is it, exactly?" asked Hunter. "What did we find?"

"It has to be the map!" exclaimed Hannah. "I'm sure of it."

"I agree," added Grandpa. "But how do we read it with the lines jumping all over the place?"

"I don't know, but look at the material. It sure looks cool with the black line moving all over the place," said Hayden.

"What if we held the material up against the wall? Do you think the light from the lamp would cast a better shadow? Maybe more of the map would show," suggested Hunter.

"I don't know, but it's worth a try," replied Grandpa. He picked up the material and held it against the wall, hoping a map would appear.

"You can't see anymore with the cloth against the wall," said Hannah, as she continued to watch the black lines jump around the cloth. "I think the wall kinda blocks the light from shining through the material."

"Well, what do we do then?" asked Hunter. "I can't think of anything else to do."

"Does the clue mention anything else?" asked Hayden. "Maybe give us a hint? Anything?"

"Yes, Hannah. Read us the clue one more time," insisted Grandpa. "Maybe we've missed something important."

Hannah again retrieved the paper from the floor and read the translation.

"'BY THE LIGHT OF THE LAMP
THAT JOSEPH SMITH OWNED,
FLICKERS THE START TO A MAP
THAT SHOWS THE WAY HOME.'"

"Okay, stop there for a second, Hannah," said Hunter. "We have the lamp, and we can see that something is flickering on the material. Now, what does the clue say next?"

Hannah continued,

"'WHILE THE LIGHT SHINES THE BRIGHTEST
WITH THE WICK FULLY SOAKED,
YOUR JOURNEY BEGINS
WHEN THE CHIMNEY STARTS TO SMOKE.'"

"And we did fully soak the wick, right Hunter?" asked Hayden, smirking, as he held up the broken brass piece.

"I think so, buddy," he replied, grinning. "What else does the clue say?"

Hannah again started reading,

"'IN THE DARK, FIND THE SECRETS
THAT WILL OPEN THE PAST
TO A PEOPLE LONG FORGOTTEN,
BRINGING FORTH ANCIENT PROPHECIES AT LAST.'"

"Okay, we've turned off the lights, but we can't find any secrets," said Hayden.

"What are we missing?" questioned Hunter. "What do you think, Grandpa?"

"I don't know for sure," he replied. "But you're doing good, so keep going."

"What does Heber say after the clue, Hannah?" asked Hayden.

"'KIMBALL POSTERITY,

REMAIN FAITHFUL, AND ALL SHALL BE REVEALED. PRAY FOR THE LORD'S GUIDANCE, AND PAY CLOSE ATTENTION TO EVERY DETAIL. SEARCH WITH THE LION, YIELDING UNENDING COURAGE.

MAKE ME PROUD,
HEBER C. KIMBALL.'"

"He tells us to pay close attention to every detail," said Hayden. "Could that be a clue?"

"I don't think that sentence is a clue, but I do think he is trying to give us some hints on how to find the clue," replied Hannah.

"What about the lion? Could that mean anything?" he asked.

"I don't know," replied Hannah.

"What if you hold the cloth over the lampshade where the lion is etched in the glass?" asked Hunter, pointing at the lampshade. "Could the picture of the lion have something to do with the clue?"

"I guess the lion could, although I really don't know how. We have nothing to lose, so let's try it and see," replied Hayden.

"Nothing except time, guys. And I'm sure the tires are close to being fixed by now," Hannah said nervously. "We need to figure this out, quickly."

Grandpa grabbed the pale-orange cloth and held the material up as close to the lamp as he could, without getting burned.

"Can you see anything?" asked Hayden, as he tried to see over Grandpa's shoulder.

"Not a lot more," Hunter answered. "Grandpa, can you get the material any closer?"

"I don't think so," he replied. "Maybe we're not on the right track, kids. I think we need to turn off this lamp and keep thinking about the clue. You know, I'm sure Joseph Smith had a lot of different lamps."

"Yeah, but this lamp has to be the right one. I think

we're on the right track," replied Hannah, not wanting to give up. "Grandpa, is the material wet at all?" she asked.

"A little—from the oil," he answered.

"What if the clue is referring to the material being soaked? Do you think soaking the material could make a difference?"

"We could try," he said. "Grab my water over by the rocking chair and let's see."

Hannah retrieved the clear, plastic bottle of water and hurried back to the table. Grandpa carefully poured a small amount of water on the material, soaking the entire cloth.

"Now what?" Grandpa asked.

"Hold it back up to the light," Hannah replied.

Grandpa again held the cloth as close as he could to the etched glass of the lamp and watched for something to happen. Slowly, the small black lines again started to dance around the material. Then suddenly, a solid black line appeared attached to another line forming a shape that flashed quickly and then disappeared.

"What do we need to do to get those lines to hold still?" asked Hayden. "I want to know what's on this clue."

"What do you think would happen if we set the material on the lamp?" asked Hannah.

"It might get burned," replied Hunter. "I'm not sure we want to do that."

"I agree. We could burn the cloth," Grandpa said nervously.

"But what if the lamp burns the map onto the material?" she questioned excitedly.

"I hadn't thought of that," said Hunter. "I wonder if that's possible."

"It could be possible, or the heat could destroy the material," replied Grandpa. "But you have a good idea, Hannah."

"Should we try it?" asked Hayden, raising his eyebrows high on his forehead.

"I think so," said Hannah. "Come on."

"I guess we could try a little material at a time and see what happens," suggested Hunter. "Maybe just a corner."

Grandpa again held the material up as close as he could to the lamp. Then he nervously placed the top edge of the material on the hot, glass lampshade.

"Hey, wait a minute, Grandpa! I had a thought," shouted Hayden, scaring everyone.

Grandpa jumped, pulling the material quickly away from the lamp.

"What is it, Hayden?" he asked.

"Should we set the map on top of the glass where the lion is etched?" replied Hayden.

"Why?" asked Grandpa.

"I don't know, I just think since we're supposed to 'Search with the lion', we should try it," he replied.

"That's true. I guess we could place the material on the lion," said Grandpa. "It won't hurt to try."

Hunter took hold of the base of the lamp and twisted it in a circle until the lion was directly in front of Grandpa. Slowly, Grandpa held the material up to the lamp and watched as the magic lines started to dance all over the cloth again. Then he carefully placed the top edge onto the hot lamp. They all watched anxiously, hoping some sort of clue would appear.

"I don't think you have enough material on the lamp yet, Grandpa," said Hannah.

"We've got to try something. Lay all the material on the lamp, Grandpa," Hunter insisted impatiently.

"All right," Grandpa replied. "Let's keep our fingers crossed we don't ruin this old cloth."

Without any further delay, Grandpa quickly laid the entire cloth across the lamp, covering the lion completely. As they nervously watched, the cloth started to change from the pale-orange color, to bright yellow, to gold. Several seconds passed and nothing else happened.

"The black lines are gone. Did we burn the material?" Hayden asked worriedly.

"I've never seen material change colors like that," said Grandpa. "That is very odd."

"The material doesn't look burned, it looks cool," replied Hunter.

Suddenly, a small cloud of smoke rose from underneath the material toward the glass chimney of the lamp.

"Uh, oh," said Hannah. "Is that smoke?"

"Looks like it to me," replied Hayden.

"Do we need to pull off the material?" asked Hunter, watching the lamp closely.

"No, not yet," replied Grandpa. "I think we're on the right track for the clue. I've never seen anything do what this material has done before."

"Hey, the smoke from the material looks like it's rising up from the chimney—just like the clue reads," said

Hannah, pointing to the wispy, white smoke cloud.

As Hannah drew shapes with her finger in the rising smoke, the material flashed unexpectedly. Frightened, Hannah pulled her hand away quickly and watched as a large cloud of dark-gray smoke covered the entire bulb of the lamp.

"What was that?" Hannah asked nervously, wondering what had happened.

"I think we just burned the material!" Hayden gasped, as he waved his arm back and forth, attempting to force away the smoke covering the material.

"You might be right," Grandpa said sadly. "Keep your fingers crossed that our first real clue is not totally destroyed."

A full minute passed before Hayden had successfully moved the smoke away from the lamp, finally revealing what was left of the cloth.

"Look," said Hannah. "Black everywhere."

"We did ruin our clue," Hayden said sadly.

"I sure hope not," replied Hunter. "I want to find this treasure the Legend talks about. Move over, and let me get the cloth off of the lamp. Maybe we can salvage some of the clue."

Hunter flicked at the edge of the material with his finger, trying to pull up the corner. As soon as the edge was free, he carefully peeled the charred material away from the hot lamp.

"How bad is it?" asked Grandpa, covering his eyes, afraid to look.

"I don't know. The smoke is still too thick to see the

material clearly," replied Hunter, waving his hand like Hayden had.

Another minute passed before the four could see the cloth.

"Oh, wow!" said Hayden. "What's that?"

"I have no idea," replied Hunter. "How did that get there?"

"I told you setting the material on the lamp might work," said Hannah, beaming with pride. "I knew something was there."

"Yeah, but I don't see a map. What are those things?" asked Hayden.

"Symbols," answered Grandpa.

"Symbols?" asked Hunter.

"Yes, symbols. Our Church uses a lot of symbolism. There are symbols engraved on the temples that have different meanings, objects inside the temples have meanings, and even words we use have symbolic meanings."

"Like what?" interrupted Hannah.

"How about the word *cornerstone?* Have you heard that word before at Church?" he asked.

"Yeah, lots of times," replied Hunter.

"Okay, the word cornerstone is symbolic to where or how something is started. The Book of Mormon is the cornerstone of the LDS religion, and four cornerstones are laid before we can build a temple."

"What else?" asked Hayden.

"The mirrors that hang on each of the sealing rooms walls in our temples—when you look into them, you can see the reflection of yourself from the mirror over your shoulder. The reflection bounces from mirror to mirror causing it to look like your reflection goes on forever, symbolizing eternity," answered Grandpa.

"What symbols are engraved on temples?" asked Hayden. "I've never noticed any."

"Well, on the Salt Lake Temple alone, there are hundreds of symbols—keystones, record stones, a hand clasp, the all-seeing eye, pillars, a compass and square, sunstones, moonstones, even the Angel Moroni," Grandpa replied. "Symbols have been used by the Lord throughout time. Having clues written in symbols wouldn't be unheard of. Especially since these four men are hiding a treasure of the Lord. The symbols on the cloth could easily lead us to the treasure."

"So, what are the symbols on the material called?" asked Hannah.

"Well, this one is squared circles," said Grandpa, as he pointed to the picture. "And this one is the hand clasp. This one here looks like the compass and square, but I'm not sure because of the frayed edges of the material."

"What about this picture, Grandpa?" asked Hunter.

"I think that is a partial picture of what is called a dedication plaque, with the pillars on both sides. I'm not sure about any of the other pictures."

"I've heard about some of these symbols before, but how do we find out what they all mean?" asked Hannah.

Grandpa laid the cloth on the table, walked over to the wall and quickly switched on the bedroom light. Then he walked to his bookcase and quietly searched through some books.

"What are you looking for?" asked Hannah, watching every move Grandpa made.

"I have a really good book on symbolism in the temples during the early years of the church," Grandpa replied, searching through every title in the bookcase.

"Can I help you find it?" asked Hannah, as she started looking without waiting for his response.

"I'll help, too," chimed in Hunter.

As they looked for the book, Hayden quietly sat at the table, staring at the cloth covered with symbols. Glancing around to make sure he was not being watched, Hayden picked up the material and looked at the amazing drawings burned into the threads. As he carefully examined each one, he rubbed his finger across the pictures. He could feel the indentations from each one and was delighted at the thought that Joseph Smith possibly held this cloth in his hands. As he rubbed the material between his fingers, he could feel marks on the other side. Excited to see more pictures, he carefully turned the cloth over and gasped, startling everyone.

"What is it, Hayden?" What did you do?" asked Hannah, jumping to her feet. "Did you do something to the cloth?"

"Nothing, I did nothing," he replied. "I promise. I was only looking at the cloth."

"What's the matter then?" asked Hunter, walking over to the table to inspect the clue.

"I found more clues. Look—there's a riddle on the back of the material," he replied excitedly. "Look!"

CHAPTER SEVEN

HANNAH AND HUNTER hurried over to Hayden, while Grandpa continued to look through the bookcase for the book on symbols. Hannah snatched the cloth from Hayden's hand, laid it on the table and carefully flattened the wrinkles.

"Hayden's right! Burned onto the back of the material is a clue," she announced excitedly. "I can't believe we found it."

"Grandpa, you had the clue all along and didn't even know it," said Hayden, grinning and pointing at the lamp.

"You could have solved the Legend years ago, Grandpa," added Hunter.

Grandpa paused from his search for the book, looked up at Hunter, smiled and said, "I can't believe I had the lamp all this time. I should have had your Grandma tell me about it years ago. I wonder if the Lord's plan from the beginning was for the three of you to help me."

"What do you mean?" asked Hunter.

"The three of you helping me solve the Legend's mysteries," Grandpa answered. "Maybe I needed you to help solve the Legend all along. Maybe the clues weren't meant to be found until now."

"I hadn't thought about that," replied Hunter, in deep contemplation. "But I bet you're right, Grandpa. I'm sure we were meant to find the Legend."

"So tell us, Hannah, what does the writing on the cloth say?" asked Grandpa.

Hannah held up the cloth and replied, "The writing is deep blue-gray and looks faded. The wording is hard to see clearly, but stretching the material seems to help a little. Let me see."

Studying the material closely, she strained to determine every letter written. Several quiet and anxious seconds passed before she finally began to read.

"THE JEWEL ERECTED
SHINES NO MORE.
IT'S HIDDEN RECORDS
RECOVERED BY FOUR.
JOSEPH AND EMMA
NOW STAND WATCH.
GUARDING THOSE SECRETS
ONCE THOUGHT LOST."

Hannah, believing she had correctly deciphered the faint letters paused, and looked up excitedly. A huge smile stretched completely across her face.

"Do you think we might actually solve the mystery or at least prove the Legend is true?"

"Hannah, with this clue, we've already proven its true," said Hunter. "Now tell us the rest of the clue."

"Oh, yeah, sorry. Okay, where was I?" she asked, frantically searching to find the place where she had stopped reading. Locating her place, she began to read again.

"'ENGRAVED IN THE GRANITE,
NEXT TO THE ASH
SHIMMER THE KEYS REQUIRED,
LIGHTING YOUR PATH.
PROMISING TO FULFILL,
ANCIENT PROPHECIES AT LAST.'"

"What does it mean?" asked Hayden.

"It sounds like a riddle we'll have to solve, Hayden," replied Hunter. "One that leads to another clue or the treasure like a real mystery!"

"We need to break the clue down, sentence by sentence, and figure it out," suggested Hannah, taking charge. "I think solving the clue will be easier if we work on it line by line."

"I agree. But what do you think about the symbols on the other side? What do they mean? Could they be important?" asked Hunter.

"I'm sure they are," replied Grandpa, holding out the book on symbols that he had finally found. "But I think we should work on the riddle first. We'll have to figure out the symbols later."

Suddenly, the door to the Blue Room squeaked loudly as it flew open, startling everyone in the room. Looking toward the door to see who was there, Hannah screamed at the unrecognizable shadow.

"Who's there?" yelled Hayden, covering his eyes from the bright hallway light.

"Oh, knock it off, you guys," said Mom, standing in the doorway with her hands on her hips. "You know who I am."

"Mom, what are you doing?" Hannah asked breathlessly.

Mom stepped in the room and looked at Grandpa and smiled shaking her head as she scouted around the room. She noticed that the blinds were closed, the lights were off, and only the lamp shone in the background.

"Why is the room so dark, Dad?" she asked, as she turned to reach for the light switch. "No wonder you couldn't see me when I opened the door."

"Did you need something, Mom?" asked Hunter.

"Time to go," she said, pointing downstairs. "Your hunt for the legendary treasure is over. The motor home is now fixed and awaiting our departure."

"You scared me, Mom," Hannah said irritably, still holding her hand to her chest.

"Sorry, honey, but its time to go," Mom replied, as she entered the room and started walking toward the map and the clues.

"We'll be right there, Mom," replied Hunter, as he quickly folded up the map and slid it into his pants pocket.

"I'm ready now! So say goodbye to your Grandpa. Give him a big hug, and then meet me outside in three minutes," she said, with a big grin in a cheery voice. "Oh, and Hunter, I'd love to hear about the item you just hid in your pocket, but you can tell me about it later."

"Oh, Sarah, leave the boy alone. We're working on confidential information, and he's only doing what I asked him," said Grandpa, ushering her toward the door.

"Then you tell me, Dad, what did he put in his pocket?" Sarah demanded.

"He's keeping the clues about the Legend safe!" Grandpa replied, smiling. "Just like I told him to do."

"I know you've never believed in the Legend, Mom, but we're making progress," said Hayden.

"Well, as long as you kids, and that includes you Dad, have had some fun with the Legend, that's great. But, it's still time to leave the treasure hunting behind—right now!" said Mom sternly, as she left the room and walked down the hallway.

"What do we do now?" Hayden asked nervously. "How are we going to solve the clue if we have to leave? I really don't want to go yet."

"Me neither. We've found something several other generations of Kimballs have never been able to find," replied Hannah, as she scrunched up her nose in frustration. "I'd really like to stay and solve the riddle, too. I don't want to go right now."

Hunter watched Hannah and Hayden's responses and felt the same way. He quietly thought for a moment and knew what he had to do. With a growing knot of nervousness in his stomach, Hunter took a deep breath and tried to build up some courage. He looked over at Grandpa and quickly asked, "Can we take the clue with us, Grandpa? I promise we'll be careful. I'm very responsible."

"Take the clue?" Grandpa asked, bewildered at the sudden request. "What do you mean, take the clue? On your trip?" he quizzed.

Hunter nodded his head.

"Uumm, Hhuumm. Well, I don't know. I finally have something to search for, kids. I've been praying to our Father in Heaven for help to find this clue for the last twenty years. I'm not sure I want to hand the clue away now."

"Please, Grandpa, please," begged Hannah. "I'm responsible, too. I won't let anything happen to it."

"I know you wouldn't purposely let anything bad happen to it. But, with all the mysterious stuff that's been happening around here, I'm very nervous you could run into problems. I believe you could be in great danger if anyone found out about the Legend or clues," replied Grandpa, not really wanting to let the clue out of his sight. "Maybe if I was going with you, helping you to solve the clues, giving you the cloth with the clue would be okay. But..."

"Well then, come with us and help us solve the Legend," interrupted Hannah. "Following the clues would be a lot easier with your help anyway!"

"I can't come right now. Besides, your mom wants to spend time with you, not me," Grandpa replied.

Grandpa then held up his hand, signaling for Hunter to hand him the material he'd put in his pocket. Hunter, disappointed, slowly reached his hand into the front pocket of his favorite faded-blue jeans. Carefully, he pulled the cloth out and handed the crumpled material to Grandpa. Hannah and Hunter watched as Grandpa took the wadded cloth and stretched it open, revealing the symbols and writing. Smiling as he read the clue silently to himself, he dreamed of the treasure that might be found by solving the riddle. The kids watched Grandpa stare longingly at the clue. Unable to wait any longer, Hunter interrupted Grandpa's daydreaming.

"Please, Grandpa. I'm old enough and responsible enough to take care of Hannah, Hayden and protect the clue. I promise we'll be careful."

"What would your mom say? You know she'll never let the three of you search for the Legend alone."

"But she'd be excited if we found the treasure, don't you think?" Hayden protested.

"I'm sure you're right. I would love for the three of you to find the treasure," insisted Grandpa. "She would have to believe then, wouldn't she?"

"Can we take it then?" Hayden asked anxiously.

Silently, Grandpa turned and walked to his rocking chair. He sat down and laid the map in his lap. As he rocked back and forth in the chair, he clasped his hands tightly together. He placed them against his lips and contemplated the fate of the newly found clue. Lifting his head up toward Hunter's face, Grandpa asked, "Are you sure you would be careful and watch for anything suspicious? Would you keep everything protected, including yourself, your family, the clue and everything to do with the Legend?"

"I promise, Grandpa," Hunter answered sincerely.

"All righty then. The three of you can take the clue, but, you've got to be very careful," whispered Grandpa. "If anyone had any idea that we'd found a clue, all of you could be in great danger. However, anything you three could do to help solve the Legend would fulfill not only my dreams, but many of the dreams of our ancestors."

"Your mom is waiting," Maria announced, as she appeared suddenly in the doorway of the room again.

Hannah, caught up in the cautious tone Grandpa had been speaking in, had not noticed Maria's mysterious appearance. Again she jumped in fright at the unexpected voice. Regaining her composure, she screamed out, "If I get scared one more time today, someone might have to take me to the hospital. My heart can't stand this kind of excitement."

"I'm sorry to scare you," Maria answered, stepping into the room. "Can I help you take anything downstairs?"

"What are you doing up here, Maria?" Grandpa asked suspiciously, as he struggled to his feet from his rocking chair. He walked toward her, preventing her from entering the room and asked, "How long have you been up here?"

"Only a moment, Mr. Kimball. Sarah is waiting for the children. She is ready to leave. She asked that you please hurry, children," Maria added, with a suspicious grin on her face. She quickly turned and left the room.

"Why does she keep coming up here?" Grandpa muttered angrily under his breath.

"She's right, Grandpa. We've gotta go before Mom gets mad," admitted Hannah. "Then she might not let us search for treasure."

"You're right," agreed Grandpa, as he walked toward the table. He turned down the lamp's wick, allowing the flame to burn itself out. "You better gather up the supplies you might need. Take the original letter from Oliver Cowdery, the second letter from Brigham Young to his son, the riddle we found in the lamp and anything else you can think of," he said, as the flame flickered one last time before finally extinguishing its light.

"Can we take the book on symbols and the book we used to translate Brigham Young's letter with us?" asked Hannah, picking up the objects. "They could come in handy on our trip."

Grandpa looked at the items on the table. Then he gathered them up, and clutched them tightly before he carefully placed them into Hunter's hands. Excited for the Kimball posterity to finally be searching for the Legend, he smiled and said, "Please take good care of them. Don't get hurt, and whatever you do, never give them to anyone or tell anyone else about them, all right?"

"I'll take care of everything, Grandpa. I promise," Hunter said reassuringly. "I'll be careful. You can count on me. I won't let you down."

"You mean we won't let him down," insisted Hannah, as she pushed at Hunter's shoulder.

"You're right, Hannah," agreed Hunter, as he laid the clues on the table and placed his arms on Hannah and Hayden's shoulders. "We won't let you down, Grandpa."

"Then take them quick," Grandpa replied. He was nervous, but excited at the possibility of finding more clues. "Get going, and find that treasure."

Grandpa watched them leave, whispering a quiet prayer for their protection and success.

Excited for the adventure ahead, the children ran nervously down the stairs and out the front door. They headed straight toward the motor home, hurrying right past Grandma, Aunt Shirley and Mom.

"Hey, wait a minute! I didn't get a kiss," Grandma called after them. "You can't leave without giving me a hug and a kiss."

Stopping dead in their tracks, Hannah, Hunter and Hayden turned around and raced back to Grandma. They each kissed her goodbye, waved at Grandpa who had finally made his way to the front door, and raced back toward the motor home.

"Come on, Mom. Let's go!" yelled Hunter.

"We'll be right there," replied Aunt Shirley, with a grin on her face. "Wow, what did you do, Dad?"

Grandpa walked toward Shirley, smiled and smugly replied, "I didn't do anything. Your great-grandfather's great-grandfather did."

"Dad," said Sarah, "what did you do?"

"I promise, girls. I didn't do anything," Grandpa replied, kissing each of them on the cheek. "Now, those kids are ready to go on a grand adventure. You better get moving."

"A grand adventure, huh?" she asked. "Thanks a lot, Dad."

"Oh, relax, Sarah," he said. "They're going to have a wonderful time. In fact, I bet they have the time of their lives."

"I don't want them to get their hopes up, only to have them crushed when they find out this Legend isn't real," she replied sadly. "I never should have let you tell them that silly Legend."

"Oh, it's real, it's very real," declared Grandpa. "If you had any faith, you would see that those three children of yours have done more to solve the clues than anyone else has in the last one hundred fifty years."

Sarah smiled. She shook her head and slowly walked toward the motor home. Aunt Shirley followed her sister. Waving as they reached the door and stepping inside, Aunt Shirley said, "I sure hope they don't get their hopes up too high."

"Yeah, me, too," replied Sarah.

"I've never heard him sound more sure that the Legend was real than I have today," said Aunt Shirley, a little concerned. "Do you think having him tell the kids was a good thing?"

"I don't know," Sarah answered, looking back at him. "I haven't seen Dad quite this caught up in this Legend for a long time. I wonder exactly what he told them. Something doesn't feel quite right," she said, as she closed the door to the motor home and stepped up the three stairs to the driver's seat.

"You're driving, Mom!" Hunter hollered, as he threw the keys to her. "I want to look at this stuff Grandpa gave us for our trip. Okay?"

Mom snatched the keys out of the air and said, "That's fine for now, but I will be needing you to help drive during some of our trip. Now, you three, tell me what Grandpa gave you."

"A book on old church symbols," replied Hannah, holding the book high in the air.

"Symbols, huh? Do they have anything to do with his silly Legend?" she asked.

"We hope so," replied Hayden excitedly, through a cheesy grin.

"Hayden, ssshhhh," warned Hannah, as she squeezed his arm. "Mom didn't want us to hear the Legend, let alone look for clues like Grandpa does, remember?"

"Oh yeah, sorry," he whispered.

Quietly, Mom climbed into the driver's seat, placed the key in the ignition and turned on the motor. As she revved the engine for a minute, her mind was deep in thought.

Aunt Shirley grabbed a bag of chips and a soda, climbed into the passenger seat and opened the road map.

"All right. We're on our way, Sarah. First stop is Arizona. We have a long way to go, so let's get started!"

Sarah remained silent, staring out the windshield deep in thought. Finally, Aunt Shirley reached over, grabbed her sister's arm and said, "All right, daydreamer. Are you okay? It is time to get on the road."

Mom turned, looked at Aunt Shirley and said, "I'm fine." Turning to the children she said, "I'm glad Grandpa told you about the Legend. Our family's genealogy is very important—especially in the early years of the

Church. But, we will not be focusing all of our time and efforts on finding something that I don't believe is real, okay?"

"I believe it's real," Hayden retorted.

Hannah reached over and pushed his arm. "Will you be quiet?" she snapped.

Mom turned back toward the windshield, ignoring Hayden's comment. She pulled the stick down into drive and said, "We'll be traveling through several states before we get to any church history locations. Because, I'm sure your grandfather gave you information about his Legend, I've decided that each of you will need to find one interesting fact about every state. As we leave each state, I will ask you what information you've learned. I expect each of you to have something to tell me, because I would hate to take away anything Grandpa gave you. That's the compromise I'm willing to make for this silly treasure hunt, and I don't want any complaining. Do you all understand?"

"Okay, Mom. No problem," Hunter replied, without taking his eyes off the riddle.

"Hannah, Hayden, I didn't hear you," she called.

"All right, Mom," Hannah answered, obviously irritated with her mom's demands.

"Yeah, Me, too, Mom. I agree," said Hayden, waving to her as she watched him in the rearview mirror.

Mom shook her head, rolled her eyes and smirked. Still smiling, she looked at Aunt Shirley and said, "All right, navigator, where do we go from here?"

"According to the map, we need to take I-15 north,

approximately one hundred twenty miles until we reach I-40. Then we need to follow I-40 until we reach our first stop in Arizona," she replied, reading the map.

"This trip is going to be so great," Mom said excitedly. "We're on our way, guys. Are you ready?"

"We're ready, Mom," replied Hannah, unable to mask her newfound excitement.

CHAPTER EIGHT

HAYDEN QUICKLY cleared the food and supplies off the table and watched impatiently as Hannah and Hunter carefully laid out everything Grandpa had given them.

"Okay, let's see. Where do we start?" asked Hunter, excitedly holding the cloth and looking at the clue.

"I'm not sure," replied Hannah.

"I know," squealed Hayden. "Let's start with the riddle we found inside the lamp."

"Is that the best place, or should we start back with Brigham Young's letter to his son?" asked Hunter.

"No, I think Hayden's right," answered Hannah, holding up Brigham Young's letter. "I don't think we will even need his letter, but I thought we should bring everything about the Legend with us, in case we need it later."

"Do you want me to set it aside for now?" asked Hayden, holding his hand out to Hannah.

"That's fine." She replied. "Set this paper on the bunk

bed over the driver's seat. That's the place we'll keep all of the information we're not working with. I think it will be safe there," Hannah added.

She handed Hayden the paper and motioned for him to take it to the bed. Then she continued, "Hayden's right, Hunter, we've got to figure out the riddle so we'll know where we should look next."

"I agree," replied Hunter, as he pulled the small cloth clue to the center of the table.

As Hunter and Hannah looked at the clue, Hayden ran to the front of the motor home and jumped into the small area above the driver's seat. Lying on his stomach, he slithered to the pillow and pulled back the covers. He carefully laid the paper on the bed and set the blanket and pillow back into place. He patted the pillow as he maneuvered backward off the bed.

Mom looked up and noticed Hayden's legs dangling over the edge of the bed.

"Hayden, what are you doing?" Mom asked.

"Uuummm," he answered, thinking for a minute. "I put a paper on the bed so I wouldn't lose it."

Jumping down he hurried back toward Hunter and Hannah.

"What paper, Hayden?" Mom called.

"One Grandpa gave us," he replied evasively.

As Hayden slid into the bench next to Hunter, he asked. "Read the clue again please, Hannah. I can't remember everything that was written."

Hannah glanced toward Mom and Aunt Shirley, then she carefully picked up the cloth and started reading.

"THE JEWEL ERECTED
SHINES NO MORE.
IT'S HIDDEN RECORDS
RECOVERED BY FOUR.
JOSEPH AND EMMA
NOW STAND WATCH,
GUARDING THOSE SECRETS
ONCE THOUGHT LOST.
ENGRAVED IN THE GRANITE
NEXT TO THE ASH,
SHIMMER THE KEYS
LIGHTING YOUR PATH.
PROMISING TO FULFILL
ANCIENT PROPHECIES AT LAST.'"

"This is so cool. I wish Mom would've told us about this before!" said Hayden. "We probably would have discovered the treasure by now."

"Me, too," agreed Hunter. "I would've paid more attention in church and seminary."

"I've never heard of a Jewel associated with the Church. Have you Hunter?" asked Hannah, contemplating the first line of the clue.

"No."

"What do we know about the first line?" asked Hayden. "'The Jewel erected'—that means something has been built, right?"

"Yes, and 'shines no more' means whatever it was is no longer there. What else?" asked Hannah.

"In the early years of the Church, a lot of the

members' buildings—their homes, churches, businesses and stuff—were destroyed," said Hunter. "How do we know which structure the clue is written about?"

"The clue refers to it as a 'Jewel'," said Hannah. "We need to find out what the 'Jewel' means."

"How are we going to do that?" asked Hunter.

"Let's worry about that later. How does the next line of the clue read?" asked Hannah, as she handed Hunter the cloth.

"'It's hidden records recovered by four.' I think whatever was hidden in the 'Jewel' was found by four people," continued Hunter.

"That's what it sounds like to me, too," agreed Hannah.

"What people, though?" asked Hayden, a little confused. "The clue is vague. It could be referring to anyone."

"I think the any four men the Lord asked to recover the hidden records," suggested Hannah. "That's makes sense to me."

"Who could they be?" asked Hayden.

"The Three Nephites and Joseph Smith," replied Hannah. "Or apostles during that time, anyone really."

Hayden shrugged his shoulders, smiled and nodded. Then he quietly asked, "But wasn't Joseph Smith killed before that letter was written by Oliver Cowdery?"

Hannah looked up at Hayden, raised her eyebrows and answered, "Yes, he was, but I think the hidden records could have been moved before he died."

"Or, Joseph Smith may not have been involved at all. I'm not sure we'll ever know," she replied.

"You know, I think you're right, Hannah. Let's keep going, what does the third line say?" asked Hunter, shaking with excitement.

"'Joseph and Emma now stand watch,'" Hayden read slowly. Confused, he thought for a minute and then asked, "They are both dead. How can they stand watch over anything anymore?"

"Duh! The clue has to be talking about their gravesites," said Hunter, as he reached over and ruffled Hayden's hair.

"Do you mean someone could have placed the clues there after they died?"

"I'm sure someone did," replied Hannah. "I bet the clues were thought of and agreed upon by those four men before they died, and I bet that together they decided where to place all of the clues. In fact, I'm sure Oliver's letter to Heber was suppose to be the last clue to be delivered. That's why Oliver's wife took the letter to Heber C. Kimball after he died. The four men had planned it out that way."

"Do you really think so?" asked Hayden, intently interested in Hannah's theory.

"Hannah is pretty smart, Hayden. You know she's got to be right," said Hunter, smiling and ruffling Hayden's hair again.

Hayden pushed his arm away and said, "Stop it, Hunter, I'm trying to help."

"Come on, you two. Stay focused. I want to find this treasure," Hannah whispered angrily, "before Mom says we have to stop, okay?"

"Okay, okay. Hunter's right. I bet Joseph and Emma watch over the clue," agreed Hayden, straightening his light-brown hair with his hands.

"Yeah, and according to the next line, they guard something secret that everyone thinks is lost. Maybe lost as the 'Jewel' was destroyed," offered Hunter.

"I think that sounds right," replied Hannah. "And according to the next line, whatever those secrets are, they were taken and engraved into the granite next to the ash."

"What does that mean?" asked Hunter. "I don't get that line."

"I don't know for sure," replied Hannah, scowling as she concentrated on the clue.

"What granite do you think the clue is referring to, and what could be engraved in it?" asked Hayden.

"Good question," admitted Hunter. "That's what we're trying to figure out. We know that Joseph and Emma are guarding the secrets, so could granite be at their gravesite?"

"Why would there be granite at their gravesite?" asked Hayden.

"I guess their tombstones could be made out of granite," said Hannah. "Isn't granite a kind of rock?"

"Hey, that's possible. Granite is a rock. The clue could be referring to their headstones and whatever part of the clue is there, has to start with Joseph and Emma's grave," declared Hayden.

"Where are they buried?" asked Hunter. "We're gonna have to start there."

"I wonder where we're going first," said Hannah.

"This could be a long trip if their graves are the last thing we see."

"Not to mention that if they're the last thing, we'll never have the time to solve the Legend," added Hayden.

"Hey, Mom!" yelled Hunter. "Where are we going to stop first?"

"We're stopping in Arizona," she answered.

"No, I mean with our church history stuff. Where is our first stop on the tour?" asked Hunter.

"Oh, uumm, I think," she said, pausing to look at Aunt Shirley, "I don't know for sure. Where is our first church history stop, Shirley?"

"Well," Aunt Shirley replied, looking at the map. "I believe our first stop will be Nauvoo, Illinois," she answered.

Hunter turned to Hannah and asked, "Do you happen to know where Joseph and Emma are buried? Are their graves possibly in the small, quaint town of Nauvoo?" he asked jokingly, with an English accent.

"I don't know," she replied, smiling at Hunter's straight face.

"How are we going to find out?" asked Hayden. "Do you think Mom knows?"

"I don't know, but we could ask her. She may know," suggested Hunter, shrugging his shoulders.

"Boy, I sure wish I had my computer," said Hayden, frowning. "I wish Mom would have let me bring it on our trip."

"Why is that?" asked Hunter.

"Well, I'm sure I could find the information we need

listed on the Church's web page. In fact, I bet I could find a ton of information about the word 'jewel' on the Internet," he added.

"Don't worry, I'm sure we can figure this out if we think about the clue for awhile. We are pretty smart," said Hannah.

They all sat quietly for a long time, trying to find a solution to the questions they needed answered. Hunter even dozed in and out of consciousness several times, when Mom surprised them as she yelled, "We will be out of the state of California in approximately five minutes. I sure hope the three of you have paid attention to the sites we've already passed. I would hate to have to tear up your clue."

"We're almost out of California already?" Hunter asked, rapidly rubbing his eyes.

"We sure are. Can you believe it?" asked Aunt Shirley, as she walked to the refrigerator. She opened the door and grabbed a bottle of water before walking back up front.

"No, I can't. Do you know how long we have been driving already?" asked Hannah.

"Almost three hours," replied Aunt Shirley from the front of the motor home.

"What sites have we passed?" whispered Hayden, afraid the fun of the clues might be over before they even started looking.

Hannah quietly stood up from the table and looked north out the window. Then she walked to the back of the motor home and looked back to the west. Calmly walking back to the table, she sat down and said, "Okay behind us was the little town of Portersville, you know, where Mom likes to shop. The sign next to the road on the north had an arrow pointing to the Mojave National Preserve, and right before we leave the state is the Parker Dam."

"How do you know all of that," asked Hayden, surprised at her knowledge.

"Well, I'm smart," she replied grinning. "Hunter's already told you that."

"And?" asked Hunter, holding his head to the right and smirking.

"And, I can read the road signs!" she said, as she laughed.

"Nice job, Sis," declared Hunter, giggling.

"Watch this," Hayden whispered. "So, Mom, do you want us to tell you the sites now, or should we wait until we pass the state line?"

"If you know them, now will be fine," Mom replied, excited to hear what they had to say.

Hannah chuckled and started, "Well, Mom, I saw the Mojave National Preserve."

"And I saw the Parker Dam," Hunter offered confidently.

"And your site, Hayden?" Mom asked.

"My site is the town of Portersville," Hayden answered proudly. "You know, where you go to shop."

"Well, you three must have really watched closely," said Mom. "So tell me, did you solve any of the clue that Grandpa gave you? I know you didn't spend any time checking out the sites, especially since we haven't even passed the Parker Dam yet."

Aunt Shirley covered her mouth laughing at Mom's comments. "What did Grandpa say about the Legend of the Lamp?" Aunt Shirley asked. "You guys whispered so much, I couldn't hear anything you were saying."

"That was the idea, Aunt Shirley," replied Hayden.

"Well guys, were you able to figure out Grandpa's old Legend?" asked Mom.

"Do you know a lot about the Legend, Mom?" asked Hannah.

"Yes, I do. Maybe even a little more than you do. When I was younger, the Legend was all Grandpa would ever talk about. He wanted so badly for it to be real that he has spent his whole life trying to find a clue. So tell me, what are the new clues he's found?"

"Nothing really," replied Hunter, not wanting to give information to anyone.

"Nothing? And you're this excited about nothing?" she asked. "So excited that you would risk having the clue destroyed by your mother? Or that you would ignore my one request to pay attention to the sites, and instead spend all your time trying to figure out the clue?"

"We didn't ignore you, Mom," Hunter insisted. "This is the first time we've ever heard about the Legend, and we're kinda excited."

"We didn't know we would be out of the state so fast," added Hayden. "We thought we had a few more hours before we had to start watching."

"I'm still waiting. Tell me about Grandpa's clue," Mom demanded.

"Yeah, I want to hear," said Aunt Shirley. She turned around backward in her seat. Crossing her legs in front of her, she peered over the headrest.

Hannah shrugged her shoulders at the boys and whispered, "Should I tell them?"

"Yes," answered Aunt Shirley. "Tell us. We're descendants of Heber C. Kimball, too."

Not wanting to upset Mom, Hunter and Hayden reluctantly nodded in agreement.

"Okay, we helped Grandpa translate a new clue he recently found. He actually had most of the clue, which he found in a letter, translated before we got there. Surprisingly, that clue led us to Joseph Smith's lamp—the lamp that Grandma has owned for years. After we found the lamp, Hunter was messing around with it and broke off the wick lever. But inside the lever hole we discovered a small cloth with another clue. After reading that clue, we learned that we needed to find something the early members of the church built—something that has since been destroyed, but was referred to in the clue as the 'Jewel'," Hannah explained in one long breath.

"Really? You found that much already?" questioned Mom. "I didn't think any clues had ever been found."

"Yep," replied Hunter.

"And you broke Grandma's lamp?" asked Aunt Shirley. "Which one?"

"Kinda, but I didn't mean to," Hunter replied defensively.

"Which one?" insisted Mom.

"The one Grandma kept in the armoire," answered Hannah.

"The one with the lion etched into the glass bulb?" asked Aunt Shirley, in a high, squeaky voice.

"Yes, but I really didn't mean to," replied Hunter.

"Oh, boy. That's Grandma's favorite lamp. That's the lamp that Heber C. Kimball's wife passed down through the Kimball family," said Mom.

"I think it's the lamp that belonged to Joseph Smith, and was used when he translated the Book of Mormon," added Aunt Shirley. "I'm sure that lamp is her favorite family heirloom."

"That's why the lamp was locked in the armoire," said Mom. "Does Grandma know it's been broken yet?"

"Not yet," Hunter answered nervously.

"That could be explosive," said Mom.

"Grandpa said he thought he could fix the small piece of metal that came off," insisted Hunter, trying his hardest to look innocent.

"You better hope so. If Grandma finds out, she'll never let you go in the Blue Room again," teased Mom. "In fact, I can't wait to hear what she is going to say."

"Well, whatever it is, you know she is going to say a lot," added Aunt Shirley, trying to hide a smile.

"All right, now tell me what you were looking for in the lamp. A clue?" asked Mom.

"Yes, and we found the clue when Hunter broke the lamp," Hannah replied.

"You asked about a word from the clue. What was the word?" asked Aunt Shirley.

"Something called the 'Jewel'," replied Hannah.

"The 'Jewel'? Let me think," Aunt Shirley said

thoughtfully. "And it has something to do with church history. Hhhmmm." Aunt Shirley sat motionless for several minutes before she asked again, "'The Jewel'?"

"Yes. Have you ever heard of anything called the 'Jewel'?" asked Hayden

"I know I've heard of something called the 'Jewel', but I can't remember what," she replied. "Can you, Sarah?"

"I'd have to think about it for a while," she replied. "I'm like you—I know I've heard that word before, but I can't remember what it means."

"That's okay. But we're going to keep working on the clue, if that's all right with you," said Hunter. "Maybe if we're lucky, we can find another clue to take back to Grandpa."

"Have fun," replied Mom, still shaking her head. "Promise you won't get your hopes up too high. I think in one day you have already found more information than has been found by multiple Kimball generations."

Hannah, Hunter and Hayden hurried back to the small table in the kitchen area and got busy attempting to figure out the clue. Silently staring at the clue for quite awhile, and wondering how to find the answers, Hayden listened to his stomach growl ferociously for the last time. He could not stand the hunger pains any longer. He jumped up from the table, grabbed a bag of chips from the counter and the bottle of salsa from the refrigerator. He placed them in the center of the table and said, "I know I think better when I'm full and my stomach isn't growling, so maybe this food will help."

"Good idea, Hayden," said Hunter, as he pulled open

the bag. "I'm starving, too."

"Back to work. Where were we?" asked Hayden, smiling through a mouth full of chips.

"Let me read the clue again," said Hannah, placing the cloth back onto the table. "'The 'Jewel' erected, shines no more. It's hidden records recovered by four. Joseph and Emma now stand watch. Guarding the secrets once thought lost. Engraved in the granite, next to the ash. Shimmer the keys lighting your path. Promising to fulfill ancient prophecies at last.'"

"I guess we really need to find out where Joseph and Emma were buried. I really think the location the clue refers to is their gravesite," said Hayden.

"I think so, too. When we get there, we can see if the headstones are made of granite. If they are, we can start looking for the keys that are supposed to be engraved in them, and that hopefully light our path to the next clue," suggested Hannah.

"I wonder what ancient prophecies are supposed to be fulfilled?" asked Hunter. "You know both clues have ended in that same sentence, and I think Oliver Cowdrey's letter said something about prophecies fulfilled."

"I don't know, maybe the end of the world," said Hayden, through a big cheesy grin.

"Yeah, right," replied Hannah. "Do you really think that is the prophecy that's supposed to be fulfilled? If so, maybe we don't want to be the Kimballs that find the Legend."

"Nah, there has to be something else," insisted Hayden. "That's too scary. That can't really be it. I was only joking."

"Hey, guys," interrupted Aunt Shirley. "I think I found the 'Jewel' you were talking about."

"Oh, yeah? So, what is it?" Hunter asked eagerly.

"Really?" Hannah asked excitedly.

"Come here, and look at this book your mom brought. It's a little old, but it has good information about the Nauvoo Temple. I knew I'd read something about a 'Jewel' before," she said. She pointed to a passage written in the book and read, "'The Nauvoo Temple, also known as 'The Jewel of the Mississippi', was restored and opened today to the public for guided tours until the day of dedication.'"

"So, the Nauvoo Temple is the 'Jewel'?" asked Hunter.

"I guess so," Aunt Shirley replied, shrugging her shoulders. "That's what this book says."

"So, we're going to Nauvoo first, right Mom?" asked Hayden. "We could go and see the 'Jewel'."

"That's what Aunt Shirley, our road trip navigator, said," she replied, pointing to Aunt Shirley.

"Is the old temple site one of our scheduled visits?" asked Hunter.

"It sure is. We can't go to Nauvoo and not see the temple," Aunt Shirley replied.

"What about Joseph and Emma's gravesites? Are they in Nauvoo?' asked Hannah.

"I don't know for sure, but your Mom brought a book on church history. You could read through the book and find out," suggested Aunt Shirley, as she handed the large book to Hannah.

Hannah took a deep breath, looked at Aunt Shirley

and asked, "Are you sure you really don't know?"

"Nope! But have fun looking," Shirley replied.

Hannah reached out and took the book from Shirley's hand. Unfortunately, the book was a little heavier than she thought. She had to quickly support the weight with both hands. Carefully, she opened the book and gazed at the drawings inside. "Well, hopefully the information will be in here," she muttered under her breath.

Walking slowly to the couch, she sat down and turned to the index. She searched under the listing of Joseph Smith and found multiple references listed in almost every chapter. Scanning them, she found several references to the martyrdom of Joseph Smith. She quickly turned to Chapter Fourteen. Then she started reading from the beginning of John Taylor's account of the last few hours of Joseph Smith's life.

"How much farther do we have?" asked Hunter.

"You can go to the back room and sleep if you want to, Hunter," replied Mom.

"No, I can't. Dad said I wasn't to leave you two up alone after dark. So how much longer until we're there?"

"Only about an hour," Mom replied. "Where are Hayden and Hannah?"

"Hayden went to sleep a while ago, and Hannah is reading the book Aunt Shirley gave her."

"Did she find the information she needed to help you with the clue?"

"I don't know. I don't think so," Hunter replied, shrugging his shoulders. "If she had, we would all be working on solving the clue."

Hunter walked from the kitchen area to a small recliner in the sitting area and sat down. With nothing else to do, he turned on the television. After scanning through the channels, he settled on ESPN. He searched for the results from the NBA's basketball games that day. He dozed in and out of consciousness as he watched the sports announcers ramble on about the day's events.

Mom finally reached the campground and hurried to her assigned camping space. She needed a good night's sleep before continuing on their long journey the next day.

"Hunter, help me get parked please," Mom called loudly, rousing him from his semi-conscious state.

"Okay," was all Hunter replied, blinking his eyes wildly as he walked out the door.

As Hunter guided, Mom cautiously pulled into the space. Hunter quickly placed blocks behind the wheels and checked to see if the motor home was level. Inside, Mom and Aunt Shirley pulled out the beds and tucked Hayden and Hannah in. They threw on their pajamas and waited for Hunter to lock the door. Then watched as he climbed into the loft and fell asleep, before he could get the words, "Good night," out of his mouth.

"We've got a long day ahead of us tomorrow," said Aunt Shirley, crawling under the covers.

"And the sun is going to rise before we're ready for its light to shine," added Sarah, as she, too, snuggled into the warmth of her bed.

CHAPTER NINE

MORNING CAME EARLY for Hunter. He was still curled up asleep on his bed when he heard the first rattling noises of the day. Not ready to be awake, he pulled his pillow over his head, hoping to block the light and noise. Unable to muffle the sounds very well, he was forced to listen to the annoying sound of clanging dice as Hannah and Hayden played a game of Yahtzee. Irritated that they woke him up, he raised his hand to shield his eyes as he slowly opened them, anticipating the sun's bright glare. Pleasantly surprised at the darkness, he gazed around the loft and noticed that the sliding curtain was closed.

"What time is it?" he thought. "Why did they wake me up so early? I could have easily slept until after ten!"

Kicking the covers off his feet, he sat up and rubbed his face. As he leaned forward, he hit his head on the low roof of the motor home. Now angry he was awake, he tilted his head to the side and wondered, "Why did they pull the curtains shut, and why is the motor home moving? It can't be later than 7A.M."

He leaned forward and forcefully ripped the screens open. Shocked by the sudden burst of bright light, he covered his eyes and asked, "What time is it? Where are we? And why are you two up so early?"

"Good morning, sunshine," replied Aunt Shirley. She then started singing, "Good morning, good morning. Ain't it great to stay up late? Good morning, good morning, to you."

"Do you sing that dumb song like Mom does, too?" asked Hayden.

"I sure do," answered Aunt Shirley. "Grandpa used to sing us that song as he ripped the covers off every morning when he came in to wake us up for school."

"I've always hated that song," admitted Hayden.

"Hey, what time is it?" demanded Hunter, still covering his eyes.

"It's one o'clock in the afternoon," replied Hayden. "You've been sleeping all day."

"One o'clock. Are you serious?"

"Yep. You have been asleep forever," said Hannah. "We've made our beds, had breakfast, lunch, watched TV and now we are playing a game."

"I know!" declared Hunter. "The clanging of the dice woke me up."

"Maybe it's a good thing they started playing," suggested Aunt Shirley. "Otherwise, you might have slept all day."

Hunter took a big breath and dropped down on the bed, still rubbing his eyes. "Why didn't anyone wake me up?" he asked.

"'Cause, you needed the sleep, and I knew I could handle it until you woke up. You can take over for awhile now," answered Mom from the driver's seat.

"Sorry I slept so long, Mom," said Hunter. "Give me a minute to get dressed and get something to eat, and then I'll take over."

"Okay, that will work great, we've almost made it to Amarillo," replied Mom.

"Amarillo? What happened to New Mexico?" questioned Hunter.

"You slept all the way through it!" answered Hayden, smiling.

Hunter climbed carefully down out of the loft. He shook his head, hoping to clear the cobwebs from his mind. "I can't believe I slept so long," he said.

"And you didn't find any interesting facts in those states, so Mom said we had to stop working on the Legend," Hannah said sadly.

"Mom, are you serious?" demanded Hunter. "You know, I would have found some facts if you'd woken me up earlier."

Before Mom could answer, Hannah said, "Hunter, wait. Mom didn't say that. I was only joking."

"Nice one, Hannah," said Hunter. "You know, you just about gave me a heart attack."

"Well, Hayden and I still had to watch for interesting sites," she replied.

"While you two were messing around today, did you happen to discover anything new with the clue?" Hunter asked, as he passed her and headed toward the back room to change his clothes.

Hannah held her hand to her lips, signaling Hunter to be quiet, and then replied, "Not much more than what we knew yesterday."

"Do you want breakfast or lunch?" Aunt Shirley teased, as Hunter pulled the door closed.

"Well, what do you have to eat?" Hunter asked.

"Waffles and turkey sandwiches and chips," replied Hayden.

"How about a sandwich?" Hunter yelled through the door.

"I'll make it for him, Aunt Shirley," offered Hayden.

Aunt Shirley smiled and agreed. Then she quickly walked to the front of the motor home to talk to Mom. Once she left, Hayden started to make Hunter's sandwich.

When Hunter returned, dressed, hair combed, and still sleepy, Hayden quietly whispered, "Hunter, Hannah found something while she was reading last night, go check it out."

Suddenly wide awake, Hunter asked, "What was it? What did you find?"

Hannah sat down at the kitchen table and flipped open the cover to the large brown book, entitled *Latter-Day History.* She rummaged through the pages, finally finding the page she wanted. Then she motioned for Hunter to sit down next to her.

"This church history book says that after Joseph was killed, he was taken to the Nauvoo House for the viewing. Then Joseph and Hyrum were secretly moved to the Mansion House, where they were buried in the basement for a while. When it was safe, sometime later, the brothers were moved across the street to the Homestead and reburied," whispered Hannah.

"What about Joseph's wife?" questioned Hunter. "The clue refers to Joseph and Emma."

"You're right, but Emma wasn't buried until years later. When she was, she was also buried next to Joseph."

"At least they're buried together. That's good," announced Hunter. "Now, do we know how far away the temple is from the Homestead?"

"It's hard to tell with this map, but I think the Homestead is about seven or eight blocks south and three blocks east toward the Mississippi River," Hannah answered.

"Hannah, show him what else is in the book," Hayden coaxed impatiently.

Hannah turned the page and pointed to a small picture in the top right corner.

"What is it?" asked Hunter, squinting to see the details.

"This is a picture of Hyrum, Joseph and Emma's gravesites," she replied. "If you look closely, you can see that the headstones are made of granite."

"Oh yes, this is going to be easy!" he said excitedly. "I thought with as much trouble as the Kimball Family has had solving this Legend, we were going to have a really difficult time as well. But everything so far has been a complete cake walk."

"Don't get over confident, we've barely started," insisted Hannah.

"That's it, Hunter. I really need a break," called Mom, as she pulled into the gas station. She stood up from the driver's seat, shaking her legs as she walked to the back. "It's your turn for a while, I'm taking a nap."

"I got it, Mom. No worries," Hunter said. He jumped up from the table, shoveling the last bite of his sandwich into his mouth.

Hannah watched as Mom staggered to the bed and fell asleep as soon as her head hit the pillow. While Hunter filled the tank with gas, she nervously hoped the gravesites would reveal the next clue. As they returned to the highway heading toward Nauvoo, Hannah continued reading the details surrounding the burial place of Joseph and Hyrum Smith. Intrigued by the stories of those closest to Joseph, she began to read the events that lead up to his martyrdom.

CHAPTER TEN 10

TWO AND A HALF DAYS after Grandpa told the kids of the Kimball Legend, Hunter excitedly announced, "We're here, Mom." We've reached the Nauvoo City limits. Where do you want me to go?"

"Well, I think we have enough time tonight to visit at least one of the historical sites you wanted to see. Which one do you want to visit first?" she asked.

"I would really like to go to the Temple," replied Aunt Shirley. "I've always wanted to see the Nauvoo Temple."

"I was kinda hoping we would have time to go to the Smiths' gravesite before it closes tonight," said Hannah softly, with a sad look on her face.

"Me, too," said Hayden, following Hannah's lead.

"That's all right with me. I'm okay to go to the Temple tomorrow when it's light outside. I will probably be able to get a better look at it if we go then anyway," said Aunt Shirley.

"Why are you so interested in Joseph's gravesite?" asked Mom. "Is it because of the Legend?"

"Well, kind of, Mom," answered Hunter. "But, that's not the only reason."

"Oh, yeah? Why then?" Mom asked, in a sarcastic tone.

"Well, because everything with the Church centers around the Prophet Joseph Smith, and I would love to feel the Spirit at his gravesite," he answered, as he continued to drive. "What a great place to start off our trip."

Mom smiled, not sure whether he was telling the truth or not, but answered, "If that's where the three of you would like to start, then we will go to the Smith family gravesite first."

Hunter smiled, and followed the signs straight toward the gravesite. After finding a parking space for the motor home in a nearby parking lot, everyone filed out the door. The kids were especially grateful the fun part of the trip was about to begin.

"Hey, Aunt Shirley!" yelled Hayden, pointing to the northeast. "Isn't that the Nauvoo Temple?"

"Yes. It's beautiful!" she exclaimed. "I can't wait to see it up close."

"Maybe if we hurry, we could at least walk around the temple grounds before it's too dark," replied Mom, seeing the excitement in Aunt Shirley's face.

"Okay, let's hurry then," said Hayden, as he raced toward the entrance of Smith Memorial Park.

Everyone watched him run through the decorative iron gates into the beautiful, lush green foliage of the gravesite. Before entering the park, Mom and Aunt Shirley walked to a restored, quaint log and rock house. Gorgeous flowers and vines surrounded it, with giant trees hanging their branches and leaves over the top, as if to protect the small house.

Mom, more interested in the treasures in the house, yelled, "Hunter, Hannah, hurry and catch up with Hayden please. Keep an eye on him, and we will see you in a few minutes."

"Okay, Mom," Hannah called back. "Hunter, let's hurry. Maybe we will have enough time to find the clue before Mom and Aunt Shirley catch up with us."

As Hannah and Hunter hurried to catch up with Hayden, they caught a glimpse of him racing around the log house.

"Hayden, you probably shouldn't run here," called Hannah.

"Why?"

"Out of respect," she answered. "This is a cemetery."

"Sorry, I'm excited," Hayden replied. "So, where are the gravesites? I can't find them."

"Look at the sign on the tree," answered Hunter, pointing to a wooden plaque. "Finding them might be easier if your pay attention and read the signs."

Hayden made a face at Hunter as he jogged toward the small wooden sign. A few feet before he reached the sign, he yelled, "Ha, I don't have to read the sign. Look, there they are."

Without another word, he took off running across the lawn. He headed toward two waist-high headstones, which were surrounded in a half circle by beautiful flowers and trees.

"He did find them, Hunter. Let's go," said Hannah, as she turned to catch up with Hayden.

"Wait, wait, wait!" said Hunter, as he grabbed Hannah's shoulder.

"What? What is it?" she asked, with a scowl on her face.

Hunter again pointed to the small wooden plaque and said, "Those are the headstones of Joseph's parents, Joseph Smith, Sr. and Lucy Mack Smith—not Joseph and Emma."

Hannah smiled and shook her head. She and Hunter watched as Hayden finally reached the head stones and discovered his mistake. He walked dejectedly back, hanging his head.

As he reached Hannah and Hunter, he asked, "All right, what does the plaque say?"

Hunter ruffled Hayden's hair and said, "There's nothing wrong with being excited. You just need to pay closer attention."

Hayden finally read the small sign and said, "According to the sign, the graves we are looking for are along the back side of the house. Come on, let's go. We've got to hurry."

As the kids reached the headstones, they were surprised by what they saw. The headstones were not typical headstones, they were complete body markers. They were made out of speckled-gray, granite, and were approximately ten feet wide, ten feet long and twelve inches thick. The markers were laid at an angle on a large cement slab.

Hyrum, Joseph and Emma were buried side-by-side inside a small plot surrounded by a picket fence. As the kids stared at the writing on the headstones, beside the names, birthplaces and dates, and death places and dates, they noticed that one other word was written on each stone. Hyrum's read *Patriarch,* Joseph's read *Prophet* and Emma's read *Wife.*

"Wow, I thought a lot more than this would be written on their headstones," said Hannah.

"I wonder why there isn't?" asked Hayden.

"I have no idea," answered Hunter. "But we better start looking for our next clue."

Hayden hurried to the side of the headstone and started looking around the granite for any indication of a new clue.

"Can you see anything?" asked Hunter, who continued looking in the front.

"Nothing yet," replied Hayden. "But I've just barely started looking."

"Hannah, why don't you read us the clue?" suggested Hunter, unaware of the numerous people around him.

"That's a good idea," she replied, as she retrieved the small cloth from her backpack.

"THE JEWEL ERECTED
SHINES NO MORE.
ITS HIDDEN RECORDS
RECOVERED BY FOUR.

JOSEPH AND EMMA
NOW STAND WATCH,
GUARDING THOSE SECRETS
ONCE THOUGHT LOST.
ENGRAVED IN THE GRANITE
NEXT TO THE ASH.
SHIMMER THE KEYS
LIGHTING YOUR PATH.
PROMISING TO FULFILL
ANCIENT PROPHECIES AT LAST."

"All right, if we follow the clue systematically, we know that the line 'the Jewel erected shines no more' is referring to the Nauvoo Temple and its destruction. And we know the second reference, 'It's hidden records, discovered by four', most likely means the records hidden at the temple were moved by four men, right?" asked Hunter.

"I think you're on the right track so far," answered Hannah. "Keep going."

"Okay. The next line is where I think this clue gets interesting. 'Joseph and Emma now stand watch'. I'm assuming this line is referencing their gravesites, where their bodies currently are laid to rest. They must be watching over the next line, which reads, 'Guarding those secrets, once thought lost.' Again, I'm assuming that line means the secrets the four men saved are placed closely to Joseph and Emma for protection," Hunter finished.

"I didn't realize you had put so much thought into this," replied Hannah, smiling.

"Me neither," added Hayden, as he wandered around to the front of the headstones.

"Excuse me," interrupted a young man, as he tapped Hannah on the shoulder.

Startled, Hannah spun around to find herself face to face with a stranger. Nervously, she stepped backward, landing right on Hayden's foot, sending him squealing in pain. Hannah turned to see if Hayden was all right and watched as he hopped around, grimacing from the pain.

"Excuse me, miss," persisted the unfamiliar voice.

Not quite so frightened this time she replied, "Yes."

"I was wondering if the clue I heard you read was a game that is available for everyone to play. And if so, do I need to go back to the Visitor's Center to get a copy? Or do you by chance have an extra one that I could have?"

Hannah nervously scrunched up the cloth in her hand and quickly placed her hand in her jeans pocket. "Oh, I'm sorry. There's not a game or clue that has anything to do with the Smith Memorial Park. My brothers and I are only playing a game," she replied, staring into his charcoal black eyes.

"That's too bad," said the young man. "I only asked because the game sounded very interesting. And a game with a mysterious clue sounds like a lot of fun. Sorry to have bothered you," finished the dark-haired man.

"No, wait," insisted Hunter, now very suspicious. "How did you know we had a clue?"

"I overheard her reading it aloud," he responded, pointing to Hannah.

Hunter nodded his head and smiled at the man. Then

they all watched as the man reunited with his friends outside the park gates.

"That was odd," said Hayden. "I don't think that guy was even in here when you read the clue, Hannah."

"Really?"

"That's why I asked him," Hunter answered.

"If he didn't hear me read the clue just now, then how would some random person in Nauvoo know that we had anything like this?" asked Hannah, holding up the cloth.

"I do not know, but it makes me nervous," said Hunter, still watching the man.

"Well, maybe we need to be a little more careful," suggested Hayden.

"We need to get back to work before Mom gets out here and wants to go," insisted Hannah. "Hunter, you were solving the clue so well, will you please continue?"

Hunter agreed and started, "I think I was on the fifth line which reads, 'engraved in the granite, next to the ash'. Now we have reached the granite, and from here I'm not sure."

"I think I know," declared Hannah. "I think the ash is not ash from a fire, but look over there," she said, pointing just outside a small picket fence.

"Look at what?" asked Hayden.

"The big Ash tree," said Hannah.

"An Ash tree," smirked Hunter. "I hadn't thought the clue could be talking about an Ash tree.

"The clue states 'Engraved in the granite, next to the Ash'," she replied proudly.

The three kids, momentarily forgetting about the

stranger, hurried behind the gravestones to the Ash tree.

"Now, 'engraved in the granite, next to the Ash', means to me that something has to be close," reasoned Hayden.

"The next line reads, 'Shimmer the keys, lighting your path,'" read Hannah.

"What keys?" asked Hayden, as he looked around the area. "Keys to a house or a car?"

"No, not like that. I don't even know for sure if people locked their houses back in the early eighteen hundreds," answered Hannah. "And we know they didn't have cars."

"Well then, what am I looking for?"

"I don't think the clue is referring to a physical key, but a key like on a map, or a key used to read or decipher something. Something like that."

"So, pretty much anything?" asked Hunter. "We better get looking. I'm sure Mom is going to be here any minute."

As they searched for any sign of engraving on the granite, Hayden was practically lying across the graves, attempting to run his fingers over every square inch.

"Get up from there, Hayden." warned Hannah.

"I can't see any engraving, so I thought I would feel for something on the granite," he explained.

"Well don't," she replied. "I've been thinking, and the clue reads, 'next to the Ash'. I think the engraving has to be somewhere on the back, not the front."

Suddenly, Hunter appeared from behind the headstones, startling Hannah. "Hey, I think I found something. Come here, quick!" he called.

Hannah and Hayden quickly maneuvered through the

bushes to the backside of the stone, trying not to step on the small flowers.

"What is it? What did you find?" asked Hayden.

"Look here—a small engraving," said Hunter, running his finger across the granite.

"Move your hand, Hunter. Let me see what the engraving looks like," insisted Hannah, squinting her eyes to get a better look.

"It's impossible to see the engraving. I can only feel that something is there," Hunter explained.

"What are we going to do?" asked Hayden.

"Relax, you two. Hayden, get me a small handful of dirt," said Hannah.

"Dirt? What is that going to do?" questioned Hayden.

"Don't ask questions, just get the dirt," insisted Hannah. "I know what I am doing."

Hayden, unsure of Hannah's plan, grabbed a handful of dirt from the garden area where they were standing and held it up for her to take. Inspecting the engraving, she took a small amount of dirt and pushed it into the open areas, filling them completely. When she was confident the engravings were filled, she pulled the sleeve of her shirt across the granite to remove the excess dirt. As she wiped away the extra dirt, the engravings revealed a message.

"I can't read the words. What are they?" asked Hunter, straining to see.

"Hopefully the writing is the beginning of a clue," Hannah said, through a big smile. "The sentence reads, 'Poor man of grief'."

"Is that right, Hannah?" asked Hunter.

"Yep, that's right," she replied.

"Is there anything else?" asked Hunter.

"Not here," replied Hannah. "But there could be small engravings like this all over this granite."

"I'll keep looking for more," offered Hayden, excitedly running his fingers across the granite.

"Wait a minute. Hayden, you take Hyrum's grave. I will check Joseph's headstone, and Hannah you take Emma's," suggested Hunter. "We can cover more area that way."

"Good idea," replied Hannah, already running her small hands over the granite of Emma's grave.

Suddenly, Hayden screamed, scaring several of the people viewing the memorial. "I found another one! I found one!"

"My goodness, son. You found another what?" asked a lady, who was holding her chest in fright.

Hayden, unaware he'd been so loud, slowly peered over the edge of the granite and said, "I'm sorry, ma'am. I didn't mean to frighten you."

"What are you doing, son?" the lady demanded, holding her hands on her hips.

Unsure what to say next, Hayden sat down quietly without saying a word.

"Son, what are you doing?" she again demanded. "Answer me."

Hayden remained quiet for several seconds. Hannah finally stood from her hiding spot behind Emma's grave and said, "We're sorry to have disturbed you. We're on a church history treasure hunt, and one of the clues is supposed to be here. He was excited to find one."

"Well, the things you are doing are very disrespectful. We have come here to pay tribute to our first prophet. If you're going to continue, please show some respect," she said angrily. She turned abruptly and walked toward the Visitor's Center.

"What did you find, Hayden?" Hunter asked, trying to be more respectful.

"Another engraving, I think," he replied, pointing at the headstone. "Quick, come look."

Hunter hurried over to Hayden and repeated the process of filling the engraving with dirt, while Hannah continued to search Emma's headstone for any other engravings. As Hunter finished filling the engraving, he quickly wrote down the sentence. Peering over the edge of the granite, they noticed Hannah excitedly motioning for the two boys to join her and see what she had found. Without waiting for them, Hannah started filling the engravings with dirt and quickly wrote down the inscription she found. Hunter and Hayden crawled over to meet her as she finished writing the clue, bringing the sentence they found with them.

Thrilled the Legend was more than Grandpa's imagination, she whispered, "Can you believe this? We've found something important that has been hidden for over a hundred years—something no one else knows anything about."

"Excuse me, you three," yelled Mom, startling Hannah. "Can you possibly tell me why my three children are hiding behind the gravesite of our prophet? And why that's remotely a normal, rational, respectful thing to do?" Mom asked heatedly.

"We were looking for…uuumm," hesitated Hunter.

"Kids, if you tell me you were being disrespectful because you were trying to find clues to that dumb Legend, I'm going to be so mad."

"We were looking for clues to solve the Legend," replied Hannah timidly.

"I told you not to tell me that. Will you please get out from behind there and show some respect to me and everyone else here?" Mom said angrily. "I never thought my teenagers would embarrass me like that. I was sure that would be the three-year-old I left at home."

"But Mom, we found…"

"STOP! I don't want to hear it right now. Get in the motor home," Mom ordered. "I do not want to hear anything else about that Legend."

Mom marched toward the motor home, as Hannah, Hunter, Hayden and Aunt Shirley watched her stomping and shaking her head all the way. She only stopped long enough to speak to a man in the parking lot.

"Take this however you want, but I recommend that the three of you work quietly on Grandpa's Legend," suggested Aunt Shirley.

"How did she find us?" asked Hannah.

"Some lady complained to the employees in the log house and Mom overheard them talking. She was hoping that you were not the kids causing a problem. She is just disappointed that it was you," replied Aunt Shirley. "She was really hoping that it wasn't."

"Sorry, we didn't mean to cause a problem," said Hayden. "I wasn't trying to be disrespectful."

"Don't tell me you're sorry. You better tell your mom," replied Aunt Shirley. "You can tell me what you found, though."

"We found another clue," Hunter replied excitedly.

"Really? Another clue? Are you sure?" Aunt Shirley asked, as they headed back toward the motor home.

CHAPTER ELEVEN

11

"WE'RE REALLY SORRY, MOM," said Hayden, as he entered the motor home.

"Really, Mom. We didn't mean to embarrass you," said Hunter, as he climbed into the driver's seat.

"I expected my teenagers to act a little more mature than this," she replied.

"Mom, I promise we weren't making a ruckus. We were only crawling around behind the graves to search for clues," said Hannah.

"You may not have thought you were being a nuisance, but you were being very disrespectful," Mom snapped.

"I promise, Mom, we won't embarrass you or be disrespectful again on this trip," said Hunter, as he pulled out and headed for the RV Park.

"No, you will not. As a matter of fact, I have been very patient with the Legend. I allowed you to work on solving the clue Grandpa gave you, even after I told you that I didn't want you to get caught up in the story. Now I'm afraid it's taking over our trip." Mom paused, took a deep breath and continued, "So, I have decided that you will need to put the Legend away and work on it another time."

"No, Mom, please. I promise, I won't let it get in the way again," pleaded Hannah. "Don't make us stop."

"Yeah, Mom," said Hayden. "I'll make better decisions."

"We got caught up in the excitement, Mom. I won't let it happen again," added Hunter. "I should have been more responsible."

Mom shook her head, puckered her lips and sat quietly the entire ten-minute ride to the RV Park. Hunter pulled into The Nauvoo State RV Park and parked in space three hundred seventy-three. Hannah quickly threw open the door, jumped outside and placed blocks behind the tires to keep the motor home secure. Hunter, only a minute behind her, checked to see if the motor home was level, then climbed swiftly back into the motor home, pushed out the side bed and opened all the windows.

Hayden helped by pulling out a pot for spaghetti and starting to boil water on the stove. He set the table, buttered and salted the garlic bread, browned the hamburger for the sauce and added the noodles to the boiling water.

"How long are you going to let them scamper around here, Sarah?" asked Aunt Shirley. "I know you're not going to make them stop working to solve the clues of the Legend."

"I don't know, I haven't decided yet," Sarah replied, smiling. "I'm trying to teach them a lesson."

"It's not like they were really terrible, you know. They were crawling around in the dirt on their hands and knees, being kids," replied Aunt Shirley. "I know you're trying to teach them a lesson, but let them have some fun on this trip. You might have some too, if you're not careful."

"I know Shirley, but what were they thinking? We could have helped them check for whatever they were looking for," she said, shaking her head. "By the way, I know they told you what they found. So tell me, did they even find anything, or was the clue they brought from home another one of Dad's stories?"

"I think they might be on to something here, Sarah. Maybe Dad hasn't been making the Legend up for all these years," Aunt Shirley replied optimistically.

"Why, did they really find something at the gravesite?" asked Sarah.

"They sure did. But I told them they better be careful. You didn't want to hear anymore about the Legend," answered Aunt Shirley, smiling.

"Oh great, Shirley, now they won't tell me anything," said Mom. "So you tell me. What did they find?"

"I don't know for sure. We didn't have a lot of time to talk about what they found."

"So, should I let them continue?" asked Sarah.

"Well," replied Aunt Shirley, standing up and walking over to the dinner table. "I can't think of a better way for teenagers to learn about church history than crawling around on their knees looking for clues." She turned to the kids and said, "Well, you guys. You are amazing. The motor home is set up and dinner is ready. What else do you have up your sleeves?" Aunt Shirley asked, as she slid into the booth.

"Come on, Mom," hollered Hunter, motioning her to sit down at the table. "Hayden has everything ready for us."

Mom, still quiet, walked over to the table and sat down. She listened as Hannah said a quick prayer over the food. Then Hayden started dishing the noodles and sauce.

"Really, Mom, we are very sorry," said Hannah. "Please don't make us stop working on the Legend."

Mom finally answered saying, "I know that you kids are having fun, but I need you to THINK about what you are doing at all times. Be courteous and respectful when we're touring through these church history sites. And no matter what, I expect you two older kids to watch out for Hayden," said Mom, pausing only long enough to take a breath. "Searching for these old treasures can be dangerous. Don't go anywhere without letting me know—ever. Do you understand?"

"Yes, I promise, Mom," replied Hunter, smiling cautiously. "So, can we continue to search for clues?"

Mom grinned at Hunter's excitement and replied, "Yes, but we will be touring all of the sites that I want you to see before you search for anything that has to do with Grandpa's silly Legend," Mom said sternly. "Is that understood?"

"Yes," replied Hunter. "Thank you."

"Good," said Mom. "And you're welcome. Now don't let me regret my choice to let you three continue with the Legend."

Hoping to change the subject for the remainder of dinner, Hayden asked, "Mom, was there anything cool in the log house back at the park?"

"Actually, yes. We saw replicas of the clothes that Hyrum and Joseph were wearing when they were martyred. That was a little eerie. We also saw some letters that Joseph had written. Then the tour guide showed us some really neat antiques that originally belonged to various Smith family members. I wanted to take pictures, but they don't allow pictures inside."

"I would've liked to have seen those things," exclaimed Hannah. "I love the old antiques and stuff."

"You would have loved this old house, Hannah. But the most interesting thing in the store was an ink drawing that hung on the wall. It was drawn by Sutcliffe Maudsley between 1842 and 1844. The drawing detailed Joseph Smith, the man, shortly before his death," said Mom.

"Why was this picture so interesting, Mom?" asked Hannah. "You've seen pictures of the prophet before."

"Well, I've never seen a life-like portrait of him in which he was dressed up so formally. The picture was life size. He was wearing a three-piece suit with long tails—like a tuxedo. He was holding a beautifully engraved wooden cane that had tassels tied around the top. A pocket watch hung from a chain above his waist and a small representation of the Nauvoo Temple was sketched just to the left of his leg. He looked very distinguished," Mom said, as she finished her description.

"I read the plaque mounted underneath the picture," said Aunt Shirley, "and the information referred to personal preferences of Joseph and images that have never been reproduced. I've heard many things about Joseph Smith, but these facts were much more personal.

"For instance, did you know that Joseph loved to wear a stovepipe hat and would always wear one when riding his horse? Sometimes he would even hide his most important papers in the hat. Joseph was also a playful and cheerful person, who loved to indulge in harmless jokes.

"I already knew he had leg surgery as a child, but I did not know that he used a cane quite often—and especially enjoyed canes that were beautifully handcrafted. Joseph's canes were actually some of his most prized possessions, and he even made most of the canes he owned. I guess the portrait of him helped me get to know him a little better. It was much more than just another picture of him," added Aunt Shirley.

As they finished dinner while talking about the prophet, Hayden could only think about translating the next clue. He raced through his food, slurping down his spaghetti noodles, until Hunter wanted to tape his mouth shut. Hurriedly clearing his plate, Hayden motioned for Hannah to hurry as well. As Mom and Aunt Shirley popped in the DVD of *The Work and the Glory,* Hannah, Hunter and Hayden finally had a chance to look at all of the engravings together.

"So show me already, Hannah," insisted Hayden, as he climbed up to the kitchen table.

Hannah smiled as she continued to dig through her backpack for the papers they had written the clues on.

Anxiously, he waited until she finally laid the papers on the table. He grabbed them, not giving the other two even a moment to view them.

"Come on, Hayden. Let us see, too," demanded Hunter. "Lay them back on the table."

"I'm sorry, but I'm so excited, I can hardly stand it," Hayden admitted.

"So are we, but you need to calm down," reassured Hunter, patting his brother's head.

"I want to solve the Legend so Grandpa can see what it is before he dies," said Hayden.

"Me, too," replied Hannah. "Now, do you want me to read what we have?"

"Yes, read the clues," replied Hunter. "I'm ready to hear them"

"We found the first clue on Joseph's grave. The engraving read, 'Poor man of grief.' The second engraving, the one you guys found on Hyrum's grave, reads, 'Cemented in time.' The last clue, which I found on Emma's grave, reads, 'Signature and key.'"

"Is that everything we found?" asked Hunter.

"Yep, that's all we found," answered Hannah.

"That can't be all of the riddle," said Hayden. "The phrases don't make any sense."

"Read all three of them again, will you please, Hannah?" asked Hunter, in a disappointed voice.

"'Poor man of grief, Cemented in time, and Signature and key,'" she replied.

"Hayden's right. We didn't get everything we needed," muttered Hunter.

"So, what do we do now?" asked Hayden. "Mom is never going to let us go back and crawl around again."

"We have to go back. It's easy to see we don't have everything we need yet," said Hunter.

"Mom might let us go tonight, but, we're going to have to ask," warned Hannah. "I'm not going to do this with out her permission."

"Then you ask her, `cause I'm not going to," announced Hunter. "She is never going to let us go back to the gravesites this late at night."

"Why?" questioned Hannah.

"So ask her then," said Hunter.

"Fine, Hunter, you big chicken, I will," said Hannah, whispering under her breath as she walked nervously toward Mom.

"Mom," said Hannah quietly.

"Yes, Hannah, what's up?" Mom asked, still trying to watch the movie.

"I know you don't want to hear anything about the Legend, but I was wondering if you would let Hayden, Hunter and I go back over to the gravesite tonight. We're missing part of the riddle. I guess we didn't find all of the engravings," Hannah quietly explained.

"Go where?" asked Mom, looking up curiously at Hannah.

"Back to Smith Memorial Park," Hannah answered.

"Hannah, have you looked at the time?" asked Mom, looking down at her watch.

"We could be really fast, Mom. Please," Hannah pleaded.

"Hayden can't go this late, and I don't want you and Hunter out alone in an unfamiliar area either. What would I tell your Dad if something happened?" Mom replied.

"Aunt Shirley could walk with us," suggested Hunter. "And you could stay here with Hayden."

"Have you even asked Aunt Shirley if she would be willing to go with you?" asked Mom, looking at Shirley with a tell-them-no look on her face.

"Well, we do have a tourist map, and I could use the exercise," replied Aunt Shirley.

Mom shook her head and smiled. "You can only go if no one gets hurt and you're not gone very long,"

"We'll hurry, Mom, I promise," replied Hunter, as he slipped on his shoes.

"Nice one, Shirley," whispered Mom, as Hannah and Hunter walked out the door.

"Oh, come on, Sarah. You used to love adventure," teased Shirley. Then smiling she added, "I didn't know you had gotten so old."

"Funny, Shirley," called Mom, as Aunt Shirley, Hunter and Hannah disappeared into the misty night.

"I really wanted to go, Mom," Hayden said sadly.

"I know son, but you're not old enough to be wandering around a strange city at night. Let's watch a show while we wait for them to get back. I'm sure they won't be gone very long," Mom said, as she threw her arm over his shoulder.

The gravesites were located about one mile southwest of the RV Park. Aunt Shirley, Hunter and Hannah hastily made their way through the unfamiliar town and were surprised by the number of people on the streets. As they reached Smith Memorial Park, they were surprised to see several people wandering around and looking at the statues, plaques and gravesites.

"Now tell me, where did you find the clues you have?" asked Aunt Shirley.

Standing at the foot of the gravesite, Hannah walked to the side. She fell down on her knees, crawled through the bushes and wiggled around to the back. Aunt Shirley followed Hannah's lead as Hunter stood watch.

"Show me what you've got," asked Aunt Shirley.

Hannah flipped on a small reading light and shined it on the granite where she had previously filled the engraving with dirt.

"Look, right here," said Hannah, pointing to granite.

Aunt Shirley gazed upon the engraving and said, "I bet Grandpa would love to see this."

"I bet you're right," agreed Hannah.

"Okay, this engraving reads, 'Poor man of grief'. Was there anything else on Joseph's grave?" Aunt Shirley asked.

"No, not that we found," answered Hannah, squinting her eyes as she studied the clue.

"Look! Something shimmers when you move the flashlight around," announced Aunt Shirley. "What is it?"

"I don't know. We couldn't see the granite shimmer at all during the day," Hannah replied. She moved the light so it shined at several different angles.

"I think whatever is shimmering is the missing part of your riddle," said Shirley, wiping away the extra dried dirt from around the engraving.

"I can't see anything," Hannah complained. "Where?"

"Look, here underneath the engravings you filled

earlier today is another sentence that can only be seen when you shine the flashlight on it," replied Aunt Shirley.

"Nice work, Aunt Shirley," said Hannah. "I didn't even see anything shimmering."

"If you look close…I think the line reads, 'His journey ended'. Does that make sense?"

"The sentence at least sounds complete now," admitted Hannah.

"Where is the next engraving?" Shirley asked, excitedly. "Let's see if there are more shimmering words."

Hannah pointed the way and they quickly started reading more sparkling words, which were written below each of the engravings on the other headstones.

Coming back around to where Hunter was, Aunt Shirley excitedly said, "Finding real clues is kind of fun. Before we leave, let's make sure we have everything you need. Hannah, why don't you read the entire riddle?"

Hannah nodded her head and said, "Any idea what order I should read the lines?"

"Good question," replied Aunt Shirley. "That's a hard one."

"That's not hard!" exclaimed Hunter, taking the paper from Hannah's hand. "Start with the clue we found on Joseph's grave, followed by Hyrum's, and then Emma's."

"Why?" questioned Hannah.

"Because that is the order of the graves. Joseph is in the middle with Hyrum on the right and Emma on the left," said Hunter, handing the paper back to Hannah.

"Okay, let's try it in that order. Read the riddle that way Hannah," agreed Aunt Shirley.

Hannah shrugged her shoulders and started reading the riddle the way Hunter suggested.

'POOR MAN OF GRIEF,
HIS JOURNEY ENDED,
CEMENTED IN TIME,
SAFELY PROTECTED,
SIGNATURE AND KEY,
CONCEALED BY FATE.'"

"The clue sounds like it's in the right order. But, I still feel that something is missing," said Hunter.

"I agree. The riddle doesn't sound complete," said Aunt

Shirley. "Are you sure you found all of the engravings?"

"We thought so, but maybe not," answered Hannah. "Should we feel around for any more of them before we go?"

"We better. Hunter, look on the face of the granite. Hannah and I will look on the back and side," said Aunt Shirley.

Finding nothing further in the back, the girls crawled out into the open and started helping Hunter with his search of the front.

"Nothing is engraved on the front of Hyrum's grave," said Hunter, almost lying on the granite and stretching to reach the top.

"And nothing is engraved on the front of Emma's," replied Hannah.

"Well, come look at this. I've found something on Joseph's grave. Hunter, grab a little moist dirt will you?" asked Aunt Shirley, anxious to discover if the newly found engraving was part of the clue.

Hunter grabbed a handful of dirt from the flower garden behind the graves and watched as Aunt Shirley pressed it firmly into the holes.

"What does it say?" asked Hannah.

"'Left for the righteous'," responded Aunt Shirley.

"Is that it?" asked Hannah.

"Until you give me the light," replied Aunt Shirley, smiling and holding out her hand.

Hannah quickly flashed the light on the engraving. Just below the dirt, the remainder of the sentence appeared. She whispered as she read the words.

"UPON THE DREADFUL DATE
6-27-18+44
V1, V2, V6."

"What does all that mean?" asked Hunter.

"Write it down, we can figure out what it means when we get back to the motor home," replied Aunt Shirley.

As Hannah finished writing the clue, Aunt Shirley again said, "Read through the clue one more time. We need to check to make sure the riddle sounds complete."

"Where should I add this sentence?" she asked.

"At the end. That way, the riddle starts and ends with Joseph," suggested Hunter.

"Okay, that sounds good," replied Hannah, as she read the entire clue aloud for Hunter and Aunt Shirley to hear.

"POOR MAN OF GRIEF,
HIS JOURNEY ENDED,
CEMENTED IN TIME,
SAFELY PROTECTED,
SIGNATURE AND KEY,
CONCEALED BY FATE,
LEFT FOR THE RIGHTEOUS,
UPON THE DREADFUL DATE,
6-27-18+44
V1, V2, V6."

"This is so cool," said Hunter. "I'm so glad Grandpa told us about the Legend."

"Come on, we better get back before your Mom starts

to worry," suggested Aunt Shirley, as she turned to leave the park.

"Wait a minute," said Hannah. "We can't leave the engravings filled with dirt. Someone will see them—especially here on the front."

"You're right," replied Hunter. "What are we going to do?"

"Hannah, I put my water bottle in your backpack. Pull it out, and let's use it to wash out the dirt," suggested Aunt Shirley.

"Good idea," Hannah replied, as she knelt down on the cement. She unzipped her pack and handed Aunt Shirley the water bottle.

Aunt Shirley quickly sprayed the water over one of the engravings, washing away the dirt. As the dirt washed down the side of the granite, the mud revealed more writing engraved in the granite.

"Hannah, look," Aunt Shirley said excitedly pointing to the words. "There's more writing."

"What does it say?" Hannah asked smiling nervously.

Aunt Shirley set the water bottle down, grabbed a small handful of dirt and carefully rubbed it across the area revealing two more lines.

"This clue is a little different," said Aunt Shirley as she wrinkled her nose and squinted up her eyes.

"Why?" asked Hunter.

"How?" asked Hannah trying to see the writing as she peered over Aunt Shirley's shoulder.

"Well, I don't know why it's different, it starts with a symbol of a lion, then the clue reads.

'SHOW BRAVERY LIKE THE LION,
FIND THE SECRETS THAT IT KEEPS'.

Then it is followed by another symbol that looks like a circle with four small squares around it."

"Is it part of the clue?" asked Hunter.

"The writing could be an additional clue," replied Aunt Shirley.

"I wrote it down, let's figure everything out when we get back," suggested Hannah.

"I agree, let's get back," said Aunt Shirley. "Let's get all these clues washed out before we go."

Hunter nodded in agreement. Picking up the water bottle from the ground, he crawled to the back of the graves. The girls stood in the dark for several minutes before Hunter finally finished the task and returned.

"I'm done. They're all washed out in the back," said Hunter, as he stood and brushed the dirt from his knees.

"Let me see the water bottle, we still have this new one up here," said Hannah, as she took the bottle and sprayed it on the writing.

"Looks good to me," said Aunt Shirley.

"Let's get back then," said Hannah, looking around nervously. "I don't like being in a cemetery at night."

They left the park and cautiously started the walk back to the RV Park where Hayden and Mom were waiting for their return. Excited about the new clue, but afraid to talk about the Legend in public, Hunter, Hannah and Aunt Shirley remained quiet.

"We need to talk about something," Hannah

said enthusiastically. "Like the weather or sports or something."

"Yes, we should," said Aunt Shirley. "And that might relieve the nervous tension you two have."

"We have? I think you're just as nervous as we are," said Hannah, as she pushed Aunt Shirley's shoulder, knocking her into Hunter.

"Careful, guys," Hunter replied, barely looking at the girls.

"What is it, Hunter?" asked Hannah, recognizing something was bothering him. "What's the matter?"

Hunter again looked over his shoulder at the people on the street. Seeing nothing suspicious, he replied, "Nothing, I guess."

"What does that mean?" asked Aunt Shirley.

"I have an uneasy feeling, like a knot in the pit of my stomach. I think we were being followed or something," Hunter responded.

"Have you seen anyone?" asked Hannah, getting paranoid.

"No, I guess I'm just excited about the clue," he replied, not convinced that was the problem.

Hannah, now anxious about her surroundings, picked up the pace as she started to look over her shoulder as well. Not watching where she was walking, she almost ran over an elderly lady who was out for a stroll in the cool, crisp evening air.

"I'm sorry," Hannah said softly, as she stepped around the woman.

"No problem, honey," the woman replied sincerely.

"Hunter, do you think there are people here in Nauvoo right now who know we are looking for this treasure?" asked Hannah.

"I don't think so, but anything is possible," he replied. "Why?"

"I don't know. I got a funny feeling when I bumped into that lady," answered Hannah, looking over her shoulder.

"What do you mean?" asked Aunt Shirley.

"I'm not sure. Something about her wasn't right. Her voice didn't fit or something," said Hannah.

"Her voice?" asked Aunt Shirley.

"I don't know for sure. Something just wasn't right," Hannah said, as she shrugged her shoulder.

"Well then, let's hurry and get back as fast as we can. I don't want to take any chances with the riddle," said Aunt Shirley, as she started to run.

CHAPTER TWELVE

THROWING OPEN THE DOOR, Hannah raced inside the motor home yelling, "I win! I win!"

Seconds behind her, Hunter raced through the door yelling, "Oh, you little cheater. You tripped me!"

"No, you tripped over your own feet. Don't blame that on me," replied Hannah, trying to catch her breath.

Finally, a full minute later, a tired and breathless Aunt Shirley pulled herself through the door.

"You're not that old, Shirley," teased Sarah smirking. "I thought you were in better shape than that."

"So did I," she replied, between gasps for breath.

"Tell us! Tell us! Did you find more engravings?" asked Hayden, eager to hear the news.

"We sure did," replied Hannah, holding up the paper with the riddle. "We had missed clues on all the graves."

"Let's figure it out," said Hayden, trying to grab the

paper from Hannah's hand. "Come on, I want to find the next clue to the treasure."

"Let's not," replied Mom. "I already let you stay up late and go back down to the park to search for clues to a treasure that you know I'm not really excited about. Besides, we have a lot going on tomorrow."

"Only for a few minutes, Mom. Please," begged Hayden, clasping his hands in front of his chest.

"Kids, it's nearly eleven o'clock. Our Nauvoo tour starts at nine o'clock sharp," she replied hesitantly. "I've already paid for the tour, so we can't change the time."

Hayden, Hunter and Hannah quietly stared at Mom with begging eyes. She took a deep breath and said, "Oh, all right, guys. You have until the TV news ends and then, no matter what, you are going to bed. Is that understood?" Mom said.

Hannah jumped with excitement and raced to the table, sliding into a chair as fast as she could. She quickly laid the paper on the table and started to read the riddle.

'POOR MAN OF GRIEF,
HIS JOURNEY ENDED,
CEMENTED IN TIME,
SAFELY PROTECTED,
SIGNATURE AND KEY,
CONCEALED BY FATE,
LEFT FOR THE RIGHTEOUS,
UPON THE DREADFUL DATE,
6-27-18+44,
V1, V2, V6'.

"Then Aunt Shirley found another clue that reads,

'SHOW BRAVERY LIKE THE LION,
FIND THE SECRETS THAT IT KEEPS'."

"What in the world does this mean?" asked Hayden, with a perplexed look on his face.

"That's what we have to figure out," replied Hannah. "Solving this riddle is gonna take some work, and it's not going to be easy. But anything worth getting is going to require some work, right?"

"Yeah, I know," Hayden replied.

"Okay, we can solve this. I need to think. Give me a minute," said Hunter, standing up from the table. He paced through the kitchen and then back again.

"What does 'Poor man of grief' mean?" asked Hayden, staring at Hunter as he paced back and forth.

"It sounds like something to do with Joseph Smith," replied Hannah. "I know that he was killed on June 27th, 1844, and that date is referenced at the end of the riddle."

"If the riddle is about Joseph, then 'Poor man of grief' must be talking about him, right?" asked Hayden.

"I think so," said Hannah. "'Poor man of grief, The journey ended' has to be referring to the grief he suffered and then his journey on this earth ending—or his death."

"'Cemented in time, Safely protected'. Does that mean after his death he is finally safe?" asked Hayden.

"I'm not sure. Hunter, what do you think?" asked Hannah.

"I'm working on it. Give me a minute," replied Hunter, pausing only briefly from his pacing.

"'Signature and key, Concealed by fate'. What does that mean?" asked Hannah.

"Well, what has both a signature and a key?" Hayden asked thoughtfully.

"Hey, that's it. Good job, Hayden," said Hannah.

"That's what?" Hayden asked, obviously baffled.

"Well, think about both words—signature and key. The only thing that I know of that uses those words is written music—like piano songs," reasoned Hannah.

"What does a song have to do with this clue?" Hayden pressed.

"I know what the clue means!" Hunter shouted excitedly, slapping Hannah on the back.

"Man, Hunter, you scared me!" Hannah shrieked.

"But, I know what the clue means!" exclaimed Hunter, as he sat down at the table.

"So, tell us. What does it mean?" asked Hayden.

"'Poor man of grief'—that is the song that Joseph and Hyrum had John Taylor sing over and over right before they were killed."

"Is there really a song with the title 'Poor man of grief'?" Hannah asked.

"Poor Wayfaring Man of Grief. Come on, Hannah. You attended Seminary this year, didn't you?" scolded Hunter. "Didn't you listen to Brother Hutcheon?"

"I listened," Hannah said defensively.

"He was talking about church history the last day of

class. Do you remember? You had to teach part of Seminary that day," joked Hunter.

"Funny, Hunter," replied Hannah.

"Well, I think that's when he told the story of Joseph in Carthage Jail," said Hunter.

"Hey, that's right. He did talk about a song John Taylor sang. The song has to be what the riddle is talking about!" exclaimed Hannah. "So, if that line in the riddle is referencing the song, and it is talking about both the signature and key, we need to see the hymnbook, don't you think?" asked Hannah.

"Mom, do you happen to have your little hymn book with your scriptures?" asked Hayden.

"Yes, it's zipped in the case," she replied.

"Can I borrow it for a minute?" he asked.

"Only if you promise to put it back," Mom replied.

Hayden hurried to find Mom's scriptures. He unzipped the light pink scripture cover and removed the small hymnbook. He finally found the song 'A Poor Wayfaring Man of Grief', and rushed back to the table.

"I found the song. Here it is, Hannah," said Hayden, holding open the book for her to see.

Hannah took the hymnbook and looked over the notes. "All right, the song has four flats," she mumbled, as she studied the key signature. "I think with four flats, the key for this song is A flat major. Could that be the information we need?"

"I don't know. Read the first couple of sentences again, Hayden," Hunter said.

Hayden, excited to help, picked up the paper and read,

"POOR MAN OF GRIEF,
HIS JOURNEY ENDED,
CEMENTED IN TIME,
SAFELY PROTECTED'."

"Stop there a minute, Hayden," said Hunter. "All right, I think the line, 'Poor man of grief', is talking about the song. The second line, 'His journey ended', is talking about Joseph being killed. Right?"

"Sounds right to me," answered Hannah.

"I think these two lines are leading us to the location of the next clue, which I believe is Carthage Jail," suggested Hunter.

"Hey, I think you've got that right," said Hannah. "Now what?"

"Well, the third and fourth lines go together—'Cemented in time, Safely protected'. A possible meaning could be, something of importance, which has been cemented in time, and keeping it safely hidden forever. Something like that," said Hunter.

"I didn't know you were this smart," teased Hayden. "I think you might be right."

"Should I go on, or do you want to take over?" Hunter asked, grabbing Hayden's neck.

"You're doing so good, I wouldn't want to slow you down," replied Hayden, as he tried not to choke.

Hunter squeezed Hayden's shoulders tightly in torment and said, "Could you read the rest of the lines, so that I can use my superior knowledge and solve the rest of the clue."

"Why, sure, Hunter," replied a smirking Hayden.

"'SIGNATURE AND KEY,
CONCEALED BY FATE,
LEFT FOR THE RIGHTEOUS,
UPON THE DREADFUL DATE,
6-27-18+44
V1, V2, V6'."

"All right, line five, 'Signature and key', might be guiding us to the song talked about in line one. I think line six, 'Concealed by fate', is referring to when Joseph was killed. A lot of information died with him."

"Let me try the next line, Hunter," offered Hannah.

"Okay, what do you have for us?" he asked.

Hannah took a deep breath and started, "Line seven, 'Left for the righteous', could mean that Joseph left a clue at Carthage that only the righteous will find. And line eight, 'Upon this dreadful date', is self-explanatory; it was the day the clue was left behind."

"Wow, I didn't know both of you were so smart," Hayden said mockingly. "But, if you are so smart, tell me, please, what do the last two lines mean?"

"Well, I know that '6-27-18+44' is the day Joseph was killed. But I have no idea why the 18 and 44 are split with a plus sign," said Hannah.

"And I have no idea what V1, V2 and V6 reference," said Hunter. "Could they have anything to do with the song?"

"I guess they could be referencing the verses, although I don't know exactly how," Hannah replied.

"Could there be a clue in each of the verses?" asked Hayden.

"That's possible," said Hannah. "I hadn't thought of that."

"Okay, someone read the verse, and let's see what we can find," suggested Hunter.

Hannah flipped the hymnbook to the right page and began to read. "'A poor wayfaring Man of grief hath often crossed me on my way…" She paused for several seconds, staring at the text with a confused look on her face. "Hunter, there are seven verses in this song with more than fifty words per verse. Hiding a clue in each verse is a good idea, but the clues would be almost impossible to find without some sort of key to decipher where the clues are hidden."

"You know, Hannah, I think the date 6-27-18+44 has to mean something. The plus sign is in a strange place," reasoned Hunter.

"What if the date is the key?" asked Hayden. "You know, like the number six stands for the sixth word or something like that?"

"Hey, you really are smart," joked Hunter. "Hannah, let's try using the numbers like that. What is the sixth word?"

"In verse one or what?" she asked.

"Yeah, in verse one," Hunter replied.

Hannah quietly counted out the numbers one through six and answered, "The sixth word is 'grief'."

"Okay, what is the twenty-seventh word?" asked Hunter.

"In verse one or verse two?" she asked.

"Well, 'V1' is listed under the number 6. 'V2' is listed under the number 27, and 'V6' is listed under the numbers 18+44. So, let's look in those verses."

Hannah counted the words until she came to the twenty-seventh. "The twenty-seventh word is 'it'. Grief it? What does that mean?"

"Look up the next word. Let's see if they make sense together," suggested Hayden.

"What number do I look up—18 or 44?" Hannah asked.

"Try the numbers 18 and 44," replied Hayden.

"All right. The 18th word is 'lying', and the 44th word is 'flesh'. 'Grief it lying flesh'. That can't be right."

"Try adding the numbers together and looking up that word. The clue says 18+44, so look up word 62," suggested Hunter, shrugging his shoulders.

"There's not a 62nd word," said Hannah, as she reached the end of the verse.

"We're not doing something right," said Hayden.

"What else could the numbers stand for?" asked Hunter.

"Hey, I have an idea," said Hayden. "What about the sixth letter? Could that spell a word?"

"Good idea. Let's try that," said Hunter. "Hannah, what is the sixth letter?"

Hannah, already looking, excitedly answered, "The sixth letter in the first verse is 'w'."

"And the 27th letter?" asked Hayden.

"That letter is 'e'," she replied.

"Okay, and the last one. What is the 62nd letter?" asked Hunter.

Hannah counted as fast as she could, looking for the sixty-second letter. She finally said, "The letter is 'l'."

"Well, what does that mean?" asked Hayden.

"I'm not sure," replied Hunter. "Could it be short for another word?"

"No, Hunter, do you remember in class a few days ago when we were talking about Joseph Smith's death?" asked Hannah.

"Yeah, right after he told us the story is when he got a little frustrated and you had to go to the front of the class and tell everyone what Brother Hutcheon had been talking about," Hunter replied.

"The information I read to the class was how Joseph Smith fell out of the second story window and crawled to a well before he died."

"Do you think the clue is talking about the well at Carthage?" asked Hayden.

"Yes, I do, and I think the lines, 'Cemented in time, Safely protected', are referring to a clue left in the well," Hannah squealed excitedly.

"Nice job, guys," said Hunter. "I guess we need to go to Carthage Jail and find the well. The next clue has to be there."

"Mom, are we going to go to Carthage Jail tomorrow?" asked Hannah.

"Come on, Hannah. We can't go on a church history trip and not visit Carthage Jail," answered Aunt Shirley, looking up from the television.

"I guess not. I don't know what I was thinking," replied Hannah, with a grin on her face.

"When are we going?" asked Hayden, as he turned around and looked over the seat.

"Tomorrow sometime," Aunt Shirley replied.

"Mom, do you know?" asked Hunter.

"I think sometime in the afternoon," she answered. "I know first thing in the morning we're going on the tour of Nauvoo. It is supposed to last between three and a half and four hours. I heard the tour takes us to Heber C. Kimball's home. Then we'll have a quick lunch, followed by a stop at the Nauvoo City Cemetery. Once we've found what Grandma needs from the cemetery, we will leave for Carthage and visit the jail. After we've seen the jail, we will be on our way to Kirtland, Ohio."

Hunter nodded and said, "Okay, thanks Mom." Disappointed, he turned to Hannah and said, "We're gonna have to wait all day."

"No were not, did you hear what Mom said?" Hannah asked.

"No, what?" replied Hayden confused at Hannah's excitement.

"The second part of the clue refers to, 'Bravery like the lion," she answered.

"Yeah, so," responded Hunter.

"Well, I've been thinking about the two lines. 'Show bravery like the lion. Find the secrets that it keeps'. In the letter that Heber C. Kimball wrote to his posterity, it states that we have to show bravery like the lion. What if this clue has two parts and one is found in Heber's home and the other part is at Carthage Jail?"

"Hey good thinking!" said Hunter. "I bet you're right and that is why the writing wasn't the same."

"I bet we have to find something from Heber's house that a lion is keeping secret," said Hayden.

"That is how it sounds to me," agreed Hannah.

"Then I guess we might as well put the clues away until tomorrow," said Hannah. "Then watch out, we've got two clues to find."

CHAPTER THIRTEEN

"COME ON, YOU TWO. You've got to get up. We're going to be late if you don't hurry," said Aunt Shirley, pulling at their blankets.

"I'm tired. Leave me alone," said Hayden, as he pulled the covers over his head. "What time is it, anyway?"

"It's time to get up before Mom gets angry," answered Hunter. "Now, come on, get out of bed."

"Remember guys, you told her you'd get up on time and be happy. She doesn't want to be late for the tour," added Aunt Shirley.

Hayden moaned as he sat up in bed. He looked around the room, blinked his eyes several times and said, "I don't want to get up, I'm just too tired."

Hunter, already out of bed, started singing, "Good morning, good morning."

"Oh, not you, too!" exclaimed Hayden, covering his ears with his pillow.

Laughing at Hayden's response, Hunter asked, "Aunt Shirley, what did Grandpa do after he sang you that song?"

"Don't you even think about it, Hunter," insisted Hannah, holding on tightly to her blanket. "Mom's told us those stories, and you better not touch my covers."

Hunter smiled as he softly tugged on her blankets. "Well, you only have ten minutes to get up, get dressed, eat breakfast and be ready to go before Mom gets back from her morning walk," he said.

Hannah rubbed the sleep out of her eyes and groaned as she kicked the covers to the bottom of the bed. Slowly, she climbed out of bed and sleepwalked her way to the bathroom. She barely opened her eyes as she got dressed and brushed her hair. As she bumped her way back to the kitchen, she asked, "Aunt Shirley, are you sure I have to be awake today?"

"Yes, Hannah," Aunt Shirley replied.

"Well, what about Hayden? Why is he still in bed?" Hannah asked.

"Because, Hannah, I slept in my clothes," announced Hayden, as he stuck his leg out from underneath the blanket, showing her his jeans. "So, I can stay in bed a few minutes longer."

"No you can't. Now get up, Hayden, before I help you get up," threatened Hunter. "I would like to surprise Mom today."

"Get your clothes changed, and get over here for

breakfast, Hayden. I have warm pancakes ready," said Aunt Shirley, as she scooped a pancake from the pan and flipped it up into the air.

"Do I have to Aunt Shirley?" asked Hayden.

"Yes, Hayden, right now," she replied.

Moaning, he let his legs fall over the edge of the bed and stood up slowly.

As they sat at the table quietly eating their pancakes, the door flew open and Mom yelled, "Hey, sleepyheads, you told me you would be up on time, so be prepared to have a bucket of water dumped on your heads."

"We're all up, dressed and eating breakfast. Do you want some?" asked Hunter, holding up the plate for her to see. "We told you staying up late wouldn't be a problem."

"That's right, Mom. We're all awake and ready," said Hannah.

"Wow, I'm impressed, kids!" exclaimed Mom. "I was sure you would all still be asleep."

"Is it time to leave?" asked Hayden, as he smoothed down the hair on the back of his head.

"I found the ticket office while I was out on my walk this morning, and it's closer than I thought. So I checked all of us in early. All we have to do now is meet the tour guide at nine o'clock," she replied, pouring a glass of orange juice. "I think, since the office is so close, we should walk and leave the motor home here. That way we don't have to try and find parking for this big old boat. What do you think of that idea?"

"That's a good idea, Mom," replied Hunter. "Parking this motor home is a giant pain."

"So, how long until we need to leave?" asked Hannah, still rubbing her eyes.

"Fifteen minutes. That's just enough time for all of you to fold up your blankets and make your beds."

"Now?" grunted Hayden. "Can't I just rest?"

"Now!" replied Mom.

Hayden moaned again, as he carried his plate to the sink and headed for his bed. When he paused to argue with Mom, Hunter quickly grabbed Hayden's shirt and said, "Come on, I'll help you."

Hayden agreed, grateful for the help.

"Can you help me, too, Hunter?" begged Hannah, struggling with her bed. "I have the bed cleaned off, but I guess I'm not strong enough to push it closed."

"The bed should slide fairly easily," said Hunter, as he threw the folded blankets into the closet.

"It's not moving anywhere," said Hannah, using her legs to help her push. "I think it's stuck."

"Hold on a minute, I'll be right there," replied Hunter, putting away the last blanket. "Wait, don't break anything."

"Very nice, kids. I love the way you are all working together," said Mom. She gathered her sunglasses and purse, and then sat down to change her shoes.

Without a word, Hunter walked to Hannah's bed, grabbed the handle and pushed. He used the same force he had used earlier to pull out the bed, but it didn't budge. He took hold again with a better grip and lifted the bed slightly as he tried to push it closed. Nothing happened—the bed still did not budge. Scowling, he pushed again with all his might. The bed shifted slightly, squeaked, and then squealed abruptly as the rollers gave way, allowing the bed to slam shut.

"Nice job, Hunter," said Hannah. "I've never had a hard time closing the bed before. Thank you."

Hunter brushed off his hands and said, "No problem. You just needed a man to do the job."

"Funny, Hunter, ha, ha," replied Hannah.

"Okay, kids," said Mom, walking out the door. "We need to get moving."

Aunt Shirley, Hannah and Hayden followed Mom outside, while Hunter quickly closed the windows, made sure the stove was turned off, and locked the door. Pulling the keys from the lock, Hunter handed them to Mom, and they started on their journey through the historic sites of Old Nauvoo.

An unexpected summer rain storm cooled the air making the heat tolerable. Until the wind started to blow, causing a shiver to run through Hannah's body. Her teeth chattered as she walked. The rhythm of the noise reminded Hayden of a song, and quickly he was singing, 'I Wear My Pink Pajamas'—one of Grandpa's favorite songs. Sarah and Aunt Shirley smiled as they led the way toward the Nauvoo Historic Tours Office. They enjoyed the early morning rain, and watched as the sun finally broke through the hazy clouds.

As they started down a gentle sloping hill, Hunter stopped and looked across the green valley to see the steam rising off the Mississippi River.

"This is so cool," he mumbled under his breath, as he hurried to catch up with Hannah and Hayden.

"Hannah, Hayden, wait for me!" he called. Quickly catching up, he said, "Kinda neat out here, huh?"

"Yep, even I have to agree. Being on the trip has been better so far than I thought it would be," replied Hannah, shrugging her shoulders.

"Hey, I meant to ask you something. Did you bring the clues and stuff?" Hayden asked.

"Oh, no! I forgot," Hannah replied frantically. "Give me the keys, and I will hurry back and get them."

"Mom's got the keys," he answered, biting his lip. He was suddenly a little nervous to have left the clues unattended.

"Where did you leave them, Hannah?" asked Hayden.

"In my backpack."

"They should be safe in there, shouldn't they?" asked Hayden. "You locked everything up in the motor home, right Hunter?"

"Yeah, I locked everything up," he answered.

"You know, I think I should hurry back and get them anyway. I would feel better if I kept them with me," said Hannah, walking toward Mom.

"Mom, I need to run back to the motor home really quick. I forgot my backpack. I'll hurry as fast as I can," Hannah promised, holding out her hand for the keys.

"Not a chance, dear," answered Mom. "We're getting on the bus right now."

"Please, I'll run really fast," begged Hannah.

"No, honey, you can't go back to the motor home. Go get your brothers, and get on the bus, right now," Mom said sternly.

Hannah turned dejectedly and walked back to Hayden and Hunter. "Mom won't let me have the keys. She said I can't go back to the motor home."

"Don't worry, I'm sure everything will be okay," said Hunter, as he climbed up the steps of the bus.

The kids followed Mom and Aunt Shirley to the middle of the bus and sat in the row directly behind them.

"Isn't this exciting, guys," Aunt Shirley asked through a wide grin.

"Mom, what are we going to see today?" asked Hayden, looking out across the valley.

"I guess we'll find out," she replied, pointing to the tour guide standing at the front of the bus.

"Hello, everyone," announced the tall, thin, dark-haired man. "My name is Darrell, and I will be your guide today. Before we begin, I have three rules that will help us stay on time and remain safe on our excursion. First, while the bus is in motion, please remain seated. I will be sure to give each of you ample opportunity to view and take pictures of the historic sites I talk about. Second, we will be touring several locations today. While we're off the bus at each location, please remain together as a group. Don't wander off, we don't want to miss any of our scheduled stops. Lastly, as you know, the sites we're visiting are over one hundred years old. I know this request sounds silly, but please, please, please don't remove anything from these historic sites. You will have the chance to purchase souvenirs from one of the many gift shops we will visit today. With that said, everyone sit back and enjoy your journey into the life and times of Old Mormon Nauvoo."

"I'm so excited to go on this tour," said a smiling Aunt Shirley.

"The tour guide seems to have a fun personality," replied Sarah. She turned to the kids and said, "Are you ready?"

"Yep, we're ready, Mom. So where's our first stop?" asked Hunter, as he scanned through the fifty other people on the bus.

"I'm not exactly sure, but I'm excited to find out," she replied.

The tour guide stood and switched on his microphone. "Our first area today is what's known as the Old Commerce area. Coming up on our left is the Sarah Granger Kimball home, wife of Hiram S. Kimball. Sarah was instrumental in founding the Nauvoo Female Relief Society. She was present with the Prophet Joseph Smith, on March 17, 1842, for the first official meeting, at which time Emma Smith was set apart to preside over the organization," Darrell said, as the bus pulled to a stop in front of the small, white, one and a half story home.

Hannah turned around as a member of the tour group asked a question. "Is this her original home?" the familiar voice asked.

Unable to see anyone that she knew, she turned back around and looked up at the tour guide. "You don't know anyone here, quit being paranoid," she thought to herself.

"Yes, this is her original home, it has been restored and is open to the public, but it is not one of our scheduled stops today," Darrell replied, motioning for the driver to continue.

"Coming up four blocks ahead of us is the Nauvoo Restoration, Inc. Visitors Center. Nauvoo Restoration, Inc. (NRI) is a non-profit organization that was formed September 4, 1971. The LDS Church began buying historic sites in 1905, when it purchased Carthage County Jail. Small parcels of land in the area around the temple block were later acquired as they became available. Dr. James Leroy Kimball founded NRI to 'acquire, restore, protect, and preserve, for the education and benefit of its members and the public, all or part of the old city of Nauvoo.' Since that time the NRI has acquired more than one thousand acres of land, all of which were originally purchased by Joseph Smith to build the City of Nauvoo. We will not be stopping here today, either. This is, however, a great site to see during your extra time in Nauvoo.

"We're now moving into the East Flats area. This area has several structures to see, all located within two blocks. We will be exiting the bus at the Joseph Coolidge home, then we'll walk to the Noble-Smith home, Brickyard, Porter Rockwell marker and the Heber C. Kimball home. The bus will be waiting to pick us up at the Wilford Woodruff Home site.

"We have only thirty minutes to tour these sites. So, on this stop only, you may either stay with me and listen to the additional information I give, or you may tour through the homes on your own. Either way, please do not be late returning to the bus," finished Darrell. The bus door opened, and he quickly exited.

"What are we going to do, Mom?" asked Hannah.

"Well, I would like to hear the information Darrell knows about these places," she replied, picking up her bag and walking to the front of the bus.

"Would it be all right with you if we hurried to the Heber C. Kimball home?" asked Hunter. "We would like to spend our time there if that's all right with you."

"I'm fine with that, as long as you have fun, don't get into any trouble and stay together," Mom replied excitedly.

"Thanks, Mom," called Hayden, as the kids ran toward Heber's home.

"Remember to stay together!" yelled Mom.

"Do you think any secrets could be hidden in Heber's home that have to with the Legend?" asked Hannah.

"I don't think so," replied Hunter. "Grandpa said only the Kimball posterity is aware of the Legend."

"Where exactly are we going?" asked Hayden.

"Look, Hayden, right there," said Hannah, pointing to the large, two-story, brick home.

"Wow!" Hayden exclaimed, looking up at the chimney. "This house is big."

Hunter jumped over the three-foot-tall picket fence and raced toward the pillars surrounding the front balcony.

"Wait a minute!" cried Hannah. "Wait for us, Hunter."

"I'm waiting, but hurry, will ya?" he yelled, standing at the foot of the front porch.

As Hannah and Hayden reached the front porch, they

excitedly walked up the stairs to the front door.

"Do we walk in or ring the door bell?" asked Hannah.

"Door bell? They didn't have door bells back then," said Hayden, laughing hysterically.

"Well then, what is this?" asked Hannah, holding a string that was attached to the wall.

Hayden shrugged his shoulders. Hannah pulled the string that ran into the house through a small hole, and suddenly a bell in the house rang.

"That is so cool," said Hannah. "I bet Heber's was the only house that had a door bell."

"I wonder if he liked to invent stuff like I do," said Hunter excitedly, as he turned the small brass knob and pushed open the door.

As they entered the house, they walked into a large parlor area. The parlor was a bright white, with beautiful hand carved oak, shadow boxes hanging on the wall. As they moved out of the parlor, they stepped into a large family room with a beautiful river-rock fireplace at the far end. Next to the family room was the kitchen, followed by a small wash area.

"This is amazing," said Hannah, as she walked around the house.

"Look at this!" Hayden yelled from the study. "Isn't this a chair like the one Grandpa was rocking in?"

"They kinda look the same," replied Hunter, examining the rocker. "Only I think the one Grandpa has is made from a different color of leather."

Hayden shrugged his shoulders and nodded as he continued to wander around the room.

"This must be where Heber would work," said Hannah, staring at the numerous books on the shelves. "I wonder if the attendant sitting in the front room would know any special information about the house or this room?"

"Possibly, why?" asked Hunter.

"She may know if there's a lion," Hannah replied, as she walked into the front room.

"Excuse me, ma'am," said Hannah.

"Yes," she answered.

"You work here, right?" asked Hannah.

"Yes, how can I help you?" she replied.

"I was wondering if there is anything in the house that is special or different?" Hannah asked excitedly.

"Special? Different? What do you mean?" the woman asked, obviously puzzled.

"I mean something like…you know, engravings in the walls or carvings in the wood—possibly something only this house has compared to others in the area," replied Hannah.

The woman sat quietly for several minutes, squinting her eyes as though deep in thought.

"Well, the only special or interesting thing that I'm aware of, and I'm not sure it's exactly what you are looking for," said the woman, as she climbed the stairs to the second floor, "is this lion that was hand carved into the wooden planks of the floor in Heber's bedroom. Could this be the unique item you're looking for?"

"Yes, this is perfect," answered Hannah, kneeling down to take a closer look at the engraving.

As the attendant turned to leave, she stopped, looked back at the kids and added, "I believe the lion symbolized courage to Brother Kimball."

"Thank you," said Hannah, glancing back over her shoulder. "You know, guys, Heber's letter to his posterity said something about having courage like the lion."

"We better get over to Wilford Woodruff's home," said Hayden, as he looked out the window across the block. "I don't want Mom to be mad if we're late, and I can see the bus already parked there."

"Are you serious?" asked Hunter, as he hurried to the window. "We've only been gone ten minutes. I thought Darrell said the bus would meet us there in thirty minutes. I'm sure it's just waiting for us to return."

"Maybe we better check," suggested Hayden.

"Wait a minute," Hannah said softly. "There's something funny about the wood where this lion is engraved."

"Like what?" asked Hunter.

"Watch," said Hannah, as she rubbed her finger around the outline of the lion. Smiling, Hannah looked at Hunter and said, "Did you see that?"

"Did I see the tail move?" asked Hunter.

"That's what I thought, too. But look—the tail doesn't move. A small piece of wood underneath the tail moves very quickly."

"Move the wood again," Hunter said excitedly.

"When I do, Hunter, try to stick your finger into the opening."

"My finger? What if something is inside of it?" he asked nervously.

"Then I guess whatever it is will bite off your finger," replied Hayden, grinning.

"Funny," Hunter replied sarcastically.

"Are you ready, Hunter?" asked Hannah.

"Ready," he replied, holding his finger directly above the tail.

Hannah slowly slid her finger across the lion's outline and watched as Hunter was successful in catching the tail's opening with his finger.

"I got it," Hunter squealed excitedly.

"What's in there?" asked Hannah. "Can you feel anything?"

Hunter wiggled his finger around the opening, but he couldn't feel anything but wood. Not wanting to pull his finger from the hole and have it close again, he pushed his finger in as far as he could and felt around again.

"Hey, I can feel something," called Hunter.

"What is it?" asked Hayden.

"I'm...not...sure," he replied slowly, as he stretched his finger to reach the object.

Suddenly, a loud POP sounded in the room, startling the kids. Hannah, grateful no one was in the room, but afraid the attendant heard and would walk through the door any second, looked at Hunter and asked, "Did the wood break?"

"I don't think so," he replied, carefully pulling his hand away from the hole.

They stared at the floor in silence. Hannah leaned

over to inspect the damage, when she suddenly felt a sharp poke in her side.

"What's going on up here?" asked Aunt Shirley, in a sinister voice. "What have you kids done?"

Not recognizing the voice at first, Hannah nervously said, "We are very sorry, we didn't mean to break anything."

"So, now what'd ya break?" Aunt Shirley asked suspiciously as she tried to peek over Hannah's shoulder.

Hannah, realizing she had been fooled, turned around to see Aunt Shirley. "Oh, I tricked you!" Hannah said.

"What?" Aunt Shirley asked.

"I tricked you, Aunt Shirley. You thought I didn't know who you were," replied Hannah, pointing toward her face. "Ha, ha, I tricked you."

Aunt Shirley looked suspiciously at Hannah, then at Hunter and finally at Hayden before she replied, "Something fishy's going on up here you three. Why don't you tell me what you're doing?"

"Where's Mom?" asked Hayden, completely ignoring Aunt Shirley's question. He walked toward her, covering the opening on the floor with his size-ten shoe.

"She's waiting downstairs. She said to tell you to hurry up." Then grabbing Hunter's arm, she said, "Now, tell me what you're doing."

"We're not doing anything. Tell Mom we'll be there in one minute, Aunt Shirley. I promise, we'll be right there," replied Hunter, pulling his arm from her grip. "We've got to finish one thing."

"One thing, huh?" she asked suspiciously. Then you

have one minute to finish. We'll be waiting downstairs," she said, as she walked out of the room. "Don't get into any trouble."

"We won't," replied Hayden, waving goodbye.

"Nice job, Hannah. Quick thinking. I was sure we were caught," said Hunter, as he turned to look at the hole in the floor.

Hannah pushed Hayden's foot away from the hole and wondered how they were going to quickly fix the opening. Sure they had destroyed the engraving of the lion, she quickly surveyed the damage. She ran her finger along the edge of the wood. As she examined the opening, she discovered that the wood flooring was not broken at all. The wood engraved with the lion swung back and forth inside the opening. A secret trap door had opened, leaving a four-inch by four-inch hole. Hannah reached anxiously into the opening to pull the trap door closed when she felt something in the hole.

"Hey, something's in here," she said, looking up at Hunter.

"Really? What is it?" he asked, kneeling down next to her.

"I don't know. Should I pull it out?" she asked.

"Hey, it sounds like someone is coming. You two better hurry," said Hayden, as he walked toward the door.

"Keep watch for us Hayden," said Hunter. "Whatever is in here has been here for more than one hundred years. We need to get it out."

Hannah reached her hand into the opening and took hold of the contents. She eagerly pulled her hand out of the hole clutching a small, round, wooden medallion. As she opened her hand to show Hunter the hand-carved object, the wood panel with the engraved lion snapped unexpectedly back into place, closing the hole as abruptly as it has opened.

Whistling a song loudly, Hayden tried to signal Hunter and Hannah of approaching people. Hannah jumped to her feet, swiftly hiding the object in her jeans pocket. She glanced at where the opening had been in the floor, but the trap door had shut. She smiled and motioned for Hunter to follow her into the hallway.

"What'd ya find? Show me," whispered Hayden.

"Not until we get back on the bus," said Hannah, holding onto the object tightly.

"I didn't expect to find anything," said Hunter, as he walked down the stairs. "I wonder if it has something to do with the treasure?"

"We've got to get back to the motor home and find out. Heber talked about a lion," replied Hannah.

Catching up with Mom and Aunt Shirley, Hunter grabbed Mom's arm and said, "Time to get on the bus, let's go."

"So, what have you three been up to now?" she asked.

"Not much, really. We had fun looking at Heber's house. It's very cool to think that our relative built this house over a hundred years ago."

"Time to leave, everyone back to the bus!" called Darrell, holding open the front door.

Everyone from the tour group quickly filed out of the house and walked across the block toward the Woodruff house and the bus. As several members of the group stopped and looked at the Woodruff house, Hannah, Hunter and Hayden moved as fast as they could toward the bus. They pushed open the bus door and climbed to their seats as quickly as they could.

Sitting down, Hayden said, "I want to see what you found, show me."

Making sure no one could see them, Hannah slid her hand out of her pocket and showed Hayden the round, wooden medallion.

"Look, there are symbols engraved on it, like the clue we found in the lamp," said Hayden, pointing to the ball.

Suddenly, Aunt Shirley popped her head over the seat and asked, "What are you doing?"

Hannah, closing her hand, to hide the medallion, replied. "We're waiting to hear where we're going next."

"Are you having any fun?" she asked.

"I am," replied Hayden. "Where are we going next?"

"Everyone, please hurry and take your seats, we're already running a few minutes behind," Darrell announced over the microphone.

The bus driver immediately started the engine and pulled onto the city street. Darrell spoke into the microphone and said, "We're moving into Main Street Flats. This area is rich in early church history. As we travel south on Main Street, on the left you can see the George C. Riser Boot and Shoemaker Shop. On the right, we're passing what was known as Widow's Row. These homes housed many women who'd lost their husbands.

"Watching on your right, you will see several more

homes that line the street before we come to the drug store, school house, mercantile storehouse and then the Cultural Hall. As we move into the Southwest Flats of Nauvoo, we will pass both the Blacksmith Shop and the Seventies Hall on the left.

"Our next stop is located in Upper Nauvoo. As you can see, not as many homes are left standing here in Upper Nauvoo as there are in some of the other areas we've passed. However, you can see several markers telling of the Pratt home, the Nauvoo Historical Building, and the City Cemetery, where many of the early saints were buried. Please refer to the maps I gave you earlier for additional information on these sites.

"Finally, we have reached our last destination—the one you have all been waiting for—The Nauvoo Temple. The temple story began in 1840 with its construction, and continued until October 1999 when the Nauvoo City Council granted permission for a building permit to rebuild the once beautiful 'Jewel of the Mississippi'.

"Hey, did you hear that?" asked Hayden. "Darrell just called the temple the 'Jewel'."

"I heard him, sshhh," whispered Hannah, pressing her finger across her lips. "I'm trying to listen."

"I want to thank you for joining us today. I hope you join us again on Nauvoo Family Tours," finished Darrell.

"Oh great, what did I miss?" Hannah asked, looking at Hunter.

"Nothing, really. We're on our own to tour the temple," Hunter replied, as he gathered his water bottle.

"Come on, kids. Let's get moving! This is what Aunt

Shirley has wanted to see since we arrived in Nauvoo," called Mom. She stepped off the bus and headed toward the temple.

Everyone was stunned at the beauty of the temple. The group wandered around the temple grounds, mesmerized by the beautiful surroundings. Hannah, Hunter and Hayden were amazed by the symbols that adorned almost every stone. They saw moonstones decorating the base of the pillars surrounding the temple, sunstones at the top of the pillars and trumpetstones that will be used one day to announce the beginning of holy days. Starstones were scattered across the eves, reminding onlookers to watch the heavens for the signs that will be sent foretelling of the Lord's Second Coming. They also saw a compass and square, a flame, the all-seeing eye, a handclasp, the dedication plaque, and even the Angel Moroni.

As the group wandered around the grounds they were amazed at the beauty and quiet of the area.

"Even the temple grounds have a wonderful feeling," said Aunt Shirley.

"It is very peaceful," replied Mom.

Excited to read Grandpa's book on symbols, Hannah asked, "Isn't it time to go, Mom?" "We've been wandering around here for almost thirty minutes."

"Yeah, Mom, if we still need to stop at the cemetery, we've got to get going," agreed Hunter, pointing at his watch.

"Oh my, you're right, we need to get moving," replied Mom. "The cemetery is on our way back to the motor home. If we hurry, we can get the information that Grandma needed before we leave."

Mom grabbed Hayden's hand and hurriedly walked beyond the temple fence toward the Nauvoo Cemetery. Aunt Shirley and Hunter hurried to follow.

Hannah watched as Hunter tried to skip with Aunt Shirley. Shaking her head in amusement she opened her water bottle and took a long drink, thirsty from the hot summer sun. Not wanting to get too far behind Mom, she quickly poured some water into her long hair, tied it into a knot and hurried to catch up with everyone.

CHAPTER FOURTEEN

14

AS SHE WALKED THROUGH the small metal gate, Hannah was stunned by the beauty of the cemetery. She scanned over the area and noticed several tall trees that hung over the gravesites, as if to shelter them. The flowers were unusually vibrant, and the shadows from the scattered clouds in the sky cast soft, floating images in the deep, rich, green grass. Hannah was surprised to see a stream meander its way down the center of the cemetery. It seemed to play soft music as it fell over the obstacles in its path. She picked up a small pebble and tossed it into the passing stream. She smiled as the ripples from the rock disrupted the water, causing it to sparkle as it continued on toward the Mississippi River.

Hannah patted her jeans pocket, excited about their newest clue to the Legend. She impatiently waited for Mom to locate the names Grandma needed from the cemetery. Twenty anxious minutes passed as Hannah,

Hunter and Hayden watched Mom and Aunt Shirley search every headstone for the right name.

Unable to wait any longer, Hannah asked, "Mom, how many names are you trying to find in this cemetery?"

"Only two here in Nauvoo, we need seven in Kirkland," she replied, without stopping her search.

"Two?" Hannah mouthed silently to the boys. "We're gonna be here forever. I want to re-read the clues, not search for names," Hannah whispered.

"Mom, I have an idea," Hunter said.

"All right, let's hear it," she replied, still searching the headstones.

"What if Hannah, Hayden and I, head back to the motor home? We can get everything packed up, check out of the RV Park, fill the motor home with gas, and pick you and Aunt Shirley up in about an hour. That way, you've got more time to search, and we won't end up having to cut short our visit of Carthage Jail," Hunter suggested.

"Yeah, Mom, I don't want to miss going to Carthage Jail," agreed Hannah.

Mom smiled at Hannah's excitement to see more church history sites. She hesitantly reached into her purse, pulled out the keys, held them tightly in her hand and replied, "Are you sure you can handle everything, Hunter?"

"No problem, Mom. With all of us helping, we'll be fine," he replied.

"Well, since I would like to have a little more time in Carthage as well, I'm going to take you up on your offer, the three of you can get the motor home ready to leave," Mom replied, happily handing Hunter the keys.

"Great! Now let's hurry," said Hayden, looking over his shoulder. "Something in this graveyard is giving me the chills. I'm ready to get out of here anyway."

Aunt Shirley placed her arm around Hayden's shoulders and teased, "Don't leave me here alone, Hayden. I need a big, strong guy to protect me in case something tries to get me. Please stay, Hayden," she teased.

"Oh, leave me alone. Quit teasing, I'm really serious. Someone or something is watching me. I can feel it," he replied fearfully.

As Hunter took the keys from Mom's hand, he yelled to Hannah and Hayden, "Quit messing around, you two, let's get moving. We've got stuff to do. See you in about an hour, Mom."

Hayden pulled away from Aunt Shirley and quickly ran to catch up with Hannah and Hunter. Sarah and Aunt Shirley paused and watched as the three ran east toward the town and RV Park.

"You can't blame then for not wanting to be here," said Aunt Shirley, as she started searching the headstones again.

"I don't. If I were their age, I'd want out of this creepy, old cemetery too," replied Mom, grinning.

"I'm so excited!" announced Hannah, waving her hand and the medallion in the air. "Let's go check out this cool thing."

"I wonder if the medallion has anything to do with the treasure," Hayden said.

"I can't wait to find out," added Hunter as he stopped abruptly.

Hayden crashed into his brother's back and fell to the ground. "What's wrong, Hunter? Why did you stop?" he asked.

Without saying a word, Hunter pointed to the motor home.

"I thought you locked the door, Hunter!" yelled Hannah, as she started to run toward the motor home.

"I did," Hunter replied, running after her.

Hayden jumped up and quickly followed them toward the front door of the motor home.

"Wait for me, Hannah. I'm sure I locked the door, so, if it's open, someone could still be inside," Hunter called.

Hannah reached the door first and cautiously peered through the opening, trying to see if anyone was there. With no one in sight, she carefully pulled the door open wider and maneuvered up the stairs as quietly as she could. Several tense minutes passed as Hannah checked the front of the motor home while Hunter checked the bathroom and back bedrooms for any sign of an intruder.

With no sign of anyone inside, Hannah called to Hayden and said, "Doesn't look like anyone is here, come on in, Hayden."

"Oh no! Look at this place! It's destroyed!" exclaimed Hayden. He walked inside and tripped over several bowls strewn on the floor.

"Do you think someone knows we're searching for treasure?" asked Hannah.

"Someone must know!" exclaimed Hunter, looking at the mess.

"What are we going to do, Hunter?" Hayden asked nervously. "Do you think Grandpa was right? Maybe, searching for this treasure is too dangerous for kids our age."

"I don't know! No! I don't think it's too dangerous," replied Hunter. "At least, I didn't think searching would be to dangerous."

"What do we do?" asked Hayden, bewildered at the mess.

"I'll tell you what we have to do," Hunter replied matter-of-factly, as he rubbed his hands together. "We've got to get this place cleaned up fast, if Mom sees any of this, we won't need to worry about bad guys. Our treasure hunting will be over for sure."

Overwhelmed by the mess, Hannah was not sure where to start.

"Who would do this?" asked Hayden.

"Are you sure who ever broke in was looking for the clues, or do you think they just broke in looking for money?" asked Hannah.

"The clues!" Hunter shouted frantically. "Hannah, where's your backpack? Did they get all of our clues?"

"I forgot. I don't know where I put it. Help me look!" she squealed.

"Where did you leave it?" asked Hunter, shuffling through the clothes, food, blankets and mess on the floor.

"Try looking next to my bed," Hannah replied nervously, as she kept searching.

"I can't see it. Oh, please tell me someone didn't steal the clues," begged Hunter, throwing the clothes as he looked.

"Grandpa is going to be so disappointed. What are we going to tell him?" asked Hayden, frantically searching the back room.

"I don't even want to think about that," Hannah cried.

"Well, don't get mad at me for asking," Hayden replied. "You're the one that left the backpack behind."

"I didn't do it on purpose," Hannah cried, as tears started to well up in her eyes.

"I'm sorry, don't be sad," Hayden said. "I'm just disappointed, I really wanted to search for the treasure."

"I'm not sad. This isn't a sad face, Hayden," explained Hannah. "This is a scared face. I promised Grandpa we wouldn't let anything happen to his stuff."

"You promised?" snapped Hunter. "I guaranteed him I wouldn't let anything happen to the clues."

"How about instead of getting mad at each other, we keep searching for the backpack," Hayden suggested.

Hunter took a deep breath and replied, "You're right, Hayden. Maybe if we calm down, we'll find the backpack."

There was no sign of the pack anywhere. They hoped they might find it as they cleaned up the mess. Hayden started cleaning up the back room. He re-made the bed, hung up Mom's and Aunt Shirley's clothes, picked up the papers and miscellaneous items, and straightened the bedroom so that nothing was out of place. Meanwhile, Hannah started cleaning the kitchen area and then fixed the beds. Hunter cleaned the driver's seat and the loft. They cleaned the motor home better than they ever had before. But still, there was no sign of the blue backpack anywhere.

Hannah's cell phone rang, startling everyone.

"It's only my cell phone, Hayden," said Hannah, holding it up for him to see.

Hayden wrinkled up his nose and replied, "I know, I just wasn't expecting it to ring."

Hunter was sure the thieves had gotten away with the clues. He grabbed Hayden's arm as Hannah answered her phone and said, "Help me outside, we need to make sure everything is put away and locked up. Mom's going to wonder where we are if we don't hurry."

Sure they'd lost everything, the boys walked outside. Hayden rolled up the extension cord while Hunter disconnected the water. With all the storage containers locked up, they walked back inside to find Hannah crying.

"What's the matter, Hannah?" asked Hunter, as he sat down next to her on the sofa. "Who was on the phone?"

"It was Grandpa who just called," she replied.

"You didn't tell him we lost everything did you?" Hayden asked frantically.

"No. I couldn't. He was so excited to hear if we had discovered anything, that he could hardly talk," she replied.

"So, what did you say?" asked Hunter, in a panicked voice.

"I told him we'd found the next clue with Aunt Shirley's help at the Smith Memorial Park. He was so thrilled. I told him I would let him know if we found anything else," she replied quietly, as tears started to well up in her eyes again.

"Relax, Hannah, everything will be okay. Maybe we can solve the treasure without the clues we already found. I think we should try to remember the last riddle. Then we would at least be able to keep searching for the treasure," suggested Hayden, looking for a paper and pen.

"Hang on, Hayden. We need to get over to the cemetery to pick up Mom and Aunt Shirley first, before we have an even bigger problem," said Hunter. He jumped into the driver's seat and grabbed the parking permit.

"Hannah, warm up the engine for me while I check us out of the RV Park, will you please?" asked Hunter, as he tossed her the keys.

"Sure, Hunter," Hannah replied, through soft sniffles. "I was so excited to search for the Kimball Legend, I'd forgotten how miserable I thought this trip would be. I'm sorry I forgot my backpack this morning, guys," she said, as she stood up and walked over to start the engine. "This is all my fault."

"Knock it off, Hannah," said Hayden. "This is nobody's fault. Let's just figure out where we need to go from here and keep searching for the treasure."

Hannah smiled slightly and quickly turned the key. "Hayden, everything is cleaned up, right?" she asked.

"Yep, I think so," he replied. "Mom shouldn't notice anything out of place."

"Hunter should only be a few minutes, Hayden. Help me to back the motor home out of the camping spot, please," Hannah said, as she scooted the driver's seat forward.

"You're not old enough to drive," answered Hayden.

"I'm almost sixteen, and I have my driver's permit. Now get out there and guide me out of here," Hannah insisted.

"You better be careful, Hannah. You're gonna get into trouble if you hit anything," replied Hayden, as he turned to walk out the door.

"I won't hit anything if you do a good job guiding me!" Hannah yelled, as the motor home door slammed shut.

Slowly, Hannah backed the motor home out of the campsite, as Hayden directed her. She maneuvered safely onto the road and waited for Hunter to return.

Suddenly Hunter burst through the door and said, "Good job, Hannah. Did you hit anything?"

"No, I didn't, Hunter," growled Hannah. "I was really careful."

"I'm teasing, Hannah, you did a good job," said Hunter, as he climbed into the driver's seat. "We're all checked out and ready to go. Let's get moving, we still need to get gas before we pick up Mom and Aunt Shirley, and we've been gone close to an hour and a half."

Shifting the RV into gear, Hunter pulled out onto the street. Hannah and Hayden watched out the back window. They hoped the lost backpack would somehow magically appear.

Hunter signaled and pulled off Main Street, into the Travel Center and Gas Station. Turning off the motor, he wiggled out of the driver's seat and hurried to fill up the gas tank. He slid the credit card into the machine, pulled out the nozzle, opened the gas tank and slid the nozzle inside the tank. Listening to the gurgling sound of the gas as it poured into the tank, Hunter's mind wandered.

"Who could know about the Legend? Who would know we were looking for the clues to solve the Legend?" he contemplated. As he stood in a daze and waited for the gas tank to fill, he suddenly screamed, bringing Hannah and Hayden outside to see what was wrong.

"Hunter, I'm sorry," said Aunt Shirley, through uncontrollable laughter. "I really didn't mean to scare you, sweetie."

Holding his chest in fright, Hunter could feel the rapid pulse of his beating heart. "Aunt Shirley, I am so gonna get you. You scared me to death!"

"When I heard you scream, I thought maybe someone was after you," said Hayden, scowling at Aunt Shirley who was still giggling.

"I'm sorry, boys, I was only playing," she said. "Why are you two so nervous?"

"We're not nervous," Hayden replied defensively.

"How did you know we were here, anyway?" asked Hannah.

"As we were walking back to the RV Park, your Mom and I saw you pull into the gas station," she replied.

"Where is Mom?" asked Hunter, looking around. His breathing and heartbeat were slowly returning to normal.

"She ran into the travel store to buy some treats for our ride to Carthage. She'll be right back," answered Aunt Shirley, as she put her hand on Hunter's shoulder.

"Did you find the names at the cemetery that Grandma needed?" asked Hayden.

"Yes, we did," she replied. "So tell me, were you able to get everything ready to go?" asked Aunt Shirley.

"I think so," answered Hunter, worried something could still be out of place. "Filling the motor home up with gas was the last thing we needed to do."

"Good, let's get on the road then," said Mom, surprising everyone as she walked up to join her family.

"What is it? Why is everyone trying to scare me?" asked Hunter, holding his chest again.

"You really are nervous, Hunter," said Aunt Shirley. "I've never seen you so jittery."

"I'm not jittery," Hunter responded angrily.

"Well, kinda," replied Hannah. She walked over to Hunter, took his arm and tried to calm him down. "Everything's all right, there's nothing to be afraid of," she teased.

"Oh, everybody's a comedian," Hunter said sarcastically, as he winked at Hannah and climbed into the motor home. "Do you want me to drive, Mom?"

"Would you, please?" she asked. "I was hoping to take a nap before we get to Carthage Jail. I need some energy so I can keep going today."

"Sure, Mom. No problem," Hunter replied, as he jumped into the driver's seat and started the engine.

"I'm gonna take a power nap, too, if you're all okay with both of us being asleep," said Aunt Shirley.

"Sure, we're okay," Hannah replied through a grin. "We're not old enough to need midday naps like the two of you."

"Hey, you're not funny!" laughed Aunt Shirley. "I'm not old like your mom, I just didn't want her to feel bad that she's the only one sleeping."

"I heard that, Shirley!" Mom yelled from the back room. "And I am not OLD!"

Shirley held her hand to her mouth, trying to muffle her laughter, as she opened the refrigerator and grabbed a bottle of water.

CHAPTER FIFTEEN

EAGER TO REACH Carthage Jail and search for the next clue, but frustrated at the loss of the other clues, Hannah climbed into the passenger seat next to Hunter and asked, "Can you remember any of the clue we found at Joseph's grave?"

"Not a lot, but some," answered Hunter, keeping his eyes on the road.

"Do you have any idea who might know we're trying to solve clues to the Legend?" whispered Hannah.

"Not one. I keep wondering if we need to ask Grandpa if he might have any idea," replied Hunter.

"I don't want to do that!" exclaimed Hannah. "Grandpa will make us stop looking. He seemed to be really nervous about us getting hurt before we left."

"I agree. That's why I think we need to ask him," said Hunter. "I think he knew more than he was telling us."

"Really?"

"Hey, Hannah, can you help me for a few minutes?" interrupted Aunt Shirley, as she placed her hand on Hannah's shoulder.

Spinning around quickly, Hannah replied, "You scared me, Aunt Shirley."

"I'm sorry."

Hannah rubbed the sweat from her head, took a deep breath and replied, "Okay, what can I help with? What's up?"

"Your roll-away bed seems to be stuck. I can't get it to budge," she answered. "Can you help me with it really quick?"

"Oh, sure, hang on," Hannah answered, as she quickly crawled out of the front seat and headed back to help her aunt. "We had some problems closing the bed earlier."

Relieved she had not broken the bed, Aunt Shirley replied, "Good, I thought I had done something wrong."

Hannah shook her head, scrunched up her face and said, "Nope, you didn't break anything."

Hannah looked at the bed for a minute, then took the bottom edge and pulled with all her strength, but the bed would not budge. Hannah motioned for Aunt Shirley to take hold of the bottom while she grabbed hold of the top.

"Are you ready?" Hannah asked, looking up at Aunt Shirley.

"Yes."

"On the count of three, pull as hard as you can. Let's see if we can get the bed out by pulling together," replied Hannah.

"Okay, I'm ready," Aunt Shirley replied.

Hannah smiled, and then said, "One, two, three, pull."

Together, they pulled with all their might. The bed squeaked and moaned several times under the pressure. Suddenly, the bed's wheels popped off their tracks and the bed slid out.

"Uh, oh! Did we break the bed?" asked Aunt Shirley.

"No. I'm sure the wheels just slid off their tracks, I think they're easy to get back on," replied Hannah, as she picked up the blanket and looked underneath the bed. "Yep, the wheels slid off their tracks."

"Can I help you get them back on the track?" asked Aunt Shirley.

"No, I've fixed the bed before, it just takes a minute. I have to make sure the tracks are clean first, so the wheels don't get stuck again," Hannah explained, as she reached down to clear the track.

Hurrying to the other side, she checked the last track, finding something in the way. She looked closer and found a long, black strap on the track.

"What is this?" she mumbled to herself. Pulling at the strap, she screamed, "I found it! I found it!"

"Found what? Why are you screaming?" asked Aunt Shirley, puzzled by Hannah's strange behavior.

Hannah tugged under the bed several times, before she finally freed the straps to her missing backpack. Holding it up proudly, Hannah yelled again, Hunter! Hunter! I found my backpack!"

"Way to go, Hannah!" he called, unable to look over his shoulder to see her excitement.

"All right, we're back in business," announced Hayden,

as he grabbed the bag and helped Hannah to her feet.

"The bed works now, Aunt Shirley. You can take your nap," said Hannah, as she jumped back into the seat next to Hunter. "Hayden, let me see my backpack," she called.

Hayden set the backpack in her lap and asked, "Is everything there? Did they take anything?"

"Did who take anything?" asked Aunt Shirley, surprising everyone.

Hannah looked up, shocked to see Aunt Shirley looking over Hayden's shoulder. "What are you talking about, kids?"

"We thought someone broke in while we were gone and took my backpack, but I guess we were wrong," replied Hannah.

"Hmmm, are you sure?"

"Yep. I couldn't find my backpack, and I was sure someone had stolen it because Grandpa's clues were inside," Hannah answered.

Aunt Shirley looked suspiciously at all of them, then quietly walked toward the bed and sat down. "You three would tell me if you were in trouble, right?" she asked, as she leaned against the pillow.

"Yes, if we get into any trouble that we can't handle, we will tell you," said Hunter.

"I promise, Aunt Shirley," said Hannah.

"You better," she warned. She closed her eyes and quickly fell asleep.

"Hannah, are the clues still inside the pack?" Hayden asked impatiently.

"I'm looking, buddy, hang on a minute," she replied.

She unzipped the pack and searched through the contents.

"Well?" asked Hunter.

"Here's the cloth we found in the lamp, the letters from Oliver Cowdery and Brigham Young, the books we borrowed from Grandpa and our clues! Yep, everything is here," she answered, smiling from ear to ear.

"So, the backpack was under the bed the entire time?" asked Hunter. "I bet that's what was in the way when we tried to close the bed this morning."

"Yes, I think you're right. Can you believe how lucky we are?" asked Hannah.

"I'm so glad," said Hayden, puffing his cheeks and blowing a big burst of air.

"We must be getting help from up above to keep this information safe," said Hannah.

"I agree," added Hayden.

"We're going to have to keep in mind that there's a good chance that who ever broke in looking for the clues will be following us," whispered Hunter. "So, whatever we do from now on is going to have to be secret. I don't want anyone to get hurt."

"I thought we were keeping everything secret already," replied Hannah. "I haven't said a word to anyone."

"Evidently, we're not being quite secret enough," answered Hunter. "Hayden, do you have any good ideas that we might be able to use for security?"

"You bet, some of my inventions would work great for security," he replied. "I'm gonna get started now on which ones to use before we get to Carthage," he said, as he turned toward the back of the motor home to find a pen and paper.

"Great, Hayden. Thanks," replied Hunter. "Hannah, why don't you read through the clues and see if there's any reference to the medallion we found earlier at Heber's house."

"Good idea," replied Hannah. She pulled the medallion from her pocket and held it up for Hunter to see.

"Look, Hunter, the medallion shines in the sun," she said.

As Hunter looked over at the medallion, he noticed a light-blue Corolla following closely behind.

"Hannah, do you remember the color of the car that belonged to that guy who asked you about the clue back at Smith Memorial Park?"

"No, I don't. Why is there a problem?" she asked, looking into the side mirror.

"No, I think I'm just seeing things," said Hunter, as he rubbed his eyes and glanced in the side mirror again.

"Do you want me to look out the back window?" asked Hannah.

"No, I'm sure we're fine. If I see the car again, maybe I will have you look. I'm just really glad we got the motor home cleaned up before Mom or Aunt Shirley saw that someone had broken in," whispered Hunter. "Now that we found the clues, we can still keep searching for more."

Hannah shook her head and said, "Someone's really looking out for us."

CHAPTER FIFTEEN

"We're here," announced Hunter, waking Hannah from her deep sleep. "Go wake up Mom and Aunt Shirley.

Hannah blinked her eyes twice and looked over at Hunter. She nodded in agreement and quickly climbed out of her seat, heading back to wake everyone.

As Hunter found a parking spot, Hannah leaned over and whispered, "Mom, we're here, time to wake up."

Opening her eyes and slowly sitting up, she replied, "I'm awake, I'll be right there."

Hannah turned to Aunt Shirley, who was already sitting up, and asked, "Are you ready to go?"

"We've seen so many great sites today, but I'm still excited to see more," said Aunt Shirley, as she stood up from the bed. She shook out her hair, picked up her backpack, threw it over her shoulder and said, "Well, come on, let's go."

"Everyone ready to go?" asked Mom, as she opened the door.

"I'm ready, let's go," said Hayden. He picked up Hannah's backpack and handed it to her saying, "Let's not forgot this again."

Hannah took the backpack from Hayden's hand,

smiled and walked outside into the warmth of the late afternoon sun. "Everything is so pretty and green out here," she said, as she looked over the area.

"That must be the Carthage Jail," said Hayden, pointing to a two-story, brick building.

"I thought the jail would be a lot bigger," said Hunter, catching up with everyone after he locked the motor home door.

Hayden pulled open the door to the building and held it as everyone walked inside. Once inside, they noticed a small desk centered in the back of the room.

"Are you here for a tour?" asked a small, elderly woman looking up from behind the desk.

"We sure are," answered Mom, walking toward her "Are we in the right place?"

"Yes," the white-haired woman answered, looking down at her watch. "Wait right here, and I will start the tour in a moment."

They watched as she hurried behind the counter, grabbed a piece of paper, looked it over, pushed it into her apron pocket and then hurried over to start the tour.

"Is everyone here that is going with us today?" she asked.

Mom looked around, checked to see that everyone was ready and said, "I think so."

"Great, my name is Thelma, and I will be your tour guide. As we start our tour, please remember not to touch anything. Everything we have in the jail is of the time period and could be damaged if touched." She looked up and smiled as she removed the chain blocking the main floor and said, "Please follow me."

"This jail is kinda spooky," whispered Hayden.

"The Carthage Jail was built in 1840 at a cost of $4,105. The foundation is three-feet deep. The walls were built three-feet thick on the first floor and two-feet thick on the second floor. The interior of the jail originally had seven rooms, including living quarters for the jailer and his family.

"As we climb the stairs to the second floor, you will see one large room. This room was equipped with a fireplace, beds for the men, a washbasin and several comforters."

As Thelma paused to open the door to the eastern room, she pulled the paper from her apron, scanned through the words and pushed it quickly back into her apron pocket.

"Everyone, please find a seat on the benches," Thelma instructed, as she opened the door to the next room. "This is the room where the story really begins. As you look around the room, you can see that the prison quarters were kept fairly comfortable. According to the accounts of those that were present during the martyrdom and the story written in church history, Jailer George W. Stigall, fearing for the men's lives, asked the prisoners to move to the dungeon on the main floor for more protection. Joseph Smith agreed and said they would move after dinner. The men never made it downstairs.

"On June 27, 1844 at approximately five p.m., John Taylor had just finished singing 'A Poor Wayfaring Man of Grief' at the prophet's request. There was a little rustling at the outer door of the jail, and the prisoners heard a discharge of three or four firearms. The mob encircled the building, and some of the men broke into the jail. They pushed passed the guard, threw the jailer aside and climbed the stairs to the second floor.

"Hearing some of the mob rush up the stairs, the prisoners tried desperately to hold the door closed. However, the unruly men were able to force a gun through the partly opened door. Firing blindly into the room, their murderous intent was to kill Joseph and his brother, Hyrum Smith.

"Hyrum retreated back from the door, when a lead ball from a gun struck him in the left side of the nose. He fell on his back saying, 'I am a dead man!' As he fell, another lead ball from outside the room entered his left side, and another grazed his chest and entered his head through his throat. Finally, a fourth bullet struck him in the leg. Joseph raced to the door and discharged his six-shooter into the hallway, hoping to slow down the mob. However, his gun misfired and only discharged three or four rounds into the crowd.

"Elder John Taylor rushed to the window in hopes of escape. A bullet fired from inside the jail hit his left thigh, striking the bone. In agony, he fell against the windowsill. Suddenly, a ball from outside the jail struck him in the chest, forcing him back into the room. Amazingly the lead ball hit his pocket-watch, and the bullet was deflected, miraculously saving his life. He was struck by two balls from inside the jail causing horrible wounds, in excruciating pain he rolled under the bed by his side.

"Joseph, seeing there was no safety in the room, and wanting the mobs to follow him, hopefully saving the lives of the other men in the room, turned calmly from the door. He dropped his pistol on the floor and sprang to the east window. Two balls instantly pierced him in the back. Another one entered his right chest from outside the window, and still another struck him in the collarbone. He fell out the window exclaiming 'Oh, Lord, my God!' to the ground two-stories below, landing next to the well. He tried to raise himself up on the well, but only able to raise one leg and one arm, he fell back to the ground.

"Willard Richards rushed to the window and looked down upon the man he loved. He had miraculously escaped the bullets of the assassins, as Joseph had prophesied. John Taylor was the only other man who survived the deadly gunfire in the attack that day.

"Please take time to look around the room and throughout the jail. Take special notice of the original door, the bullet holes from that dreadful day still remain. If you have any questions, I am here to help you. Thank you for your attention."

The kids noticed Thelma take a deep breath and let out a sigh of relief. She quietly walked to the back of the room, obviously relieved to have finished her presentation.

Did you hear that, Hannah?" asked Hunter, walking toward the window.

"You mean the well?" she asked.

"Yeah, that has to be the well from our last clue, don't you think?" he asked.

"Yep, I bet you're right," she answered, as they looked out the window to the well below.

"Mom, were going to walk outside for a minute, is that okay?" asked Hayden.

"That's fine, honey, we'll meet you down there in a minute," she replied. She continued to walk around the room, asking the tour guide questions.

Once outside, Hayden asked, "What are we looking for?"

"I have no idea," Hunter replied. "Hannah, why don't you read us the clue again?"

Hannah unzipped her backpack, removed the paper and read the clue.

'POOR MAN OF GRIEF,
HIS JOURNEY ENDED,
CEMENTED IN TIME,
SAFELY PROTECTED,
SIGNATURE AND KEY,
CONCEALED BY FATE,
LEFT FOR THE RIGHTEOUS,
UPON THE DREADFUL DATE,
6-27-18+44,
V1, V2, V6'
WHICH TRANSLATES TO 'WEL'."

"I'm sure that the clue is referring to the well, where Joseph fell and died. The clue states that something is 'Cemented in time, Safely protected'. So, could that mean the clue is cemented in the well?" asked Hunter.

"How could that be? Most of the well is made out of wood," said Hayden, as he looked at the structure.

"Where is there cement?" asked Hannah, sitting on her knees, staring at the base of the well.

"All right, the well is made out of wood from the wooden platform on the bottom to the trough and pump. It has a water spigot on one side and a wooden handle to pump out the water on the other," said Hunter, as he slowly walked around the well.

"This doesn't make sense," complained Hayden. "Why would the clue lead us to the well that has no cement?"

"We're missing something," insisted Hannah. "But what?"

"Mom is going to be down here any minute, we've got to hurry," said Hayden anxiously. "Maybe we didn't solve the clue correctly, and now we're in the wrong place."

"No, I'm sure we're in the right place. We're just missing something important, I can feel it," replied Hannah.

"But what?" asked Hunter, as he sat down next to Hannah and stared at the well.

More than fifteen minutes had passed when Aunt Shirley walked outside.

"Have you found your clue?" she asked, cautiously optimistic.

"No, I think we're at the wrong place," announced Hayden.

"Are you sure?" she asked.

"Well, Hannah doesn't think so, but the well is not made out of cement," explained Hayden.

"As I sat upstairs listening to our tour guide, I was surprised to find out that this well has been covered by wood to protect the integrity of the cement engravings that were found after Joseph was killed," she said smiling.

"What?" asked Hunter, jumping to his feet.

"The tour guide told us that if you remove the top of this wooden box, the cement well has secrets that someday she hopes are solved."

"What secrets?" asked Hannah.

"I don't know, maybe you should remove the top and find out," suggested Aunt Shirley.

"Can we do that?" asked Hayden, nervously looking around.

"Yes," Aunt Shirley replied. "The tour guide said if you lift this handle, the entire box lifts off," she said, pointing to a small wooden handle on the top of the box.

Hannah almost screamed in excitement as she pulled the handle and lifted off the wooden top. Hayden and Hunter then carefully lifted the box up and off the small cement well. Quickly walking around the well, Hannah scanned for any sign of a clue.

"Look, another lion," she said excitedly.

"Where?" asked Hunter.

"Here, in the brick," replied Hannah, pointing to the gray and black square.

"I think the clue is cemented in the brick," said Hannah. "Hayden, give me your pocket knife, quickly."

"My pocket knife? What for?" he asked.

"Just give me the knife, and hurry—before we get in trouble," she demanded.

Hayden pulled the knife from his pocket, handed it to Hannah and watched anxiously as she carved away the mortar from around the edge and wiggled a brick from the well. When she finally pulled the brick free, she reached her hand into the dark hole and felt around for a clue.

"You better hurry, Hannah," said Aunt Shirley. "I'll go and see where your mom is."

"Could you slow Mom down for us, or at least give us a warning when she is coming?" called Hunter, as he watched Aunt Shirley turn and hurry back toward the jail.

"Sure, I'll see what I can do," she replied, as she turned the corner and headed back into the jail.

"Is there anything in there, Hannah?" Hayden asked anxiously.

"I'm looking," she replied. "The opening inside is bigger than this brick.

"Search faster, Hannah, I don't want to get in trouble," insisted Hayden.

"Can I help?" asked Hunter.

"No! I'm going as fast as I can, you two. Give me a minute," she anxiously replied.

Suddenly, they heard Aunt Shirley whistling loudly, signaling that Mom was approaching.

"Here they come. Hurry let's put everything back, the clue must already be gone," said Hunter.

"Wait! I think I have something," replied Hannah.

"Hurry! Hurry!" yelled Hayden.

"I am, I don't want to damage it," Hannah replied.

"I can see them, they're almost here," said Hayden frantically.

"I've got it, I've got it," she whispered, as she pushed the brick back into place, just as Mom and Aunt Shirley appeared around the corner.

"What are you three doing?" Mom asked suspiciously.

"Nothing, we're just checking out this cool old well," Hunter replied casually.

"Aunt Shirley told us that the wooden covering could be removed, so we pulled it apart to check it out, I hope that was okay," Hannah said innocently.

The tour guide smiled and said, "Usually we like to do that for you, but it looks like you've been careful."

"We'll put everything back together right now," offered Hayden, as he motioned for Hunter to help him with the wooden covering.

"That would be helpful, kids," replied the elderly woman. "Especially since this is my first day and my very first tour."

"I wondered why you kept looking at that paper," said Hannah, as she walked over to the woman.

"Yes, I wanted to make sure I didn't miss anything important," she replied.

"Oh, you were wonderful," said Mom reassuringly. "I appreciate all of the extra information you gave us."

As the boys quickly put the box and lid back over the small well, Mom, Aunt Shirley and Thelma walked to the front of the building.

"That was close," said Hunter, as he wiped the sweat from his forehead.

"What happened?" asked Hayden, grimacing as he examined his sister's arm.

"Those bricks can be sharp," Hannah replied, as she dabbed some blood from her arm. "I'm all right."

"So, show me what you found!" shrieked Hayden, excited to see the next clue.

"Hang on, I don't know what we have yet. I haven't had a chance to get a good look at it," Hannah answered. She reached inside the pocket of her jeans.

"All right, Hannah, enough suspense. Let's see this clue already," demanded Hunter, excited to see what they had found.

Hannah opened her hand slowly to reveal a small cloth, almost identical to the cloth they had found inside the lamp.

"Not that one, Hannah," said Hayden, annoyed that she was teasing him.

"This is what I found, Hayden," she replied, scowling.

"That's the clue we found in the lamp, isn't it?" asked Hunter, somewhat confused.

"No, this is the clue we just found in the well," she replied.

"Is it a map?" Hayden asked.

"More symbols?" asked Hunter. "What's on it?"

"I'm looking, just a minute," snapped Hannah, as she tried to flatten out the crumpled cloth.

"The material is frayed on the edges like the one from the lamp. I wonder if the two pieces of cloth fit together," questioned Hannah.

"Making a map?" Hayden asked, hopefully.

"Could be," replied Hannah.

"Come on, let's get back to the motor home and find

out," suggested Hunter, as he started walking toward the parking lot.

"Thank you," Hannah called to Thelma, as they walked through the front gate.

"Thanks for coming," she called back, and waved.

"We'll meet you back at the motor home, Mom!" called Hannah, as she started running.

CHAPTER SIXTEEN

"WHERE IS THE OTHER CLUE?" asked Hunter, as he walked through the motor home door.

"In my backpack, right here on my back," replied Hannah. She quickly slipped the pack off her shoulders and threw it on the kitchen table.

"Get the cloth from the lamp. Let's see if they are from the same cloth, maybe they go together," said Hayden.

Smiling, Hannah grabbed a paper towel, wiped the blood from her arm, then walked to the table and unzipped her backpack. She rummaged through the papers and found the original, carefully folded clue. She gently laid the old material on the table, reached into her jeans with the other hand and retrieved the new clue. She placed the new clue right next to the one on the table. They were all delighted to see that the edges of one piece matched perfectly with the other piece.

"Look, more symbols," said Hayden, pointing to the new cloth. "I bet a clue is on the other side."

"I bet you're right, Hayden," replied Hunter. "Hannah, turn both pieces of cloth over and let's take a look."

Hannah turned the cloth over and yelled, "A new clue!"

"Read it," demanded Hunter.

Hannah picked up the cloth and squinted at the faded writing. "Write this down, Hunter," she said.

"PROPHECIES REVEALED TO MAN,
BROUGHT LIGHT UNTO THE WORLD.
EIGHTY-NINE WAS SOON RECEIVED,
WHERE 'LECTURES OF FAITH' UNFURLED.

LEGENDS LIE IN RAFTERS OLD,
MARKED BY SILENT STRENGTH.
REFLECTIONS CAST, SILENT IMAGE SHOWN,
OPENING HIDDEN AT GREAT LENGTH."

Hannah finished and looked up at Hunter. "That's all of the clue, it's really not very long."

"Are you sure?" Hunter asked, with a confused look.

"What does it mean?" questioned Hayden. "I don't understand any of it."

"Don't understand what?" interrupted Mom, as she climbed into the motor home, startling the kids.

"Nothing," replied Hayden.

"I know you're talking about something," she teased, in a spooky voice.

Mom grabbed the keys from the counter, climbed into the driver's seat and started the motor.

"Nothing, really, Mom," replied Hayden.

"So, I'm guessing this has something to do with Grandpa's Legend," said Aunt Shirley.

"I'm sure it does," Mom interjected. "Anything else, and they would be asking for our help."

The sisters laughed as Mom pulled onto the road headed for Kirtland, Ohio.

"Funny, Aunt Shirley," Hayden said sarcastically. "You know Grandpa told us to keep the clues confidential."

"Does that mean you found another clue?" asked Mom, intrigued by their success.

"Yes, we did!" announced Hannah. "You should be proud of us."

"I am very proud," replied Mom. "You've done more in the last few days than any other Kimball has done in a lifetime."

"Does that mean you believe the Legend, Mom?" asked Hunter.

"Uuummm, I'm not sure of that," Mom replied, crinkling her nose and mouth. "I'm just glad you're having fun and learning some church history."

"Come on, Mom," said Hayden. "You've got to believe the Legend is true by now."

"Maybe I will when you find the treasure," she replied, smiling and shaking her head.

"How long is our drive to Kirtland, Mom?" asked Hunter.

"I think we need to travel about 500 miles. So, we will

have to drive for about eight hours or so," answered Aunt Shirley.

"There you go, Hunter, we have about eight hours of driving ahead of us," said Mom.

"Good, we have plenty of time to work on the next riddle then," Hayden replied excitedly. "Let's get to work."

"Wait, wait, wait," insisted Mom. "Before you start with another clue, I need..."

"I know, what new thing have we learned about this state, right?" interrupted Hunter, somewhat irritated. He walked to the window to look outside.

"No, Hunter," responded Mom. "I can see that you three are paying attention to our travels, so I'm letting you off the hook—for now. "I want all of you to start dinner. I don't know about you, but I'm starving."

"So am I," squealed Aunt Shirley, looking to Hunter with a big, cheesy grin on her face.

Hunter shook his head and smiled. "You know, I'm starving, too," he said.

"All right, then, I thought tacos would taste good tonight. Can the three of you handle making those by yourselves?"

"Sure, Mom, no problem," replied Hannah. "What time do you want to eat?"

"Well, it is 4:30 P.M. now, why don't we snack on the vegetable tray in the refrigerator until six o'clock?" she asked.

"Okay, no problem," Hannah replied.

Hannah pulled the hamburger from the freezer, and

she placed it onto a plate and put it into the microwave to defrost. Then sat down at the kitchen table.

"What do you want me to do?" asked Hayden. He was immediately disappointed that they did not have time right then to work on the clue.

"Nothin' right now. Tacos only take a few minutes to prepare, so we have a little bit of time before we need to start," replied Hannah.

"Enough time to work on the clue?" Hayden asked excitedly.

"You bet," Hannah answered.

"Great!" added Hunter. "Where do we start?"

"I'll read the clue again," Hannah offered. She picked up the small paper Hunter had written on and began to read.

"'PROPHECIES REVEALED TO MAN,
BROUGHT LIGHT UNTO THE WORLD.
EIGHTY-NINE WAS SOON RECEIVED,
WHERE 'LECTURES OF FAITH' UNFURLED.

LEGENDS LIE IN RAFTERS OLD,
MARKED BY SILENT STRENGTH.
REFLECTIONS CAST, SILENT IMAGE SHOWN,
OPENING HIDDEN AT GREAT LENGTH.'"

"Hannah, do the two pieces of cloth fit together?" asked Hunter.

"They look like they do fit together," she replied.

"Then, I was wondering, when the two pieces of cloth

are placed together, is there any more information to the riddle?"

"Oh, good idea, let me put them together again and see," she said excitedly.

Carefully, she laid the two pieces together on the table, adjusted the pieces the way she thought they fit together.

Hayden peered over Hannah's shoulder watching as she moved the pieces around, unexpectedly he squealed, "Stop, go back! When you put them side to side this way, the symbols on the back look like they kinda form the number ten."

"Nice job, Hayden," said Hannah, patting him on the head.

"I wonder what the number refers to, if anything," said Hunter.

"Maybe we'll figure out information about the number as we solve more of the riddle," suggested Hannah.

"Hey, I'm sure the meat is thawed by now, it's been defrosting for twenty minutes. Are you kids going to start dinner, or do you want to drive, Hunter, and I will start dinner?" asked Mom.

"We'll have it ready by six o'clock," replied Hannah, as she looked at her watch and gulped at the time. "Come on, guys, we better hurry. Mom's letting us spend a lot of time on Grandpa's Legend, so we don't want to upset her now."

Hunter and Hayden both quickly agreed and jumped to their feet. Hayden pulled the dishes from the cupboard as Hunter cleared and wiped down the table. Hannah quickly pulled the lettuce, tomatoes, cheese and taco shells from the refrigerator and placed them on the counter. Then quickly opened the package of hamburger, dumped it into a pan then salted it and stirred.

"Hunter, cook the hamburger while I cut up the vegetables," suggested Hannah, as she handed him the wooden spatula.

"What do you want me to do, Hannah?" asked Hayden.

"Pull out three bowls and then open a can of refried beans and warm it in the microwave," she replied, as she took a sharp knife from the utensil drawer.

Dinner was ready just as the clock reached six.

"Everything's ready, Mom," called Hunter, as he scooped the hamburger into the pre-made taco shells.

"Good job, guys, I can't believe how well you've been working together these last few days," Mom replied, smiling. "There is a rest stop five miles ahead, I'll pull over there."

"Is there anything else you want us to have ready for dinner?" asked Hannah.

"I can't think of anything, sweetie," Mom replied. "Shirley, Shirley," she said loudly trying to wake her sister.

"Yeah?" Shirley replied in a groggy voice.

"Time for dinner."

"Wow! Already?"

"Yes, look at those three back there. I can't believe how Dad's Legend has brought them together," said Sarah, as she pulled off the highway into the rest stop.

As they sat down to eat, Aunt Shirley asked, "Now tell me, what is the new clue you found?"

"We're supposed to keep the clues a secret," teased Hunter. "You know, searching for treasure can be dangerous if you're not careful."

"Cute, Hunter," replied Aunt Shirley. "You know that I am a Kimball, too."

Smiling, Hunter motioned for Hannah to read the clue.

"I can't quite figure out where this clue is leading us," said Hannah. She carefully opened the cloth and read.

"PROPHECIES REVEALED TO MAN,
BROUGHT LIGHT UNTO THE WORLD.
EIGHTY-NINE WAS SOON RECEIVED,
WHERE 'LECTURES ON FAITH' UNFURLED.

LEGENDS LIE IN RAFTERS OLD,
MARKED BY SILENT STRENGTH.
REFLECTIONS CAST, SILENT IMAGE SHOWN,
OPENING HIDDEN AT GREAT LENGTH."

"You kids found this clue?" asked Mom.

"Back at the jail," replied Hayden. "It was by the well."

"I'm so impressed," Mom said.

"Are you going to help us solve the riddle?" Hannah asked.

"I could try."

"Hunter, you did such a great job with the last clue, what is your feeling on this one?" asked Hayden.

Hunter rubbed his chin between his thumb and forefinger and strutted around the room like Sherlock Holmes. Finally, he answered, "Well, Doctor, I believe that the first two lines, 'Prophecies revealed to man, Brought light unto the world', are referring to, none other than, the Prophet Joseph Smith. The next line that reads, 'Eighty-nine was soon received'—well I, quite frankly, have no idea."

"Oh, Hunter, you make a lousy Sherlock Holmes," said Aunt Shirley, through her uncontrollable laughter.

"Could the clue be referring to people?" asked Hayden, determined to solve the riddle.

"It very well could be, my good man," replied Hunter, still mimicking the detective.

"Quit messing around, Hunter," insisted Hannah. "We need to get this riddle solved."

"Sorry, sis, I'm just playing," replied Hunter. "What are the next two lines again?"

"'Eighty-nine was soon received, where 'Lectures on Faith' unfurled'," read Hannah.

"I'm going to let the smart people figure this out," said Aunt Shirley, as she stood from the table. "I'm finished eating, Sarah, give me the keys, and I'll start driving."

"The keys are in the ignition," replied Mom, as she pointed toward the front of the motor home.

As Aunt Shirley headed for Kirtland, Hannah, Hunter, Hayden and Mom continued to decipher the riddle.

"I believe the 'Lectures on Faith' have something to do with Joseph Smith in the early years of the Church," said Mom, as she stood up and cleared her plate. "I bet if you look up 'Lectures on Faith' in my church history book, you could find some good information."

"Where is the book, Mom?" asked Hayden, ready to run.

"Right up in the front seat," she replied.

As Hayden returned with the book, Hunter grabbed it out of his hands and quickly looked up 'Lectures on Faith' in the index. "Page one hundred sixty-nine," he said, flipping to the page. "'Lectures on Faith were a series of lectures given by Joseph Smith at the School of the Prophets. These meetings were held in a small room above the kitchen in the Newel K. Whitney store in Kirtland, Ohio.'"

"Okay, the 'Lectures on Faith' were unfurled in a small room in Kirtland. But, the clue starts with 'Eighty-nine was soon received'. What does that mean?" questioned Hannah.

"Can you think of any historical events that deal with the number eighty-nine?" asked Mom, as she started to wash the dishes.

"Like what? Eighty-nine important men or something?" asked Hayden.

"I have no idea," answered Hunter, with a confused look on his face. "I don't know of anything that had a large, specific number attached to it in church history."

"What about men that attended the School of the

Prophets? Did eighty-nine men attend?" questioned Hannah. "Does the church history book have any other information about the 'Lectures on Faith'?"

Hunter scanned through the pages, but found nothing more about the lectures. Quietly pondering where else he could look, he suddenly had an idea. Searching through the index for the 'Newel K. Whitney Store', he was excited to see a reference. He flipped to the page and scanned the information. Several seconds passed before he read. "According to the book, sometime in February 1833, Joseph and several other brethren in Kirtland were meeting in the School of Prophets when Joseph received an important revelation—Section 89 of the Doctrine and Covenants, also known to us today as the Word of Wisdom."

"I should have known that," shrieked Aunt Shirley.

"Me too!" added Hayden.

"'Eighty-nine was soon received'—why does solving the clue always seem easy after you figure it out?" asked Hannah. I can't believe I didn't think about the scriptures."

"Read us what we have figured out so far, will you please, Hannah?" asked Hunter.

Hannah picked up the paper and read.

"PROPHECIES REVEALED TO MAN,
BROUGHT LIGHT UNTO THE WORLD.
EIGHTY-NINE WAS SOON RECEIVED,
WHERE 'LECTURES ON FAITH' UNFURLED.'"

"What is the rest of the clue?" asked Hayden. "Hannah, will you read it to me, please?"

"You bet. The remainder of the clue reads,

"'LEGENDS LIE IN RAFTERS OLD,
MARKED BY SILENT STRENGTH.
REFLECTIONS CAST, SILENT IMAGE SHOWN,
OPENING HIDDEN AT GREAT LENGTH.'"

"I bet that part is telling us where to look and what to do when we get there," suggested Hunter.

"Yeah, I agree," said Hannah. "'Legends lie in rafters old'—that has to be referring to the location, which we've decided is the Newel K. Whitney Store."

"Mom, were we planning to stop at the store?" asked Hayden, yawning uncontrollably.

"I'm sure the store is on our list," she replied, as she bundled the laundry.

"Could it be our first stop?" asked Hayden.

"We'll figure that out in the morning," she replied. "Now it is time for you to get to bed. We'll arrive in Kirtland in a few hours, and you need some sleep."

Hayden, barely able to keep his eyes open, agreed. He brushed his teeth and put on his pajamas. Mom tucked him into bed, and he was asleep before she could say good night.

"All right, you two, tell me, where are you getting these riddles?" Mom asked suspiciously.

"We're solving the clues which lead us to new clues," replied Hannah.

"We started with the first riddle Grandpa gave us," answered Hunter. "Why? Afraid the Legend, that you were sure wasn't true, might be?"

"That was a little sarcastic, Hunter," Mom replied sternly. "I don't want to hear that attitude again, or it won't matter whether I believe the Legend or not. You're Legend finding days will be over."

"Sorry, Mom," he replied.

"We're really just solving the clues and using the information to find the next one," insisted Hannah. "The next clue we've got to find must be in the rafters of the Newel K. Whitney store, we hope."

"I'm very proud of you two," she replied, smiling. "And I love that you're having to study a little church history in order to figure out the clues.

"Mom," said Hannah. "Do you think there's a treasure at the end of these clues?"

"I'm not sure, honey. I can't believe after all these years that you kids are the first to find some of these old clues," she replied, taking in a deep breath. "And I'm afraid the mysterious treasure could already have been found."

"But, there's always the possibility the treasure is still waiting for someone to find it," Hunter said optimistically.

"We could be the first, right?" asked Hannah.

"You could be!" said Aunt Shirley. "And wouldn't that be exciting?"

CHAPTER SEVENTEEN

17

MORNING CAME TOO EARLY for Hannah, as Hayden loudly pulled the pans for breakfast from underneath the counter. "I wonder where we are," she thought, not wanting to open her eyes.

Hayden continued noisily with breakfast, until Hannah finally pulled herself from underneath the blanket, stood up and walked into the kitchen and asked, "Hayden, what time is it?"

"We've all over slept!" was his irritated response. "We've got to get moving."

"Hayden, most of us were up until after two this morning, I think it's all right if we sleep in until at least nine. Now tell me, what time is it?" she snarled, trying to focus on the clock.

"Hannah, it's already nine-thirty," he replied, as he cracked an egg. "And you're the first one I've seen get out of bed."

"I'm exhausted, and Mom and Hunter were still driving when I went to bed. Give us all another thirty minutes, will you please?" she begged.

"I guess," he replied coolly. "But I would like to find our next clue before too long."

Hannah nodded, then turned and walked back to her bed. Falling on top of the covers, she was asleep before her head hit the pillow.

"Hannah, time to wake up!" yelled Hayden from the doorway.

"Hayden, I said another half hour, now leave me alone," she snarled.

"Leave you alone? Hannah, it's now eleven o'clock. You've been asleep another ninety minutes," Hayden snapped.

"He's right, honey, we need to get up and start moving," called Mom. "We're going to miss all of the sights on our itinerary today."

"Okay, Mom," Hannah replied, as she tried to lift her head from the pillow. "Where are we?" she called, as she sat up and stretched.

"We're in Kirtland," Mom replied.

"When did we get in this morning?" asked Hannah.

"About three-thirty or so," Mom answered.

"Then how are you awake? I went to bed around two, and I can barely keep my eyes open."

"Were not traveling as far tonight, so I'll try to catch

up on some sleep then," she answered.

"Where is everyone?" asked Hannah, as she slowly emerged from the room.

"They've gone out already," answered Mom, as she handed Hannah a plate of food.

"Gone where?" she asked.

"Hunter wanted to go scout out some of the sights, so he and Aunt Shirley left about an hour ago," Mom replied.

Hannah walked to the kitchen table and sat down to eat, followed by Hayden, who was now eating lunch.

"Why didn't you go, Hayden?" Hannah asked.

"'Cause I thought I would read up on the some of the sights in Kirtland, to see if there were any others that we needed to check out while we're here," he replied.

"Did you find any?" she asked.

"I sure did!" he replied excitedly. "Look," he said, as he showed her a book on Kirtland. "We're in a camp ground about two miles south of town. If we head north on Chillicothe Road, which is the main road through town, we will pass the Temple Quarry, which is now called the Chapin Forest Reservation Park. Beyond that, about one block on the left is the Hyrum Smith home. About another mile on the east is the Sidney Rigdon home, and on the west side is the Kirtland Safety Society, the RLDS Kirtland Temple Historic Center and the Kirtland Temple," he explained, looking up at Hannah.

"Nice job, Hayden," she said. "What else? Did you find the Whitney Store?"

"Yes, I did," he replied. "If we keep traveling north on

Chillicothe Road, just past the Temple and turn on Maple Street, we will see the cemetery, the John Johnson Home and the Parley P. Pratt Home. If we stay on the main road, we will pass the Joseph Smith, Sr. Home on the west, and the Joseph Smith Variety Store on the east. The William Smith Home, is also on the west side of the street."

Mom, aren't we related to Parley P. Pratt?" asked Hannah.

"Actually, we're descendants of Orson Pratt, so I guess that would make Parley a great uncle," Mom replied, as she washed the dishes.

"Okay, what's next, Hayden?" asked Hannah.

"Maybe a mile or two further on Chillicothe Road, there's a major crossing. Chillicothe Road crosses Kirtland-Chardon Road. At the crossing is the LDS Visitor's Center, Whitney Home and Whitney Store," Hayden replied.

"Great! When do we get started, Mom?" asked Hannah.

A loud knock on the door startled everyone.

"Are you expecting anyone, Mom?" asked Hayden, as he stood up from the table and walked toward the door.

"Nope," she replied.

Hayden timidly pushed the door open. As he did, someone from the outside pulled the handle with great force. Hayden was ripped down the steps and outside.

Nervously, Mom rushed to the door. Unable to see who was outside, she hesitantly asked, "Who's there?"

Jumping from behind the door, Hunter screamed, "It's me! Are we ready to go?"

Frightened, Mom screamed, "Aaaaaaahhhhhhh!" She threw the dishtowel in the air and jumped away from the door.

"Mom, Mom. It's just me," said Hunter. "I'm sorry, I didn't mean to scare you."

Mom sat on the couch, trying to regain her composure. She breathed hard for several seconds before she could finally speak. "That was a good one, Hunter, but don't think I'm not going to get you back for that!"

Hunter smiled and said, "Sorry, Mom."

"Okay, what's the plan for today?" asked Aunt Shirley. "We can't sit around here all day!"

"Did you find anything interesting while you were scouting around outside?" asked Hannah.

"We found a map with directions to the Temple Quarry, Kirtland Safety Society, the Kirtland Temple and a few other sites. The map looks kinda interesting. Should we start by following the sites it has listed?" asked Hunter.

"Well, Hayden has also been studying a map of the area. I think he has some really good ideas on where we need to go," said Hannah. "I think he should be in charge as we view the sites today."

"Good idea!" Mom shouted from the bedroom. "Hayden, why don't you lead us on a tour today?"

Hayden excitedly agreed. Mom grabbed her purse and climbed out of the motor home. She was followed quickly by, Aunt Shirley, Hunter and then Hannah. Hayden was the last to exit, handing Hannah her backpack as he closed the door.

"Don't want to forget this," he said smiling.

"Nope, not again, thanks," Hannah replied.

"Where to first?" asked Aunt Shirley.

"We need to catch a taxi or tour bus—one that allows us to get off and back on again at each stop," said Hayden.

"We saw a bus like that this morning," said Hunter, trying to be helpful. "I think the bus stop is a block north on this road."

"All right, let's go!" shouted Hannah, as she started running up the street.

"I'll race you, Mom," Hayden said through a big grin.

"You're on!" she called, as she started running.

"Wait a minute. That's cheating!" yelled Hayden, as he ran to catch her.

"I guess we better run, too, Hunter," said Aunt Shirley. They quickly chased after the others.

Hayden caught the sightseeing bus just before the driver closed the doors. Mom quickly paid the money for everyone to get an all-day bracelet for the bus. Hayden led the way to several open seats at the front and they all quickly took their seats.

"For your information," the bus driver announced, "my name is Scotty, and I drive one of the four buses that follow the Chillicothe to Kirtland-Chardon Road Express Tours. You have the option to stay on the bus and view the sights as I drive by and talk about the rich history in this valley, or you may exit during our brief stops and explore any of the areas. You can catch one of the other buses when you are ready to continue the tour.

"From start to finish, there are eleven stops—making

traveling through the area very convenient to get off and on throughout the day. As we start the tour, my advice is to ride the tour bus to your final destination first. This makes duplication of stories told by your bus driver fewer as you enter and exit the bus. We will be picking up a few more passengers at the Joseph Smith Variety Store. You, of course, are welcome to exit the bus there. However, my tour will start at the LDS Visitor's Center, which is our second stop."

"So, what are we going to do, Hayden?" asked Mom. "Get off at the Joseph Smith House, or should we start at the Visitor's Center?"

"I think we need to start at the Visitor's Center," he replied.

"Good! That's where we'll start," replied Mom. She turned to watch the scenery out the bus window.

"Look, Hannah," said Hunter, holding up the map. "The LDS Visitor's Center is down the street from the Whitney Store."

"Perfect, we'll be able to find the next clue before we tour the area. I wanted to find the clue fast, so this is great!" she replied.

"When Aunt Shirley and I were out on our walk this morning, I'm almost positive I saw the same car that was following us yesterday," whispered Hunter.

"Are you kidding? Are you sure someone is following us?" asked Hannah.

"No, I'm not positive I saw the same car, so I'm not sure if I'm being paranoid after the motor home was broken in to or what," Hunter replied.

"What do we do?" asked Hannah.

"Help me keep a close eye on the people around us today. Make sure we don't say anything important around other people as we search for the clues," he replied.

As the bus horn honked, the tour guide yelled, "Second stop, folks!"

"Here we go," announced Aunt Shirley, jumping from her seat.

As everyone got off the bus, Hannah asked, "Where are we starting?"

"I think we should start with the Visitor's Center, and then tour the other homes in this area," answered Hayden. "Follow me."

Hayden quickly crossed the street to the Visitor's Center, and everyone followed closely behind. As they looked at the newly constructed building, they were surprised at the curious construction. Walking inside the doors, they were immediately greeted by an elderly couple from Vidor, Texas.

"Hello, how are ya'll?" asked the man.

"Fine," replied Mom, shaking his hand.

"We're Elder and Sister Torres, and if there's anything we can do for ya'll, or if you have any questions we can answer, let us know," said Sister Torres.

"Actually, we're here for the first time, where do we start?" asked Hayden.

"I suggest you start with the short film covering the history of the saints in Kirtland. It's starting in three minutes over in the film room," replied Brother Torres, pointing to a room in the distance.

"After you're finished, take some time to look around the Center. You'll see pictures of early Kirtland and a large mural of the Kirtland Temple that is being assembled right now," added Sister Torres.

"Following that, be sure to take the ninety-minute guided tour around the Kirtland Historic Village," said Brother Torres. "Now hurry, the movie is about to begin."

Everyone hurried to the film room and watched a short movie on the history of the Saints in the area. After the movie they wandered around the Visitor's Center looking at all the interesting pictures.

"Hunter, look at this," said Hannah, pointing to a map on the wall.

"Look at what?" he asked.

"Heber C. Kimball had a home here that was destroyed, all that is left is a marker of the home site."

"I hope there were no clues inside it," Hunter replied, as he walked to the next picture on the wall.

Over the loudspeaker came the announcement, "The guided walking tour is getting ready to leave. If you are interested, please report to the Information Desk located near the front door."

"Mom, are we going on the tour?" asked Hannah.

"Yes, let's go," she replied. She quickly took Hayden's arm and walked to the desk. Aunt Shirley, Hannah and Hunter followed.

"Our first stop in the Historic Kirtland Village is a new addition to the area," said Brother Torres. "The newly-rebuilt, water-powdered sawmill, located directly behind the Visitor's Center, was originally built in 1834 by Joel Hills Johnson. Lumber cut at the mill was used not only in the construction of homes, but also for many businesses and the Kirtland Temple. The sawmill provided much needed employment for the new members entering the area."

"Does the sawmill work?" asked Hunter.

"The sawmill is in working order. However, at this time, there is no need for it to be used," Brother Torres replied.

"The next building you see is the newly restored Ashery. Rebuilt on its original site, this Ashery is the first of its kind to be restored in North America. The Ashery was important for both financial and practical reasons. The early saints would bring ashes from their homes and trade them to the Ashery for goods available at the store," said Sister Torres.

"What is made at an Ashery?" asked Hayden.

"Potash," she answered, smiling.

"Potash? What is potash?" asked Hannah.

"Potash is made by soaking ashes in water. The Potash was then used to make soap, glass and fertilizer for crops," she replied.

"Now, as we continue on our tour, this next home is built on the foundation of the original Sidney Rigdon Tannery. The tannery was used to stretch and dry leather and tan them for multiple purposes, such as satchels, blankets and other useful items. This home is owned and maintained by the LDS Church. Currently, it is being used for housing and is unavailable for viewing on our tour, so let's quickly move on to the next site," said Sister Torres.

"This is one of my favorite sites to visit," said Brother Torres, as he walked to the door and pushed it open. "This is the Newel K. Whitney and Company Store. In 1988, President Ronald Reagan awarded the President's Historic Preservation Award to the LDS Church for its authentic restoration of the store. Using the original journals and meticulous records of Brother Whitney, every effort was made to stock the shelves with items that would have been sold in the store during the 1830's.

"As we move into the southeast room, you can see that this room was used as a Bishop's Storehouse. Saints would also work here and trade labor for goods. Bartering was commonplace during that time. Saints would bring in their excess goods, hoping to trade them for something they needed. This room was the beginning of the current Church Welfare Program. Saints would also hold a fast meeting on the first Thursday of each month. Items donated for their fast were sorted here and given to those in need.

"As we move into the main part of the house, you can see a family also lived here in the midst of the hustle and bustle of the store. During the years between 1832 and 1834, the Prophet and his family lived here with the Whitneys. Going upstairs, the northwest room was Joseph and Emma's bedroom. Their son, Joseph III, was actually born here. On the original wood floor, you can still see the tulips Emma painted with pigment from flowers and buttermilk.

"The northeast room housed the School of the Prophets from January to April 1833. Doctrinal discussions, spiritual preparedness, as well as revelations were received in this tiny room. Notice the open ceiling exposing the rafters, this was sometimes done to give the room a larger feel," explained Brother Torres.

"This is the place we have to look," Hannah whispered.

"Where?" asked Hayden. "Read the clue again will you, Hannah?"

Hannah rifled through her backpack and found the last clue and without hesitating she whispered,

"PROPHECIES REVEALED TO MAN,
BROUGHT LIGHT UNTO THE WORLD.
EIGHTY-NINE WAS SOON RECEIVED,
WHERE 'LECTURES ON FAITH' UNFURLED.

LEGENDS LIE IN RAFTERS OLD,
MARKED BY SILENT STRENGTH.
REFLECTIONS CAST, SILENT IMAGE SHOWN,
OPENING HIDDEN AT GREAT LENGTH.'"

"As we continue moving to the southwest room...," started Sister Torres, turning toward the door.

"Mom, can we catch up with you in a minute?" asked Hannah. "Hunter and I wanted to check out this room for a few minutes."

"I guess," replied Mom. "But don't be too long."

"You won't have more than five to eight minutes before the next tour group comes through, so please catch up quickly," interrupted Sister Torres.

"Thanks, Mom," said Hannah, smiling as they walked back into the room. "I promise we'll catch up in a few minutes."

The kids watched as Sister Torres led the tour group out of the room and down the hallway toward another room. When he was sure they could not be seen or heard, Hayden said, "We better hurry you guys." He quickly stepped up on a chair, sure they needed to start in the rafters. "Where up here do you think we need to start looking?"

"I don't know where, other than in the rafters, and we've got to look for something of strength," replied Hannah, as she pulled a chair to the corner of the room.

"What do you think the clue means where it reads, 'Silent in strength'?" asked Hayden.

"I'm not sure, but I think that based on where we found the last clue inside the lion, the clue must be marked by something that symbolizes strength," said Hunter. "So, look for anything engraved or that looks really strong."

"I think there's a ledge next to the rafters that surrounds

the room. I might be able to fit and crawl along the edges," said Hannah. "Hunter, come lift me up."

"Hayden, stand by the door and keep a look out," said Hunter, as he took a hold of Hannah's waist and hoisted her to the rafters.

Reaching to take a hold of the closest rafter, Hannah pulled herself onto the eight-inch ledge. Carefully steadying herself, she crawled slowly. She searched every inch of the rafters. As she reached the first corner, she struggled to stay on the ledge.

Frightened, she yelled, "I can't do this!"

"Come on, Hannah," reassured Hunter. "I am right here to catch you if you fall."

Hannah took a deep breath and began to search. "Hey, there's something up ahead," she said excitedly.

"What is it?" Hayden asked from the doorway.

"I'm not sure," she replied, still moving slowly across the ledge.

"Someone's coming!" exclaimed Hayden.

"Be quiet, Hannah, someone's coming," whispered Hunter.

"They passed this room and went to the one next door, hurry up!" insisted Hayden.

"Hurry, Hannah, we're running out of time," said Hunter.

"I found it!" she said trying not to talk too loudly. There's a lion head carved into the corner rafter. The lion looks like its standing up and roaring with its mouth open wide."

"Can you see any clues?" asked Hayden, looking up in her direction.

"I can't see anything else," she replied.

"Is there something inside its mouth?" asked Hayden.

"There could be, but that seems almost too easy," she answered skeptically.

"Check," pleaded Hayden. We don't have a lot of time."

"What if there's something scary inside its mouth?" she asked, hesitant to stick her hand inside.

"Come on, Hannah, what's going to be inside?" asked Hunter.

"Oh, I don't know—bugs, spiders, snakes, creepy things," she answered sarcastically.

"Well, you've got to try, we don't have a lot of time," replied Hunter.

"Come on, you three, it's time to go," Mom called from the hallway.

"We'll be right there, Mom," replied Hayden.

"Come on. We've got to go. If you can't do it, we'll have to come back later," Hunter said to Hannah.

"Give me a second," Hannah insisted, as she gingerly reached her small hand into the lion's mouth.

"There's something here," she exclaimed. She pulled out her hand and revealed a small leather bag. "It's here, this has to be the clue," she announced excitedly. "We did it! We found the clue."

"Yeah, this clue was way too easy to find," Hunter said nervously. "I hope we're not missing something."

"Maybe this clue was meant to be easy, because the next one is not going to be," suggested Hayden.

"Could be," replied Hannah, holding the small bag tightly.

As Hunter helped her climb down off the ledge, Mom walked back into the room and said, "I said let's go. Right now! Everyone is waiting for you three."

"Sorry, Mom, we're coming," replied Hayden, as they walked out the door.

"Yeah, sorry, Mom," said Hannah.

CHAPTER EIGHTEEN

18

EVERYONE IN THE GROUP watched as the kids walked out the front door of the Newel K. Whitney Store.

"Sorry to have held up the tour," Hunter said apologetically.

"No problem," said Brother Torres. "Let's move on to the Newel K. Whitney home. This home was once used as a Visitor's Center for the LDS Church, but it has recently been restored to its original condition inside and out. The Whitney's were very gracious to Joseph and Emma Smith. They allowed the couple to live here for a few weeks before the Smiths took a more permanent residence upstairs in the store."

"As we continue on our tour, you can see the first brick building built in Kirtland. Originally built by Peter French as an inn, the building was ideally located on a small piece of land at the intersection of Chillicothe and Kirtland–Chardon Roads. The LDS Church purchased the Inn from Peter French in 1833, to help provide temporary housing for the Saints. Brother John Johnson was later given the stewardship of the building," finished Brother Torres.

"Wasn't a temporary printing office here for a while?" asked Aunt Shirley.

"Yes, I'm surprised that you know about that," replied Brother Torres. "Very few people are aware that after the Church's printing press was destroyed in Independence, Missouri, a temporary printing office was set up here inside the inn until a permanent location could be acquired."

"I read that computer stations inside can be used to do genealogical research as well," Mom added.

"Yes, the Church set up several computers inside the inn, and they are hooked to the Church's Genealogical index. These computers allow visitors, who are looking for their ancestors, to check for relatives that may once have lived in Kirtland or the surrounding areas," Sister Torres explained. "After the tour, you are welcome to come and spend time searching if you would like."

"As we walk back to the Visitor's Center, you will notice markers for a few other homes in the area. Unfortunately, they no longer exist making them of course unavailable for viewing, but we hope there will be a replica built in the near future. However, I can tell you what we do know about each of these markers," said Brother Torres.

"The Warren Parrish Home was located north of the

Whitney Store. Warren Parrish acted as scribe to Joseph Smith from 1835 to 1837, and he was one of the signers of the Kirtland Safety Society Notes. The Nathaniel Milliken Home, was just to the north of the Newel K. Whitney Store, is said to be where the Prophet Wilford Woodruff was introduced to his soon-to-be bride, Phoebe W. Carter."

"Another home to visit, and located about one mile northeast of the Visitor's Center, is the Isaac Morley Farm. After Morley joined the Church, he provided temporary housing on his two-hundred-sixty-acre farm to the Saints who had recently moved into the area, until they were able to secure a place of their own. Joseph and Emma also lived at the Morley Farm in 1831, from March to September," said Sister Torres.

"On a final note, the sites that we've seen today—the Sawmill, Ashery, the Whitney home and Schoolhouse—were all dedicated recently by our Prophet, Gordon B. Hinckley. They are now referred to as Historic Kirtland Village," Brother Torres said.

"As we complete our walking tour of the Historic Kirtland Village, we hope that we've answered at least some of your questions regarding Kirtland. We hope you enjoy the remainder of your stay in the Kirtland area," finished Brother Torres.

"Thank you for taking us," said Mom. "We appreciate your knowledge of the area."

"Brother Torres, do you know of a good place to eat?" asked Aunt Shirley.

"Yes! I'm glad you asked. There is a restaurant just

down the street from the Kirtland Temple called R.J's Diner. They serve the best BBQ ribs, they're wonderful," he replied.

"And they are so good to our missionaries," included Sister Torres.

"Really, how?" asked Aunt Shirley.

"The restaurant is normally closed on Thanksgiving, but for our missionaries, they open and serve the best Thanksgiving dinner ever," she proudly replied.

"I can't wait to eat there, thanks for telling me about it," Aunt Shirley said smiling.

Brother and Sister Torres shook hands with some of the people in the tour group, then, quickly disappeared behind the tinted windows of the new Visitor's Center.

"That was neat," Aunt Shirley commented.

"Neat?" teased Hunter. "You mean cool, don't you?"

"Nope, I'm old enough to think that was really neat," Aunt Shirley replied, grabbing Hunter's neck.

"Have we seen everything in this area that you wanted to see, Mom?" asked Hayden, looking down at his map.

"I think so, honey," she replied.

"Good. Let's get moving, then," said Hunter. "I want to finish and get back to the motor home as soon as we can."

"There's the tour bus. We can take it down to the next stop if we hurry!" shouted Hannah, as she ran to catch the bus.

"Hannah, slow down!" yelled Aunt Shirley. "Why are you running?"

"I want to hurry and see all the sites so we still have time to figure out the riddle before we leave, just in case we need to find another clue," Hannah replied.

"You found another clue?" Aunt Shirley asked excitedly. "Where?"

"We found another piece of cloth back at the Newel K. Whitney Store," Hannah replied, as she patted her jeans pocket.

"Good job, Hannah, I can't believe how many clues you've found," said Aunt Shirley.

They all climbed on the bus, showing their passes as they entered.

"Can I see it?" asked Aunt Shirley, as she sat down in the seat next to Hannah.

Hannah raised her eyebrows and said, "Sure, I guess."

She carefully pulled the small, leather pouch from her pocket, slid open the leather drawstring and reached inside. Excitedly, she pulled a small cloth in the shape of an "L" out of the pouch. The material was three inches wide by eight inches long with frayed edges along the sides and bottom.

"I think this is made from the same material as the other two clues we found," said Hannah.

"The others weren't in this shape, were they?" asked Aunt Shirley.

"No, they were square, about the size of a napkin. I was thinking maybe all the material clues might fit together to form a square about the size of a piece of paper," said Hannah. "But, I won't be sure until I can put them all together."

Aunt Shirley handed Hannah the clue and said, "You three kids are amazing, I can't believe you've been so successful finding clues to the Legend."

"Well, we really are smart, you know," Hannah replied, with a huge grin across her face.

"Have you told Grandpa yet?" Aunt Shirley asked.

"No, we we're hoping to surprise him when we've deciphered all the clues and solved the mystery," Hannah replied.

"What about this clue? Does it have any other information?" asked Aunt Shirley.

The tour bus came to an abrupt stop and sounded two loud blasts with its horn. Startled, Hannah looked toward the front of the bus to see what had happened.

The tour guide announced, "We have reached the next stop on our route, which includes the Smith Family home on the west and the Joseph Smith Variety Store on the east and to the south, you can also see the Kirtland Temple.

"The next tour bus should be through this area again in approximately forty-five minutes and another in an hour and a half. That will be the last bus through for today. If you need to ride the bus to a different location, you will need to make sure you're on the bus at 5:30 p.m. If you are staying on the bus with me now, we will be continuing on to the Temple Quarry Chapin Forest Reservation Park. Please be careful as you exit."

"Come on, let's go. I want to see the Kirtland Temple," Hannah said, as she hurried to the door.

"What's the rush?" asked Hunter, as he stepped off the bus.

"The Kirtland Temple has amazing symbols that cover the outside and inside," she replied.

"We can't go inside the temple," said Hunter.

"I know that, Hunter. I've been reading about all the symbols on the temple, and I'm excited to see if what I've read is actually true," Hannah explained.

"We need to stop at the Smith home before we go to the temple," said Mom.

She paused and quietly read the plaque outside the Joseph Smith Variety Store.

Hunter, unable to hear her, said, "Mom, read the plaque loud enough that we can hear what you're saying."

Mom started again, this time a little louder. "'Based on the knowledge currently available, the building erected on this site used the original foundation belonging to the Joseph Smith Variety Store before it was destroyed.'"

"How do they know that it is the original foundation of the Variety Store? Do the Church historians know where everything was because they have pictures?" asked Hayden.

"Pictures, journals, members' writings and things like that, Hayden," replied Hannah.

"So, anything that has been restored looks like it did when it was originally built?" he asked.

"Yep."

"So, is the Smith home an original or a rebuilt home?" asked Hayden.

"Let's go find out," said Aunt Shirley. "The home is open for tours."

"Wait, Shirley," called Sarah. "They're only open for tours from nine a.m. to one p.m."

Aunt Shirley and Hayden stopped running down the sidewalk to the home.

"Serious?" whined Hayden, as he turned around and looked at Mom.

"Sorry, guys. We were a little late getting out this morning, and we missed a few of the homes on this tour. I can read the plaque if you'd like me to," Mom said.

"Yeah, read it, Mom," Hayden said, as he walked back toward her.

"Okay, I just need my glasses," she said, as she searched through her purse.

"They're on top of your head, Mom," said Hannah, trying not to laugh.

"Oh, you're right, here they are. Okay, the plaque reads, 'Scholars disagree whether the Smith home was the residence of the Joseph Smith, Sr. family or of Joseph Smith, Jr. family. However, much of Joseph Smith, Sr.'s work was completed in the upstairs room, and Joseph Smith, Jr. is thought to have translated the Egyptian writings from the Papyrus there also.'"

"I've heard about the Papyrus, but what is it?" asked Hunter.

"I don't know much about it," said Mom. "I need to do some studying to find out for sure. What I do know is that the Papyrus was a scroll brought from Egypt to Joseph Smith. Some man, and I don't remember his name right now, asked Joseph to look at it because he had heard that Joseph was able to translate old writings. We'll have to ask someone to tell us the story. Maybe Dad will know what happened."

"We should get moving," said Hayden. "I really want to see the stone quarry and how the Saints found all the stones they needed for the temple."

"All right, let's go see the temple, then," said Aunt Shirley, as she started walking down the asphalt path.

Hannah ran to catch up with her. "I'm so glad you came, this trip has actually been kinda fun."

"I'm glad I came on this trip, too," replied Aunt Shirley. "Now, while no one is here, you were going to tell me about the new clue."

"I haven't had a chance to look closely at it yet, but it has writing and more symbols on the cloth, just like the other two we found," Hannah replied, as her eyes twinkled with excitement. "There is one symbol I have never seen before that looks kinda cool."

"What does it look like?" asked Aunt Shirley.

"I can't explain it, I'll have to show it to you later," Hannah replied.

Hannah and Aunt Shirley paused at a sign just outside the temple grounds.

"Hey," Hannah called to Mom, Hunter and Hayden. "This signs reads, 'To visit or take a tour of the Kirtland Temple, proceed to the Kirtland Temple Historic Center operated by the Community of Christ Church. Tours available Monday through Saturday nine a.m. to five p.m.'"

"What time is it?" asked Hayden.

"4:30—we better hurry," replied Hunter.

Everyone quickly followed the signs leading the way to the Historic Center, hoping there was still enough time to tour the temple grounds. As they hurried through the door to the center, a short, white-haired, elderly man greeted them.

"Welcome to the Kirtland Temple Historic Center, we're glad you're here," he said, as he handed Mom a handful of literature on the Community of Christ Church.

Graciously, Mom took the information and said, "We're excited to be here, have we missed all of the tours of the Kirtland Temple today?" Mom asked.

"No, we have one that started just a moment ago. If you hurry, you will be able to catch up with them," he replied, walking toward the group. "Quickly, purchase your tickets then follow me."

"Thank you," said Mom, as she quickly purchased tickets and followed the man.

"Here you go. They're just about to walk up to the temple right now," the man whispered, as he turned to walk back to the front door.

Turning their attention to the tour guide, they all listened intently.

"...By far, the most important building in Kirtland during the Mormon period was the Kirtland Temple. The Saints began construction in 1833 and dedicated the temple on March 27, 1836, when the Prophet was only thirty years old.

"The dedicatory service was a memorable experience for the Saints. At seven a.m., approximately five hundred

Saints gathered at the door—an hour before the temple opened. When the doors opened, the Saints filled every seat, and many had to stand outside during the ceremonies. Because of the number of people who were forced to remain outside, a second service was held on March 31, 1836. The congregation sang several new hymns from the first hymnal, which was compiled by Emma Smith and published in 1835. If there are no questions," said the tour guide, "follow me, and we will enter the temple and start our tour. For those of you who just joined us, my name is Bill."

Quietly staring at the beautiful surroundings of the temple, the tour group walked the fifty yards to the temple doors. Bill opened the door, surprising Hannah.

Nervously, she turned to Mom and asked, "Are we really going to go inside?"

"Honey, this is no longer a working temple. The LDS Church does not own it, and I'm sure the Community of Christ Church uses the temple as a source of revenue, because of all the LDS people who would like to see it," Mom whispered.

"Something doesn't feel right about going inside, Mom," said Hunter.

"Hunter, the Kirtland Temple is more like a meeting house—somewhere you would go for Sunday meetings."

Hunter shrugged his shoulders as he followed the tour guide inside.

"This is the Assembly Room. As you look around the room, notice the choir lofts, the four-tiered Melchizedek Priesthood pulpits located on the west end and the

Aaronic Priesthood pulpits on the east end. These bottom-tiered pulpits have a drop-leaf table which was used for sacrament," said Bill, as he pointed to the pulpits.

"Rollers in the ceilings held curtains which divided the room into four sections. The benches in this room could be moved to allow seating in any direction. The second floor in the temple is similar to the first floor. On the third floor, there are five rooms. They were used for offices, ordinances and schooling for the early Saints.

"Joseph used the far west room, also know as the President's Room, for his office. Many significant events took place in that room, including translation work, the teaching of Hebrew, and the receipt of several revelations including the vision now recorded in Doctrine and Covenants Section One Hundred Thirty-Seven. Also, in LDS church history books and personal writings of the men closest to Joseph Smith, it is recorded that Joseph saw his deceased brother Alvin in the Celestial Kingdom.

"Please take a few moments to look around on the main floor, then, we will return to the Historic Center. There I will show you early artifacts and pictures from the 1830's before we finish our tour," finished Bill.

"This is really awesome, Mom," said Hayden, looking around the room at all the historic artifacts.

Hannah, quietly walked through the room pondering everything on display. She marveled at the intricate hand-carvings on the stairs, pews, pulpit and even the doors. She was amazed at the large windows and the light they allowed to enter the rooms. She especially enjoyed looking at the Priesthood pulpits. A beautiful, rounded window cast a halo of light onto each pulpit, showing the awesome detail of the intricate hand-carved engravings in the wood.

As she studied the details, a knot formed in her stomach. She frantically looked around the room for Hunter. Motioning for him to come over, she pointed to the carving.

"Can you see that engraving on the wood? See the one that looks like a circle with four square marks?" she asked anxiously.

"Yes," he replied.

"That symbol is on the new clue," she said.

"Do you know what it means?" she wondered.

"I don't, did you look it up in the book Grandpa gave you?" Hunter asked.

"No, we haven't been back to the motor home yet," she replied.

"Well, I guess we better hurry and get back. Are you ready to go?" Hunter asked.

"I think so, but do you think there could be a clue up there by the engraving?" she asked.

"I doubt it, but if we need to come back, I'm sure we can talk Mom into returning here in the morning," replied Hunter.

Hannah looked over at Mom and knew she would let them return in the morning if they asked. She knew her mom loved church history, stories and artifacts of the early Saints.

"Come on, we better get moving," said Hunter, as he turned to leave. "Bill is waiting at the door."

"Hunter," Hannah quietly said, as she grabbed his arm. "Look over there, by Mom."

Hunter quickly looked toward Mom and gasped. "Oh, no! Who is that guy?"

CHAPTER NINETEEN

19

HANNAH AND HUNTER quickly grabbed Hayden's arm and headed for the door.

"Wait...what...I was trying...," stammered Hayden.

"Be quiet, and walk with us, Hayden," whispered Hannah.

"Why? What's up?" he asked. "Is there a problem?"

"I don't know," Hunter replied. "That guy who asked Hannah about the clue back at Joseph Smith's gravesite is here."

"And the lady I ran into the night we went back to the grave with Aunt Shirley is here, too!" Hannah exclaimed, pointing to the woman.

"Do you think they're following us?" asked Hayden.

"Maybe this is all coincidence," said Hannah. "But it sure seems odd."

"Do you have the clues?" asked Hayden.

"Safe and sound in my backpack," Hannah replied, as she pulled the bag from her shoulder.

"Where is the new clue?" asked Hunter.

"It's in my backpack, too," Hannah answered.

"If I can have your attention!" called Bill. "The Historic Center will be closing in ten minutes. If you would like to follow me back now, we will still have time to finish our tour."

Almost running to keep up with Bill, Hannah and Hunter kept a close eye on the two mysterious people. Hannah could not shake the feeling that she knew the elderly lady. More interested in keeping tabs on the two people than listening to the tour guide, Hannah and Hunter barely heard anything Bill said as he finished the tour. Almost the last person to exit the Historic Center, Hannah was grateful she could no longer see the two suspicious people.

"We have about twenty minutes before the tour bus comes. Are there any other sites you'd like to see, Mom?" asked Hayden.

"Well, I was hoping we had enough time to look through the Kirtland Safety Society Bank Historic Site. Grandpa has an old bank note at home that he used to show me—one that came from this bank," Mom explained.

"Cool, let's go," said Hunter. "Where is it? Look at your map, Hayden."

Hayden pulled out the map and quickly scanned for the Kirtland Safety Society. "I can't find it, Mom," he said. "Do you know where it is supposed to be?"

"I'm not sure, I thought it was somewhere close to the temple," she replied.

"Hey, come look at this!" yelled Aunt Shirley, from down the street.

"What's up?" asked Hayden.

"Yeah, what's up?" asked Mom, mimicking Hayden.

"Sarah, listen to this. The Safety Society building once stood south of the temple, where the circular walkway is now located. The bank opened on January 2, 1837, with Sidney Rigdon as chairman and Warren Parrish as secretary. The bank struggled and was finally closed in November of that same year."

"That's too bad," Mom said sadly. "I was hoping to get more information than that. Your grandpa's note had a really cool symbol drawn on it that I thought you kids might like to see," Mom replied.

"What did the symbol look like?" asked Hannah.

"Oh, I can't remember exactly, a circle with four corners, I think," she replied.

"How can a circle have four corners, Mom?" asked Hayden. "Isn't a circle round?"

"Maybe we will be able to find a replica of one in the gift stores in the area," said Mom. "Then I can show you what I'm talking about."

"Hey, there's the bus," squealed Hunter. "If we don't hurry, we're going to miss it."

Aunt Shirley glanced up the street and said, "I guess

it's early, we better hurry."

Hayden ran to where the bus was parked and quickly climbed inside. Once inside, he saved seats for his family. They all climbed inside and showed the bus driver their tour bracelets. Finding their way back to Hayden, they all sat down and waited for the driver to continue with the excursion.

"Hannah, let's see the clue now," insisted Hunter, as he squished into the seat. He pinned her against himself and Hayden.

Hannah picked up her backpack, unzipped the main pocket and searched for the soft, leather bag. Finally finding it, she pulled it from the pack, re-zipped the pocket and set the bag on the floor between her feet. She loosened the soft, leather strings, opened the bag and pulled the cloth from inside. Laying the cloth out on her lap she smiled and said, "This is the most awesome thing I have ever done in my life."

"Does this cloth have a clue on it like the other two did?" asked Hayden.

"This is really the first time I've had a chance to look at it," replied Hannah. "The only thing I've seen is this really neat symbol," she said, pointing to the cloth.

"Hey, that looks like Mom's squared circle," he replied.

"You're right, I wonder what that means," Hunter said.

"Turn it over, I want to hear the clue," Hayden demanded.

As Hannah started to turn over the cloth, the bus driver called, "Attention! We are headed to our last stop at the Temple Quarry. You will have fifteen minutes, and then the bus will be leaving. There will not be another bus through the area tonight. So, unless you're planning on walking to your hotel tonight, please don't be late."

With that, there was a sudden jolt as the bus lunged forward, toward the last stop.

"Hurry, Hannah, read the clue," urged Hunter.

"All right, just a second," she replied. "She stared at the cloth. "This clue is written differently than the others," she said. "Look."

Hunter and Hayden looked at the writing and were both perplexed at what the words meant.

"You're right, Hannah. Something doesn't look right," replied Hunter.

"Read it anyway, maybe the words will make sense," suggested Hayden.

Hannah nodded and started reading the clue.

"'OF VISION
WORDS OF GOD.
RECORDS WRITTEN
SHOWN ON PLATES OF GOLD.

IS REQUIRED
YEARS TO WAIT.
WATCH FOR BRICK AND MORTAR
WHERE HE SHOWED THE EIGHT
HIDES THE OPENING
HOLDS THE CANE
PROPHECIES FULFILLED'"

"Then across the bottom is the sentence,

'BRINGING BACK THE LORD TO RULE AND REIGN.'"

"What does it mean?" asked Hayden. "I don't understand."

"Neither do I," replied Hunter.

The bus came to an abrupt stop and the driver called, "We're at the Temple Quarry! Please remember, I will be leaving in fifteen minutes sharp."

"Hurry, you three," insisted Mom, as she stood up from her seat. "I want to see this."

"We're coming, Mom," replied Hannah, scrunching up the cloth in her hand.

"Hannah, put the clue back in the leather bag and put it away, quickly," said Hunter, as he stood. "I'll walk Mom to the quarry. Hayden, stay with Hannah and meet us as quick as you can."

Hannah nodded and watched as Hunter hurried to Mom and Aunt Shirley, who were waiting outside the bus. He ushered them toward the large, granite historical marker that was a hundred yards in the distance. Hannah placed the clue inside the bag, and then put it back inside her backpack. She zipped the outer pocket, tossed the bag over her shoulder and hurried to catch up with Hunter.

"What does the marker say?" asked Hayden, resting his hands on his knees as he tried to catch his breath.

"I'll read it," Mom offered, pulling her glasses from her purse. "Okay, the plaque reads, 'When the Temple was planned, the brethren desired to construct it out of brick. When the stone quarry was discovered within an easy distance, the idea to build the temple out of brick was abandoned.'"

"Carrying the stones more than two miles is easy?" asked Hayden.

"Well, I doubt they carried the stones, Hayden," replied Hunter.

"I'm sure they used wagons, honey," said Mom.

"Oh, yeah, I forgot about wagons. I bet you're right," agreed Hayden.

"Everything is lush and green out here, Mom," said Hannah, looking around the area.

"Yes, it is very pretty," Mom replied.

"We better get back to the bus," warned Aunt Shirley. "I really don't want to walk back to the camp ground tonight."

"Me neither," agreed Mom.

"I'll race ya, Hunter," said Hannah, as she started to run.

"Hey, no fair!" he yelled, as he ran to catch up with her.

"You'll never catch me, Hunter!" Hannah hollered over her shoulder. "You know I'm faster than you."

"We'll see about that!" yelled Hunter, trying to catch his sister.

With her long, beautiful hair flowing in the wind, Hunter could almost grab the strands with his hand, if he stretched his arm hard enough. "I could stop her really fast," he thought, smiling. "All I have to do is catch that hair."

Hannah tagged the front of the bus as she ran by yelling, "I win! You lose, Hunter."

Hunter shook his head, rolled his eyes and said, "Oh, come on, Hannah, you know I let you win."

"Only in your dreams, Hunter," she replied, as she climbed onto the bus and strutted her way back to a seat.

"I can't believe how much fun they're having, Sarah," said Aunt Shirley, as they watched the kid's race.

"Me neither," Sarah replied. "I really thought we were going to have a battle on our hands for the whole trip."

"Maybe it was a good idea to have Dad tell them about his Legend," said Aunt Shirley.

"I think you're right. I'm glad you talked me into having Mom say something," she replied, smiling. "I really didn't want them to wonder about the Legend like we did when we were kids. But, I think telling them really sparked an interest in church history."

"And, not only that, look how much fun they are having together. No fights—nothing," said a smiling Aunt Shirley.

As Sarah and Aunt Shirley sat down, Hayden asked, "Mom, what's next on the list?"

"Well, I don't know about you, but I'm starving," she replied. "And I think we've seen everything that I wanted to."

"I'm ssooo starving, too," agreed Hayden.

"Me, too," said Hannah, holding her stomach.

The bus ride back to the campground was a short five minutes. As they hurried off the bus and back toward the motor home, a nervous lump formed in Hunter's throat.

"I hope no one tore up the motor home today, Hannah," whispered Hunter.

"I hadn't thought about that," she replied. "I hope everything is all right."

As they reached the motor home and Mom unlocked the door, Hunter was relieved to find everything in its proper place. Mom hurried to the refrigerator and pulled out the fixings for hamburgers. Hannah quickly set the table and Aunt Shirley prepared a salad and vegetable tray.

"What are the plans from here, Mom?" asked Hayden. "Where is our next stop?"

"I believe that we're going straight to Palmyra, is that right, Shirley?" Mom asked.

"Yep, Palmyra is our next stop," Shirley answered as she looked at the map.

"How long is the drive to Palmyra, Mom?" asked Hannah.

"About four hours, sweetie," Mom said, as she flattened the meat into patties and dropped them into the frying pan.

"So, when are we leaving?" asked Hunter. "Do I need to get the motor home ready to go?"

"Well, we could leave tonight, but then we would have another long night of traveling without sleep. I thought we would stay here tonight, have a good dinner, and maybe play some games before bed. Then, after a good breakfast in the morning, we could leave for Palmyra at about nine or ten o'clock," Mom replied.

"That's a great idea," agreed Hayden. "That gives us plenty of time tonight, and the ride to Palmyra in the morning, to solve the next clue."

Hannah looked angrily at Hayden and said, "Can you ever be quiet and keep a secret Hayden?"

"You found *another* clue?" Mom asked. "Really?"

"We sure did," answered Hunter proudly. "I just know we're going to solve the clues that lead all the way to solving the Legend, I can feel it."

"Feel what, Hunter?" asked Aunt Shirley.

"I don't know for sure," replied Hunter. "I'm sure that we're going to find the clues that no other Kimball could."

Mom smiled as she cooked the meat. She listened to the kids excitedly describe to Aunt Shirley how they had found the last clue, and how Hannah had to balance on the ledge in the rafters of the Newel K. Whitney Store.

"Is that what you were doing when I came back up to get you?" Mom asked, eavesdropping on the conversation.

"Yes, we were really hurrying though," replied Hunter. "We couldn't go much faster, Hannah was way too nervous."

"Hunter," Hannah squeaked. "I wasn't that nervous."

"Yes, you were too," he countered, smiling from ear to ear.

"Is everything else ready for dinner?" interrupted Mom.

"Yes," answered Hunter. "Ready and on the table."

"Everyone sit up to the table, I'm bringing over the hamburgers right now," Mom said.

Hungry from the long day of touring, everyone sat up to the table. Aunt Shirley quickly offered the blessing on the food, and without a word, everyone began eating.

Several quiet minutes passed before Mom asked, "Can I see your new clue?"

"You bet," replied Hannah, reaching underneath the table to pick up her backpack and retrieve the clue.

"Have you figured out what the clue means yet?" asked Aunt Shirley, anxious to see the clue as well.

"We're having a hard time with this one so far," replied Hannah.

"Yeah, the writing doesn't make a lot of sense," interrupted Hunter.

"We haven't tried really hard yet," said Hayden. "We've only had a minute to look over the clue."

Hannah retrieved the L shaped cloth she had pulled from the leather bag and displayed it for everyone to see.

"That's an odd shaped piece of cloth," said Mom. "Does that shape have any significance to the clue?"

"We're not sure yet," replied Hannah. "That's what we're hoping to find out."

"The shape almost has to mean something, doesn't it?" questioned Hunter. "I mean, the other two cloths we found were square not L—shaped."

"I think we better start by reading the clue and go from there," said Hannah. "That way we don't get ahead of ourselves."

"If you decide you need some help with the clue Aunt Shirley and I know a little about church history," offered Mom as she stood up from the table, grabbed her cup and filled it at the sink.

"Before you start working on the clue, will you at least read it to me?" asked Aunt Shirley.

Hannah smiled and nodded. She quickly located the clue on the cloth and read,

"'OF VISION
WORDS OF GOD.
RECORDS WRITTEN
SHOWN ON PLATES OF GOLD.

IS REQUIRED
YEARS TO WAIT.
WATCH FOR BRICK AND MORTAR
WHERE HE SHOWED THE EIGHT
HIDES THE OPENING
HOLDS THE CANE
PROPHECIES FULFILLED'."

"Then across the bottom section of the cloth is the sentence, 'BRINGING BACK THE LORD TO RULE AND REIGN.'"

"Wow!" exclaimed Aunt Shirley. "You're right, that clue doesn't seem to make a lot of sense."

"Sounds like you're gonna have to work hard if you want to solve this riddle," said Mom.

CHAPTER TWENTY

20

RUSHING TO FINISH DINNER, the kids sat in silence pondering Mom's statement about how to solve the clue. Hunter cleared their plates while Hannah rinsed and loaded the dishes into the dishwasher. Hayden helped by gathering all of the trash and taking it out to the camp dumpster.

Mom and Aunt Shirley studied the road map and planned the next day's adventure, occasionally glancing up to check on the kids' kitchen progress.

"Sarah, how about we have fortune cookies for dessert?" whispered Aunt Shirley.

"You have fortune cookies, and you haven't shared any with me, Shirley?" asked Sarah.

"The fortune cookies are a new church game. You

break the cookie open, and inside, instead of a fortune, you have to answer a Book of Mormon question," Shirley replied, talking softly. "I thought playing with the kids would be a lot of fun and of course, we'll have to eat the cookies."

"Everybody ready to play a game?" asked Mom, as Hannah put away the last dish.

"Mom, how about you and Aunt Shirley play for a little while? We were hoping to work on the clue for a few minutes, if that's okay," Hunter said hopefully.

"I guess for a while, but we want to have a real competitive game before bed tonight. One you've never played before, agreed?"

"Agreed," answered Hannah. She sat down on the couch, unzipped her backpack and removed all the clues, books and paperwork Grandpa had given her.

Mom smiled and grabbed a deck of Rook cards. "I guess Shirley and I will play alone for now."

"That's all right, Sarah. You can teach me how to play again before those three kids of yours humiliate me," Aunt Shirley replied, with a smirk on her face.

"All right, let's get this crazy clue solved," suggested Hayden.

"Where do we start?" asked Hunter.

"We need to start by reading the clue again," answered Hannah. She cleared her throat and started to read.

"'OF VISION
WORDS OF GOD.
RECORDS WRITTEN
SHOWN ON PLATES OF GOLD.

IS REQUIRED
YEARS TO WAIT.
WATCH FOR BRICK AND MORTAR
WHERE HE SHOWED THE EIGHT
HIDES THE OPENING
HOLDS THE CANE
PROPHECIES FULFILLED.

BRINGING BACK THE LORD TO RULE AND REIGN.'"

"So, where do we start?" demanded Hayden. "I still don't know what to do."

"We start at the beginning," replied Hunter, with the first line. Evidently, there's something there that we're missing."

"Something important," said Hayden.

"Where are the other clues?" asked Hunter, as he stared at the L-shaped cloth.

"Right here," replied Hannah, picking them up from the couch and handing them to Hunter.

"With the newest clue in such an odd shape, do all of these clues fit together like a puzzle?" questioned Hunter.

"I don't know," replied Hayden, peering over Hunter's shoulder.

"Why don't we try to put them together like a puzzle?" replied Hannah. She carefully placed all three pieces of cloth on the couch. "Putting them together only makes sense."

"Does it look like any of them might fit together?" asked Hayden.

"Hold on," replied Hannah. "I can't tell by just looking at them."

Hannah worked for several minutes, trying to fit the three frayed pieces of cloth together. She tried over and over, but nothing looked right.

"I don't get it, the newest clue seems to be the perfect place to fit the other two clues. But with the frayed edges on the pieces, I can't tell for sure," said Hannah, obviously frustrated.

"Do any of the symbols fit together?" asked Hayden. "Maybe that's what we're missing."

"Oh, good idea, I'll try to match the symbols rather that the edges," said Hannah.

Again she worked, trying to position the material together, so that the symbols formed something recognizable. "This isn't working either," she said angrily.

"Now what?" asked Hayden.

"Let's think for a minute," said Hunter, as he stood up and started pacing back and forth.

Hannah and Hayden watched Hunter impatiently pace while he rubbed his chin. Suddenly holding his finger up he yelled, "I've got it!"

"What? What have you got?" asked Hannah, startled by his sudden outburst.

Without responding, Hunter knelt down next to the couch. He picked up each piece of cloth and laid it back down on the couch—this time with the clues facing up.

As he paced back and forth, trying to mimic Sherlock Holmes, he said, "I had a thought."

"You actually had a thought cross your mind, Hunter?" interrupted Hannah.

Hunter did not even look up, but continued, "I was thinking, as we read the new clue, not one of the words starting each sentence is capitalized. Although that could mean whoever wrote the clue had bad grammar, I hoped it could also mean that, when the cloth is lined up correctly with the other clues, they might have an additional word or two that begins each sentence," Hunter explained.

Hunter fiddled with the all three cloths for a minute or two before he said, "Okay, tell me what you think about this."

"Think about what?" asked Hannah.

"I'm gonna read you the new clue by adding the new words to the end of each line from the old clues. Does that make sense?" he asked.

"I think so," replied Hayden.

Hunter scowled and said, "Pay close attention. The first line of the clue we found back at Carthage reads, 'Prophecies revealed to man'. Do you remember?"

"Yes," replied Hannah.

"Okay, I am going to take that line on the cloth and match it with the line on the new cloth that reads, 'of vision.' Do you understand?" he asked.

"Yeah, I get it, then the clue will read, 'Prophecies revealed to man of vision.' Right?"

"Yep, only, if you look at the first two clues, you will see that the last word is set apart from the sentence more than it should be. So, instead of 'Prophecies revealed to man of vision', I think the clue reads, 'Man of Vision'."

"So the second line would read, 'Received words of God'?" asked Hannah.

"That's it, you've got it," replied Hunter.

"That's actually a good idea, Hunter," said Hayden. "How did you think of it?"

"Oh, funny, Hayden," Hunter replied. "Well, I used my powers as a master detective. You may not know what those are since you are so young, your powers may not work yet," Hunter joked.

Hayden shook his head and said, "You know, Hunter, you can actually be funny every now and then. I'm just trying to figure out if now is one of those times."

Hunter reached over and tousled Hayden's hair. "I kinda like you every now and then, too," he said.

"All right, let's get this clue translated," said Hayden.

"Too late, boys, I've already got it done," announced Hannah.

"Nice work, Hannah," said Hunter. "Read it to us."

Hannah picked up the paper with her scribbles and said, "This is what I came up with. Tell me if you think it's right."

"'MAN OF VISION
RECEIVED WORDS OF GOD
OLD RECORDS WRITTEN
SHOWN ON PLATES OF GOLD.

MORE IS REQUIRED
FOUR YEARS TO WAIT
WATCH FOR BRICK AND MORTAR
LOST WHERE HE SHOWED THE EIGHT
ASH HIDES THE OPENING
PATH HOLDS THE CANE
LAST PROPHECIES FULFILLED

BRINGING BACK THE LORD TO RULE AND REIGN.'"

"So what do you think? Does that sound right?" Hannah asked.

"Yes," replied Hunter. "That sounds right to me. Now all we have to do is figure out where the clue wants us to go."

"That actually sounds right to me, too. That was a great idea, Hunter," said Hayden excitedly. "How did you come up with it?"

"Cute, Hayden," retorted Hunter.

"The clue didn't sound hard, in fact, it seems pretty

simple, guys," said Aunt Shirley, startling Hannah.

"What is it around here? Does everybody think they need to scare me?" asked Hannah.

"Sorry, Hannah," replied Aunt Shirley. "I thought you knew I was standing behind you."

"Nope, I didn't know that," she said, still holding her hand to her chest.

"What's simple about this clue, Aunt Shirley?" asked Hunter.

"Listen to the first four sentences," she replied.

"'MAN OF VISION
RECEIVED WORDS OF GOD
OLD RECORDS WRITTEN
SHOWN ON PLATES OF GOLD.'"

"That says Joseph Smith to me, clear as a bell," Aunt Shirley replied, smiling.

"Hey, I think you're right, Aunt Shirley," Hayden said excitedly. "He was a man of vision, he received words from God, and he was shown old records that were written on plates of gold."

"What about the next four?" asked Hunter. "I don't think they're as easy."

"I bet I can figure them out," said Hannah.

"'More is required'—I think that meant more from Joseph. 'Four years to wait'—If I remember correctly, I think Brother Hutcheon said that is how long Joseph had to wait before the Angel Moroni finally let him take the Gold Plates from the Hill Cumorah. 'Watch for brick and mortar'—I'm not sure on this line. But I'm sure I know the next line. 'Lost where he showed the eight'—I'm sure that line is talking about the eight witnesses. We need to find out where Joseph showed the eight witnesses the Book of Mormon. I bet by the brick and mortar, something is lost or hidden."

"Nice job, Hannah. You've been reading that church history book I gave you," said Mom.

"Actually I have, some of the stories in the book I've never heard before, and they're kinda interesting," Hannah replied, beaming with pride.

"I'll try the next few lines," said Hunter. "'Ash hides the opening'—wherever Joseph showed the eight witnesses the Gold Plates, must have been close to brick and mortar. Brick and mortar are usually items needed to build a fireplace. And when wood is burned inside a fireplace, ash is created. Now, according to the clue, ash is what is hiding a secret opening."

"Wow, you kids amaze me," said Mom, interrupting Hunter. "I never knew you were so smart."

"Let me try the next one," insisted Hayden. "'Path holds the cane'—I think the clue is hidden in the fireplace and is found by following the path, until we find a cane. Once we find the cane, the 'Last prophecies are fulfilled, bringing forth the Lord to rule and reign again on the earth.'"

"Shirley, did you know I have brilliant kids?" asked Sarah.

"I sure did, Sarah," she replied. "And they're really cute, too."

"Sorry to have interrupted," said Mom, as she turned and walked back toward the kitchen table. "We were just wondering if you were about ready to start playing games soon."

"You know after ten o'clock, I turn into a pumpkin," added Aunt Shirley.

"We'll be over in three minutes, Mom," replied Hunter. "I want to check in the church history book to see if it provides any information on where the eight witnesses viewed the Gold Plates."

"Okay, but try to hurry, it's getting late, and I would like to get to bed fairly soon. I want to be on the road no later than ten o'clock in the morning," said Mom. "I would really like to leave earlier if we can."

"We'll hurry, Mom," replied Hayden. "I promise."

"Hannah, run and get the church history book you've been reading, and let's see what is written about the eight witnesses," Hunter suggested anxiously. "Maybe it will give us some information that can help us."

"I'm already ahead of you," she answered, holding up the book.

"Is there anything there that talks about where Joseph showed the eight witnesses the Gold Plates?" asked Hayden.

"I can only find one small paragraph about the location," she replied. "The statement reads, 'Joseph was relieved when he was given permission to show eight men other than himself the Gold Plates. The Plates were then shown to eight men in his father's home a few days later.'"

"The book doesn't say anything else?" asked Hunter.

"Nope, nothing more about the location," replied Hannah, still searching.

"Well then, we need to go to the Joseph Smith, Sr. home," announced Hunter, walking toward Mom. "I think that's where the next clue is hidden."

"Well, then I guess you're in luck," Mom replied. "We're on our way to Palmyra in the morning."

"I can't believe how everything has worked out to find all these clues," said Hannah. "I just hope we have this next clue right."

"I know were right," replied Hunter. "I think the Lord is helping us."

"I bet you're right," agreed Hannah. She stood up from the couch and walked to the kitchen table, looking at the cards Mom had dealt already. "All right, who wants to lose at a fun hand of Rook?" she asked.

"There's no way you can win, Hannah, I've been having lessons for the last hour," replied Aunt Shirley. "I think I'm gonna beat everyone here tonight."

"Well, we'll just see about that," declared Hunter, as he sat down at the table. "I think Hayden and I are going to be the run away winners tonight."

Excited to have solved the next clue, everyone sat down to a fun game. They ate popcorn, joked together and played for nearly two hours, before Mom finally said, "So much for our going to bed early. It's time for you to brush your teeth and get into bed. As usual, we have a full day ahead of us tomorrow."

CHAPTER TWENTY-ONE

FRUSTRATED THAT SHE could not sleep, Hannah climbed out of bed and headed for the kitchen. She shielded her eyes from the light of the freezer as she searched for the Rocky Road ice cream. Locating it quickly, she closed the door, grabbed a spoon and sat down at the kitchen table in the dark.

As she scooped the top layer of ice cream with the spoon and took a bite, a faint light a few feet outside the window caught her eye. She lifted one of the small slats from the blinds to see what was outside. Spotting the shadow of a person, she tried to determine who it could be. Unable to see the mysterious person's face, or tell for sure what the person was doing, she squinted her eyes and moved closer to the window to get a better look.

Suddenly, the shadow's flashlight shined up at the blinds. Startled, Hannah released the slat and leaned away from the window, afraid whoever was outside might see her. Several tense seconds passed as the light continued to shine on the blinds. Finally, the light moved away from the window and Hannah breathed a cautious sigh of relief.

She slowly lifted one of the slats on the blinds, revealing the shadow of the mysterious person right outside the motor home. Afraid to let the shadow out of her sight, she continued to watch the person's every move. She watched as the shadow rifled through their campsite trashcan and then fiddled with something on the right, front side of the motor home.

"Who is that?" she thought. "And what is he doing?"

She quietly watched the shadow for nearly five minutes before the person turned away from the motor home and disappeared into the darkness. Concerned about what the shadow was doing at the front of the motor home, Hannah cautiously unlocked the side door and slowly pushed it open. Positive no one was around, she opened the door just wide enough so that she could slide outside.

She walked quickly to the front of the motor home and scanned the area for anything suspicious. Unable to find even the tiniest scratch, she shrugged her shoulders, turned and quickly walked toward the door.

"I wonder who that was," she thought. "Maybe a homeless person?"

Uncertain what to do, she wiggled back inside and locked the door. With one last peek through the blinds, she wondered, "Did I imagine I saw something?"

Still shaken, she walked back to the table and sat down. Hoping the ice cream would bring her some comfort, she picked up the spoon and slowly scooped bite after bite until the ice cream was gone.

Deep sleep never came for Hannah. She tossed and turned, fading in and out of consciousness. She briefly dreamed about the mysterious shadow she saw that night.

Hunter watched Hannah's eyes move rapidly back and forth. Her body shook abruptly, as though she was fighting. Concerned about her, he placed his hand on her shoulder and asked, "Are you all right, Hannah?"

Ripped from another horrible dream, she sat up and almost started crying. Tears welled up in her eyes as she looked at Hunter and realized he was her brother and not the shadow.

"What's the matter, Hannah," he asked. "Are you okay?"

"I think so," she replied, wiping the beads of sweat from her forehead. "What time is it?"

"About six o'clock in the morning," Hunter replied.

"Why are you up so early?" Hannah asked.

"You were making noises, and I thought maybe you were sick," Hunter replied. "Besides, I've had a hard time sleeping tonight."

"Me, too," Hannah said. "Falling asleep has been almost impossible. I got up about two o'clock this morning and I saw the shadow of a person outside the motor home. I don't know if it was a man or a woman, but I watched the person for a while. After he or she left, I walked outside and checked the motor home to see if everything was all right."

"And what happened?" asked Hunter curious.

"I couldn't see that anything was wrong with the motor home, but, I can't shake this sick feeling in my stomach. I'm still concerned that someone was messing around at two in the morning."

"I'll check everything later this morning," said Hunter, sitting down on Hannah's bed.

"Do you think we translated the clues right?" he asked.

"I sure hope we're right," said Hannah, reaching underneath her pillow for the clues.

"We have to be right," replied Hunter. "Where else could the clue be hidden?"

"He's right, Hannah. Joseph showed the eight witnesses the Gold Plates while he and his family lived in the home Alvin started to build in hopes of giving his mother and father the life that he thought they deserved," assured Hayden, in one big breath. "At least, that is what is written in this book about Old Palmyra. I think the house is referred to as the frame house."

"How long have you been up, Hayden," asked Hunter.

"Since about four o'clock," he replied. "I couldn't sleep last night. I have a really anxious feeling in the pit of my stomach and I'm not sure if that's good or bad."

"Wow! All of us had a hard time sleeping last night," said Hunter. "Don't you think that is kinda odd?"

"Yes, it is odd, but, I think we're nervous because we're getting close to solving the clues of the Legend," Hannah replied.

"I'd have to agree with you. I have this feeling that we're almost there. In fact, I think we're really close," said Hunter.

"The sooner we get up and get ready, the sooner we'll get to Palmyra," said Hannah, sitting up and stretching. "I know I won't be able to fall back asleep now, I'm too nervous and excited."

"Do you think we could find the treasure today?" whispered Hayden.

"You know, I think we have all the clues to the map now, we've got to be getting close," replied Hunter.

"We've got a fairly long drive ahead of us. Let's see if we can't get ready to go quickly. Maybe by the time Mom and Aunt Shirley get up, we'll be ready to pull out."

Hayden and Hunter nodded in agreement. They quickly got dressed, made their beds, and even helped straighten up before Mom awoke.

Excited to see Mom finally appear from her room a little after seven, Hayden excitedly told her the motor home was ready to go. In fact, they had already eaten, cleaned up, and packed.

"Why didn't you wake me up earlier?" asked Mom. "We could have gotten on the road before now."

"You looked like you needed the sleep," replied Hunter.

"All right. I'll get dressed really quick and get something to eat, then we can leave," said Mom.

Thirty minutes later, with everything and everybody ready to go, Mom pulled the motor home onto the highway headed for Palmyra.

The anticipation of solving the clues to the Legend was more than Hayden could handle. He laid on the couch, unable to sleep during the entire drive to Palmyra. "Are we getting close?" he asked anxiously.

Hannah glanced out the window just in time to see a sign that read, 'Palmyra three miles'.

"We're here," announced Hannah excitedly, ready to get to work on the clue.

Mom exited the freeway and followed the signs toward Palmyra.

"Where are we going first, Mom?" asked Hayden.

"For food," interrupted Hunter. "I'm starving."

"We need to check in at the RV Park first. Then, we can get some food," replied Mom.

"Mom, are we going to visit some of the historical sites today?" Hannah asked anxiously.

"Well, your dad and Uncle Gary are flying in tomorrow, and I know that they both want to tour some of the sites with us, but I thought we could go see a few today," replied Mom. "Where do you want to go?"

"I want to go to the Joseph Smith Farm," she replied.

"All right, why don't we find the Wayne County Fairground RV Park on West Jackson Street and check in?

Then we can stop at Mark's Pizzeria or The Hot Spot for lunch, before we head to the Joseph Smith Farm," suggested Aunt Shirley as she read the information packet the Palmyra Chamber of Commerce had sent to Sarah.

"Mark's Pizzeria sounds great, let's go there," replied Hannah.

"Okay, pizza for lunch, then on to tour the farm," agreed Mom.

The kids watched anxiously as Mom wandered her way through the streets of Palmyra. Finally finding Jackson Street, she located the RV Park and pulled up to the front office.

"I'll go check in and be right back," said Mom, as she hurried out the door.

Almost five minutes passed before she returned. "We're in space number one hundred twenty-one, straight up this trail," she said, pointing north.

"The first camp site is one hundred, so it can't be too far up the road," said Hunter, sitting in the passenger seat.

"Up on the right, Mom!" yelled Hayden. "There it is."

"Good, go place this reserved tag on the sign and we will get going," said Mom, as she handed Hayden a small, yellow card.

Hayden slid the card into the sign and hurried back to the motor home. Throwing the door open he yelled, "All done, let's go eat."

"Pizza, here we come," added Aunt Shirley.

Mom found her way back to Main Street on Route Thirty-one and quickly spotted the restaurant. She parked, and everyone hurried into the air-conditioned building. Glad to be inside out of the heat, they ordered the best homemade pizza they had ever tasted. Mom even found a well-stacked salad bar.

"That was a great meal," said Hayden, as he licked his fingers. "We're going to have to bring Dad here."

"Yeah, and I wouldn't mind eating here again either," said Aunt Shirley.

"You know, I bet the farm tour is only open for a few more hours, we probably need to go, I want to have time to look for the clue," said Hannah.

"Let's get moving then," replied Mom as she stood.

They hurried back to the motor home and Mom followed Main Street to Stafford Road, then followed Stafford Road about three blocks to the Smith Farm Welcome Center and turned into the parking lot.

"Wow, there are a lot of people here," said Hannah. "More than we've seen anywhere else."

"Are they all here for the Pageant?" asked Hayden.

"I'm sure they are," replied Aunt Shirley.

"When are we going to the Pageant?" asked Hunter.

"Tomorrow, for my birthday," replied Hannah, in a sarcastic tone.

"When do we pick up Dad?" asked Hunter.

"Tomorrow morning," replied Mom.

Entering the Welcome Center, they noticed countless pictures hanging on the walls.

"I wonder how many relatives we have hanging on these walls," said Aunt Shirley. She was in awe of the amazing pictorial history of Palmyra.

"Good afternoon," said a tall man with sandy blond-hair. "My name is Elder Cahoon. Welcome to the Joseph Smith Farm Welcome Center, can I answer any questions for you?"

"Where do we start? What do we do?" quizzed Mom.

"You can always take a map of the farm and wander around on a self-guided tour, however, my recommendation is to take a free-guided tour with Elder Leatherman. He is our best guide and he's starting a tour right now."

"Thanks," replied Mom, taking the map from Elder Cahoon.

They hurried to catch Elder Leatherman. They joined the tour group just as the people exited the Welcome Center doors.

"Directly to the west is the Sacred Grove. That area only has a self-guided tour. If you do tour the grove, please remember to walk only on the established trails. leave all materials, dead or alive, in the grove, and please refrain from carving on or marking any of the trees.

"As we walk to the log cabin, let me tell you some interesting facts about it. The log home is one of the most sacred sites of The Church of Jesus Christ of Latter-day Saints. Located here on this property, it is an exact replica of the log cabin the Smith family lived in during the time they lived in the village of Palmyra," said Elder Leatherman, as he opened the door to enter.

"As you can see, the cabin was small, and on more than one occasion, this small log home housed more than twelve people. This is also the location where Joseph

Smith, as a young boy, lived when he prayed in the Sacred Grove and where he was visited several times by the Angel Moroni. Please take a moment to look around especially upstairs in the loft where Joseph slept. Don't hesitate to ask questions."

"Elder Leatherman, are you sure this is not the original home?" asked Hayden.

"I'm sure," replied Elder Leatherman smiling. "Our current Prophet, Gordon B. Hinckley, had this replica log home rebuilt a few years ago."

Confused, Hayden turned to Hunter and said, "This is not the real log home."

"I heard that," said Hunter.

"Now what? If the home no longer exists, what do we do now?"

"I'm not sure, buddy," replied Hunter. "Maybe this is where the Legend ends."

"That would be a real bummer," he answered, wrinkling his nose trying not to cry.

"Yes, it would," agreed Hunter.

"You two aren't serious are you?" asked Hannah.

"What do you mean?" asked Hunter.

"We talked about this earlier today. The home where Joseph showed the Gold Plates to the eight witnesses was the frame house, not the log house."

Excitedly Hayden turned to Elder Leatherman and asked, "Is the frame house the original house? Or a replica, like the log house?"

"The frame house is the original home," replied Elder Leatherman. "It has, however, had a few minor renovations over the years and is currently under complete renovation."

"Are we going to tour it?" asked Hannah.

"We are going to see only the main family room and possibly one room upstairs. Everything else is currently under construction," he replied.

Elder Leatherman raised his hand and called. "If you will turn your attention to me, those of you who would like to continue on to the frame home built by Alvin Smith, please follow me. The rest of you, please enjoy your stay here in Palmyra. Have a safe journey home, wherever that may be."

With that, he opened the door and quickly disappeared outside.

"Are we going to continue with the Elder, Mom?" Hunter asked, nervous that Elder Leatherman was getting too far ahead.

"No, I would love to stay here in this cabin for a little while," replied Mom.

"Can we continue with him to the frame house?" asked Hunter. "I would really love to hear what he has to say about it."

"Why? I thought you wanted to get out of here as fast as possible," teased Aunt Shirley.

"Well, I did in the beginning. But, we've had a lot of fun touring through all the old historic sites so far and we're anxious to see some more," replied Hunter.

"Oh, okay," answered Aunt Shirley, with a smile.

"Kids, it's fine if you want to go with Elder Leatherman to the frame house, but please don't leave the frame house until we get there. We'll catch up in a little while," said Mom. "And remember be on your best behavior."

"Thanks, Mom, we will!" hollered Hayden, rushing out the door of the cabin.

"Meet you in a little bit, Mom," Hannah said excitedly.

"Wish us luck on our next clue," whispered Hunter.

"Good Luck," whispered Mom.

CHAPTER TWENTY-TWO

HANNAH SMILED from ear to ear as the kids raced to catch up with Elder Leatherman and the rest of the group. Hannah's images of a horrible church history road trip were completely wrong. The trip had actually turned out to be fun and exciting. Even the long hours in the motor home seemed to pass by quickly as she worked together with her brothers attempting to solve the clues to the Kimball Family Legend.

Catching up with the tour group the three kids followed Elder Leatherman down the path toward the Smith Family frame home, listening intently to every detail the Elder said regarding the history of the home. They hoped he might unknowingly give them the information they needed to find the whereabouts of the next clue.

As the group reached the house Elder Leatherman stopped them at the burgundy-colored front door and said, "Due to the renovation and construction being done in the home, the areas inside that we will be able to tour are limited. Please stay with me at all times and I will try to cover all of the information I have about the closed areas."

Hannah, excited to enter the home pushed past Elder Leatherman as he opened the door and walked inside. She scanned the area searching frantically for anything that matched the clue.

"What is this room, Elder?" asked Hannah.

"As soon as everyone comes in, I will tell you all about it," he replied, surprised at her curiosity.

Hannah impatiently waited for what seemed like hours for the Elder to begin. Sure she could not wait any longer she turned to Hunter and said, "We're never going to find the clue at this rate."

Hunter smiled and said, "Relax Hannah, I'm sure he's going to start any minute."

Hannah breathed a sign of relief as seconds later Elder Leatherman finally began.

"The frame house of Joseph Smith, Sr. was built over a period of approximately four years. The house was planned by Alvin Smith, Joseph's oldest brother. The design of this New-England-style farmhouse was brought to life by Alvin's desire to provide a comfortable home for his aging parents, Lucy who was forty-five and Joseph Sr. who was fifty."

"Hannah, how old is Mom?" asked Hayden.

"She's forty-two, Hayden," Hannah softly answered snickering. "Should we tell her that back in the 1800's she would be considered old?"

"Quiet, you two," whispered Hunter. "I'm trying to listen."

"Sorry," mouthed Hannah, turning her attention back to Elder Leatherman.

"Having apprenticed as a builder, Alvin managed the initial construction himself, positioning the home to face west and look out towards the Sacred Grove. By the fall of 1823, the heavy timber frame had been raised and the house was starting to take shape. Unexpectedly, in November of that same year, Alvin died, and construction lay idle for several months. Wanting the home to be completed Joseph, Sr. hired Mr. Stoddard who lived down the road to finish the construction. Finally in late 1825, two full years after Alvin had passed away, the Smith family moved into the home, even though much of the finish work still remained undone.

"Joseph received the Gold Plates from the Angel Moroni about two years later while still living in this home.

"Here on the main floor was where the family spent most of its time. As you can see, the kitchen area is fairly large, making it possible to accommodate the numerous people that lived here and it still features the original soapstone sink that the family used while they lived here. You can also see the original red clay bricks that make up the hearth and fireplace. The fireplace was not only used to heat the home but cook the meals as well. It had a custom oven built on the right side of the open pit allowing Lucy to bake bread a lot the way we do today."

"Is that what the small red door is?" asked Hayden.

"Yes," replied Elder Leatherman as he walked to the fireplace and pulled open the oven door. "This fireplace is also where it is believed that Joseph Smith hid the plates beneath the hearth to hide them from the mob."

"Do you know where in the fireplace the Gold Plates were hidden?" asked Hunter.

"No one knows for sure," Elder Leatherman replied.

"Are there any loose bricks?" asked Hunter.

Elder Leatherman nodded as he walked to the hearth and wiggled several loose bricks located in the center of the hearth just outside the brass log holder. "There are several loose bricks here," he replied. "Including my favorite brick with the small engraving of a lion on the front."

"A lion?" quizzed Hayden.

"Yes, a lion," he replied.

"Have you ever removed the bricks to see if anything is there?" asked Hannah.

"No, I've never wanted to disturb the clay bricks," he replied. "Clay this old could be very fragile. I would hate to be responsible for crumbling the bricks and ruining the fireplace."

"Is this all we get to see in the house?" asked an elderly lady from the group.

Positive the voice sounded familiar, Hannah turned quickly toward the voice, hoping to recognize who was speaking. Unable to see the face of the woman speaking, she turned to Hunter and asked. "Can you see who's talking?"

Hunter looked toward the woman but he too was unable to see her face. "I can't see her, why?"

"I'm not sure, her voice just sounds really familiar, I thought maybe someone we knew was here." Hannah replied.

"Actually, there's one small room upstairs where the renovation has been completed. If you're interested we can walk up there," Elder Leatherman replied.

"I'd like to see it," said a man from the crowd.

"And so would I," said another woman.

"Then follow me, but please be very careful as we will be passing some of the renovation areas," he replied, as he quickly walked to the stairs. "The upper bedroom in the Smith house is one of the areas still under construction. However, as we pass the door, notice the richness of the colors and the light that is cast into the room through the windows.

"As we continue to the renovated back room, look closely at the wood flooring we're walking on. Notice how the Smith brothers pieced the planks together with different sizes and widths of wood. Money was scarce for them and the desire to complete the project that had gone on for so long was great, leaving the family with limited supplies and resources.

"Miraculous events took place in this home, including the Lord's hand in protecting the Gold Plates. This is the small bedroom that we can visit on our tour. The story is told that in this room, Joseph Smith hid the plates between his two nieces, when the mob came to find them. Joseph's sister asked the mob to search any place in the house they would like, but please don't wake the children. The mob surprisingly agreed and the plates were kept safe."

"Does anyone know if that story is really true?" interrupted Hayden.

"I'm not sure, but, I have been told the Smith Family said the story is true," replied Elder Leatherman.

"Is there a fireplace anywhere upstairs?" asked Hunter.

"No, the only heat source in the house is the fireplace on the main floor, located in the kitchen," he answered.

"Hunter, the clue is in the fireplace downstairs," whispered Hannah.

"I know it," he replied. "Any ideas on how we're going to move the bricks and find the opening without anyone seeing us?"

"We're going to have to wait until everyone is gone," he replied.

"How are we going to do that?" Hannah asked, annoyed at Hunter's response. "People come in and out of this house all day long."

"I know how," whispered Hayden, from behind Hannah, startling her.

"Hayden, don't sneak up on me," she snapped. "You scared me half to death."

"Sorry, Hannah, I didn't mean to scare you," he replied.

"Oh, you're okay, Hannah," said Hunter. "Now Hayden what's your idea?"

"Elder Leatherman told me that the tour we are on is the last tour for the day. However, the farm remained opened for self-guided tours for several more hours. So, I was thinking, when he takes the tour group and heads back to the Welcome Center, you and I can move the bricks while Hannah stands watch outside," said Hayden.

"That's a pretty good idea," said Hunter. "When we find the opening I can hopefully find the cane the clue talks about, while you stand watch from inside as well."

"I want to help find the cane," said Hannah. "Not stand watch outside. That's no fun."

"Fun?" asked Hunter. "I thought we were here to find the next clue and prove the Legend was true."

"You're right," replied Hannah dejectedly. "I'll keep watch, I'm just anxious to help."

"I know," said Hunter. "But I think Hayden is right, the bricks are going to be a little heavy and awkward and if the opening requires you to crawl inside with bugs and stuff I'm not sure how much you 're going to love that."

Hannah rolled her eyes and replied, "All right, boys you can find this clue, but you know I'm not really afraid of bugs and stuff."

"Now, if there are no more questions," said Elder Leatherman, "the guided portion of this tour is over. You are welcome to stay here, or wander through any of the other open structures on the farm or stay with me as I will be returning to the Welcome Center momentarily, where I will begin telling stories about the pictures that hang on the wall, hopefully some you've never heard before," he said smiling.

Elder Leatherman walked downstairs to the front door and opened it, allowing a burst of hot air to travel into the room. "If you're coming with me, let's go." With that he disappeared outside into the hot summer's heat.

The kids wandered around the house pretending to look at the interesting relics that adorned the home, anxiously waiting for everyone to leave. More than five minutes passed before the last person shut the door behind him as he left.

"I thought he would never leave," said Hayden.

Hunter hurried over to the fireplace, heading straight for the bricks that Elder Leatherman had shown them were loose. Nervous to touch them, but anxious to find the next clue, he pried the first brick off the ground.

"Hannah you better keep watch, we don't want anyone to know we're searching for treasure," said Hunter.

"Wait!" insisted Hayden. "Before you leave, will you read us the last clue one more time?"

"Sure," said Hannah, throwing her backpack to the ground. She fumbled through the paper for several seconds before she found the L shaped cloth.

"All right, here is it," she said as she started to read.

"'MAN OF VISION
RECEIVED WORDS OF GOD
OLD RECORDS WRITTEN
SHOWN ON PLATES OF GOLD.

MORE IS REQUIRED
FOUR YEARS TO WAIT
WATCH FOR BRICK AND MORTAR
LOST WHERE HE SHOWED THE EIGHT
ASH HIDES THE OPENING
PATH HOLDS THE CANE

LAST PROPHECIES FULFILLED
BRINGING BACK THE LORD TO RULE AND REIGN.'"

"Okay, so I need to find an opening then follow a path?" said Hunter.

"Yep," answered Hannah. "Now, I'm going to go keep watch. Is there anything you need before I go?"

I don't think so," said Hayden.

"If someone starts to come, how do you want me to warn you?" she asked as she opened the door.

"Good question," replied Hayden. "What should she do, Hunter?"

Hunter thought for a few seconds before he smiled and said, "Why don't you text message me. I will give Hayden my cell phone and if we hear it beep, we'll know someone is coming."

"I think that just might work, nice call Hunter," she said, as she walked outside and closed the door.

"Okay Hayden, let's get to work," said Hunter as he removed another brick.

"Does it look like there's an opening?" asked Hayden.

"I can't see anything yet," replied Hunter, carefully removing another brick and handing it to Hayden.

Hayden carefully laid each brick, side-by-side, writing on his hand where each brick needed to be returned. As Hunter handed Hayden the ninth brick he startled him when he yelled, "Hey, I found something."

"What? What did you find?" asked Hayden anxiously.

"I don't know, but look, I think the plywood can be moved," replied Hunter.

Hayden watched as Hunter stuck his finger into the opening of a small knot in the wood. "My fingers are too big," he exclaimed.

"I bet I can fit mine," Hayden replied excitedly. He carefully moved closer to the plywood and easily stuck his finger into the hole. Sliding his finger inside the hole as far as he could, he bent his finger at the knuckle and gripped the wood. Sure that he had a good hold on the wood, he lifted his hand, hoping that it would follow. To his surprise and delight the square lifted, revealing an opening underneath the house.

"Oh, wow! We found the opening," exclaimed Hayden excitedly, as he handed Hunter the wood piece. "I can't believe it, this is so cool!"

"We've got to hurry, so I'm gonna try to climb down there," said Hunter poking his head through the opening into the darkness.

"How are you going to find the cane?" asked Hayden. "It's dark in there."

"I'll figure that out when I get in there," said Hunter, sliding his legs into the small opening.

"Be careful," warned Hayden as he watched Hunter's head disappear into the dark.

Suddenly, Hunter's phone rang, startling Hayden. "Oh no! Someone is coming," he thought, jumping to his feet and running to the window. Quickly he pulled the drapes aside to see Mom and Aunt Shirley thirty yards away talking to Hannah.

Not sure what to do Hayden ran back to the fireplace and yelled, "Hunter, Mom's coming, what do you want me to do?"

"Cover up the opening, quick," Hunter called.

"What? Close you up inside?" he asked, bewildered at the request.

"Yes, I'll be fine and I haven't found the cane yet. Now hurry, cover up the opening, Hayden."

Hayden practically threw the wood back over the opening and cautiously placed each brick back into the spot Hunter had pulled them from. As he laid the last brick into place, the front door creaked opened. Hayden quickly jumped to his feet and turned away from the fireplace toward the old sink.

"Hayden," called Aunt Shirley. "Are you having any fun?"

"I sure am," Hayden replied nervously.

"Where's your brother?" asked Mom, looking around the room.

"I'm not sure where he's at," Hayden replied.

"So, what are you doing?" asked Aunt Shirley suspiciously.

"I was waiting for you and Mom. You said to wait for you here, right?" he quizzed.

Mom and Aunt Shirley looked at each other, not quite sure what to believe.

"Something sounds a little fishy, doesn't it, Shirley?" asked Mom.

"Yeah, I was thinking that same thing. Hunter is nowhere to be found, Hannah is supposedly tanning in the hundred-degree weather and Hayden is standing in here like he's Mr. Innocent," answered Aunt Shirley.

"I think something is real fishy."

"Should we start upstairs?" asked Mom. "Maybe we'll find Hunter up there."

"I bet we find him in one of the rooms being renovated," said Aunt Shirley.

"I'm sure looking for another clue," replied Mom.

"Well, let's be really quiet and sneak up there, maybe we can scare him," said Aunt Shirley, tip toeing toward the stairs with a wide grin on her face.

"He's not upstairs," insisted Hayden, trying to block their path.

"I don't want to hear any bird calls to signal him we're coming, Hayden," said Mom, pushing Hayden out of her way.

"Well don't get mad at him then," said Hayden. "'Cause he's gonna be mad at me for not warning him that someone is here," he said making the straightest face he could.

Mom and Aunt Shirley quietly sneaked up the stairs in search of Hunter while Hayden stood at the bottom of the stairs smiling.

"I've got to get him out of there quick," thought Hayden, hurrying toward the fireplace once Mom and Aunt Shirley were out of sight. Removing the bricks and placing them in the same order side-by-side, Hayden pulled the plywood off again and looked into the opening.

Suddenly Hunter appeared, shining a light right in Hayden's eye. Surprised, he jumped backwards hitting his head on the mantle, knocking him to the floor.

"Hayden, it's just me," called Hunter quietly. "I've

found the cane, give he a hand so I can get out of here."

Hayden crawled quickly back to the opening grabbed Hunters' hand and said, "You scared me, Hunter.

"Sorry," he replied, trying to wiggle out of the hole.

"Did you get it?" Hayden asked.

"I sure did," replied Hunter as he crawled out.

"Where is it?"

"I tied it to my shoe strings," replied Hunter, pulling on the string until a beautiful, hand carved, wood cane appeared.

"Mom and Aunt Shirley are upstairs looking for you," said Hayden. "We've got to hurry and get these bricks back where they go."

Hunter untied the cane and leaned it up against the wall as Hayden dropped the plywood into place. Quickly the two boys set the bricks into the opening making sure they were all replaced in their proper position. Hunter brushed the small amount of red dust that had fallen from the clay bricks into the fireplace, stood up and grabbed the cane.

"How are we going to get that out of here?" asked Hayden. "It's not like anyone is going to let us take it."

Hunter nodding in agreement thought for a moment, then smiled and said, "I know."

Hayden watched as Hunter slid the cane inside the waistband of his baggy blue jeans and then down the leg of his pants until it could no longer be seen.

"That work's," replied Hayden, shaking his head and smiling.

"So, there you are, Hunter," said Aunt Shirley surprising the two boys.

"Here I am," Hunter replied, trying not to look nervous.

"All right, tell me where you've been?" Aunt Shirley asked. "You weren't down here when we came in a few minutes ago."

"Sure I was," answered Hunter, slowly walking toward the door. "You just didn't see me."

"Something is going on around here and I'm gonna find out what, even if you don't tell me," Aunt Shirley declared.

"Tell Mom we're going to head over to the Sacred Grove, will you?" Hunter asked, as he opened the door.

"I'll tell her. We'll meet you there in a little while and then I expect to hear all about what you three have been up to," replied Aunt Shirley.

Hunter nodded and smiled as the two boys walked outside.

"That was way too close," said Hunter, struggling to walk. "Thank goodness I found the cane quickly."

"Yeah, tell me where in the world did you find, a flash-light?" questioned Hayden.

"It wasn't a flashlight. I was checking my pockets for a match, when I remembered that Mom has one of those small lights on her key chain. Talk about luck, the light worked and I was able to find the cane hanging on the wall," Hunter replied as he hobbled down the path, unable to bend his knee. "Where is Hannah?"

"She was right here talking to Mom when she sent the text message," said Hunter looking around puzzled as to where she would have gone.

"She didn't go back in the house, did she?" asked Hunter, confused as well.

"No," replied Hayden.

"Are you sure this is where she was?" asked Hunter.

"Yeah, look," said Hayden pointing to a paper on the ground. "She was sitting on the grass like she was tanning, pretending to read a paper or something. Hayden grabbed the small envelope and handed it to Hunter.

Hunter looked at the envelope and then again scanned the area for his sister.

"Did she leave us a note?" asked Hayden.

Hunter shrugged his shoulders and said, "I don't even know if this was hers."

There was no writing on either side of the dirty, white envelope. Hunter, curious to see if Hannah had left them a note, opened the flap and retrieved a lined three-by-five card from inside.

Hayden watched the color drain from Hunter's face as he read the note. Worriedly he asked, "What's the matter? What does it say?"

Hunter, unable to speak and suddenly sick to his stomach, handed Hayden the note and said, "We've got to get to the motor home quick.

Hayden turned the card over and read the writing.

"'WE'VE GOT HER. IF YOU WANT HER BACK SAFELY, BRING EVERYTHING YOU HAVE ABOUT THE KIMBALL LEGEND TO THE DIRT PATHWAY THROUGH THE SACRED GROVE. FOLLOW THE PATH UNTIL YOU REACH A CLEARING. WAIT THERE. REMEMBER COME ALONE OR SHE'S DEAD.'"

Hayden looked up from the note to see Hunter wobbling as fast as he could toward the parking lot outside the Welcome Center.

As Hayden caught up he looked at Hunter and asked. "Who knows that we're working on the Legend?"

"I have absolutely no idea," Hunter quietly replied.

"What are we going to do?" asked Hayden. "We're not giving them the cane, no matter what."

"I don't want to give them anything, but I don't want Hannah to get killed either," replied Hunter, obviously upset.

"Should I go get Mom and Aunt Shirley?" asked Hayden. "They would know what to do."

"You read the note. Didn't it specify to come alone?" asked Hunter angrily.

"So, what are we going to do then?" asked Hayden.

"Well, I'm gonna take the cane back to the motor home and hide it. Then I guess we're going to take them everything else we have about the Legend," he replied.

"How are we going to do that?" questioned Hayden. "Hannah has everything in her backpack."

Hunter slid the key into the motor home door, took a deep breath, shook his head and said, "I completely forgot about that."

Hunter opened the door and hurried inside. Once inside he pulled the door closed tightly behind Hayden and motioned for him to close the blinds. As Hayden twisted the lever, tightly closing the slats of the blinds in the kitchen, Hunter pulled out the hidden cane from inside his jeans. Shaking the cramps out of his leg and knee he quietly stared into space.

"Hunter, what are you doing?" asked Hayden.

Blinking his eyes he looked over at Hayden and replied, "Do you know how hard it is to walk without bending your knee?" Hunter replied.

"What do we do know?" asked Hayden worriedly.

"We find a safe place to hide this," Hunter replied, holding up the cane.

"Why don't you pull Hannah's bed out and hide the cane along the backside of her bed," suggested Hayden. "The bed did a pretty good job of hiding her backpack."

"That's not a bad idea," replied Hunter, as he walked to her bed, pulled it away from the wall, lifted the covers and slid the cane between the box spring and the mattress. After pulling the covers into their proper position, Hunter, pushed the bed back against the wall. He looked up at Hayden smiled and said, "Don't worry, I have an idea."

"What? Tell me what it is?" requested Hayden. "I don't want her to get hurt."

"Go get your small blue backpack, the one that looks like Hannah's. Then grab Mom's church history book, the one Hannah's been reading the entire trip. I will grab several of Aunt Shirley's, 'Places to see' papers," said Hunter, as he shuffled through every kitchen drawer.

"Here you go," said Hayden holding out his backpack.

Hunter took the pack, unzipped the front pocket and placed three things inside.

"What was that?" asked Hayden.

"I cut a few pieces off of Hannah's tan, suede skirt. I think the material looks similar to the cloth from the clues we've found," replied Hunter.

"She is going to kill you, Hunter," said Hayden.

"I know, but I don't know what else to do," he said as he threw the backpack over his shoulder and walked outside.

"I'm a little scared, Hunter," said Hayden, as he watched him lock the motor home door.

"Me, too, Hayden," said Hunter. "But I don't want Hannah to get hurt and I'm sure we're smarter than whoever has kidnapped her."

Following the signs around the farm they hurried toward the dirt path leading into the Sacred Grove.

"Here we go, Hayden," said Hunter as they entered the first grove of trees.

"I don't understand what our plan is," whispered Hayden.

"I'm going to try to get the kidnappers to trade Hannah and her backpack for this pack," replied Hunter holding back a tree branch as Hayden hurried by. "Now be quiet, I don't want anyone to overhear our conversation," said Hunter.

The boys wandered along the path about a hundred yards when they reached a small clearing. They looked around but could see no one.

"Is this the right place, Hunter?" asked Hayden as he scanned the area for any signs of the kidnappers.

"I hope so, the note said to wait here," he replied.

Nearly five minutes passed when Hunter noticed something moving in the trees and brush to the east of the clearing.

"Is that Hannah and the kidnappers?" whispered Hayden, through a squeaky nervous voice.

"I don't know," replied Hunter, squinting to see their faces.

Hunter lifted his hand about waist high and waved when he finally saw Hannah's face. She startled the kidnappers and the boys when she screamed louder than anyone had ever heard before. The kidnapper quickly covered her mouth and warned her not to scream again.

Hunter watched every move they made, but was unable to see the faces of the two people holding Hannah. As they moved closer he could see that they both had baggy clothes and ski masks covering everything on their face but their eyes, which were covered with dark sunglasses. The tall kidnapper motioned for Hunter to come closer, so cautiously, he started walking off the path and into the cover of the forest.

About ten yards from Hannah, Hunter could see that the kidnapper was holding a gun at her side.

"Do you have the clues?" hollered the man, in a deep booming voice.

"Yes," replied Hunter, pointing to the bag on his back.

"Pull them out and show them to me," growled the man.

Hunter pulled the backpack from his shoulder and set it down on the ground. Slowly he unzipped the front pocket and retrieved the look-a-like material he had cut from Hannah's skirt, and held it up for the man to see.

"I can't see it, bring it to me," he demanded.

"No! You release my sister first or you don't get to see anything," Hunter boldly answered.

The kidnapper grabbed Hannah's arm, pushed the gun firmly into her ribs and said, "Walk."

Hannah walked nervously toward Hunter. About fifteen feet apart, the kidnapper stopped her and said, "Now you come the rest of the way."

Hunter and Hayden walked toward Hannah.

Suddenly the kidnapper pulled his gun away from Hannah's ribs and yelled, "Not both of you, only you," he said, pointing to Hunter.

Hunter took a deep breath, looked at Hayden and said, "Move back, I'll go from here."

Hayden moved quickly back to the clearing and watched as Hunter walked closer toward Hannah with the backpack thrown over his shoulder.

As Hunter moved closer he stared at Hannah's eyes and motioned discretely with his eyes for Hannah to put her backpack on the ground. She nodded slightly to Hunter, hoping the kidnappers wouldn't recognize their signs.

Hunter, only a foot away from Hannah, set the back-pack on the ground next to her feet and asked, "How did you know we're searching for the treasure to the Kimball Legend?"

"That is none of your concern," the kidnapper replied.

"Yes it is," Hunter snapped. "Unless you are from the Kimball family you shouldn't know about any of this."

"Quit talking and let me see what you have found," he demanded again, pushing the gun into Hannah's ribs.

Hunter knelt down next to the backpack opened the front pocket, only this time of Hannah's backpack, and again held up material for the kidnapper to see.

"Read to me the clue," insisted the man.

"No! You read it and figure it out for yourself," replied Hunter, sliding the real clue back into Hannah's bag.

Standing up quickly he pushed Hannah's bag toward her as he picked up the bag with fake clues inside and pretended to slide the clue back inside.

"Wait a minute. Let me see that again," demanded the man.

Hunter, not holding the real clue any longer, flashed the fake material quickly in front of the kidnapper and said, "If you want to see anymore, we need to make the trade, you take the bag and I will take my sister."

The kidnapper, holding tightly on to Hannah's arm, pushed her closer to Hunter. She carefully picked up her bag from the ground as the kidnapper placed the gun in his waistband and held out his empty hand for the bag.

Hunter, pretending to be scratching his back, motioned for Hayden to start backing up. Then, with a firm grip on the bag, he held it out for the kidnapper to take and boldly took hold of Hannah's arm.

"On the count of three you let go of my sister, and I will let go of the bag," Hunter suggested.

The man nodded and said, "You better not be tricking me boy. Now, I will count. One...Two...Three!"

Hunter watched as Hannah pulled her arm free and

ran toward Hayden as fast as she could go. Hunter paused only for a moment to see Hannah was free before he too let go of the bag and took off running.

"Hurry, run!" yelled Hunter knowing they only had a few seconds before the kidnapper knew that he didn't have the real clues."

Almost back to the entrance to the Sacred Grove, a shrill scream sounded causing all the birds to suddenly squawk and fly off.

"Don't stop now," insisted Hunter, running faster. "He just found out that all he has is Mom's history book and a few pieces of useless material."

"By the way Hunter, that material you were holding up looked awfully familiar," said Hannah, through gasps for air. "Please tell me that wasn't my new suede skirt."

"I'm sorry Hannah that was all I could find the right color and texture to trick the kidnapper."

"Hunter, I just got that from Grandma for my birthday," she screamed, glad he had rescued her, but sad to have lost her new skirt.

"I was trying to save you, Hannah," Hunter replied angrily.

"I can hear someone behind us. Quit fighting and hurry up," said Hayden. "We're almost to the safety of a public place."

"Ouch," screamed Hannah, reaching for her shoulder. "Ouch, ouch," she screamed again as they rounded the corner and ran as fast as they could toward the parking lot.

"What's the matter?" asked Hayden.

"I think I got shot?" she replied, pulling her hand away

from her shoulder, sure it would be covered with blood.

"I can't see anything," said Hunter. "If you're shot I don't know what kind of gun hit you."

"Look there's Mom and Aunt Shirley," said Hannah, pointing twenty yards in the distance.

Hannah continued holding her shoulder, sure she had been hit by something, as they reached Mom and Aunt Shirley who were walking toward the Sacred Grove.

"Are you three going to go back into the Grove with us?" asked Aunt Shirley.

"I think the Sacred Grove might be more fun if we wait to go with Dad," said Hayden, out of breath. "The shadows this late in the afternoon are kind of scary."

"I'll protect you, Hayden," teased Aunt Shirley. "Come on let's go check it out."

"No, he's right, Aunt Shirley," added Hunter. "Because of the shadows we couldn't see a lot. I think the Sacred Grove might be better tomorrow."

"Well, I guess we can go when your Dad gets here," said Mom, as she turned toward the parking lot. "So are you three ready to go, you've seen enough here?"

"I know I have," replied Hannah, swiftly walking toward the motor home.

"I guess were going, Aunt Shirley," said Mom, as she tried to keep up with their swift pace.

"What do you think those three are up to, Sarah?" asked Shirley as they walked toward the motor home.

"I don't know. They either did something they shouldn't have and they're trying to get away before they are caught or they found the next clue," replied Sarah.

"Let's go find out, should we?" asked Aunt Shirley smiling.

They hurried to catch the kids and followed them quickly inside the motor home. Hayden dropped down on the couch and took big breaths hoping to slow his racing heart. Hunter checked Hannah's shoulder and was shocked at what he saw.

"You've got several big welts, but I don't see where anything broke the skin."

"What's the matter?" quizzed Mom.

"My back is hurting in a few places and I thought maybe I'd been bit by a bug or something," replied Hannah.

"Let me take a look," said Mom. She turned Hannah to the side and said, "Wow! Where did you get that?"

"I don't even know what it is," replied Hannah. "I don't think it's a bug bite, but, I don't know for sure what else that could be."

"You know what that mark looks like?" asked Aunt Shirley.

"No, what?" asked Hayden.

"That looks like the welt I had when you guys shot me with your air soft pistols," she replied as she rubbed her hand across Hannah's shoulder.

"Who would be shooting an air soft pistol in the Sacred Grove," asked Hannah, sure she knew the answer.

"You wouldn't think anybody would, would you?" asked Aunt Shirley, as she climbed into the passenger seat.

Mom started the engine and asked. "Should we get

settled at the RV Park for tonight, get some dinner and play a few more games before we go to bed?"

"I think that's a great idea," replied Hunter, afraid the kidnappers might have followed them to the motor home. "Let's get moving fast."

"Okay then, on our short ride back why don't the three of you tell me what you were really doing back at the Sacred Grove," said Mom, as she pulled out of the parking lot onto the main road and headed back toward the RV Park.

CHAPTER TWENTY-THREE

QUIETLY PONDERING the events that had just transpired, the kids sat in silence for several minutes, nervous about who had tried to kidnap Hannah and how anyone knew they were searching for clues to the Kimball Legend.

"Well?" said Mom, interrupting the quiet, nervous feeling in the motor home.

"What? What did you say, Mom?" asked Hannah, shaking the fog from her head.

"Tell me what you found and what you three have been doing," she replied.

"Well, we found the cane and we're just excited to get working on finding and solving the next clue," Hunter replied, as he placed his hand on Hannah's shoulder for comfort.

"You found the cane?" asked Hannah, suddenly excited.

"I thought you were with the boys, Hannah," said Aunt Shirley, positive the kids weren't telling them the entire story.

"I..., I ran into the Sacred Grove by myself for a few minutes and I wasn't sure if Hunter had actually found the cane or not," Hannah replied evasively.

"Hmmm," replied Aunt Shirley, still very suspicious.

"So, where is this cane you've found?" asked Mom, excited to see what they found. "Let me see what it looks like."

Hunter walked to Hannah's bed, grabbed the metal frame and pulled it away from the wall. He moved aside the blankets and slid his hand in between the box spring and mattress. As Mom parked in their campsite at the RV Park, Hunter located the cane between the mattresses and excitedly held it up for everyone to see.

"WOW!" said Aunt Shirley, jumping to her feet. "Where in the world did you find that?"

"Back at Joseph's Frame home," Hunter replied proudly.

"Where?" asked Mom, looking closely at the cane.

"You really wouldn't believe me if I told you," answered Hunter, hoping to avoid the question.

"So, this is information you really don't want me to know?" asked Mom, raising her eyebrows as she looked at Hunter.

"Yep," Hayden answered. "He really doesn't want you to know how we found the cane."

"Then that's exactly the information you need to tell me," she insisted. "Where did you find the cane, Hunter?"

Hunter could tell that Mom was serious by the look on her face. Afraid she wouldn't allow them to continue with the Legend if he didn't tell her everything, he replied, "We found the cane right where the clue indicated it would be."

"And where was that?" Mom asked.

Hunter took a deep breath as he smiled at Mom, hoping to relieve the tension in the room and replied, "After we moved a few bricks from the hearth of the fireplace, there was a small square opening that led to a dark, musty room. I climbed in through the opening to a small room and found the cane hanging on the wall inside."

"You tore apart the fireplace inside the Joseph Smith house?" Mom angrily asked.

"No," replied Hayden. "I was very careful with the bricks. I made sure they didn't get damaged."

"What else did you do?" asked Mom, worried the kids might have destroyed important church history.

"Nothing, that was it and we made sure we were careful with the fireplace," replied Hunter reassuringly. "I promise we were very careful."

"Does the cane have a clue with it? Like the others do?" asked Aunt Shirley eagerly.

"We haven't even had a chance to look at the cane yet," replied Hannah. "But, I can't wait to find out."

"You know you three are really lucky?" said Aunt Shirley.

Hunter grinned and replied, "Lucky? No, we're, blessed!"

"I agree!" said Aunt Shirley, taking the cane from Hannah's hand.

"How about Aunt Shirley and I start on some dinner, and you three take a few minutes to check out the cane. Maybe it will give you ideas about what you need to do next," suggested Mom, taking the cane from Aunt Shirley and handing it to Hunter. "Because tomorrow, we will be returning the cane to the appropriate person back at the Smith Farm."

"But, Mom," squealed Hannah.

"No, you three know that it is wrong to take something that does not belong to you," she said.

"The cane is part of the clue, Mom. No one ever would have found it if we hadn't solved the clues," screeched Hayden.

"You may look at the cane tonight, I will talk to your father tomorrow to decide what we need to do with the cane," Mom sternly replied. "Now go look and see if there is a clue while Shirley and I make dinner."

"Thanks, Mom," Hannah said. "I'm sorry we've upset you."

"I'm not upset Hannah, I just want to make sure we do the right thing, whatever that is," she replied.

"So you're not mad?" Hayden asked confused.

"No," answered Mom.

"Really?" quizzed Hayden. "You sound kinda mad."

"Really," she whispered with a smile. "I'm not mad."

Hunter carried the cane to the kitchen table and sat

down. Hannah and Hayden followed closely behind, determined to figure out what the cane was for and hopefully find a clue that would lead them on in their quest.

Mom and Aunt Shirley started on dinner watching the excitement of the Legend drive all three kids to study more about church history.

"The clue must be engraved on the cane," said Hayden.

Hannah nodded in agreement, picked up the cane and started to search the detail and engravings for any sign of a clue.

"Hey, there's a lion engraved on the cane. It's a little smaller, but it looks the same," she said excitedly. "We are so on the right track to solve the Legend."

"Cool! What else is there?" asked Hayden.

"At the top there are two rows of wavy lines, with alternating circles and squares, about every two inches around the cane. About two inches underneath that is the lion, followed by the symbol of the squared circle."

"What does the squared circle mean," asked Hayden. "I can't remember."

"It has something to do with the scattered tribes of Israel," replied Hannah. "I'd have to find it in Grandpa's symbol book to read it word for word."

"Okay what else is there?" quizzed Hunter. "Keep going."

"Well," she said pausing for a few moments.

"Come on, Hannah, I can hardly stand this. What's next?" asked Hayden impatiently.

"I think it's the clue," she responded shaking from excitement.

"Tell us," insisted Hunter.

"Okay, below the squared circle are several engravings written in a circle around the cane. They look like rings, but the rings are actually sentences, see," said Hannah, holding up the cane and pointing to the engravings.

"What do they say?" asked Hunter in a deep demanding voice. "What is written?"

Hannah excitedly started to read the words.

"THE LEGEND IS WITHIN YOUR GRASP,
BUT YOUR JOURNEY'S JUST BEGUN.
WITH MORONI WILL YOU ENTER,
RIGHT BEFORE THE DAY IS DONE.
JOSEPH'S CANE AND THE MEDALLION,
WHEN TOGETHER LONG SHADOWS CAST.
AT HIS FEET LOOK FOR THE LION,
ITS MOUTH LEADS TO RECORDS PAST.
ONCE INSIDE THE HILL CUMORAH,
HANNAH'S..."'

Puzzled, Hannah abruptly stopped reading.

"Why did you stop?" asked Hayden.

"Did you hear what I read?" she asked.

"Yes," Hayden replied. "So why did you stop?"

"My name is written in this clue," she quietly replied.

"So?" said Hayden.

"Keep reading the clue, Hannah. Let's find out what else is written," suggested Hunter.

Hannah looked again at the cane and continued reading the clue.

"'ONCE INSIDE THE HILL CUMORAH,
HANNAH'S WATCH WILL BE YOUR GUIDE.
TRUST THE DIRECTION THAT IT LEADS YOU,
OR FOR YOUR SAFETY YOU MUST HIDE.'"

"Is that everything?" asked Hunter.

"Yes, that's all of the clue," replied Hannah. "There are another couple of squiggly lines with circles and squares after the last line of the clue followed by..."

"Followed by what?" asked Hayden anxiously.

"Followed by the engraving of, *Joseph Smith, Jr. 1829,*" Hannah replied, looking up at Hunter.

Hunter shook his head and said, "I don't know what we ever did to be worthy of all these cool things."

"I think Heber C. Kimball was the worthy one," replied Hannah.

"Who are you two kidding, I'm a saint," said Hayden smirking.

"Oh yeah, that's what I'd call you, Hayden, a saint," said Hunter, reaching across the table trying to grab his shirt.

Hayden leaned back in his chair just out of Hunter's reach and teased, "Well, you can't hide perfection. I guess you two are just lucky that I'm here to help you with all these clues, otherwise I don't think you'd ever made it beyond the first one."

"Now you're getting on my nerves, Hayden," said Hannah, still staring at the cane.

"I'm only teasing," he replied grinning from ear to ear.

"You'd better be Hayden," replied Mom. "Cause I know for sure that you're not a saint. Do you want me to start telling stories about when you were a baby?" she asked as she placed the garlic bread in the center of the table, returning quickly to the kitchen.

"No, please not the baby stories," Hunter cried, teasing Hayden. "I'm not sure I can handle hearing those stories again," he said plugging his ears.

"It's not very often I get to tease Hunter, Mom," called Hayden. "Let me have some fun."

"Hunter, when I read the clue, did you write it down?" asked Hannah.

"No, you didn't ask me too," he replied.

"I'll read the clue again really quick. Would you please write it down for me," Hannah asked. "We need to figure out where we need to go next and why my name is part of the clue."

"Sure," answered Hunter. "I'd be glad to."

"Here's a paper and a pen," Hannah said, holding them out for Hunter to take.

"Okay, I'm ready," said Hunter, as he drew a circle on the paper making sure the pen worked.

Hannah again started reading.

"THE LEGEND IS WITHIN YOUR GRASP,
BUT YOUR JOURNEY'S JUST BEGUN.
WITH MORONI WILL YOU ENTER,
RIGHT BEFORE THE DAY IS DONE.
JOSEPH'S CANE AND THE MEDALLION,
WHEN TOGETHER LONG SHADOWS CAST.
AT HIS FEET LOOK FOR THE LION,
ITS MOUTH LEADS TO RECORDS PAST.
ONCE INSIDE THE HILL CUMORAH,
HANNAH'S WATCH WILL BE YOUR GUIDE.
TRUST THE DIRECTION THAT IT LEADS YOU,
OR FOR YOUR SAFETY YOU MUST HIDE."

"That's everything, right?" asked Hunter, as he wrote down the last sentence.

"That's it," Hannah replied.

"Time for dinner guys," interrupted Aunt Shirley. "Here are the plates and cups, set them around the table for me, please?" she asked as she laid them down.

Hannah stood from the table, propped the cane against the couch, picked up the dishes Aunt Shirley had set out and quickly helped with dinner.

Excitement filled the air as the kids waited for Mom. Finally, she placed the Lasagna on the table and sat down. Hunter moaned as Mom assigned Aunt Shirley the prayer, excited to tell Mom about the clue, he knew Aunt Shirley would pray for at least five minutes. When she finally finished Hunter blurted out, "We found the clue."

"You found the clue?" asked Aunt Shirley.

"We sure did," replied Hayden.

"Do you know what you need to do?" asked Mom as she handed Hannah the Lasagna dish.

Hannah took a big spoonful and replied, "We haven't figured that out yet. We're gonna have to do that next."

"Good job, guys! I can't wait to see what you bring back next," said Aunt Shirley.

"Me either," said Hayden through a mouth full of food.

"Can Aunt Shirley and I hear the clue?" asked Mom.

"Yeah, I'll read it," replied Hunter, as he picked up the paper and read.

"THE LEGEND IS WITHIN YOUR GRASP,
BUT YOUR JOURNEY'S JUST BEGUN.
WITH MORONI WILL YOU ENTER,
RIGHT BEFORE THE DAY IS DONE.
JOSEPH'S CANE AND THE MEDALLION,
WHEN TOGETHER LONG SHADOWS CAST.
AT HIS FEET LOOK FOR THE LION,
ITS MOUTH LEADS TO RECORDS PAST.
ONCE INSIDE THE HILL CUMORAH,
HANNAH'S WATCH WILL BE YOUR GUIDE.
TRUST THE DIRECTION THAT IT LEADS YOU,
OR FOR YOUR SAFETY YOU MUST HIDE."

"Hannah's watch will be your guide?" said Aunt Shirley, confused by the sentence. "Hannah, your name is in this clue?"

"I guess it's referring to me," she softly replied. "Kind of freaky, huh?"

"Yeah, totally freaky," answered Aunt Shirley smiling. "It's almost like the Legend wasn't meant to be solved until the three of you were old enough to work on the clues."

"Have you decided where you need to go to solve this clue?" asked Mom.

"No, we're starting on that now," replied Hannah. "Can we discuss the clues while we eat?"

"Sure," replied Aunt Shirley. "I'd love to hear you three work on the clue."

Hannah glanced at Mom looking for her approval. Mom nodded slightly, causing Hannah to smile uncontrollably.

"Let's get started," said Hannah.

"The first line is pretty straight forward," said Hayden. "'The Legend is within your grasp,' that can only mean that we are close, right?"

"I think you're right, Hayden," said Hunter. "But, I guess our 'journey's just begun."

"What does that mean?" asked Hayden confused.

"It must mean that even though we've proven the Legend is true, we must have more to do or find," he replied. "What do you think, Hannah?"

"I agree," she replied. "What about, 'with Moroni you will enter'?"

"I think either Moroni is going to be at the opening and we will enter the Hill Cumorah with him, or, it is a clue to the location, maybe a statue of Moroni, something like that," replied Hunter.

"What about the Hill Cumorah? I bet there's a statue of Moroni somewhere on the grounds," suggested Hayden.

"Hey, good idea, Hayden," said Aunt Shirley, who was listening intently to the conversation. "Who knew you kids were so smart? I think you found the location of the next clue."

"And if you're right Aunt Shirley, we've got to be at the statue of Moroni, 'right before the day is done'," said Hunter.

"Does that mean sunset?" asked Hannah.

"I think so, that's how I understand the line," he replied.

"Okay, what does the clue say next, Hunter?" asked Hannah.

"'Joseph's cane and the medallion, when together, long shadows cast.' I'm not sure what that means," said Hunter.

"What if you put the cane and the medallion together somehow?" asked Hannah.

"That's a good idea, Hannah," said Hunter. "And maybe when we put the two together they cast long shadows that lead us to the next clue."

"And that is done, around sunset with the Angel Moroni," included Hayden.

"You kids are so smart!" insisted Aunt Shirley. "I never could've figured out all the things you have for the Legend."

"What is the medallion that you keep talking about?" asked Mom as she walked into the room.

"We found a round wood medallion with beautiful

engravings back at the home of Heber C. Kimball,"' replied Hannah. "It is kinda the shape of a ball, only flat."

"A flat ball?" she quizzed.

"Not a ball, but round, about the same size and one-inch thick," answered Hunter.

"Can I see it?" Mom asked, confused by Hannah's description.

"Sure," replied Hannah, as she searched through the contents of her backpack.

Intrigued, Mom watched as Hannah quickly found the medallion and held it out for her to take.

"This is beautiful. Where did you find it?" Mom asked.

"At Heber C. Kimball's home," replied Hayden, as he squished an entire slice of bread into his mouth.

"Please tell me you didn't destroy anything to find this?" Mom asked nervously.

"Nope, we didn't," said Hayden. "Actually the medallion was hidden in a secret compartment. Hannah figured out how to open the compartment and Hunter grabbed the medallion."

Mom studied the intricate engravings on the medallion for several minutes before she handed the wooden object back to Hannah.

"You kids are really amazing. Grandpa is going to be so excited when you show him what you've found," said Mom.

"I can hardly wait to tell him about everything we've found," said Hunter.

"I'm looking forward to watching his reaction as you show him," said Aunt Shirley.

"We're never going to get the clue figured out if we don't keep working on it," said Hannah anxiously.

"You're right, tell me what's next?" asked Hayden.

"I'll read the next two lines," replied Hannah. "'At his feet look for the lion. Its mouth leads to records past.'"

"At whose feet?" asked Mom.

"The Angel Moroni's feet," answered Hayden.

"How do you know that?" she asked, with a perplexed look on her face.

"The beginning of the clue," replied Hayden.

"I must not have been paying very close attention," reasoned Mom.

"Okay, what do we know so far?" asked Hunter, looking up at Hannah.

Quickly answering his own question he started, "First, we know we're close to confirming the Legend. Second, we know we've got to find the Angel Moroni. Third, we know the opening is located somewhere near Moroni's feet, marked by the symbol of the lion, whose mouth somehow leads to records past. From there, we need the cane and the medallion and together they will form a shadow leading us to the next clue."

"You know, Hunter, you could be pretty close," said Mom, standing from the table and placing her dishes in the sink.

"What's next?" asked Hunter.

"'Once inside the Hill Cumorah, Hannah's watch will be your guide," read Hayden. "I don't understand what Hannah's watch has to do with the clue. Do you, Mom?"

Mom shrugged her shoulders and replied, "I don't know, honey."

Hannah, looking at her most prized possession, smiled and said, "There's nothing special about my watch, other than Grandma gave it to me."

"There must be something special about the watch," said Aunt Shirley as she stood from the table and carried her dishes to the sink.

"I'm not sure what," replied Hannah as she held up her arm to display the watch.

"Well, we can try to figure that out later. What's left of the clue?" asked Hunter.

"'Trust the direction that it leads you, or for your protection you must hide'," said Aunt Shirley, reading the clue over Hayden's shoulder.

"My watch is not a compass," Hannah said bewildered by the clue. "How can it lead us anywhere?"

"Maybe as we get closer, those lines will make more sense," suggested Hunter. "I think we know where we have to go."

"And where's that?" asked Mom.

"We've got to look for the next clue somewhere at the Hill Cumorah—possibly by a statue of Moroni," he replied confidently.

"When are we going to the Hill Cumorah?" asked Hannah, still looking for anything special about her watch.

"Tomorrow, after we pick Dad up from the airport," replied Mom, as she wiped down the kitchen table.

"I guess we have a starting point," said Hayden optimistically.

Overwhelmed at the day's stressful events, Hannah excused herself from the table and headed for bed.

"Where are you goin', Hannah?" asked Aunt Shirley. "I was getting ready to beat everyone in a game of Rook."

"I'm really tired, Aunt Shirley, maybe, tomorrow," Hannah replied.

"Tired? It's only nine o'clock, Hannah," said Mom.

"I'm still exhausted, see you in the morning," she called, as she changed into her pajamas and fell into bed.

"Hannah has the right idea, Mom," said Hunter. "I think I'm going to skip the games and go to bed."

"I guess we could all use the extra sleep," replied Mom. "I'll lock everything up."

"I'm not tired!" announced Aunt Shirley.

"Then I guess you and I will have a fierce battle of war," replied Mom, smiling.

CHAPTER TWENTY-FOUR

ROCHESTER AIRPORT was crazy, and finding a place to park the motor home was even more nerve racking. Unable to locate a parking spot, Mom circled the airport waiting for Dad and Uncle Gary to arrive. After more than thirty minutes and ten laps circling the airport, the two finally appeared in the passenger pick-up area. Aunt Shirley squealed excitedly as she spotted them. As Mom maneuvered the motor home up to the curb, Aunt Shirley threw open the door and raced to her husband, hugging him tightly.

As they climbed inside Hayden yelled, "Hi, Dad!" As he threw his arms around his dad's neck.

"I'm so glad you're here," said Mom, thrilled not to have to drive the motor home anymore.

Hannah waited patiently for her turn to say hello, silently hoping Dad would remember that today was her birthday.

As everyone hugged Dad, an airport security guard approached. "This is a loading-only zone, you need to keep moving, folks," he said, as he motioned for them to continue out of the area.

"Sorry, Sir, we'll be on our way as soon as everyone is loaded," Dad replied.

The guard nodded his head and replied, "Hurry please, this is a very busy airport and for security reasons you need to move on."

Dad nodded to the guard then glanced around the motor home and asked, "Where's my birthday girl?"

"I thought you forgot," Hannah replied, as she stood up from the kitchen table and walked toward him.

"How could I forget? You're sixteen and trapped on a horrible family vacation!" he replied.

Hannah smiled. "Actually, Dad, I've been having a pretty good time."

"That's what you're mother has been saying, but just in case, I brought you the best sixteenth birthday gift I could think of."

Hannah's eyes instantly lit up in excitement. She watched in nervous anticipation as Dad moved aside and pointed to the baggage claim door where her best friend, Alli was standing.

"Alli? How? What are you doing here?" Hannah screamed, rushing out the door, surprised to see her best friend.

"We've had this planned for two months, Hannah," squealed Alli as she raced toward the motor home.

"And you didn't tell me? Some best friend you are," teased Hannah as she hugged her. "You should've told me!"

"That would have ruined your birthday surprise," Alli replied as she climbed inside.

Suddenly, there was a loud bang on the driver's window.

"You've been here long enough, please get this RV moved before I have to give you a ticket," insisted the guard.

"I guess that means now," said Dad, as he carried Alli's bags inside. He quickly moved into the driver's seat, and pulled the motor home away from the curb.

"Where am I heading?" he asked, unfamiliar with the area.

Aunt Shirley grabbed her map, handed it to her husband, Gary, and said, "You're the co-pilot now, go help him with directions."

"Where am I going, Sarah?" called Dad.

"To the Hill Cumorah," responded Hannah.

"How about food first, and then the Hill Cumorah?" suggested Uncle Gary. "I'm starving, that is a very long flight."

Everyone agreed.

Dad quickly found a small, hole-in-the-wall Mexican restaurant and pulled over. Without a word he jumped out of the car and raced into the restaurant. A few minutes later Dad return with a bag full of chips, salsa and taquitos.

Hannah and Alli grabbed a handful of taquitos and headed for the privacy of the back room in the motor home. Hannah was excited to hear about all of the events that had happened back at home while she had been gone. But she couldn't wait to tell Alli about the Kimball Family Legend.

More than thirty minutes had passed before Dad announced they were close.

"I'm so excited," Hannah announced.

"Why?" asked Alli. "I thought you didn't even want to be here?" she teased.

Hannah about to answer, paused. "Hold on, I'll be right back," said Hannah, excusing herself from the room.

She hurried into the bathroom, closed and locked the door behind her. Dialing Grandpa on her cell phone she was excited when he answered.

"Grandpa, I have a question," she said rapidly.

"Hannah, is that you?" he asked.

"Yes, Grandpa, I have a question," she repeated.

"What is it, Hannah?" he asked.

"May I please tell my best friend Alli about the Legend?" she asked. "Mom and Dad brought her to New York for my birthday and I was hoping I could tell her."

"That's right, it's your birthday Hannah, Happy Birthday!"

"Thank you, Grandpa. But I'm hiding in the bathroom and I really need to know if you will let me tell her about the Legend," she asked again.

"Can she be trusted?" he asked.

"Yes," Hannah replied.

"If you trust her, then I guess Hannah if you explain to

her how important it is not to tell anyone about the Legend, you can tell her," Grandpa answered.

"Thanks Grandpa, I love you," said Hannah.

"I can't wait to hear how you are doing," said Grandpa.

"I promise, we're close to finding the treasure, and when we do, I will call," whispered Hannah.

"Goodbye, Hannah, I love you." said Grandpa.

Hannah smiled as she closed her cell phone and hurried back into the room with Alli.

"You know how I didn't want to be here at first? Hannah asked.

"Yes," replied Alli.

"Well, my grandpa told us about a Legend, I've had, no...we've all had, a great time solving clues and trying to find the treasure," said Hannah excitedly as she and Alli walked to the kitchen.

"So, what is this Kimball Legend, Shirley has told me about?" asked Uncle Gary, as he opened the refrigerator and grabbed the milk.

"Supposedly a treasure, hidden long ago," Hannah replied. "But I don't know what kind of treasure."

"Shirley said you've had some luck finding clues, do you think you're close to finding the treasure?" he asked.

"I think so," replied Hunter.

"When we get to the Hill Cumorah, Hunter, Hayden and I have another clue to find. Do you want to come with us, Alli?" asked Hannah.

"Sure, I'd love to," she answered. "But, I'm not a Kimball, is that going to be all right?"

"Yep," Hannah replied, as she watched nervously out the window as Dad made his way to the Hill Cumorah.

The Hill Cumorah was more beautiful than Hannah ever imagined. "Maybe it wasn't such a bad place to be on your birthday," she conceded. As she scanned the area, she noticed that the north end of the hill jetted up suddenly from the flat lands, forming a peak. The peak was covered in deep-green, wavy grass, while the east and west sides dropped off sharply. Scattered on the south side of the hill were beautiful trees and thick foliage.

"The area of flat lands was cleared of trees, but only for ease of passage for the tourists," Hannah read from the brochure, as she looked silently out at the valley.

"What is that statue out there?" asked Hayden, pointing up the hill.

"That's the Angel Moroni," replied Dad, as he placed his hand on Hayden's shoulder.

"That's so cool," said Hunter.

"I haven't seen it myself, but I understand the monument is absolutely amazing at sunset, when the spotlights shine on Moroni," said Aunt Shirley.

"We'll be able to see that in a couple of hours," said Hannah, looking down at her watch.

As she looked at her watch, she noticed the two small spindles in motion. "Wow, they've never done that before," she thought, tapping the face of the watch with her fingernail. "Maybe the battery is going dead."

Hurrying to catch up with everyone, Hannah again gazed out at the Hill Cumorah. Chills ran up her spine as she thought about everything that had happened in the last one hundred and fifty years on this hill.

Hannah looked at her watch again. "Wait a minute—my watch doesn't use a battery!" she thought. "This is odd, why are the spindles on my watch going crazy?"

"Hannah, Hannah!" yelled Alli.

"What, Allison?" asked Hannah, looking up from her watch with a confused look on her face.

"Come look at this quick," she called, pointing to something on the ground.

"Look at what?" Hannah answered, smiling as she walked toward her friend.

"I found an old Birch log, you know, like the one we learned about in Seminary. Joseph hid the plates in a Birch log so the mobs wouldn't find and steal them," Alli excitedly said.

"I doubt that is the actual log Joseph used," replied Hunter, shaking his head. "I'm sure that log is long gone."

"Well, I know that, Hunter," Alli replied through a scowl. "But, what if this was the same Birch log?"

"You know it's not," he answered, teasing her.

"Hey, Hunter, come here a minute, will you?" asked Hannah.

Hunter could tell by the look on Hannah's face and the sound of her voice that something was wrong. He quickly walked to her and asked, "What's up?"

"Look at this?" she said, holding up her wrist.

"Wow! That's really cool, Hannah. How long have you had an arm now?" he asked sarcastically, not understanding what she wanted.

"My watch, Hunter, not my arm," she replied, still holding out her watch for him to see.

Hunter took her arm and pulled her wrist close enough to see the watch clearly. "What am I looking at?" he asked, staring at the watch.

"Do you see something that doesn't look right?" she asked, annoyed that he couldn't see the problem.

"With what, Hannah?" he asked totally confused. "What are you talking about?"

"My watch, Hunter. My watch!"

Hunter, still not sure what he was looking for, took her wrist again and examined the watch. Studying the face, he wrinkled his nose and asked, "Should I notice something?"

"Come on, Hunter, look at the spindles," Hannah replied, pointing to her watch.

Finally noticing he asked, "What happened? Why are the spindles spinning like that?"

"I don't know, they weren't spinning like that earlier," she replied. "They started when we got to the Hill Cumorah."

"What about the kidnappers, Hannah, have you seen them anywhere?" asked Hunter.

"No, but I never got a look at their faces," she replied. "And there are so many people here, I'm not sure I would recognize them."

"Kidnappers? What do you mean?" asked Alli.

"Hannah was sort of kidnapped yesterday," replied Hayden quietly. "But don't say anything, we don't want anyone to worry."

"What?" asked Alli, as she turned and looked at Hannah. "Are you okay?"

"I didn't get hurt and the boys saved me," she replied confidently.

"Are we all ready to go?" interrupted Mom, as she threw her arms around Hunter's shoulder.

"What's the plan? Where do you want to go first?" Mom asked as they walked toward the Cumorah Visitor's Center.

"We're hoping to search the area around the Angel Moroni so that if we're in the right place, we can be prepared right at sunset to use the cane and medallion to find the opening," Hunter replied.

Mom walked quietly for several moments before she answered, "I've given you three lots of freedom to work on the Legend—more than I wanted to. Luckily for you, Aunt Shirley was here and she talked me in to allowing you kids to play with this Legend. But, your dad is here now and I would really like to spend some time together as a family."

"Does that mean we can't work on the legend anymore?" asked Hayden, choking back the tears.

"No, you can still work on the legend for a little while," Mom replied.

"Do we have three or four hours?" asked Hannah.

"Hannah, I would suggest you don't push your luck?" answered Dad, startling Hannah, surprised he was standing behind her.

"Dad, Aunt Shirley, Uncle Gary and I are going over to the Visitor's Center, you are welcome to come with us or work on the clue," said Mom.

"If it's okay, can we head over to the statue of Moroni?" asked Hunter.

"Yes, do you have your cell phone with you?" Mom asked.

"Yes," replied Hunter.

"And I have mine as well," added Hannah.

"Good, call me in two hours and we'll decide what we're doing from there," Mom said. She turned, took Dad's hand, and walked along the path toward the Visitor's Center.

Ready to find the next clue and hoping this one would take them to the treasure, the kids waved at Mom and Dad and hurried toward the statue of Moroni on the hillside.

"Do you think we're in the right place, guys?" asked Hayden.

"I do," Hunter answered confidently.

"Do you think we'll find the treasure this time?" Hayden asked hopefully.

"Yes, I do!" he replied confidently.

"Where exactly are we going?" asked Alli.

"According to this map, if we stay on this path a little longer, we'll reach the bottom of the hill. From there, the statue looks to be about three-quarters of the way to the top next to some trees," replied Hunter.

"Do you think Joseph Smith walked this same path to find the Gold Plates?" asked Hannah.

"I'm sure he did, but he wasn't able to remove them for four years," replied Hunter.

"Brother Hutcheon said Joseph returned the same day every year for fours year until the Lord allowed him to take the Plates, so I'm sure he walked the same path as we are," added Alli.

"Look, there's the statue," called Hayden.

Moving up the hill quickly, the four kids stood at the base of the fifty-foot statue.

Staring in awe at the beautiful surroundings, Hannah said, "It's easy to see why the Plates were hidden in this hill."

"You know, church history is very cool," said Alli.

"I don't think I could've done what Joseph and the pioneers did back then," confessed Hannah, as she walked around the statue.

"I know I couldn't have done it," said Alli.

Hunter quietly searched the base for any sign of the symbol of the lion. As he circled the statue with no luck, he took a deep breath, blew it out quickly and started his search again. As he completed his second time around the statue with no luck he looked up to Hannah and Hayden and said, "We might find the lion faster if you two would help!"

"Where do you want us to look?" asked Hayden.

"You know, I'm not sure, pick any place," he answered angrily.

Hayden dropped to his knees and crawled around the grass at the base of the statue, moving the grass and flowers. Hannah walked ten feet away and circled the area searching. Hunter searched the cement base of the statue again scouring every inch from the bottom up about three feet. While Alli walked into the scattered Birch trees to the west. No one was having any luck.

Frustrated, Hunter called, "We've got something wrong!"

"Hannah read the clue for us, please?" asked Alli.

Hannah nodded, pulled her backpack off her shoulder, unzipped the front pocket and found the clue.

"THE LEGEND IS WITHIN YOUR GRASP,
BUT YOUR JOURNEY'S JUST BEGUN.

WITH MORONI WILL YOU ENTER,
RIGHT BEFORE THE DAY IS DONE.
JOSEPH'S CANE AND THE MEDALLION,
WHEN TOGETHER LONG SHADOWS CAST.
AT HIS FEET LOOK FOR THE LION,
ITS MOUTH LEADS TO RECORDS PAST.
ONCE INSIDE THE HILL CUMORAH,
HANNAH'S WATCH WILL BE YOUR GUIDE.
TRUST THE DIRECTION THAT IT LEADS YOU,
OR FOR YOUR SAFETY YOU MUST HIDE.'"

"It has to be here somewhere, I know we're in the right place," Hunter said, frustrated that he couldn't find the lion.

"I'm not sure what I'm looking for, but I saw something in the trees over there," said Alli, pointing.

"The lion?" asked Hunter excitedly.

"No, I don't think it was a lion," she answered.

"In the trees isn't at Moroni's feet either," said Hayden.

"Well it is kinda, at your feet can mean a lot of things," insisted Alli.

"I'm going to keep looking over here, Hannah you check it out, you know what we're looking for," suggested Hunter.

"Show me what you saw," said Hannah, walking toward the trees.

Alli, annoyed at Hunter's response, walked toward Hannah and said, "You know I can go with your mom if he doesn't want me here."

"Come on, Alli," said Hannah. "I know you've seen him get mad and frustrated before."

"Yeah, but he's never directed his frustration at me before," she replied sadly.

"So, show me, what did you find?" asked Hannah.

Alli walked to a thick stone that was round in the middle and thinner toward the edges. She walked around the north side and brushed away tree leaves to reveal a grapefruit-sized engraving. "This is what I saw," she replied. "It's partially covered with dirt so I can't tell for sure what it is, but I don't think it's a lion."

Hannah knelt down excitedly and frantically brushed the dirt away. Still unable to determine what the picture was, she pulled her water bottle from her backpack and rinsed the area off. Rubbing the dirt as she poured the water, she could finally see the symbol.

"Hunter, Hayden, come look, quick!" Hannah yelled.

The boys rushed to see what Hannah had found.

"What is it? Did you find the lion?" Hunter asked.

"I didn't find the lion, Alli did," Hannah replied smiling at her friend.

Hunter knelt down next to the rock and examined the picture. "That's the lion, all right, good job Alli."

"Look at its mouth, it's huge!" exclaimed Hayden.

"The clue referred to the lion's mouth didn't it?" asked Hayden.

"Yes, the mouth is supposed to lead us to records past," replied Hannah.

"How?" asked Hunter.

"Come on guys, doesn't the mouth look about the

right size for Joseph's cane?" said Alli.

"Hayden, let me see the cane," insisted Hunter.

He took the cane and tried to fit the bottom into the lion's mouth. After several failed attempts, Hunter finally moved the cane in the right direction causing it to slide easily into the opening.

"What do we do with the medallion now?" asked Hannah, holding it up for everyone to see.

"The cane and the medallion are supposed to work together," said Hayden. "So how can we fit them together?"

"What about on the handle of the cane?" asked Hannah. "There is that little knot on the end, could the medallion fit on there somehow?"

Hunter took the medallion from Hannah and said, "Hold the cane steady for me while I see if I can fit the medallion and cane together."

Looking over the medallion for a few seconds, Hunter noticed a small opening about the size of a pencil eraser. Carefully he pushed the opening over the knot on the cane. Hunter, wanting the two pieces to fit together, applied more pressure and pushed them together.

Suddenly there was a loud snap. Hunter closed his eyes, afraid to look, sure he had snapped the medallion in half. Several nervous seconds passed before he finally pulled his hand away from the medallion, expecting it to fall to the ground in pieces.

"Look, it fits!" announced Hayden. "Now what do we do?"

"We wait until sunset," answered Hannah.

"Well, how long until then?" Hayden asked, disappointed they couldn't continue.

"Hunter!" screeched Hannah. "We we're supposed to call Mom fifteen minutes ago."

Hunter looked at his watch, grabbed his cell phone and hurriedly dialed Mom's number.

Three rings passed before she answered. "Hello?"

"Hi, Mom, it's me, we're checking in," Hunter said calmly.

"You're late son!" said Mom.

"Sorry, Mom, we just remembered," replied Hunter. "What's the plan?"

"Well, we are about to go into a fifty-five minute movie presentation here at the Visitor's Center. We will be finished about eight o'clock. Why don't you meet us at the gate and we'll find a place to watch the Pageant at nine."

"That sound's great, Mom," Hunter replied, excited she was going to let them continue working on their clue.

"Are you having fun?" asked Mom.

"We are, and we're getting closer to finding the next clue," Hunter replied.

"Oh, guess who I saw here" said Mom.

"Who?" asked Hunter.

"Maria, your grandmother's housekeeper," Mom replied. "Can you believe she's here? I told her she ought to come and see you kids."

"Did you tell her where we were?" Hunter asked nervously.

"Yes, up by the Moroni statue. Maria and her husband sounded excited to see you. I'm sure they'll go up there. I've got to go, everyone is entering the theatre. See you in a little bit." said Mom.

"See ya," replied Hunter.

Turning off his cell phone, Hunter turned to Hannah and said. "I think I know who is following us and who kidnapped you."

"Who?" asked Hannah anxiously.

"Maria, Grandma's housekeeper," Hunter replied. "Mom said she just saw her at the visitor's center and told her we were up here."

"Where is she now?" asked Hayden.

"I don't know, I'm sure on her way up to us to take the clues," replied Hunter.

"What do we do?" asked Alli.

"We're gonna have to hide until just before sunset and then see if we can follow the shadow before they find us," Hunter replied.

"At least we have some cover from the trees," said Alli.

"Not enough to keep us safe," replied Hunter, as he took the cane from Hannah, careful not to knock off the medallion, and walked deeper into the trees.

"I never would have thought Maria was the one trying to steal the clues from us," said Hannah in shock. "In fact, I didn't think she would tear up the motor home or kidnap me either."

"You know it makes sense. She always seemed to be upstairs when we were at Grandpa's house," said Hunter.

"And all those times I thought I heard a familiar voice, I bet it was her," added Hannah.

"Clever of her, I wonder what she knows?" asked Hunter.

"Hey Hunter," whispered Hayden. "Isn't that Maria?"

Motioning for everyone to scrunch down in the weeds Hayden peered out from behind a tree and saw Maria searching around the area.

Several minutes passed before Hunter saw her turn and start down the hill. He watched her until the trees blocked his view.

"I'm sure she's not gone for long," said Hunter. We're gonna have to be very careful now."

CHAPTER TWENTY-FIVE

NOT WANTING MARIA to find them, the kids hid in the trees and discussed all the events of the trip. Hannah was angry that she had not discovered Maria earlier. As the sun began to set, Hunter carefully scoured the area for any sign of Maria and her husband. Unable to locate them anywhere close by, the kids hurried back to the rock at the edge of the trees.

"Get the cane back in the lion's mouth and let's see what happens, Hannah," requested Hunter.

Hannah held the cane as steady as she could, hoping to allow the reflection of the sun to shine through the medallion. The kids hoped they had solved the clues correctly and that the light would reveal the hidden path.

Impatiently they waited as the sun's final rays of the day shone through the leaves on the trees, every minute brought the light closer until suddenly it hit the medallion and sent a bright beam thirty feet into the woods.

"Hunter, can you see that?" asked Hannah."

"I can," he replied.

"Follow it, quick!" yelled Hayden.

"I will, Hayden. You watch for Maria, I don't want anyone to sneak up on us now," Hunter asked as he turned and quickly followed the bright orange beam cast through the trees by the medallion.

"Hannah, can you tell where it stops?" yelled Hunter.

"You're pretty close. Go about five feet farther and then two feet to your right," Hannah replied.

"I hope we've got this clue right," said Alli, as she watched Hunter.

"Can you see an opening, Hunter?" asked Hayden.

"I don't know what I'm looking for," Hunter replied. "Give me a minute."

"Hunter, hurry I can see Maria at the bottom of the hill," yelled Hayden quietly.

"What?" asked Alli.

"Look!" whispered Hayden as he pointed to the woman. "That's Maria."

"You better hurry, Hunter," said Alli, "They're only fifty yards away."

"Hunter, should I move the cane so they don't see it?" asked Hannah nervously.

"No, I'm almost…Yeah…I found something," Hunter said excitedly. "Everybody, come look."

"Can I come?" asked Hannah. "Am I okay to move the cane and medallion?"

"Yeah, hurry up and get over here," Hunter replied.

Hayden, Hannah and Alli, hurried toward Hunter, wondering why he was on his hands and knees in the tall grass.

"What are you doing, Hunter?" asked Hannah.

"The ray of light stopped right here," he explained, pointing to a small area at the base of the hill. "The area is covered in tall grasses and surrounded by protective trees on all sides. This has to be how we enter the Hill Cumorah."

They watched as Hunter carefully felt around in the grass, searching for an opening. He crawled between the trees, continuing his search. Suddenly a small opening, about the size of a bike tire, appeared.

"This has to be it," he squealed. "Hurry, everyone follow me! Quick before Maria finds us."

Hunter led the way through the opening. Hayden was close behind, with Alli and Hannah bringing up the rear. They crawled in the dark along a winding path for more than fifty feet.

"Oh, I hope there aren't bugs or slimy things in here," whined Alli. "I just can't do snakes, I hate them."

"Can you see how much farther, Hunter?" called Hannah. "My knees are killing me."

"I can see a faint light about ten feet ahead, keep moving, I think we're almost there," he replied.

Unsure what to expect, the kids moved slowly toward the light. As Hunter reached the light, the tunnel opened into a large room.

Hunter stood in silence, staring in amazement at the treasures in the room, as Hayden, Hannah and Alli finally made their way through the opening and into the giant room inside the hill.

"Wow!" exclaimed Hannah. "Look at all this stuff."

"Are these the Gold Plates?" asked Hayden, pointing to an enormous stack of records.

"Is that the breast plate?" asked Alli, pointing to an object on the wall.

"The Legend was true, the clues did lead to a great treasure," yelled Hunter.

"Can you imagine how excited the Prophet is going to be to see all this stuff?" exclaimed Alli.

"How will anyone ever be able to deny the Church is true? You know physical evidence eliminates the need for faith," said Hayden. "And here we are, looking at all the proof."

"I wonder how we are going to get all this stuff outside through that little hole we crawled in through," Alli said.

"I'm sure we can do it, I brought Joseph's cane in with me," Hannah replied, holding it up for Alli to see.

"Look, Hunter, a sword!" Hayden yelled excitedly.

"Does it say whose sword it is?" asked Hunter, walking to the small table in the middle of the room.

Hayden gasped. "It's the Sword of Laban," he replied.

"This is so amazing, I can't believe we actually found our way inside the Hill Cumorah," said Hannah. "Grandpa is going to be so proud of us."

"I can't wait to tell him," said Hayden. "He's been waiting all his life to solve the clues from the Legend."

"Look, there's a handwritten letter on the table next to the sword," said Alli.

"Is the writing in English?" asked Hannah.

"Not only is it in English, but the letter is addressed to all of us," answered Hunter, as he picked the paper up from the table. "And it is signed by Joseph Smith, Jr."

"What?" asked Hannah. "My name is on that letter?"

"Yes," answered Hunter.

"And my name, too?" asked Hayden.

"Yours and Alli's," replied Hunter.

"My name is on the letter? How would anyone know that I was going to be here with you?" Alli asked.

"The Lord knows everything, Alli," replied Hayden. "Why wouldn't he tell Joseph you were going to be here with us?"

"You didn't know I was going to be here with you," she answered.

"You're right, I didn't, but the Lord did," Hunter answered.

"I'm kinda nervous," she said, afraid to move her feet.

"What does the letter say?" asked Hayden.

"Would you like me to read it?" asked Hunter.

"Yes, and hurry! If Joseph wrote me a letter, I want to hear what he wrote," insisted Hannah.

Hunter held the paper up, cleared his throat and started reading.

"'Hunter, Hannah, Hayden and Allison,

As I sit alone inside the Hill Cumorah, secluded from the eyes of any mortal, I contemplate the feelings of my heart in meditation. I am overjoyed to write this letter to you. Much favored of the Lord, I have been allowed to see, in vision, the things which are to come. As I watch the hardships that you face each day in the world in which you live, I feel encouraged to know the true conviction of your hearts is to build up Christ's Kingdom on the earth.

"'I feel as though I have known you all my life, and I look forward to the day when I will be able to throw my arms around you. Remain steadfast in your commitment to the Lord. Endeavor to fulfill His every commandment, and the Comforter will always be at your side.

"With that said, your immediate assistance is required. The world has been waiting for you to wax strong in your testimonies of the gospel, and that day has finally arrived. As you look about your surroundings, you will see many treasures. Many of the treasures that lie hidden in this room, are the treasures spoken of by prophets of old. But they are of no importance at this time and they are not the true treasures hidden in or spoken of with regard to the Hill Cumorah. They are not to be removed from this room for any reason. Should you attempt to do so, your punishment would be severe. The Lord would most surely erase your memory of this place and how to return here. You are also forbidden to reveal this location or speak of the treasures inside—unfortunately, even to your grandfather at this time.

"'As you look upon this room, you will notice ten separate openings scattered about the walls. Each opening is marked with a small, gold plate engraved with the name of the tribe that resides deep within the cave. Your task will be one of peril—surely full of hardships should you choose to endure it. Yet, each house must be returned for the fullness of the Lord to continue.

"'Therefore, your charge, should you choose by your own free will to accept it, is to return to your day the Scattered and Lost Tribes of Israel from the four corners of the earth. Bring at least two—one man and one woman—who may show the path to their people. Be aware as you make your decision that the adversary will do everything within his power to stop you from completing the tasks which the Lord hath placed before you.

"Your lives may be in grave danger on many occasions. Know also that if your trust is placed in the Lord, righteousness will prevail. Whatever your choice, I cannot wait until such time that I have the opportunity to shake your hands and reside in the company of such worthy Sons and Daughters of God. You are those that he has sent forth—his most noble and valiant soldiers—to reside on the earth during these last days.

"'I know you will fulfill the mission you were sent to earth to accomplish. Humble yourselves before the Lord, that He may guide you in your journey to return our lost brothers. May the Comforter always remain at your side. Remember to keep your eyes single to glory of our God.

Your eternal brother,
Joseph Smith, Jr.'"

"What are we supposed to do?" asked Hayden.

"Find each of the ten lost tribes of Israel, I guess," replied Hannah, shocked at what Hunter had just read.

"How?" Hayden asked.

"Are you sure you read the letter correctly, Hunter?"

interrupted Alli, shaking her head. "I'm a big chicken. I can't travel to an unknown land in search of people I don't know, and then tell them they have to come to a world they don't know."

"Hunter, how are we supposed to do this?" asked Hannah, almost in tears.

"I guess we travel through these caves to find them," he replied, walking toward the openings.

"Hunter, we can't just leave. We're already going to be in trouble when Mom and Dad find out that we haven't been watching the Pageant," said Hannah.

"I'm not sure why we have to go now, but, I do know that the Lord will provide a way for us if it's His will that we do this thing," he replied.

"Don't you think I'm a little too young for this?" asked Hayden. "I could go back and pretend like I never saw anything."

"Your name was on the letter, too, I guess that means that the Lord thinks you're old enough," replied Hannah. "Besides, you're bigger and taller than I am."

"What does being big and tall have to do with anything?" he snapped. "I'm a lot younger."

"I want to go home," cried Alli. "This is scary enough without you guys fighting."

"Sorry, Alli," said Hunter. "I think we're all a little afraid. I know this wasn't exactly where I thought the Legend and clues would bring us."

"Me neither," admitted Hayden. "I thought we would get to bring an artifact or something like that back to the Prophet."

"Well, I don't know about the rest of you, but if the Lord asks me to do something, I plan on doing it," said Hannah. "So, Hunter, hand me that letter. I better know exactly what I'm doing before I head off into dark caves toward who knows where or what," she said, holding out her hand.

"Wait a minute. Don't think you're going alone. Besides the fact that Dad would kill me if I let you get hurt, I actually think this could be really cool," replied Hunter. "So I will read Joseph's letter one more time."

"I want to go if you will let me," said Alli, in a small, timid voice.

"The more the merrier," answered Hunter. "What about you Hayden? Are you going or staying?"

"I'm scared, but I'm in," he replied nervously. "If I go back, Mom's going to ask a lot of questions, and I know I can't lie to her."

"Okay, let me find in the letter where it tells us what we need to do," offered Hunter, clearing his throat and scanning through the letter.

"'Hunter, Hannah, Hayden and Allison,

As I sit alone inside the Hill Cumorah..., the hardships that you face everyday in the world in which you live... Endeavor to fulfill His every commandment

With that said, your immediate assistance is required... As you look about your surrounding you will see many treasures... They are not to be removed from this room for any reason. Should you attempt to do so, your punishment would be severe... You are also forbidden to reveal this location or speak of the treasures inside, unfortunately, even to your Grandfather at this time...

As you look upon this room, you will notice ten separate openings scattered about the walls. Each opening is marked with a small gold plate engraved with the name of the house that resides deep within the cave. Your task will be one of peril—surely full of hardships should you choose to endure it. Yet, each house must be returned for the fullness of the Lord to continue.

Therefore, your charge, should you choose by your own free will to accept it, is to return to your day the Scattered and Lost Tribes of Israel from the four corners of the earth. Bring at least two—one man and one woman—who may show the path to their people. Be aware as you make your decision that the adversary will do everything within his power to stop you from completing the tasks which the Lord hath placed before you. Your lives may be in grave danger on many occasions. Know also that if your trust is placed in the Lord, righteousness will prevail... I know you will fulfill the mission you were sent to earth to accomplish...

Remember to keep your eyes single to glory of our God,
Joseph Smith Jr.'"

"We can't tell Grandpa anything. I didn't hear that part the first time," admitted Hayden. "What are we going to say to him?"

"Nothing right now, we'll worry about that later, after we get back," said Hunter.

"How do we do this? One cave a time?" asked Hannah.

"Well, I'm not splitting up, so we can just forget that idea," Alli protested.

Hannah smiled and said, "All right, let's pick a cave and get started."

"I agree," said Hayden. "But which one?"

"I wish I could read these gold engravings," said Hunter. "That way, we would at least know which tribe we're looking for."

"Let's start with this one," said Hayden. "The writing of the name looks pretty cool."

"Okay, let's go," said Hannah, as she stepped into the cave. "How hard could this really be? We've got to be smart enough to bring home the Lost Tribes."

"Are you sure, Hannah?" asked Alli, still a little nervous.

Hayden and Hunter watched as Hannah grabbed Alli's wrist and pulled her into the cave.

Hunter shook his head at Hannah's determination and wondered, "How long will it be before she needs my help?"

"Aaaaaaahhhhhhhhh!" suddenly echoed from the darkness of the cave, followed by another scream and then another.

Hunter's heart dropped into the pit of his stomach. "What's the matter?" he yelled, jumping to his feet and quickly running into the cave after the girls. "Are you okay?"

"Hannah, Alli!" yelled Hayden, who was following closely behind Hunter. "Where are you?"

Again the boys heard, "Aaaaaahhhhhhh!"

"Hunter, I can't see a thing. Can you see the girls?" asked Hayden.

"No, I can't see very well either," he replied. "Where could they be? They sounded really close."

"Hunter, they're not here, and they're not answering. What do we do?" Hayden demanded.

"We keep searching, Hayden," Hunter replied. "They've got to be here somewhere."

ABOUT THE AUTHOR

Although born in Provo, Utah, Tina spent most of her life in San Diego, California. Her writing is strongly influenced by her hometown experiences and her large family whose flair for story telling never ends.

As a direct descendent of Heber C. Kimball and Orson Pratt, the stories told to her by her parents about them encouraged a fascination with the Book of Mormon, Church History, and the adventures of the early saints.

Tina is the author of ***The Liahona Legacies,*** a Book of Mormon adventure series for youth.

Tina Storrs Monson currently lives in Draper UT, a suburb of Salt Lake City. She attended Brigham Young University where she met her husband, Kreg. They have been married for seventeen years and have four children.